Return to Ter Chadain © 2015
All rights reserved Craig Yelle

Previously available through Staccato Publishing
ISBN: 978-1-940202-16-7

978-0-9972821-4-6

Cover art by Suzanne van Pelt
Book cover by Amina Black

Printed in the United States of America

Return to Ter Chadain

by

C. S. Yelle

The Protector of Ter Chadain
Book Three

Character List:

Name	Title
Logan Lassain	Protector of Ter Chadain
Saliday Talis	Tarken/Tracker
Sasha	Betra/Seeker
Teah Lassain	Queen/Protector of Ter Chadain
Lizzy Bridon	Zele Magus Student
Rachel Craddick	Zele Magus Student
Morgan Task	Captain of the Morning Breeze/Tarken
Duke Banderkin	Duke of Fareband
Dezare Banderkin	Daughter of Duke Banderkin
Zeva	Magical From Caltoria
Bastion	First Protector of Ter Chadain
Falcone	Protector betrayed by Zele Magus
Stalwart	Protector betrayed by Viri Magus
Galiven	Protector killed by the Betra
Quinty	First Mate of Morning Breeze
Raven Gassler	Scalded Island magical leader of revolution
Caslor	Son of Empress Shakata
Sniffer Boskin	Sniffer in Port Shoal
Shakata	Empress of Caltoria
Berza	Female personal magical slave of Empress Shakata
Grinwald	Viri Magus
Stern Barsten	Weave Patrol Member of Stellaran
Cita Cane	Rookie Weave Patrol Member of Stellaran
Commander Wilkin	Commander of The Weave Patrol
Bristol Alabaster	Weave Tender and Leader of the Sacred City
Trevon Alabaster	Son of Bristol, next in line to lead the Sacred City
Clastis	Cousin and Friend of Trevon
Fedlen	Young Friend of Trevon and Clastis
Linell	Betrothed to Trevon
Senji	Secret Society of Assassins
Aston Englewood	Royal Englewood Line of Ter Chadain

Captain Courtney Armada	Commander of the Ter Chadain
Bethany	Oldest Child Inhabiting Zeva's homestead
Sara	Second Oldest Child Inhabiting Zeva's homestead
Zack	Third Oldest Child Inhabiting Zeva's homestead
Violet	Youngest Child Inhabiting Zeva's homestead
Emmett	Storekeeper in Port Shoal
Rudnick Curn	Crystal Council of Stellaran's Magical Member
Duchess Heniton	Duchess of Los Clostern
Miso Tallar	Headmaster of Shotwarg Cliffs
Machala	Betra/Seeker of the Protector
Abria	Girl forced to be a Sniffer in Port Shoal
The Banished Ones	10 Magicals Exiled for Treason by Tera Lassain, First Queen of Ter Chadain

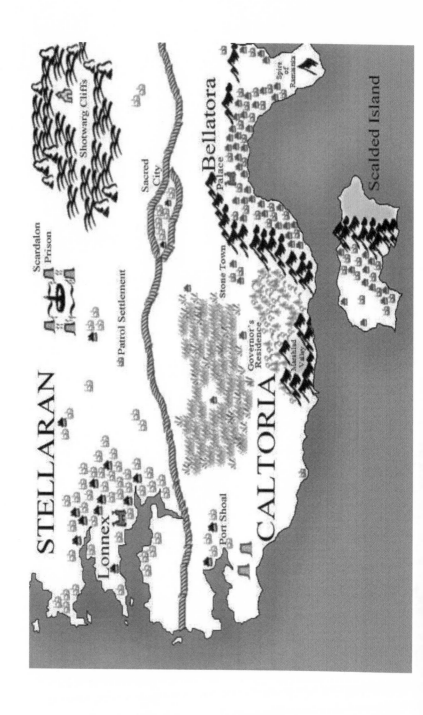

STELLARAN

Shotvarg Cliffs

Scardalon
Prison

Sacred
City

Patrol Settlement

Lonnex

Port Shoal

CALTORIA

Stone Town

Governor's
Residence

Marshland
Valley

Bellatora

Palace

Spire of
Ramantia

Scalded Island

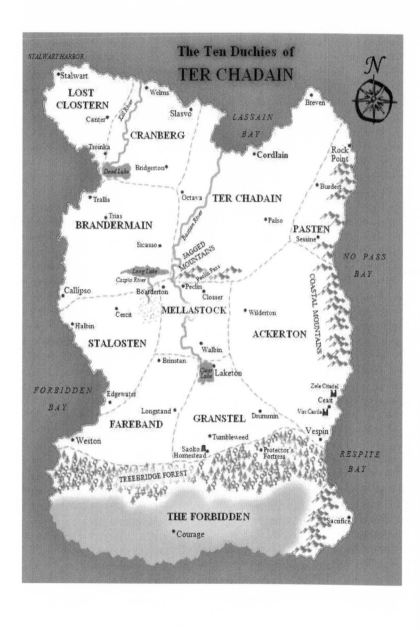

The Ten Duchies of
TER CHADAIN

N

STALWART HARBOR

•Stalwart

LOST
CLOSTERN

Canter•

•Welms

Slasvo

LASSAIN
BAY

Breven

CRANBERG

Troinka•

Dead Lake

Bridgerton•

•Cordlain

Rock
Point

•Burdest

•Trallis

Octava

TER CHADAIN

•Trias

BRANDERMAIN

Sicasso•

•Palso

PASTEN
Sessine•

NO PASS
BAY

JAGGED
MOUNTAINS

Long Lake
Caspio River

Pedlic Pass

Callipso

Boarderton

•Pedlin

Closser

•Cercit

MELLASTOCK

•Wilderton

COASTAL MOUNTAINS

ACKERTON

•Halbin

STALOSTEN

Walbin

•Brinstan

FORBIDDEN

BAY

Edgewater

Clear
Lake Laketon

Zele Citadel
Ceait

Viri Castle

Longstand •

FAREBAND

GRANSTEL

Drummin

Vespin

•Weston

Saolto
Homestead

•Tumbleweed

Protector's
Fortress

RESPITE

BAY

TREEBRIDGE FOREST

THE FORBIDDEN

•Courage

•Sacrifice

Chapter 1

Stern Barsten rode in near darkness at a leisurely pace, leaning down every so often to pat his mount's neck and give soft words of encouragement. His horse strode along favoring an injured left leg as it followed the deep rutted path worn down over centuries of constant use.

The young man straightened again, pushed his blond bangs from his eyes, and glanced around. His green eyes scanned for any sign that the "Pillars of the Weave" were somehow failing. He couldn't be blamed for his half-hearted attentiveness. Nothing ever happened along the weave, but that didn't mean they could ever stop patrolling it. Besides, the patrol was now the only occupation acceptable for his kind.

"His kind." He laughed at the thought, pulling his green travel cloak tighter around his neck as the dampness of the early morning chilled him. Where once his people ruled the land as far as the maps displayed the gifted now were more seen as oddities, destined to guard the weave between them and the land of the outcasts; the last remnant of their glorious past.

His mount stumbled on a rut and Stern jerked back to his surroundings from his daydream. He lifted his head as his horse steadied and the settlement inched into view. The streetlights and a few homestead lights flickered in the distance.

Stern sighed with exhaustion. Two days on patrol; a warm bed and hot meal would do him good. He wondered if Cita Cane was ready to head out. The newest patrol member, she still had the excitement for the ride and possible adventure that he once felt, but now knew would never come.

He plodded into the town; the houses lining the streets in neat straight lines, the yards and fences tended to and in perfect repair. He pulled up to the patrol headquarters, the two-story stone building with a few windows on the second level, but none on the first to allow for defense, stood with the two large entry doors opened wide allowing the light within to pour into the street.

He slid from his saddle landing nimbly as he lifted the reins over the horse's head and secured them to the post. He straightened, stretching the kink in his back from being in the saddle for nearly two days straight, the length of time it took to ride out to the end of the weave and back.

A tall burly man with long grey hair stood in the doorway casting an oversized shadow toward Stern as he walked up.

"Stern," the man said in a deep authoritative voice.

"Commander Wilkin." Stern nodded, only straightening enough to glance at the man's face. Stern's pace slowed as the expression on his commander's face told him he had news that Stern wasn't going to like. "No," Stern said as he passed the commander.

"You haven't even heard what I was going to say."

"I know that look," Stern said shaking his head.

"She isn't ready."

"But I've already been out on my run." Stern stopped and turned to his commander with a glare.

"You have the least seniority." Commander Wilkin shrugged. "Get some food and take an hour to rest."

"My horse can't take another run without a rest," Stern argued.

"Take my mount."

"Commander…" Stern began, but the light from the doorway glinting off his commander's eyes told him his words weren't swaying him. Stern pressed his lips together and nodded with resignation.

"Remember," Commander Wilkin said, "You were there once not too long ago."

The hour felt like a minute to Stern and soon he sat astride the commander's mount waiting patiently, as patiently as possible, as Cita scurried around her horse adjusting and tightening the straps

14

for the saddle and supply bags.

Cita pulled the strap tight on the saddle, tugging on the leather one more time before fastening it. She stood as tall as any man in the company, save for a few, and carried herself better than most of them. Stern wasn't concerned about her abilities, she could hold her own in any situation.

She had pride. Stern grinned. But he hoped it wouldn't drive him crazy on their first trip out.

In her twenties, she became the first woman to qualify for the patrol, and she held the gift stronger than any others in many years which trumped the rest of the patrol members. She pushed her long black hair over her shoulder as she pulled herself up into the saddle, draping her green cloak over her light brown trousers and thigh high black riding boots. She looked at Stern, her dark brown eyes filled with excitement.

Stern gave a weary nod, kicked his mount into a walk, and led the way onto the trail he just vacated a mere hour earlier.

Cita Cane fell in behind him, keeping pace along the worn path.

They rode in silence until Cita spoke, causing Stern to jump in his saddle, having forgotten she rode behind him.

"Do you think the weave will ever fail?" she asked.

"Ain't supposed to, so likely…no," Stern said glancing back over his shoulder.

"Then why do we do this?"

"You already questioning your occupational choice?" Stern asked with a chuckle.

"No choice. Better than a bar maid or farm hand," Cita said with a shrug.

"We do what the chairman and the Crystal Council tells us to do."

"What would happen if it did fail?" Cita continued.

Stern pulled his mount to a stop and motioned Cita next to him with a wave of his hand.

She moved beside him and stared expectantly.

"I thought they trained you about this." Stern sighed.

"Vaguely, but only a real patrol member would know the truth," Cita said.

"If I tell you, will you be quiet until we stop for camp?" He said, making an exception on this trip to stop and camp instead of riding straight through like he usually did.

Cita nodded that she would.

"If the weave between the four stones fails, there should be a patrol similar to us on the other side to keep the outcasts from coming back into Stellaran."

"You mean the gifted trapped on the wrong side when the weave closed too early?" Cita asked the fascination evident in her voice.

"So they say."

"You doubt they're there?" Cita said raising an eyebrow.

"I have my own theories on that, but now is not the time." He kicked his mount forward leaving her wondering after him.

She nudged her horse quickly catching up with him and pulled beside him again, brushing the overgrown grass crowding the narrow path out of the way with her hand.

"You doubt there are others like us on the other side of the weave?" she asked.

"Not the time to talk about it," he said and motioned with his head toward the large stone standing directly in their path ahead of them.

Cita nodded and fell in behind Stern as they approached the stone standing over twenty feet high and half again around. The path curved following the stone's surface and circled it. They remained silent as they followed the path.

Cita watched in amazement as she took in the stone for the first time. The others of the patrol explained it to her, but what she saw before her, their words didn't prepare her for. Even in the darkness, it reflected her image back to her in jagged lines as the stone curled in on it over and over as the surface displaying ridges of curved glass ringing the surface. But the appearance wasn't the strangeness she felt.

The stone seemed to pull at Cita's soul, drawing on her inborn magic as if to consume it. Her hand impulsively extended to touch the stone, but something roughly smacked her wrist, driving her arm away from the shimmering smoothness.

Cita jerked from her trance as Stern glared at her, his bow extended in his hand and anger simmering behind his green eyes.

"Didn't they teach you anything?" Stern growled.

"Sorry, I forgot," she said shamefully.

"Forgetting can leave you a burnt out husk."

"But the trainers said it wasn't dangerous," Cita said and regretted it as Stern stiffened in his saddle.

"What trainers? The ones from the council? Those fools shouldn't train children to eat, much less a gifted to be a member of the patrol," Stern shouted. "The stones were designed to take the inner magic of the stone and amplify it across miles to create and hold a weave strong enough that nothing can cross it or destroy it. That kind of power would suck your magic from you along with your life."

A low humming vibration suddenly filled the air sending the forest creatures on the edges of the path scampering. The stone began to glow, brightest along the peaks of the curves and less on the valleys of the grooves. The resonating vibration increased in volume sending out waves that reverberated in Cita's and Stern's chests.

"What did you do?" Stern said, trying to keep his mount from bolting like a wild animal.

"I didn't do anything," Cita shouted as her horse darted to the grass opposite the path and the stone.

The stone shone brighter and brighter, forcing both Stern and Cita to shield their eyes from the intensity. Then, as quickly as it began, the light vanished into the depths of the stone, but the sound continued to resonate louder and louder.

Stern's eyes opened wide as the energy inside the stone released in an outward rush. Cita raced to Stern, crowding as close to him as possible and then threw up a wall of magic she drew upon when the stone began to glow.

The stone's energy impacted her barrier sending woman, man, and horses alike into the trees in a jumbled heap and then everything went silent.

Stern pulled himself from the rows of thorn bushes he unfortunately landed in, ignoring the scrapes and imbedded thorns and lifted Cita out of the bushes with one hand.

"Thank you," Stern said as Cita came to her feet.

"It's why they allowed me to join," she shrugged off the compliment.

The horses righted themselves and trotted a short distance away along the tree line, waiting obediently for their riders.

As Stern pulled the stickers from his white shirtsleeves leaving red dots of blood, Cita stared aghast back toward the stone.

Stern noticed the look on the girl's face and spun to the stone, or what was left of it. The stone was gone except for ash and a large divot in the ground. Stern walked over and inspected the spot where the stone once stood.

Cita followed him and stared in shock as he picked up the dusty ash from the hole and rolled it between his fingers in disbelief.

"What happened?" Cita whispered.

"I believe a stone has failed," Stern whispered.

"Does that mean the weave is down and the portal is open?"

Stern's head snapped up at the possibility, finding it difficult to imagine. He jumped to his feet and ran to his horse with Cita close behind. They quickly mounted and kicked their horses into a full run, racing down the path.

They rode hard for a day, pushing the horses as far as they dared and then walked them until they recovered, and then rode hard again.

Stern pulled his horse to a walk when the second stone came into view.

Cita moved beside him, sighing with relief at seeing that the stone still stood. They continued closer and a familiar ominous humming reached their ears. They raced for cover and dismounted behind some trees. Cita raised her magic to protect them just as the light burst from the stone and incinerated everything outside their barrier.

In a burst of energy, the ash covered the magical barrier and the forest went silent except for the crackling fire in the trees, their black skeletons stretching skyward.

Cita and Stern exchanged apprehensive looks and stood as Cita released her magic. They walked to the divot where the stone once stood and stared in disbelief.

"Do you think it's open?" Cita again asked the unthinkable.

"Don't say that," Stern said in a hushed tone. "The other two stones on the Caltorian side might still be holding."

"But the four stones are tied together. Two here and two on the other side," Cita reasoned. "If the two here are destroyed, the sister stones on the other side must also be destroyed."

Stern couldn't argue with her logic. He stared at the ash and ran a hand through his hair. "It is fine...everything will be fine."

"But if the purpose of the stones was to keep the rebels who tried to overthrow the Crystal Council of Stellaran from returning..." Cita pressed.

Stern spun on her, his fear masked in anger at her bluntness.

Cita took a step back, but didn't waiver in her conviction to the truth.

"Are the traitors imprisoned in Caltoria…free?"

"May the spirits of our forefathers protect us," Stern prayed.

Chapter 2

Bristol Alabaster stared at the darkness, her gray eyes narrowing as she searched back and forth. From her apartment in the deserted Sacred City, she held the perfect vantage point to monitor the weave separating Stellaran from Caltoria. Her silvering hair was pulled back from her face and tied in a neat bun. She frowned at the night, giving a shudder, and pulled the silver embroidered blue cloak around her, feeling something different; something she hadn't felt in all her sixty plus years.

She resided within these secluded walls for most of those years, taking up a calling that only a handful of magicals could. It wasn't so much her magical strength, since she possessed only modest prowess in the use of her magic, but instead it was her special ability with that magic which made her one of only seven destined to be a member of the Weave Tenders.

Bristol leaned out the window into the cool night, fighting back her fear as she urged her magic to tell her differently. She didn't want to believe that what had stood through hundreds and hundreds of years was no more. Her eyes flitted from one end of the long stone wall to the other, searching just past that wall for the weave that needed to be there.

But it wasn't there. The weave wasn't there.

She hurried to the curved horn hanging from a leather strap resting on the hook in the wall. She rushed back to the window and put the horn to her lips taking a deep breath. As her lips touched the horn, the long bellow of a matching horn sounded down the wall.

She jumped with a start and pressed the horn to her lips and blew. The eerie sound of the hollowed instrument echoed into the night, joining the first horn and then was joined by another, and another, until seven horns sounded in unison.

Many others over the years manned these walls and stood

21

watch over the weave, never needing to touch the horn. Bristol knew this changed everything. Now the descendants of those who could overthrow the Council of Stellaran were no longer barred from their homeland. But also, those descendants of the members of the council who were trapped so many years ago could return home and leave this horrible place of slavery and death for all magicals in Caltoria.

The door flew open, banging against the stone wall of the apartment causing Bristol to spin around in surprise as her son rushed in, his face a mix of horror and exhilaration. Their eyes met and he stopped and nodded. His small, muscular frame shuddered as he exhaled and eased into a chair.

"So it's happened," he stated and lifted his brown, tear filled eyes to his mother's and brushed his long brown bangs from his face.

"Yes," she whispered.

"Now we find the traitors who trapped us here," he said as he wiped a tear from his cheek.

"Trevon, you mustn't think that way."

"We've heard the stories and it hasn't taken all these years to figure out what happened. The council was betrayed that day. It was no accident that only those with magical ability were trapped on this side of the weave." He stared hard at her, his tears drawing back into his eyes as his emotion turned to anger.

"There is only our small group still alive with the knowledge of those times," Bristol said. "We must return to Stellaran to share this knowledge and bring justice to the council."

"Now is the time we need to find out. If the weave is down, that means the stones have been destroyed. That which the empress has used against us is now gone. All magical slaves should now be free. We can search for others related to the original council."

"We have spoken of this before, we need to flee Caltoria. The weave separating us from our homeland also protected us from the empress," Bristol argued.

"The chairman's weave around our sacred city is now gone as well?" Trevon asked.

"He bent the weave barring access to Stellaran around our city to protect us. The weaves are one in the same."

Fear filled Trevon's eyes.

"We must gather everyone and flee north into Stellaran," Bristol instructed. "Hurry, we have little time to lose. The empress has wanted us for a long time; we should not be here when her troops arrive."

****

Stern and Cita rode hard, pushing their mounts to exhaustion until they feared the animals might die. They made camp to allow the horses a short rest before continuing on.

Sitting beside a small fire, each stared into the flames, contemplating what the failure of the weave might mean. To Stern, the veteran patrol member who now found himself without a purpose and Cita, the new recruit whose career guarding the Pillars of the Weave lasted less than a night, it meant that their lives would change forever.

"Will there be war?" Cita said breaking the silence.

Stern didn't look up from the flames, but gave a guttural grunt in response.

"What is that supposed to mean?" Cita said. "Is that a grunt for no or a grunt for yes?"

"Just a grunt," Stern replied. "A grunt for I have no idea."

"What is on the other side?" Cita asked motioning with a nod in the direction of Caltoria.

"No one knows," Stern admitted. "Since the weave rose over five hundred years ago there has been no contact with the other side."

"Surely there are those that possess magic guarding the other side as we are," Cita reasoned.

"Do you see them? Are they here checking to see that we are on this side of the weave?" Stern grumbled.

Cita looked into the darkness as her mind churned with the possibilities. "What could have happened to them?"

"They say the strongest of us were trapped on the other side when the weave went up unexpectedly."

"I've read the stories," Cita nodded. "The entire Council of Stellaran was on that side. They were inspecting the stone placements in Caltoria when the weave activated before scheduled. Surely they saw that the weave was patrolled."

"With the entire criminal population on the other side with them, it is reasonable to think that may have been the last thing on their minds," Stern said.

"What do you mean?"

"Do you know why the criminals were being exiled to Caltoria?" Stern asked with a frown.

"They were criminals," Cita said, but instantly knew that wasn't what he meant.

"They failed in an attempt to take over Stellaran along with killing or imprisoning every person who possessed magic in the kingdom. The council exiled them along with their extremist views."

"But instead, our strongest Council of Stellaran in history became trapped on the wrong side of the weave with them," Cita said as the pieces of the puzzle she read about many times finally fell into place.

"I believe the captors might have become the captives in this case," Stern said.

Cita looked back at the flames, her thoughts even more disturbed and chaotic than before. After staring at the fire for a long time, she looked back at Stern, her jaw clenched in determination.

Stern looked at her, confused and then shook his head as the fire flickered in her eyes. "No."

"You haven't even heard what I'm thinking," Cita objected.

"Doesn't matter what you're thinking. The answer is still no. We head back to base and inform the others."

"We need to find out who is in charge in Caltoria so we can report to Wilkin," Cita argued.

"Our job is to report that the weave has failed, nothing more," Stern said with a shake of his head.

"But if what you suspect is true, we need to warn the commander that the exiles are in control in Caltoria."

"Then what?" Stern asked flatly.

"I'm not sure, but I'd rather know what's coming...wouldn't you?"

Stern held Cita's gaze for a moment, stood, and rolled his pack up. He walked to his horse tethered next to Cita's, lifted his saddle into place, and secured the straps. Setting his bedroll behind the saddle, he tied it in place with the thin strands of leather fastened to the saddle. Stern turned back to Cita with a raised eyebrow.

Cita frowned, not understanding.

"If we move on tonight and scout the other side of the weave, we can still get to base by the same time tomorrow," Stern said and then leapt into his saddle.

Cita scrambled together her supplies, saddled her horse, and kicked dirt on the fire, the flames flickering and hissing before going out. She scurried into her saddle and followed Stern as he headed into Caltoria and the unknown that lay in the darkness before them.

****

Empress Shakata stared out over her burning city as flames engulfed the Spire on the point overlooking the harbor. Fire consumed Stone Town in the distance. She knew she should feel something…anything, but a lack of feeling, numbness, had filled her in the days since the revolt. She pulled the heavy gray woolen blanket across her shoulders closer as the damp sea breeze wafted through the open window.

The Queen of Ter Chadain and the Protector of Ter Chadain, here in my palace within my grasp, under my control…how could I let them escape?

She hung her head for a moment and then lifted it to look down along the path leading to the palace below her window. Spikes with severed heads impaled upon them lined the walkway. The one nearest her window burned her soul the deepest, but was nearly a skeleton with patches of skin here and there along with eyes. The crows picked clean everything and soon the condemning eyes would give way to hollowed sockets.

Rowan Anthony, her lover, the father of her son and the general of her army stared with empty eyes into the distance. His betrayal cut so sharply that her faith in anyone around her felt corroded forever. How could he do this to her? Hide his magical ability, plot to free the slaves, and ultimately overthrow her. He not only did this, but used her own son, Caslor, against her to reel her in and deflect suspicion away from him. And now Caslor, the only heir to her throne and a traitor himself, sped across the sea to Ter Chadain with her mortal enemies.

Berza rushed into the room surrounded by the guards who stood watch outside. Shakata trusted no magical after the stones no longer held them. The magical in her red travel cloak stood amidst the gold-clad guards with the golden eye on their breastplates looking expectantly at Shakata's back.

Shakata turned wearily to the magical who swore her loyalty to the empress as the stones failed, saving her family from a death sentence in Stone Town.

"Yes, what is it?" Shakata asked, her voice ragged with

fatigue.

"Have you slept, Empress?" Berza asked.

"I will sleep when I die."

"If you keep this up, that may be sooner than later."

Shakata looked hard at Berza who took a step back.

"What is it?"

"The weave is down," Berza said.

Shakata looked blankly at the magical.

"The weave separating Caltoria and Stellaran," Berza clarified.

Shakata's eyes shot open wide with surprise.

"What do you wish me to do?" Berza asked.

"What do you mean? What is there to do?"

"Do you want me to gather our army to invade Stellaran, or perhaps a scouting party to discover what they are preparing for us?"

Shakata stared at the magical as her mind processed this new and surprising development. A thought came to her and a smile crept across her face, a smile that made Berza cringe.

"Didn't the source stones come from Stellaran?" Shakata asked.

"Yes, Empress, they are said to have come from the mountains of Stellaran. They were mined and then brought and placed here in Caltoria."

"Along with two matching ones on the Stellaran side..." Shakata said turning back to the window and stroking her chin in thought.

"When the stones here were destroyed, the matching ones in Stellaran must have been destroyed as well, breaking the weave and removing the barrier that separated us."

"If we came into possession of another source stone could it be used in the same manner as the ones that the Lassains destroyed?" Shakata asked, the name tasting bitter in her mouth, causing her to scowl as she turned back to Berza.

27

Fear filled Berza's eyes as she nodded.

"Ha ha ha, how perfect," Shakata smiled. "Not only can we get revenge on those who imprisoned us here in this desolate land, but we can take control of the magicals once more and set the order right again."

"But what of the Lassains and Ter Chadain?" Berza asked.

"Let them have their tiny country…for now. Get a search party together tasked with seeking out a source stone." Have our generals begin preparation for the invasion of Stellaran. If my history lessons were right, the Council of Stellaran is far too interested in peace to have a fraction of the army we possess. We shall walk into Stellaran, take control, and soon have our magicals back as well. Then we will crush Ter Chadain and wipe away any evidence of the Lassain bloodline from existence."

Berza stood staring at Empress Shakata as her ruler regained her confidence and set a course for conquering anyone and anything in her path. A true ruler of Caltoria.

"What are you waiting for?" Shakata barked, jolting Berza from her horror-filled contemplation.

"Yes, Empress," Berza said with a bow. "At once, Empress." She turned and ran from the throne room. "May the spirits have mercy on us all."

****

The next morning Trevon packed frantically, throwing random items into a brown leather bag until it overflowed and had no hope of closing.

The clearing of a throat brought Trevon spinning around to the open door where a tall, slender man not much older than he stood with his arms crossed over his chest. His hazel eyes danced with amusement, betraying the frown on his face. His brown riding cloak hung open to reveal a light brown shirt covered by a darker brown leather tunic.

"Clastis, you scared me." Trevon turned back to his packing. "Bristol told me of your plans to go before the Stellaran Council and accuse their ancestors of betrayal." Clastis strode into the room and flopped down on the bed where Trevon packed.

"So? You come to tell me I'm crazy?" Trevon glared for a moment, stormed across the room to gather a canteen, then returned to toss it on the bed next to the overflowing bag.

"You *are* crazy. Everyone knows that." Clastis struggled to keep the smirk from his lips.

"Crazy or not, I won't let the council get away with what they did to us or let the empress destroy Stellaran like her and her ancestors did Caltoria. Not without trying to stop her." Trevon stared hard at him.

"Cousin, you might be crazy, but you are also right," Clastis said, unable to stop the smile that now spread across his face, his white teeth shining. "As was your father."

Trevon stopped and stared in disbelief at his older cousin, the same cousin who always picked on him as a child and teased him incessantly, until Trevon grew large enough to defend himself. Once Clastis saw Trevon as more of an equal, they had become close friends. He thought his father and his beliefs had died with him in the empress's dungeon. He always held those beliefs close and never spoke of them with others.

"Uncle told me of the history and what must be done if the weave failed. I'm behind you, as are Linell and Fedlen," Clastis said with a nod.

"Linell? You told Linell?" Trevon moaned. "Why does *she* have to be a part of this?"

"Because magic is strongest in women and she is the strongest we have," Clastis argued. "Besides, your mother wouldn't keep this from her since you two are betrothed."

"Ugh," Trevon groaned.

Clastis shrugged. "Could be worse, she could be ugly with

warts and moles with hairs growing out of them and be without magic and completely worthless to us."

"Like Marnie Moxen," a voice said from the doorway.

Clastis and Trevon turned to see Fedlen dressed in a brown riding cloak and a gray tunic over dark brown pants leaning against the door jam, hands on his narrow hips and a sly smirk on his face. He ran a hand through his straight black hair and his dark brown eyes twinkled with amusement.

"Oh, don't bring her up," Clastis moaned.

"Sorry, but anyone would rather have Linell Los as a betrothed than Marnie Moxen," Fedlen said with a laugh.

"I have to agree, Linell is much more attractive than Marnie," Trevon chuckled.

"I would like to believe there is more to me than just a pretty face," a woman's voice spoke up from behind Fedlen.

The three men looked from one to the other with shock and embarrassment before Fedlen stepped aside to reveal Linell. Her long dark hair and dark skin shone in the light as her black eyes scanned the room's occupants. Her smooth skin blended with the tight black leather bodice of her riding dress that split at the thigh to reveal shapely legs and thigh-high riding boots. Her high cheekbones displayed her attractiveness for all to see, but it was her inner strength and beauty that radiated from her giving off a sense of control and sensuality.

"Uh… hey, Linell," Trevon stammered.

"My betrothed," Linell said padding lightly to him and giving him a submissive kiss on his cheek.

The men stared at her, their confusion obvious on their faces.

Linell reached back and slapped Trevon full-on across his face, sending him spinning with a loud smack.

He turned back to her nodding with a hand to his cheek.

"That's more like it," he said rubbing his reddening face.

"I am not a piece of meat and I have enough slaps to go around if you forget," she said looking at the other two in the room.

Fedlen and Clastis put their hands up defensively before them and shook their heads.

"Are we going to get out of here before dark, or do you ladies have some more gossiping to do?"

"We're ready," Fedlen said. "The horses are saddled and we're just waiting for your 'betrothed' to get his stuff so we can go."

Linell turned to Trevon who looked back at her, the fear showing in his eyes. He slipped a leather vest on over his brown tunic and then draped his brown cloak over the top and scurried to gather his pack. Spinning, he raced past her to the door shouldering Fedlen aside on his way out.

Linell laughed as Trevon left and then motioned to Clastis and Fedlen to follow. They hurried out the door leaving Linell to close the door as she smirked and nodded to herself.

Chapter 3

Grinwald, in his gray long robe with the hood pulled up, and Raven in her brown slacks and tunic stood in the dark hallway outside the cabin door as the Morning Breeze swayed with the waves. The sounds of sleep filled the cabins around them, but the two magicals had more important things to do than sleep.

Miles out to sea and away from Caltoria, Grinwald made the decision he dreaded since discovering that both Logan and Teah possessed the protector's powers. He knew this choice needed to be made, but never dreamed the pain it caused him would be so profound.

Morgan slipped silently up behind them as they waited, stopping to secure the leather wrist guards on his arm and pull down the brown leather vest over his deep red shirt as he eyed them expectantly. The captain needed to be in on the plan and added a unique twist that ensured their success. By having the ship's cook slip a sedative into Logan's food, he assured the plan's outcome. He looked at the Viri Magus and the girl, giving them a nod.

Grinwald took a deep breath and pushed open the door, the hinges creaking in protest. He hurried into the cabin, forming the weave he needed and stepped to one side of the room toward an occupied cot.

Raven padded to the other cot and swung her arm holding a club, bringing it down on the occupant with a thud. Air released from the person's lungs, then silence.

Morgan moved to where Grinwald stood and brought his club down on the person's head as the Viri Magus released his weave. The red strands of magic hovered over the body and then eased into it. Grinwald glared at Morgan.

"Can't be too careful," Morgan whispered and gave a shrug.

Raven now stood next to the men and released a green weave

of magic around the person in the cot still covered in the blanket. The body lifted up and floated toward the door.

Grinwald scooped up the sheathed protector's blades next to the cot along with the short metal bar in its holder and followed out the door.

The three guided the floating body out the door leading from the cabins, onto the shadowed deck, and toward the rail where a small dingy leaned over the edge of the ship's rails, suspended by ropes and pulleys above the black sea.

Grinwald deposited the weapons into the dingy and stepped back.

Raven stared at the boat and then spun on Grinwald.

"What are you doing?" she asked in an intense whisper.

"I will do what I must, but I won't be a cold blooded killer," Grinwald said.

"Kind of late for that, old man," Morgan said, amused. "Don't worry, I'll make sure it is done."

Grinwald shot Morgan a hard look but the captain ignored him.

"Those weapons are gold in my pocket," Morgan complained looking at the rare artifacts as they sat in the dingy.

"We need it to seem that Logan fought and lost," Grinwald argued. "If his weapons remain, it will draw suspicion."

"Let's get this done," Raven said.

"Get what done?" a voice asked from behind them.

The three spun away from the floating body to Zeva, standing in a deep green dress with white lace at the collar and wrists with her hands on her hips, glowing with the magic she held at the ready. She looked at the three conspirators and then at Morgan's hand holding the crooked dagger of the Senji. She strode over to the covered body and pulled the blanket away revealing Logan unconscious with a large welt on his forehead. She spun to face the others in shock.

"It must be this way," Grinwald said.

"But why?" Zeva asked.

"To assure that Ter Chadain survives," Raven said, impatient. "Now step aside and let us do what we must."

Raven slipped between Zeva and Logan, pushing her away as Morgan raised the Senji blade and drove it down into Logan's chest. The blade twisted free of his hand and skittered across the deck.

"What are you doing?" Grinwald shouted.

"Making sure he doesn't come back to haunt us," Morgan nodded to Logan. "If you don't tie up loose ends, they tend to come back and tie you up...in my experience."

"Why would I waste my energy binding his powers just so you can kill him?" Grinwald grumbled.

Raven sent a weave that drew the knife back to Morgan who then plunged the knife into Logan's inner thigh.

"There, he won't die from the blade, but now we have blood to add to the story," Morgan said with a nod.

"But the poison might kill him," Grinwald argued.

"Quit being so soft," Raven chided. "It is you who said this must be done, now live with it, Viri Magus."

Zeva took advantage of their distraction and shoved Morgan aside, guiding Logan into the dingy as she untied the weave around him. Logan dropped into the dingy and Zeva jumped in, sending a weave of magic to release the ropes and drop the boat into the threatening waters below.

Raven leaned over the rail, a weave leaving her fingers and striking Zeva in the back of her head. The woman fell on top of Logan, disoriented and dazed.

The dingy pulled free of the lines tethering it to the Morning Breeze, bounced against the hull, and spun away as the ship raced off into the night.

"Quinty," Morgan shouted to his first mate manning the wheel, "turn us around."

Quinty nodded and started spinning the wheel.

"That won't be necessary. Grinwald laid a hand on Morgan's arm.

"Hold that order," Morgan shouted and the first mate spun the wheel back again. "And why shouldn't we go back and finish them?" Morgan said to Grinwald.

"We are two days from land and I have bound his Viri Magus abilities. He is no more magical than you are," Grinwald said with a sigh.

"But what if Zeva unties your weave?" Raven asked.

"She does not have the power or the knowledge. She will not succeed," Grinwald said.

"How can you be so sure?" Morgan pressed.

"If the weave is untied, it will kill Logan instantly. I'm not even sure he still has use of his protector's powers. My weave may have bound them as well."

"They are days, maybe weeks from land with no food or water," Morgan said with a nod. "They are done."

"And our story just became more believable, thanks to Zeva," Raven said with a grin.

"How's that?" Morgan asked.

"Zeva has now become our assassin who fled the ship after killing Logan and tossing his body overboard," Raven explained.

Morgan nodded with a grin and lifted the blade up to see Logan's blood clearly on the blade. He tossed it to the deck with a clang. "That should do it," he said with a nod.

"Yes, but I hope we did the right thing," Grinwald said turning to the rail and the dark night hanging over the sea.

****

Teah sat up in her bed as a rush of anxiety flowed over her. She looked to Rachel in one bed and Saliday in the other and then to Zeva's empty bed.

Something wasn't right. She felt it, but the feeling confused her.

What was that? Galiven asked.

I don't know. You felt it too? She asked.

Something is wrong, Stalwart said.

Brother, did you feel it? Teah reached out to Logan. She waited, but Logan didn't respond.

Brother?

"What's the matter?" Rachel asked, sitting up in her bed and rubbing the sleep from her eyes as she pulled her light blue dress over her head.

"I felt something strange and now…" she hesitated, remembering her connection to Logan needed to remain a secret. "I need to check on Logan."

"Something's wrong with Logan?" Saliday asked, throwing her covers off and slipping into her black pants and pulling on her brown tunic before topping it with the black vest holding her many knives. She slipped her calf-high boots on and fastened her belt with her short sword around her waist before slipping her dark green cloak on.

Teah hurried to dress in dark green pants and shirt, leaving her cloak on the chair next to her bed and strode for the door with Saliday and Rachel close behind.

They went to Logan's room he shared with Caslor and paused outside. Teah tapped on the door and waited. When she heard nothing, she turned the latch and eased the door open.

Caslor slept in his cot and the other sat empty.

Teah pushed past Saliday and Rachel, heading for the deck as the two women exchanged concerned looks and spun to follow.

Teah stepped onto the deck, expecting to find Logan leaning against the rail, staring out at the early morning sky, but scanned the deck frantically when he was nowhere to be seen. She rushed up the stairs to the wheel where First Mate Quinty stood watching the three women curiously.

"Have you seen my brother?" she inquired, the urgency in her voice causing it to quiver.

"No, mum," he said with a shake of his head.

"And you've been here all night?" Teah pressed.

"Yes, mum," he said.

"Quinty," Saliday said, doubt in her voice.

Quinty gave Saliday a sheepish look and turned back to Teah.

"Well, mum, I did step away for a brief time to, uh, relieve myself..." he said without looking her in the eyes.

"And...?" Saliday added.

"And get some refreshments," he said, his eyes staring at the deck. "I did get a might bit parched."

"Teah," Rachel called as she stood on the deck below the bridge holding up a dagger with a crooked blade.

Senji, the four protectors said in unison.

Saliday gasped at the sight of the Senji blade in Rachel's hand, following Teah as she rushed down to the deck to take the weapon from Rachel. Teah lifted the blade before her eyes to examine it. Drying blood reddened the edge of the silver metal.

"Careful, Senji blades are usually tipped with poison," Saliday warned.

Senji? Teah asked the protectors.

"That is a Senji blade," Saliday said as if reading Teah's thoughts. "They are a society of assassins who Englewood contracted to kill your brother."

"But on this ship?" Rachel asked.

"They are everywhere," Saliday said.

"But who?" Teah asked the impending question.

"Where is Zeva?" Rachel said looking around the deck as the sunrise brightened the sky in the distance lightening the darkness hanging over the ship.

"Not Zeva," Teah objected.

"And why not?" Saliday argued. "We know her least of all and Senji can be anyone."

"Get Grinwald," Teah said turning to Rachel.

Rachel nodded and hurried off below deck to the cabins, Saliday moved over to the rail.

"Where could they have gone?" Teah muttered under her breath.

"The dingy is gone," Saliday said from the rail.

Teah moved over beside her, looking at the empty pulleys the ropes holding the dingy once filled.

"Zeva's escape route. Saliday pointed to the missing dingy.

"Why would she take him with her?" Teah asked.

"She wouldn't," Morgan said as he stepped on deck and walked to them. "If she is Senji, she would have killed him, thrown him overboard, and then taken the dingy and escaped."

"Who are we talking about?" Grinwald said as he wrapped his cloak around his frail frame and fastened it with a clasp at the neck.

"It seems we are missing Zeva and Logan," Morgan said turning to the Viri Magus.

"What gives you the indication she is Senji?" Grinwald asked.

Teah held the dagger up to Grinwald and he scowled.

"That's Senji," Morgan said with a nod.

Can you sense him? Bastion asked, breaking his silence.

Teah reached out, letting her thoughts spread across the distance over the empty sea, searching for any trace, any tickle of existence from Logan.

No. She said as her hopes washed away and her fear became reality. *He's gone.*

Chapter 4

The dingy from the Morning Breeze drifted with the high waves, tossing and turning randomly as each whitecap battered the wooden boat and drenched its unconscious passengers.

Zeva lay on top of Logan where she'd landed after taking a direct hit from Raven's magic and now began to stir. The sun crept above the rough surf shining in her eyes as she fought to pry her eyelids open. After several futile attempts, they inched open in time to see the sun hidden behind the black clouds looming above them.

The spray wet them from head to toe. Her teeth chattered as the cold seawater and wind sapped every ounce of heat from her body. Even Logan's teeth chattered as he lay unconscious in a light, white shirt and dark pants soaked through with sea water.

She drew upon her magic weaving a protective barrier around them, tied it off, and then filled the space with a weave of warm air.

She leaned over Logan carefully, looking for the source of the blood mixing with the water on the bottom of the dingy, producing a large crimson puddle beneath them. She sent her magic into the wound and worked at removing the poison which treated every Senji blade. After being certain the wound was poison-free, she wove the tissue together and sealed the site.

Staring down at this boy, not much younger than she, gave her a sense of isolation as the memory of her family lost in Stone Town broke through her stoic resolve. *Gone, all of them were gone.* Her mother, father, two brothers, and sister were gone. She thought of her uncles and aunts who shunned her family once Zeva's magic became apparent when she turned fifteen. Unlike some families who abandoned a lone family member who possessed the magic, Zeva's mother and father insisted on moving to Stone Town and finding work to support her brothers and sister in order to stay close to Zeva.

Tears welled up in her eyes knowing that loyalty to her ended their days. Remaining in the small fishing town on the northwest coast of Caltoria could have saved their lives.

She lifted her head and stared out across the empty horizon. Turning her head, she could see water sprawling out in every direction and disappearing into the distance. Worry filled her eyes as she drew a hand across her face, removing her tears and hardening her to what lay ahead. She looked once more to Logan and felt sorrow envelop her.

On the ship she had listened as Logan told the crew how Grinwald, once thought lost to them, reappeared in the caves. She noted the tears of joy in his eyes as he spoke of the wonder he felt at finding his mentor once again.

And when she stepped onto the deck and found Grinwald, Morgan, and Raven standing over the form covered in a blanket hovering above the deck, she never imagined it was Logan, the boy who sacrificed everything to save his sister and in doing so, freed all the slaves of Caltoria in the process. This boy who lost yet another loved one but still gave everything for those he cared about and inspired the same from all those around him. She sacrificed herself to keep him alive. Raven and Morgan she never trusted, but how could Grinwald do this to him?

She looked closely at Logan as he lay unconscious and saw the dark weave surrounding him, hinting at its seriousness. It tied off at some unseen location along the deadly strands of magic. Apparently, he once was connected to magic, but now he would wake to find that magic severed, keeping him from that which filled every sense of who he was.

"What have you done to deserve such betrayal?" she asked, looking first at him, then staring out at the emptiness surrounding them once more.

****

Logan felt himself lolling from side to side as he slowly became aware of his surroundings. Pain throbbed in his head and his thigh pulsed in agony. He eased his eyes open to an overcast sky. Lifting himself to a seated position, the shock of being in a small boat instead of the Morning Breeze greeted him and snapped him wide awake in the here and now.

A small figure curled up on the bench seat across from him and water splashed and sprayed against the invisible magical barrier protecting them from the harsh elements surrounding them.

"Zeva?" he whispered, not intentionally, but due to the rawness of his throat.

Zeva stirred and lifted her head to look at him. Seeing him watching her, she sat up to face him, her features showing the gravity of their situation.

"How do you feel?"

"What's going on? What are we doing here? Where's the ship?" He scanned the vast ocean before turning his confused stare back to her.

She cleared her throat, but that didn't seem to help as her words still came out weak. "I'm afraid you've been betrayed."

"Betrayed? By whom?"

"Morgan," she began and stopped as Logan's eyes turned venomous.

"I might have known. Ever since he discovered Saliday had feelings for me, he wanted me out of the way."

"And Raven."

Logan's expression lost its edge and he pressed his lips together as the pain of her betrayal cut deep. He nodded as he processed the information. "That I can see…sort of, but I thought we had a connection. I always felt she might have her own agenda though…" He stared out across the water as his mind drifted.

"And…"

Logan turned back with surprise. "There is another?" His brow furrowed and he scowled at the thought of three betrayers on the ship. "One of the crew members?"

Zeva shook her head, hesitant to give him the last name. The name she knew would devastate him.

"I doubt Rachel would be party to any of this," Logan said. "Not Saliday?" Logan's face filled with fear at the mere thought that she might betray him…again.

Zeva shook her head.

"I'm getting a headache, stop making this a game and tell me," Logan insisted.

"Grinwald," Zeva whispered.

"Who?" Logan leaned close, their faces so close they could feel each other's breath upon their skin.

"Grinwald," Zeva said.

Logan recoiled as if bitten by a snake, scrambling to the other side of the dingy. He stared back at her, aghast, as she raised her sorrow-filled eyes to him.

His eyes filled with tears as he shook his head, slowly at first, but then harder and more determined. "No…no…no…*No!*"

Zeva turned away, fighting to stay composed. She needed to stay strong for him.

"I don't believe you. Grinwald would never. Why would he ever…?" the thought trailed away as the possibility hung unspoken in the dingy.

Zeva stared off into the distance and Logan went silent.

Logan sat with his eyes closed, reaching out to Teah with his mind. The effort left him feeling as if he held his head underwater, muffled and sluggish. He frowned and tried again. His thoughts seemed to reach the edge of her consciousness and then stop short.

After the protector spirits leapt from his mind to Teah's, Logan struggled to make sense of the things they normally guided him through. Not until they destroyed the source stone did he once again link up mentally with his sister, but now, that connection felt more than missing, it felt blocked, cut off, muffled. He knew it still remained, but he didn't have any way of reaching across the void to make contact.

Panic filled him as he searched the bottom of the dingy until he found his swords and bow. Scrambling the short distance to them as they lay at Zeva's feet, he snatched them up and hurried back, the fear spread across his face.

He pulled the artifacts close to him and then drew a sword to stare at it before him. He frowned when the sword did not light up with the magical glow he'd grown accustomed to. The sword still felt good in his hand, but it did not draw upon his innate magic as it did in the caves of the Mashlad.

Lifting the sword high above his head, he urged his magic into the sword, willing it to light, but still nothing came. He brought the sword down to eye level then hoisted it again, still nothing. He repeated the motion again and again as Zeva watched in agonized silence.

When he lowered the sword to his lap in defeat, Zeva's empathetic eyes beheld his crushed spirit and a tear rolled down her cheek.

"You've been bound," Zeva whispered.

Logan didn't look up but nodded, still staring at the sword resting in his lap.

"I'm sorry."

"Did you do this?" Logan asked, lifting his tired gaze to her.

"No." She shook her head as their eyes met.

"Then why are you sorry?" He held her gaze for a moment and then turned away staring at the empty horizon. "Raven."

"It is a Viri Magus magic that binds you."

Logan's eyes clenched shut as the pain of the statement cut him to the core. Grinwald was the only Viri Magus on the

Morning Breeze.

"He wouldn't do that," he said, but the tone in his voice betrayed his lack of conviction.

"I know how important he is to you, but I do not lie."

Logan turned back to her, the intensity in his eyes causing her to lean away from him.

"An easy statement when I have nothing to base its merit on."

Zeva stiffened and her hands opened and closed into fists at her side as she fought to remain in control. She leaned forward, closing the small distance in the dingy between them, matching his fierceness as she hissed through clenched teeth.

"Do not question my honor, boy, else you will be taught a lesson you won't soon forget." She held his gaze. Neither of them backed down. She spun away with a growl to face the other end of the boat.

Logan glared at her back for the longest time and finally let his anger wash from him as he began processing what happened and how he would resolve the predicament he now found himself in. He felt as he did when his protector powers first came to him...*minus the voices*...he added. He needed to treat everything around him as a threat and discover what powers he still possessed.

He looked around the small wooden boat again. He needed to be on land to do that so until they got out of this dingy, he couldn't be sure if he still possessed his protector's powers.

Until he knew what he had to work with, he couldn't afford to trust anyone, or anything, he decided with a curt nod. Logan was once again...on his own.

Chapter 5

Trevon and his friends headed for the gates of the ancient city. Built by those of the Stellaran Council within the weave, it separated the two countries for one purpose: to assure that the weave stood. Now with the weave gone, the Sacred City held no purpose and no safety for that matter. The weave that flowed around either side of the great city protected its occupants from the aggression of the rulers of Caltoria, keeping the magical occupants safe from being stoned. The magic inside each resident flowed through their blood and allowed them passage from the city through the weave and into Caltoria but did not allow any other passage into the city. That inborn magic didn't allow passage through the weave separating Caltoria and Stellaran however. That magic remained far too powerful, until now.

So now the city needed to rely on the ramparts and gates surrounding it in order to fend off the empress and her aggressions. Trevon looked up at the looming walls of yellow stone in a new light, wondering if they could possibly withstand a siege. He need never find out since their numbers continued to dwindle over the years and now only a handful of people still occupied the city. Not nearly enough to defend against the empress's assault that surely would follow.

Linell pulled up at the gate and the rest of the city's inhabitants gathered for departure stopped behind her. Trevon wove his mount from the back to the front and stopped next to his betrothed, glancing over at her as she raised an eyebrow in inquiry.

A large man wearing shiny silver armor adorned with golden bars on each shoulder, stood in the middle of their path in a heated discussion with a man in a dark brown riding cloak holding his horse's reins in his hand and frantically flailing his other arm around. The larger man dismissed the man in the riding cloak and turned, planting his hands firmly on his hips with his helm tucked neatly under one arm. His deep blue eyes looked flatly up at Trevon as his lips thinned in determination.

"Morning, Captain," Trevon greeted, his voice cracking with nerves.

"I might have suspected you'd be the first to try and flee the city," the man said, distaste in his tone.

"By the looks of it," Trevon said looking at the others gathered around, "Everyone is ready to leave." He nodded in the direction of the rider leading his horse into the stables. "What was that all about?"

"Just got word that Stone Town was destroyed," the captain said with indifference.

"What?" Linell asked from behind Trevon.

"The empress must have feared the town's inhabitants would turn on her once the weave went down and decided to lessen her risk," the captain explained.

"That's horrible, all those innocent people," Linell gasped.

"Rumor has it some royalty from Ter Chadain destroyed the stones in Bellatora," the captain continued. "Someone called the Protector of Ter Chadain or something like that."

"If the empress destroyed Stone Town, we'll be next," Clastis pointed out.

"We need to evacuate immediately," Trevon said.

"Not everyone has the stomach for war, but I would have thought with all your rhetoric about standing up to the empress, you would have a backbone to actually act on it."

Trevon's friends drew a gasp in unison at the insult.

Trevon stiffened in his saddle.

As if on cue, men exited the guard houses on either side of the gate and fell in behind their captain, snapping to attention.

"We have been over this many times, Captain," Trevon said, his tone low and steady. "If we are to survive once the weave is

46

down, we need to retreat to Stellaran and the safety of our homeland. It is impossible to stand up to the empress with our limited numbers."

"What good is that magic of yours if you can't use it to defend your home?"

"It is foolish to think that even with our magic we are a match for the empress's army," Linell spoke up.

"Cowardice," the captain spat. As the words left the man's mouth, Linell's hand shot out before her and energy glowed white on her fingertips. The captain's eyes opened wide and his jaw dropped as he gasped to breathe.

"Linell, this isn't helping," Clastis whispered. "Let him go."

Linell turned to consider Clastis for a moment, the anger smoldering in her eyes and then nodded, dropping her hand and releasing the captain from her weave without looking back at the man.

The captain dropped to a knee as he gulped in air once more.

"No one calls my betrothed a coward," Linell said, her voice trembling as she struggled to regain control.

"Linell," Bristol shouted as she rode up to the front of the group. She turned to the captain. "We wish you to come with us back to Stellaran. We will need you and your men to assure we reach safety."

"Open the gates," the captain said, glaring at Bristol with his hand to his throat. "We need not the likes of them within our walls."

The men scurried to open the gates and Linell kicked her mount into motion, speeding out of the city without another glance at the captain.

Trevon, Clastis, and Fedlen exchanged worried looks with Bristol and hurried after Linell. The rest of the people gathered followed after them, a few of the guards mounted horses and joined them as well. The captain jeered as they rode out. The gates of the city slammed behind them, echoing into the distance, making the travelers flinch as the gates to their home for so many years reverberated with finality.

They rode at a steady, but slow pace, allowing those traveling on foot to keep up with those on horseback. When Trevon and the others finally caught up with Linell, he cut his horse in front of hers, forcing her to stop.

Linell pulled up, not looking at him as he fumed.

"What were you thinking back there?"

"He called you a…"

"I'm well aware what he called me," Trevon raised his voice glancing up at Fedlen, Bristol, and Clastis as they trotted up.

Fedlen veered away from them, searching the side of the trail for unforeseen objects he needed to discover in order to avoid being included in the exchange.

"You made Trevon look more the coward than ever," Clastis said glancing at Trevon then back to Linell.

"I, I, I just lost it. One minute I was in control and the next, all I could see was red," Linell lowered her eyes in shame.

"You need to control yourself, girl," Bristol said placing a calming hand on Linell's arm.

Linell looked up at Bristol with her dark eyes and nodded, understanding the need for more restraint.

"We're going to need all the help we can get now that the weave is gone and you pick a fight with the captain of our security. Brilliant!" Clastis threw up his hands in disgust.

"None of you were going to do anything," Linell said.

"Sometimes choosing *not* to act is the best choice," Trevon said and kicked his horse into motion.

Clastis exchanged an awkward glance with Bristol and then hurried after Trevon, leaving the woman staring after them.

"Men are all about reputation," Bristol reminded. "We need to ease them into taking action so they think it is their choice, not ours."

With a nod, a sigh, and a roll of her eyes, Linell kicked her mount and trotted after them.

****

Stern and Cita rode hard until they dared not push their mounts any harder and stopped for the night curling up in their bedding without the warmth of a fire and were back on the trail again at first light without a word. They pushed forward until they encountered a well-traveled roadway, stopping just off the smooth path to let their horses rest and decide which direction to go next. Chewing on some dried meat, they looked from one direction to the next, unable to see a clear choice.

"If I am correct, the sea is in that direction," Stern said pointing to his right.

"But we can't be certain how far west we need to go to reach any kind of civilization." Cita glanced back to the left.

"If there is water, there are settlements," Stern reasoned. "We need to find the coast and there will be people. The coast should be in that direction."

"Is that what we want?" Cita looked to Stern with uncertainty.

"We need to determine the culture of the Caltorians and decide if they pose an imminent threat to Stellaran. How else will we gain that knowledge?"

"True, but do we admit openly to Caltorians that we are from Stellaran?"

"It will depend on who we meet." Stern stuffed the last bite of dried meat into his mouth with a nod. He strode over to his mount and swung up into the saddle, looking back at her expectantly.

She nodded, shoved the remaining meat into her mouth causing her cheek to bulge, and climbed up into her saddle. "Wesshhtt?" she asked past the meat filling her mouth.

"West," Stern chuckled and gave a nod. He nudged his horse

forward with a thrust of his hips and trotted along the road heading west.

Cita flicked her reins and moved her horse beside him chewing methodically. She swallowed hard to empty her mouth of the tough meat.

"What if nothing has changed?"

Stern looked to her confused.

"What if they are as against magic as they were when our ancestors trapped them here?"

"Then we report back and prepare for the defense of Stellaran," Stern said matter-of-factly.

"But Stellaran is not designed for warfare. Our patrol is the most militarized company in the country beside the Crystal Council's troops, but they are limited in number."

Stern laughed. "That isn't saying much, is it?"

"Stern, I'm serious."

"So am I." Stern pulled his mount to a stop.

Cita stopped a few paces past him and turned back.

"If the criminals isolated on this side of the weave continued on their path through the years, they may have an army large enough to crush Stellaran." Stern stared at her hard, fear showing clearly in his eyes.

"What about our magic? What if they eliminated all the magic like they wanted to in Stellaran? We would have an advantage over them…wouldn't we?" Cita's eyes pleaded with Stern to give her hope.

Stern edged his horse beside her as their eyes locked and she knew instantly that he held no such hope. She dropped her eyes in defeat.

"Don't borrow worry, Cita," Stern said reaching over and setting a hand on her arm. "We know nothing of what lies ahead. Many things may have come to pass changing that potential outcome."

"I just thought our magic…" her voice trailed off as his eyes stayed firm.

"Our magic is only a wisp of the past. If we needed to create the weave to protect us when our magic was at its strongest, without the weave we are like naked babes before the wolf."

"May the spirits prove you wrong," Cita said.

"I agree." Stern nodded and kicked his horse into motion again.

Chapter 6

Teah stared out over the ocean as the waves broke around the ship. Deep down she hoped to see the dingy drift into view with Logan waving his hands to catch her attention. But days after his disappearance, little hope remained for that outcome. The voices inside her head graciously remained silent since Logan disappeared off the ship. Teah thanked them for that. Her own thoughts echoed in her mind, heard by the spirits of the protectors, but not commented on.

To lose Logan when she just got him back seemed like a bad dream she couldn't wake up from. His voice in her mind felt refreshing once they broke the stone's spell. Their connection gave them a renewed strength that seemed to diminish the overwhelming responsibilities resting on their shoulders. Their spirits lifted with that knowledge and gave them renewed hope that they could accomplish anything.

Then, in a heartbeat, it was gone. Logan was gone. The Senji, who never forget a mark, made good on their contract to the dead King Englewood. How the assassin was able to kill Logan without him at least crying out in alarm still bothered Teah. A shout might be cut short with a well-placed blade, but a thought travels in an instant. He would have told her. But he never did.

She asked the protectors if they heard him that night. None did. It didn't feel right.

And for Zeva to be a Senji…was it possible? After all, she'd been bound in slavery to the empress with Teah; she never displayed a single clue that she was a member of the oldest society of assassins. It made no sense. But the evidence loomed before her, leaving little room for doubt.

The most important thing still didn't change no matter what the suspicions; Logan was gone.

Saliday eased up to the rail next to her and Teah glanced over.

Saliday's eyes, red and puffy, stared straight ahead across the ocean, her longing palpable as she searched the empty skyline.

Teah turned back to the ocean and the two women shared their loss in silence.

"It doesn't add up," Saliday said breaking the silence, causing Teah to jump. "He never gets caught off-guard."

"It appears this time he did."

"Caslor was knocked unconscious by the look of the welt on his head. He said he didn't hear a thing. That must be how they caught Logan unaware."

"It's hard to believe that Zeva did this."

"Is it?" Saliday turned to Teah. "No, really, how well did you know her?"

Teah frowned. "She trained me when I was a slave."

"But did you ever look deeper at her motivation, her loyalty?"

Teah looked questioningly back at Saliday, not following.

"Was her motivation to ally with us for her freedom, or to accomplish her mission?"

"I can't see her protecting me and aiding our cause just to get close enough to kill Logan," Teah argued.

"We had a Senji get caught in order to get close to Logan when we questioned him." Saliday folded her arms across her chest.

Teah's eyebrows rose in surprise and she nodded at the possibility. The protectors didn't speak, but she felt their consensus that Zeva could have had this as her ultimate goal.

Both women turned back to ponder the open water again.

"How do you move on from here?" Saliday asked with a sigh.

"I'm not sure." Teah didn't look at her. "I guess if I don't claim the throne of Ter Chadain his death would be for nothing. But it seems so pointless now."

"I loved Logan," Saliday began. "I know he loved me, at least at one time, but his passing has left a void in my heart that will always be there."

53

A long silence hung in the air and then Teah turned to Saliday.

"I know that he loved you and wanted a future with you. I ask that you aid me in seeing that his goal is achieved. Will you help me to claim the throne?"

Saliday looked at her hard as her mind churned through her future without Logan and her obligation to continue her lineage with Morgan. Her path seemed clear until that moment.

"Yes," she whispered, knowing that she needed to do this out of her love for Logan. "Yes Teah, I will aid in your quest to claim the throne."

Teah reached out and drew her into a hug, catching Saliday off guard. She wrapped her arms around Teah and hugged her tightly, a smile curling her lips. If she couldn't be there for Logan, at least she could see that his sister sat upon the throne.

****

Raven sat on the far rail with her legs hooked around the vertical spindles watching Teah and Saliday embrace. A scowl twisted her lips as she hopped down and stormed to Morgan's chambers. She rapped on the door, barely hesitating before barging in to find Morgan behind his large desk and Grinwald sitting in a chair off to one side, staring back at her in stunned silence.

"Blimey, girl," Morgan said wiping his hand across his frustrated face. "You nearly gave us a heart attack. You can't come storming in here like that else you might find a blade planted between your ribs."

"Ha," Raven laughed as she walked over to take a seat next to Grinwald seeing the man's tension ease from his features. "It will take more than the likes of you to do me in." She smiled and gave Grinwald a wink.

Morgan looked curiously to Grinwald.

"She had a shield up. Your blade wouldn't have reached her,"

Grinwald said with a nod and cautious glance back at Raven.

"A magical in the rebellion doesn't stay alive very long in Caltoria by being too trusting."

"What's going on topside?" Morgan moved the conversation onto something he felt more comfortable with instead of magic.

"It seems that Saliday and Teah found common ground and have allied."

"Damn, I was afraid that would happen with both having such deep feelings for the boy," Morgan said with frustration.

"It was inevitable," Grinwald conceded. "Now we must make sure they continue toward the path that will benefit us all."

"And what is that?" Morgan asked. "You, Viri Magus, are too slippery to nail down as to what your real intentions are."

Grinwald's eyes narrowed at Morgan and the man put his hands up to shield himself from the wizard's glare.

"I mean, you often have deeper motivations for your actions," Morgan backpedaled. When this only brought a frown to Grinwald's lips, Morgan looked to Raven for assistance.

"I think what the captain is trying to say is that Viri Magus rarely share their true motivations with commoners like ourselves."

Grinwald turned to Raven, held her attention for a moment, and then nodded at her assessment of a Viri Magus's motives. "Fair enough," Grinwald said with a shrug. "As to answer your question, our goal at this time is to place Teah upon the throne and thus activate the spell to keep Caltoria from any further infiltration into our country."

"And after that?" Raven asked.

"We go about putting the country back in order like before Englewood's rule."

"Putting the two houses of magic in control again, you mean," Morgan added.

Grinwald spun on him, anger flaring in his brown eyes but he held his tongue until the fury subsided back behind the glassy windows into his soul and forced his lips into a smile.

"If you are suggesting that the houses of magic control Ter Chadain when a Lassain is upon the throne, those thoughts could be considered treasonous. But it is true that Ter Chadain is a much safer and more harmonious country when the houses play a vital role in running the country."

"So now I need to help put a queen, who I don't trust, upon the throne and hope she is the right choice to lead Ter Chadain?" Raven asked.

"You are putting way too much thought into this, girl," Grinwald said, his tone scolding.

"I mean..." she tried to continue but Grinwald cut her off.

"You need to do as you are told. This has been laid out in prophecy and your choice has no bearing on the matter."

"I don't follow blindly, Viri Magus," Raven said with a scowl.

"You don't follow at all, is what I've heard," Grinwald said, catching her eye and staring hard.

Her steely look held his, not wavering, but burning back at him.

"Easy, girl." Morgan leaned forward across his desk, trying to break her staring contest with Grinwald. "We all do what we feel is best for our country and ourselves at the same time. It is a difficult balancing act; if you lean too far in one direction, disaster."

Raven looked at Morgan who showed genuine concern in his normally ice cold eyes. She turned back to Grinwald who was still considering her with a disapproving frown. Taking a deep calming breath, she nodded slowly.

"Contrary to what you might have heard, I think for myself and decide the path to take based on the facts, not someone's word. I have committed to this path with you, Viri Magus, and I am trusting that this is the path for the betterment of Ter Chadain, my new home."

Grinwald's expression softened and he gave a slight nod of approval.

Before Grinwald could move, Raven sprung from her chair and closed the gap between them, holding her dagger against the Viri Magus's throat.

Grinwald stiffened as a thin line of blood appeared under her blade.

"But if you even think of betraying me, I will have no qualms at removing your head from your neck. Do we understand each other?" Her words came breathy in Grinwald's ears.

He gave one ever so slight nod. She released him with a shove and strode from the room.

Morgan and Grinwald watched her leave, their mouths hanging open in shock. Grinwald dabbed the end of his sleeve against his neck.

"Are you sure we should have included her in our plans?" Morgan asked.

"She is very strong and a better ally than foe, but we need always remember how she survived her years on Scalded Island."

"And how was that?" Morgan asked curiously.

"She killed all who were a threat to her."

Morgan looked at Grinwald, unnerved, then joined the Viri Magus as they looked with uncertainty to the door Raven just exited.

****

Logan stewed. Or perhaps it was closer to a mope, but either way he stayed silent, searching for something positive in his life to latch on to as his emotions roiled inside.

With Sasha dying to protect him in the catacombs beneath the palace, Teah far from him on her way to Ter Chadain, and Saliday Talis, the first woman he ever loved, denying him for the last male

57

Tarken and a chance to continue her bloodline, he felt completely alone.

Even the spirits of the protectors who once guided him while he searched for control and balance between who he was and the newfound powers of who he was becoming now resided in Teah's mind, leaving him feeling isolated and deserted.

He stared at the protector's swords on the bottom of the boat in their black sheaths with the counterbalance ball of crystal encasing the protector's seal jutting out. Their familiarity now seemed to mock him and his failure to succeed on his mission of placing Teah upon the throne. He held the small sheath with the steel bow in his hands clasped before him.

Since he woke with Zeva in the dingy, he felt the muffled shield blocking his contact with his magic. The sensation reminded him of being underwater while someone on shore shouted his name. He still felt it, knew it to still be there, but it lay beyond his reach.

He stared at the bow again as it sat in the sheath, a solid cylindrical piece of metal. He wanted to test his protector's abilities by pulling the bow and watching it expand, but the ramifications if nothing happened weighed heavily on his confidence.

Lifting his gaze to Zeva as she slept at the front of the boat, he understood his anger toward her might be unwarranted, but he had only known her since the destruction of the two controlling stones in Caltoria. How could he trust her when she claimed that Grinwald was behind his fate? How could he believe that Grinwald would betray him so completely?

He was staring past Zeva, contemplating his life, when she stirred in his vision bringing him back to the here and now. Empathy flooded from her eyes as she saw the pain in his.

"Stop." He spoke, not sternly, but firm.

"What?"

"Stop feeling sorry for me."

"Logan, I just…"

"I know, but I have to digest this at my own pace. My fate has taken another twist and this may be the last I can stand."

"What do you mean?" her voice filled with concern.

"This protector thing has pretty much worn out its welcome."

"Does it work that way? Can you just stop being the protector?"

"I don't know, but I've done everything I've been asked to do and this is where it lands me: in a boat, adrift, no food or water, with you."

"This isn't the picnic I would have chosen to be on either," Zeva said, tears filling her eyes.

"I'm not saying I'm ungrateful for you saving me, if what you say is true…"

"How can you be so stubborn? What would I have to gain by doing this?"

"You could be bringing me back to the empress for a reward."

"That's ridiculous. I saved Teah and helped both of you escape. Why would I turn around and hand you back to her and risk being enslaved again?"

"I don't know what motivates you. I don't know you. Maybe she is holding some of your family hostage and this is the only way you can save their lives."

Before Logan finished the sentence, magic lifted him off his seat and swung him out over the ocean. The magic stopped, plunging him into the water and sending him under several feet. He struggled to the surface sputtering for air, scrambled to the boat, and pulled himself over the edge to flop into the bottom of the boat panting.

He looked up at Zeva as she towered over him. The expression on her face sent him scooting away from her without taking his eyes off her berserker eyes.

"My family was killed in Stone Town when the empress used the Spire to destroy it out of fear that you and Teah would succeed in the destruction of the source stone."

Logan reached for words, but none seemed adequate so he stared dumbfounded back up at her.

"Your actions sealed the execution of my entire family as well as thousands upon thousands of magicals and their families living in Stone Town that day. So, Protector Logan of Ter Chadain, I do not have any motivation to betray you other than because you are an ignorant, arrogant, selfish boy who doesn't deserve to be called protector at all."

She spun, took a step over the dingy seat, and sat down with her back to him without another word.

Logan stared at her in shock as his mouth hung open and then snapped it shut when he realized no words could improve things between them, at least not at this time. He lay in the bottom of the boat, the protector swords digging into his back painfully, but he refused to move, letting the pain burn deeper and deeper into him, hoping it might bring him a small sense of the agony that aiding him had brought others in the past.

A single tear fell from his eye as the thought of Sasha came to him. He mentally added Zeva's family to the growing casualty list of innocents hurt by his quests. He wasn't sure he could endure any more losses caused by his actions.

At that moment Logan made a decision. He would no longer be the Protector of Ter Chadain. From that moment on, Logan would be Logan Saolto, nothing more. He would cause no more pain to innocents. He would not put others in harm's way to defend him. From that moment on, he would fight no more.

Chapter 7

Fedlen eased his horse beside Trevon's and matched his pace. He glanced back at Clastis behind them and Linell a few paces beyond that. Bristol now rode back with the remaining group of people from the city. They numbered no more than fifty in all.

"You know she didn't mean anything by it," Fedlen said.

Trevon turned to his cousin and fought to keep the smile from his face. The youngest of his group, Fedlen hated to see anyone at odds, which was a tough task with the four of them. Trevon and Fedlen had become close over the years after Fedlen's father failed to return from a scouting excursion outside the safety of the weave. Only a few years older than Fedlen, Trevon took him under his wing and guided him along the bumpy path of living in the city and staying out of trouble.

"She does it every time, and at the worst times. Now the garrison will never take me seriously," Trevon said.

"But do you really care what they think? Are you planning on going back and leading them in battle? She showed everyone that you have someone with strength and power watching your back."

Trevon turned and considered the counsel from his cousin with surprise. When did he get so insightful? He reached over and messed Fedlen's thick head of brown hair. Just like his father's Trevon thought, recalling his uncle.

Fedlen gave Trevon a playful push and laughed.

"I know you didn't ask to be born into the Wall Watchers, but since you will one day lead all of us, isn't it good to have someone as strong as Linell beside you?"

Trevon nodded as a crooked smile curled his lips. "You've learned some things while you were so quiet."

"I found the best way to learn is to watch," Fedlen said with a chuckle.

They rode a little further in silence before Fedlen glanced back at the others again and leaned closer to Trevon who eased nearer to his cousin.

"Why do you hate her so much?"

Trevon straightened in his saddle with a shocked look at Fedlen. He glanced back at Clastis and Linell and then to his young cousin again.

"I don't hate her."

"Then why do you treat her so poorly?"

"She is so strong that I'm afraid she will swallow me whole and I will be nothing more than a shell doing as she tells."

"Don't you know that it hurts her?"

Again, Trevon appeared shocked.

"I never..."

"You never tell her and she keeps trying to do different things to get you to like her. She tried to be attentive and you told her she was smothering you. She tried to take interest in what you like and you told her she couldn't come fishing with us because it was our time. She gave you space and you said she was ignoring you. Now she is trying to show you her strength in supporting you and you say she is out of control. One could think that you hate her."

Trevon turned his stunned expression straight ahead and his thoughts inward, digesting what Fedlen said. Had he pushed her away in her attempts to be a good betrothed?

After riding a long time in silence, Trevon looked to Fedlen who still cast him the occasional glance.

"I love her more than anything in this world," Trevon said, the words somehow making him feel as if a weight lifted from his shoulders. "I feel her beauty, intelligence, and strength are too good for me. I was afraid she would reject me."

"Trevon, you are the next leader of our people and any number of women would give anything to be your betrothed. You have to give yourself some credit."

"How do you know all this?"

"I watch and listen."

"Humph, I need to try that sometime."

Trevon's head jerked up and he glanced back over his shoulder, giving a sharp chopping motion with his hand to his left side.

In unison, his entire party exited the path disappearing into the woods alongside, scattering into the trees. Trevon, Linell, Clastis, and Fedlen spun at the edge of the woods out of sight and held at the ready as a patrol of Caltorian guard numbering around eight hurried past, their shiny armor glinting in the sunlight. At the center of their patrol, a diminutive figure draped in a black cloak raised a hand and brought the company to a sudden halt.

"Sniffer," Linell hissed under her breath and then drew in her magic, closing her eyes and concentrating.

The hair on Trevon's arms stood on end as Linell's magic spread over their company. He felt his mother's magic as well as she enveloped the rest of the party with her protective powers.

The Sniffer looked toward their hiding place, squinting to see into the dense forest.

"What is it?" the apparent leader of the patrol asked, pulling his mount up next to the figure. He threw back his golden cape exposing the golden breastplate with the golden eye symbol of the empress on it and leaned down, trying to spy what the man searched for as his hand rested on the pommel of his sword.

"I felt it," the Sniffer said. "One second it was there and then…"

"And now? Do you feel it?" the man asked, sounding irritated.

"Gone." The Sniffer straightened in his saddle and shook his head.

"Then let's get moving. We need to get to Port Shoal and search for that escaped magical," the leader said before kicking his mount to the front of the party again.

The Sniffer hesitated for a moment and then followed after.

Trevon's party gave a collective sigh as the patrol rounded a bend in the road and vanished from their sight

****

Cita heard the horses coming before Stern, but only by a second. He looked back behind them and then turned to her.

"What do we do?" she asked.

"Act normal. If they suspect anything or intend to cause us trouble, we will need to deal with them so be ready."

Cita gave a nod and straightened as the party surrounded them, forcing them to stop. The lead rider of the armored patrol pulled up beside her while a small man in a black cloak grinned from beneath a darkening hood.

"What business do you have on the empress's highway?" the man asked, looking from Cita to Stern.

"Traveling to the coast," Stern said not knowing any town's names in Caltoria.

"You are too well armed for traders." The man was looking at the swords and bows hanging from Cita's and Stern's horses. "And I don't see anything to trade."

"We are new to the area looking to establish connections in port and with all the turmoil going on, felt it better to be safe than sorry," Stern replied.

Cita's hand reflexively slid to her sword.

The gesture was not lost on the man and he placed a commanding hand upon his sword. "We are headed the same way. You will come with us to Port Shoal and we shall see what connections can be made for your trading."

Cita and Stern exchanged concerned glances, knowing this was not a request.

"Very well, we are thankful for your protection." Stern gave a slight bow.

Cita pulled up on her reins and caught the eye of the cloaked man, his smile now a pleased sneer. She frowned at his expression.

"Captain," the man spoke to the leader of the patrol.

The captain turned away from Stern to the cloaked man who gave a slight nod. The captain's sword swept from its scabbard and his men quickly followed suit as the roadway rang with the sound of drawn steel.

"You thought you could fool me?" the small man asked, moving his mount beside the captain as he stared at Cita and Stern. "They are magicals. The girl is much stronger than the man, but they both are."

Cita felt a strange sensation drift over her as if a veil slid between her and her magic. Her eyes filled with panic at the lack of contact with something she'd held as long as she could remember. She turned to Stern, seeing a frown furrowing his brow.

"They are shielded," the man said proudly.

The captain motioned to one of his men who moved over and relieved the travelers of their weapons. Stern and Cita didn't resist but sat dumbfounded in their saddles.

"You will now accompany us to Port Shoal and we will decide what to do with you," the captain said, kicking his horse into motion. The rest of the company followed after, ushering Cita and Stern along with them.

****

Trevon and his party entered the roadway once they were certain the patrol was gone. They stopped, looking ahead as the near miss with the Sniffer passed.

"I never get used to that," Trevon said with a shudder.

"I'm glad I don't have a lick of magic in me. From how you look, Sniffers are very distasteful," Clastis said.

"I've learned to hide our presence from them, but they are vile," Linell said. "How anyone with magical ability can use it to seek out others and enslave them is the lowest of lows."

"Especially now when the stones are no longer in use," Fedlen said bringing everyone's attention to him. He leaned away uncomfortably. "Didn't you notice there was no stone on his forehead? This can only mean he remains loyal to the empress by choice."

"Even more reason to despise him," Trevon spat.

"Do we continue on with them ahead of us?" Clastis asked.

"We have little choice, but we need to keep a safe distance so the Sniffer can't detect any of us with his magic," Trevon pointed out.

"I'll ride ahead and keep an eye on them," Clastis said with a nod. "You stay back here a safe distance." He didn't wait for a reply but kicked his horse into motion and raced down the road.

"Thanks for the shield," Trevon said looking at Linell.

"What was I supposed to do, let us get caught?" She shrugged.

Bristol eased her horse next to Trevon's and he turned to her. "We need to head north soon and hopefully avoid any more close calls like that."

Trevon looked north into a fairly thick forest and then turned back to his mother with a raised eyebrow.

"I will cut a path with my magic," she said.

"That might alert the sniffer to our presence," Trevon argued.

"It is a chance we must take. Keep an eye out for their return," Bristol instructed.

Their attention turned to approaching hoof beats as Clastis raced up to them. He pulled up and his horse danced with adrenaline.

"Sniffer's party just took two travelers prisoner ahead, must be magicals."

Trevon exchanged concerned looks with Fedlen and Linell.

"Wait here," Trevon instructed his mother and then kicked his horse into a run followed by Clastis, Linell, and Fedlen.

****

Cita and Stern stared at the soldiers in a daze as they clamped shackles on their hands, the magic spell cast over them giving them a feeling of being in a bad dream.

The sound of riders racing toward them spun the party around just as four riders attacked without warning. The unexpected assault erupted so quickly that many of the soldiers didn't have time to react.

A burst of magic from the assailants hit the cloaked man in the chest sending him flying from his horse and into the woods lining the roadway.

Several soldiers fell under the blades of the aggressors before the captain shouted for retreat and they raced down the road and out of sight.

****

Trevon rode into the party with his sword raised, feeling the magic Linell unleashed race past his ear and strike the Sniffer in the chest. He deflected the sword sweeping for his head and countered with a strike to the soldier's body, cutting deep in the open arm hole of the armor and sending the man to the ground.

The sound of battle around him clattered as Clastis easily dispatched a soldier whose bad luck found him in the path of Clastis's broadsword as he wielded it across the man's neck, nearly decapitating him and sending him tumbling to the roadway.

Fedlen exchanged blows with another soldier who struck down repeatedly on Fedlen's raised sword in defense. Fedlen twisted nimbly in his saddle to avoid another hammering blow and swept his blade into the midsection of the soldier as he raised his arm to strike again lifting his ill-fitted armor and exposing his stomach. The man fell lifeless from his horse in a cloud of dust.

The call for retreat went up and the remaining soldiers raced away toward Port Shoal.

Trevon turned to the two captives in chains as Linell wove her magic around first the woman then the man who gave a sigh of relief as the barrier surrounding them and isolating them from their magic wafted away.

"Thank you," Cita sighed.

Stern nodded. "We are truly grateful."

"What brings the two of you along this path?" Fedlen asked boldly, causing his companions along with the newcomers to turn to him in surprise.

"Just heading to the nearest sea port," the man answered bringing curious stares from the others.

"That would be Port Shoal and known to you if you were from these parts," Trevon said. "So where are you from?"

"We are merely passing through and are new to the area," the man said.

"Not likely." Clastis glanced back at them and then turned to observe the road in the direction the patrol retreated. "You are too heavily armed for ordinary travelers. I would say you have military training and from your dress, you are not from anywhere around here."

The two glanced at their tailored green cloaks with elaborate silver embroidery down each side of the opening and then back at the loose-fitting clothing of the others and nodded to the obvious difference.

"I am Stern Barsten, member of the weave patrol from Stellaran and this is my partner Cita Cane."

"And what brings members of the weave patrol so far south?" Trevon asked.

Stern stared at Trevon and gave a glance to Cita as she gawked at him in shock.

"You aren't surprised that we are from Stellaran so you must know the weave is down, but how?" Stern asked.

"Since we are sharing, I am Trevon, and this is Linell, Fedlen and that is Clastis." Trevon indicated each member of his group.

"We are a few of a larger party still down the road. We've discovered that the weave is down and wish to return to our homeland."

"It is truly an honor to meet you and thank you once again for your help," Stern said.

"Glad to help those being hassled by the empress and a sniffer," Trevon said with a slight bow of his head.

"Sniffer?" Stern asked.

"A sniffer is a magical who uses his or her magic to seek out other magicals, kind of like a hound tracking a fox," Linell explained.

"Who would do such a thing?" Cita asked, looking disgusted.

"Some magicals did it to survive when they were enslaved, but now that the stones are gone, I've heard that some do it for money," Linell told her.

"I hated them when they were forced to 'sniff' or die, but now I really hate them," Clastis spat.

Stern exchanged a look of disbelief with Cita. If this was what Caltoria had come to, there was no way Stellaran could live in peace. Their excursion into Caltoria had provided more than enough information to report back to Wilkins.

"This is awful," Stern said.

"You should have been here before the stones were destroyed and the capital city was sent into chaos," Trevon said.

"And Stone Town was destroyed," Fedlen said, the pain heavy in his words.

"Stone Town?" Cita said looking to Linell.

"Stone Town was the largest concentration of magicals in Caltoria since magicals were required to be stoned and then become possessions of the empress and her ruling party. They lived next to the capital city of Bellatora and the empress destroyed it just before the Spire Stone was destroyed." Linell stopped and the entire party sat in stunned silence.

"We must return to Stellaran and report this," Cita said urgently.

"I agree," Stern said and then turned to Trevon. "Will you accept our offer to escort your party to our Weave Patrol camp in Stellaran?"

Trevon stared at Stern, his deep green eyes bright against weathered brown skin. The offer was tempting, but Trevon needed to find the heir to the Lassain line who possessed enough lineage and magic to lay claim to the chairman's seat of the Council of Stellaran. He also needed to get the lay of the land of Stellaran to see if a claim could even be possible.

He glanced from one of his party to the next until all nodded acceptance of his decision. He grunted approval, turning to Stern again.

"Our path lies on the same road," Trevon said with a smile. "Come and let us collect the rest of our party."

As the newly formed company filed down the road, Clastis and Linell flanked Trevon with Fedlen bringing up the rear as Stern and Cita led the way.

"Do you think this wise?" Linell asked.

"I don't know, but if we are to take back what has been withheld from us for so long, we need to know the obstacles in our path," Trevon said receiving nods of agreement from his friends.

After making the introductions of Stern and Cita to Bristol, the party gathered and followed the weave patrol members toward Stellaran. Trevon glanced to his friends who acknowledged his unspoken request and then dispersed to take up positions around the group. Trevon and Bristol followed behind Cita and Stern as they found a safe trail for their return to Stellaran.

Chapter 8

Teah leaned against the rail of the Morning Breeze staring out at the horizon as Caslor studied her. She turned and her sad expression shifted as their eyes met. His undeniable effect on her caused her skin to tingle, their connection made them both smile. But her smile came only to her lips; her eyes remained sad.

The weight of the losses over the past two years still bore deep and hung heavy on her soul. Her latest loss seemed too much to stand and she couldn't pull herself from the deep depression threatening to pull her in and consume her.

The protectors all saw the signs and did their best to bring her back from the edge of the abyss, but lately Caslor held the key. His tenderness and strength anchored her in the present, not allowing her to fall into the horrors of the past and drag her over the edge.

The fact that his loss nearly matched her own gave him insight into her pain. Caslor's father died defending Teah and Logan from his mother, the empress. That action now tied his future to Teah's forever.

"Thinking of him?" Caslor asked as he eased closer and let his hand lightly brush hers where it rested on the rail.

She took his hand in hers and nodded, not defining the "him" she thought of. Many days Logan filled her thoughts, but this time it was memories of Talesaur that saddened her. She felt his arms around her, giving her strength when she thought she couldn't go on. His kindness and love gave her the strength to accept her birthright and forge ahead.

"I'm so sorry you have to carry this burden."

"It is no greater than most on this journey."

Tears welled up in her eyes and she looked away, not wanting to reveal her weakness in front of him. A tear escaped and ran down her cheek.

Caslor reached over and caught the tear on his finger, lifting it in front of her eyes so they both could see it.

"This tear holds the pain and suffering of thousands of people who have come before us and died for a better life. That is what this quest offers, a better life for many with the sacrifice of a few."

Teah stared at him and her tears turned hard as she felt rage swell within her. She tried to stop it, but it surged past her control and erupted.

"Why Logan? Why me? What did we do to deserve this?" she shouted and gestured wildly with her arms.

"It is our bloodline that leads us down this path," Caslor said calmly.

Too calm for Teah, it fed the burning anger within and she advanced on Caslor who backpedaled until his shoulders struck the cabin wall. He cringed as Teah stopped, glaring up at him.

"My bloodline? Really? That's your only explanation for all of this? Who my parents were?" Her finger poked Caslor's chest with each question for punctuation. "There is more to it than that. I feel someone is orchestrating it all. Logan and I got the short end of the deal."

She fumed up at him and as the red rage blurring her vision cleared, she finally saw Caslor staring down at her, terror in his eyes. She stepped back, embarrassed by her outburst.

Caslor's fear vanished in that instant and he placed a hand on Teah's trembling arms, compassion filling his eyes.

"I understand that much has been set upon your shoulders, but if we let the weight push us to the ground, then who will stand for those who cannot?"

Teah stared at him with disbelief and shook her head.

"How can you be so calm about it? You, more than anyone here, have a right to be angry by fate's lot."

"I wouldn't wish my lot on anyone, nor do I place blame. To

be born a magical to the empress of Caltoria is a curse upon itself, but to have had a father who understood and helped me understand the responsibility put upon me was a blessing I will never forget."

"But you lost him to fate as well."

"I lost him to my mother, who could see nothing but hate when she knew the truth. Fate had nothing to do with it." Caslor stepped past her and walked across the deck and down to the cabins below without looking back.

Teah watched him go, ashamed.

He is wise beyond his years, Bastion said.

Teah nodded at the protector's insight.

"There's a hard one to figure out," Saliday said from where she sat on top of the cabin roof looking down at Teah.

"He is something special," Rachel said walking up along the rail.

"The son of Empress Shakata? Interesting," Saliday stroked her chin unable to curb her smile.

"He's crazy about you," Rachel said causing Teah to look at each of the women and then off in the direction Caslor left.

His love is obvious, Galiven agreed.

"No," Teah said with a shake of her head, as much to Galiven's statement as to the two women's. "I will not have feelings for someone just so they can be taken from me. I won't go through that pain again."

"The way I see it," Saliday said standing and jumping down beside Teah. As she straightened, their eyes met and Saliday held her gaze for a moment. "You don't have much of a choice in the matter." She turned and walked to the cabin entrance and went below.

Teah looked at Rachel as she stood regarding Teah with her arms crossed over her chest.

"What?" Teah sighed.

"She's right. You have no more influence in the matter than a leaf in the wind." She shrugged and walked away to the other side of the ship.

Teah's jaw clenched and her eyes narrowed as she fought to put a finger on how Caslor made her feel.

We are not able to dictate our feelings, I'm afraid, Bastion said. The other protectors didn't say a thing though their agreement radiated in her mind.

"We shall see about that," Teah said, turning to the rail and glaring out at the sea.

I was afraid she was going to say that, Galiven moaned.

"Land ho!" a voice above her shouted.

Teah looked to the crow's nest where a sailor pointed into the distance. She followed his outstretched arm and squinted to see something she hadn't seen in weeks...land.

Off on the horizon, barely discernible from her vantage point, a line rose up ever so slightly in the distance. Ter Chadain.

Excitement filled her and she raced to the cabin entrance and down the stairs scurrying along the narrow hallway to Caslor's room. She tapped once on the door and entered to find Caslor standing with his shirtless back to her, frozen with surprise by her sudden entrance.

She stopped and stared in disbelief as dark purple stripes greeted her eyes. The remnants of many years of abuse under the iron hand of his mother, the empress.

"How could she?" Teah said aghast.

Caslor turned, this time the tears shone in his eyes as he looked at her with his hands hanging at his sides.

Teah saw four bloodied, bruised, welts raised from his chest and she gasped with realization.

The protectors moaned in unison at the sight.

"Oh, Caslor, I'm so sorry..." her voice trailed off, losing its strength.

He gathered her into his arms and she cried against his shoulder.

"Sometimes loving someone hurts," he said as she sobbed deeper and he rested his lips against the top of her shaking head.

****

"Captain." A deckhand stuck his head into the room. His greasy black hair hanging down to his shoulders from beneath a gray bandana wrapped around his head.

Morgan looked up from his maps with a flat stare.

"You might want to come take a look at this." The man didn't wait for a response but pulled his head back into the hallway and closed the door.

Morgan stretched with a moan as he stood and lumbered to the door. He pulled the door open and trudged along the narrow corridor, up the stairs, and out onto the deck. Raising his hand to block the bright sunlight that greeted him, he turned to the helm and the man who stood next to the wheel.

The man pointed ahead of them and Morgan turned to see what troubled his crew.

A thick fogbank stood before them blotting out everything beyond it, disappearing in both directions to the left and right as they approached.

Morgan hurried up the steps to the helm and stared with disbelief at the thick fog.

He turned to Grinwald and Raven who already stood staring at the phenomenon with their mouths agape.

"What is it?" Raven asked, searching Morgan's face for an answer.

"I have heard about it, but never have witnessed it from the sea," Grinwald said, bringing Raven's and Morgan's eyes to him.

"What is it?" Raven pressed.

"Some ancient magic has once again been summoned,"

Grinwald said.

Raven frowned at the vague response from the Viri Magus and looked to Morgan for clarification.

Morgan shook his head.

"What? Don't you know what it is?" Raven demanded, starting to get angry.

"Of course I know what it is, girl," Morgan spat. "I grew up on the sea and have seen it many times, but not since…" he stopped, frowning at the possibility. He spun on Grinwald pointing an accusing finger at him. "I thought you said the girl was the only one who could activate the spell."

"She is," Grinwald said defensively.

"Then how do you explain that?" Morgan said gesturing ahead of them at the fog bank.

"I don't know. The only way to create the spell is if a Lassain queen sits upon the throne again…" Grinwald's thoughts trailed off.

"Then there must be another Lassain queen who has claimed the throne," Morgan shouted.

"Impossible," Grinwald whispered as his eyes lost their focus and he considered the possibility.

"What are you two talking about?" Raven stepped between them.

"This old fool has made a mistake," Morgan shouted.

"No, I have not," Grinwald said shaking his head. "Teah is the direct descendent to the throne. Only she can activate the spell."

"What spell?" Raven shouted, demanding clarification.

"When a Lassain queen is upon the throne, this fog bank is cast around Ter Chadain to protect it from Caltoria's invasions," Grinwald said.

"Fog will stop Caltoria from invading?" Raven chuckled.

"It isn't just fog," Morgan interjected. "If you don't carry a magical medallion, you cannot get through the fog bank except through the port of Stalwart."

"What happens if you try to get through the fog without the medallion?" Raven asked.

"The fog spins you around and spits you out again. It can take days to be clear of the fog, but you will never reach Ter Chadain." Morgan shook his head.

"So we need Teah?" Raven shouted at Grinwald. "How did the spell get activated?"

Grinwald stared at Raven as horror swept through his features. His eye grew wide and he turned slowly to stare out at the fog. "There must be a new Queen of Ter Chadain," he whispered.

Chapter 9

Thanks to Zeva's magic, they ate fish and stayed warm and dry for the duration of their trip. She proudly took the briny sea water and pulled the salt from it so they could drink clean water.

"A trick perfected by your ancestor, the first Queen of Ter Chadain," she said with a smile.

He was impressed. Especially now that he felt no connection with his own magic, his respect for those who could wield it grew.

Logan smiled as she did the trick again and floated a handful of clean water through the air to hover over him. He tilted his head back as Zeva lowered the water lightly into his open mouth. He swallowed, savoring the fresh, cool sensation as it went down his throat and spread throughout his chest, arms, and legs.

He looked calmly at her, giving a nod and a grin. His smile broadened as he realized that he felt much more content now that he decided to stop being the protector. His frustration with being tossed into this boat and set out to sea had long since dissipated giving him clarity on his rightful path. Peace and harmony would be his new mantra as he followed the course chosen for him.

A shimmer of anger threatened to edge through the calm as he thought of Grinwald's betrayal. If Grinwald actually betrayed him, he thought glancing over at Zeva. But she had no reason to lie since her fate now traveled along the same trail as his.

Zeva caught his eye as he looked her way. She smiled, relaxed with his recent demeanor. "What?" she asked.

"Nothing," he said and grinned with a shake of his head.

"What has come over you? These past few days you seem at peace."

"I am. For the first time in nearly two years, I feel as if the weight of a country no longer rests on my shoulders."

Zeva frowned in confusion.

"I can no longer concern myself with fulfilling a higher

calling," Logan explained. "I am out of that world and now that I'm here, I want to stay out of it…for good."

Zeva's mouth dropped open as what Logan said registered with her. "You're not saying…you can't be seriously considering…no, you aren't giving up…?"

"I'm no longer going to be the protector."

Zeva stared at him and then beyond as she tried to imagine Logan as just Logan and not the legendary warrior. She shook her head to clear her mind and bring her back to reality.

"You can't just shut it off," Zeva whispered. "It is part of you."

"A part I will no longer allow to dictate my actions."

"Logan, I know we haven't known each other long, but you are a hero. That is who you are."

"But what makes a hero?"

"Someone who acts selflessly and bravely for the good of others." As she said it, her eyes shot up to his and she went cold. "You are going to ignore the plight of others?"

"I am going to mind my own business."

"As a hermit? Because the heroes I've heard of address injustice wherever they are."

"If that is what it takes, then so be it." Logan held Zeva's stare for a long time.

"I don't agree with this, not one bit, but I will respect it. You have gone through so much for one so young; I can't blame you for wanting some peace."

"So you'll keep my secret when we reach land?"

"I'll do one better," Zeva said with a crooked grin. "I've been steering us toward my old fishing village, Port Shoal, and we will make land in another day or so. Once there, we can stay at my family's old farmstead outside of town. You should be able to avoid being a hero out in the middle of nowhere."

Logan brightened as Zeva's hopes dwindled. She wasn't sure about this idea. The world had so few heroes and here Logan was deciding to stop being one as well. She only hoped that Caltoria didn't need any, right now at least.

****

Two nights later in the dead of night as the moon shone high above them, Logan and Zeva touched the shores of Port Shoal. No pomp and circumstance greeted the Protector of Ter Chadain as he stepped upon the beach of Caltoria once more. They stretched and took tentative steps, allowing their muscles to regain their bearing on being used to walk again. Each step brought them closer to feeling like their normal selves. Only a few stray dogs paused in their searching for food along the water line to look up at the newcomers and then turn back to their foraging.

Zeva led Logan along the edge of Port Shoal; he carried his swords in his arms, wrapped in the tattered blanket that landed in the dingy when he went overboard.

He thought about leaving them in the boat for the next unlucky person to come along and gather them up, but the pain and suffering they might cause an unsuspecting person forced Logan to bring them with him. Just the mere possession of artifacts such as these would ruin an innocent person's life.

They slipped to the east of town and walked for another hour or so until reaching a small valley. Standing on the ridge overlooking a gentle stream as it meandered into the valley floor they surveyed their new home.

A clay block house stood at the far end of the valley barely visibly by the bright moonlight. What made the house stand out caused them both to tense with caution. The glow of light coming from the windows may have welcomed some travelers, but for Logan and Zeva it only meant they needed to confront interlopers if they wished to claim Zeva's heritage.

Zeva looked worriedly to Logan as the moonlight shone on his angled chin, his jaw set with frustrated determination. He turned to her and his brown eyes glinted in the moonlight. Even though he denied his title of protector, she knew that didn't mean he was weak. She shuddered at the thought of the poor unsuspecting souls in the house if they chose to reject their claims on her family's homestead.

"This is it?" he asked, not looking at her but surveying the surrounding out buildings on the property.

"Yes."

"Any relatives who have legitimate claims to it?"

"No."

He stood, unwrapped his swords, and handed the blanket to her. Strapping on his weapons, he left the handles jutting over each shoulder. He strode down toward the home, not waiting for her. She hurried after, catching up to him as he approached the first building sitting dark and empty.

Logan paused with his back to the outer wall, peering around the corner at the rest of the buildings and the main house. He noted the condition of the buildings in the moonlight. The signs of fresh paint and the absence of weeds around their foundations caused him to pause and turn back to Zeva.

"You sure there are no relatives who may have taken up residence here?" he asked and then turned back to his scanning of the buildings.

"No. My family all moved to Stone Town..." she trailed off as her voice cracked at the emotion welling up inside at the thought of her slaughtered family in Stone Town. "Why?"

"Doesn't seem like squatters to paint and weed," Logan responded without looking back at her.

Zeva looked around the homestead, noticing the pristine condition of the buildings and grounds for the first time.

He extended a hand to her. "Blanket."

She handed him the blanket and watched in silence as he took off his swords and wrapped them once again in the blanket. He slipped around the corner of the building and then stepped inside. The building housed tools that lit up in the moonlight as they hung upon the wall. Logan moved to one side and set the swords behind a box of tack next to the wall. He stepped back and gave a satisfied nod as he assured they were out of sight.

Zeva stood in the doorway watching as Logan stepped back outside and eased the door shut again.

"Let's see if the occupants have some food for weary travelers, shall we?" he said with a gesture of his hand toward the house.

Zeva nodded and led the way through the remaining buildings to the fairly sizable house. The door glowed brown with a new coat of paint and the shutters hung straight on hinges tightly sealing the inside from the elements. Flowers lined the walk leading to the door and precisely trimmed shrubs stood guard on either side of the entrance.

Zeva stopped before the door, uncertain, as Logan stepped up beside her. He paused and listened to the muffled voices from within. He rapped on the door and the voices stopped, followed by higher pitched chatter and then silence before footsteps trod to the door and the latch pulled back unlocking the door. The knob turned and the door opened quietly inward.

Logan stared at empty space at eye level until he looked down to see a child's face peering up at Zeva and then to him.

The girl, no older than ten, stared up at him with pale blue eyes filled with fear. Her small face framed by curly blond, shoulder length hair. Her body shook with fright under a clean white dress as she tried to form words with her small delicate mouth.

Logan frowned at the choice of greeter and felt uneasy as she stepped back opening the door wider to invite them in.

Zeva took a step inside, but Logan yanked her back as a broadsword came down in front of her, clipping a chunk of hair from her locks that drifted away from her as she jerked back. The sword ended its arc with a thud on the wooden floor. A mace swung from behind the door and Logan spun to roll Zeva and himself into the shrub next to the opening.

He came to his feet, hesitating just long enough to assure Zeva was unharmed, and burst into the room, kicking the door wide and sending the attacker behind it banging into furniture on the other side. He snatched the wrist of the hand wielding the broadsword and easily twisted the large weapon free of the small hand. With the sword in one hand he strode over and recovered the mace from the floor. He stood with a weapon in each hand, surveying the battleground for the first time.

A boy, possibly twelve, lay behind the door looking dazed amongst the jumble of chairs and small furniture. A girl approaching fifteen stood rubbing her sore wrist.

A thrum followed by a hissing caught his attention as a girl with a bow loosed an arrow that struck him dead center in the chest. The arrow hit his chain mail and snapped with a loud crack, falling in pieces to the ground.

By this time Zeva entered the house with her hands raised above her head, holding her magic at the ready.

Logan extended his arm with the sword and held her back so she could see their adversaries before releasing her magic upon them.

Zeva's determined expression turned from Logan back to the assailants and her anger washed from her as her hands came down, allowing the magic to siphon away.

She stared up at Logan as he considered her with compassionate eyes.

"They're children," she said aghast.

"Don't worry," Logan said taking in each of their faces. "We mean you no harm."

The expressions on the children's faces made it clear they didn't believe him.

He nodded as a crooked smile curled his lips. Handing back

the sword and mace, he ushered Zeva in and closed the door behind them.

A pot boiled over the fire in the fireplace and he smiled broadly.

"Smells good. Do you have any to spare for some weary travelers?"

The tension in the house rose as the children looked to one another.

"Lamb stew. Nothing fancy, but there is enough to go around," said the girl holding the sword with the point touching the floor.

"We would be grateful for any you can spare," Logan said.

"I love lamb stew," Zeva added with a smile.

A quick look from the girl to the other children sent them into motion as the weapons were stored, her sword taken by the little girl who answered the door, and she motioned for Logan and Zeva to take a seat at the table next to the fireplace.

"Thank you very much," Logan said with a slight bow. He strode over and sat down as Zeva followed, sitting across from him so they both could watch the children gather plates and glasses for the meal. "Welcome home," he whispered to Zeva.

"Not what I expected," she said with raised eyebrows and looked lamentingly at the missing chunk from her hair.

"Life rarely is," Logan said matter-of-factly.

Chapter 10

Trevon thought it funny a land so long beyond his reach now melded seamlessly together with Caltoria, a land he learned to despise throughout his life. The countryside remained dotted with patches of woods separated by rolling hills and fields. He didn't know when they entered Stellaran exactly, but a sense of calm crept over him at one point in the ride and he knew they now found themselves in his homeland.

He watched his new companions weave through the sparse vegetation ahead of them and his attention went from Stern, a strong and weathered man with years in the saddle to Cita. She easily maneuvered the horse with her legs letting the reins rest lightly in her hands.

His demeanor turned sour as he recalled the history of his people, trapped in Caltoria with those Stellaran meant to be exiled there. The stories rang clearly in his head of the Chairman of the Council of Stellaran making a visit to the pillars to see everything was in place and then being trapped there with his party of advisers on the wrong side of the barrier.

A direct descendant of those who accompanied the chairman that fateful day, he struggled to keep the anger and thoughts of vengeance from overwhelming him. He needed to keep a clear head. He needed to be able to assess the situation and decide if his original goal of finding a direct descendent of the chairman himself remained feasible.

His thoughts came back to the present as Cita stood in her stirrups to lean down and retrieve the reins that slipped from her grasp just moments before. Heat filled his cheeks and his ears burned as he watched the woman gracefully stretch for the straps of leather exposing her tight-fitting brown pants from under the green cloak and then settle back into her saddle without causing the horse to break stride.

Focus on the task at hand, he scolded himself.

As if on cue, Linell eased her horse beside his and looked at him questioningly.

"Why is your face so red?"

"Uh, I don't know. I'm just hot I guess," Trevon said, glancing at her for a second and then turning away to look at Cita again.

Linell followed his gaze and her eyes narrowed as she studied him.

He turned back to her with a sheepish look and Linell's eyebrows raised. Her eyes widened. She looked up at Cita and then glared at him, pulling her reins and drawing her horse back behind him.

He sighed in embarrassment at being discovered gawking at another woman in front of his betrothed and also with relief at her dropping back behind him so he needn't see her disapproving glare any longer. He soon realized that the glare, even though unseen, still raised the hairs on the back of his neck. He shook his head as he accepted this silent chastising he well and truly deserved.

They made camp in Stellaran for the night and Trevon found it strangely comforting to be back in his home country again. Bristol saw to the others while Trevon and his friends sat around a small fire with the newest members of their party. The conversation didn't come easily. Actually, it didn't come at all until Stern, clearly the eldest of the group, broke the silence.

"Tell me Trevon, where were you going before we requested that you return with us to Stellaran?" the weave patroller asked.

Cita drew in air with a hiss at the awkward icebreaker and the others just stared in silence, first at Stern and then at Trevon, as they waited for the young man's response to such a direct question.

Trevon looked to Stern and then the other members of the party as he scrambled to find the right words. He couldn't expose his true mission.

"Once the weave came down, we decided we needed to head to Port Shoal and see what effects it had on the closest port to Stellaran," Trevon said.

"And what issues did you think the weave coming down might cause in Port Shoal?" Cita asked before Stern could respond.

"We weren't sure if a port in Stellaran existed in close proximity to the one in Caltoria and needed to decide if there were going to be tensions between the ports," Linell jumped in.

Stern frowned. "In what capacity do you oversee the wellbeing of Port Shoal?"

"Uh, none, but..." Linell stumbled, caught once again speaking without first thinking it through.

"We get all of our supplies from Port Shoal. If the trade at the port is disrupted, everyone in the area would be affected. We merely wanted to assure that we could sustain the people in our town," Trevon explained.

"And what city is that?"

Trevon glanced out of the corner of his eye to his companions to see their concerned expressions. Did they want to share their origin? Would naming the Sacred City raise concern with Stern and Cita?

Trevon took a deep breath and looked back to Stern and Cita as they waited for his response.

"We live in the Sacred City," Trevon said, paying special attention to their response to the name.

Neither Cita nor Stern exhibited any emotion over the mention of the only city in Caltoria where magicals remained free and out of the empress's reach. The chairman bent the weave around their city during construction, effectively shielding the population from the exile's influence. The only contact the residents of the Sacred City had with Caltoria came in the occasional trading at Port Shoal.

"We hope that the weave coming down will allow you to come home," Stern told them.

"Thank you," Trevon said. "Now that you have asked us to accompany you, may I ask why it is so important to you?" Trevon turned the tables on the travelers from Stellaran.

Stern hesitated for a moment and went with his gut. "We not only wish to help descendants of Stellaran return home, but we have been separated for so long we need to discover what changes in culture have developed over the many years to ensure that peace is a reasonable possibility between our two countries."

"Then you should travel to Bellatora and inquire with the empress," Clastis spoke up, his mouth twisted with distaste.

"That decision will come above my station as well, but due to our close proximity to Caltoria, we felt it prudent to investigate to discover any information we could before returning to our headquarters," Stern explained.

"So we are the information you're bringing back?" Linell asked.

"You know what is going on in Caltoria first hand, what better source of information?" Cita said.

Trevon bristled. He held no love for the empress and Caltoria, spending most of his life as a prisoner inside the Sacred City, but to be taken back to Stellaran as merely a form of information made him seethe with anger.

"Time for some sleep," Trevon stood abruptly. He looked down at his three companions and they nodded their understanding. Each stood and gave a nod to Cita and Stern before moving back into the shadows away from the fire where their horses stood tethered to tree limbs.

As their eyes met, Trevon and Stern knew that this conversation did not go as well as they hoped. Stern bowed his head slightly and Trevon turned and joined his friends.

"I'm sorry," Cita said leaning in closer to Stern so the others wouldn't hear.

"People don't like to be used, even if they are using us as well. To point it out so clearly makes it that much harder to swallow." Stern held Cita's gaze for a moment, stood, and walked to his bedroll.

Cita watched him lie down and pull his blanket around his shoulders. She turned back to the fire and stared at the flames as they twisted and swirled in the light breeze before reaching through the stacked wood again.

She sat watching the flame and listening to the hissing mixed with the popping of moisture trapped inside the wood turning to steam and then escaping its confines. So consumed by the fire, she didn't notice when Trevon sat down across from her.

"How long have you been a weave patroller?" Trevon asked, breaking the silence.

Cita flinched but held her composure, not looking up, but continuing to stare at the fire. She hesitated in answering, but something inside told her she needn't fear honesty with Trevon.

"My first time out was when the weave went down."

"Kind of a short career." Trevon's voice held sympathy, not sarcasm.

"It was what I wanted my entire life and now there is nothing left to patrol." Cita sighed and lifted her eyes to meet his.

"I'm sorry about earlier," he said.

"No, I shouldn't have put it that way."

"It's just that I envisioned our returning to Stellaran to be different."

"Different how?"

"More fulfilling."

"And it hasn't lived up to what you expected?"

"I was born and raised in Caltoria, but it never was my country. Stellaran always held that place in my heart and now…" his voice trailed off as his thoughts drifted.

"Now what?"

"Now I am merely a messenger of what Caltoria is like and if it is a danger to Stellaran."

"You are helping your homeland."

"As an informant. Not what I had planned."

"Then what is your plan, Trevon?"

Once again Cita caught Trevon off-guard by her directness. He couldn't tell her that he wanted to return with the descendent of the chairman and claim the council for his people who lived as prisoners between their homeland and the land of the exiles.

"I don't have a plan," he said, but as the words came out of his mouth, they sounded insincere to himself; he only imagined how they sounded to Cita.

"If you say so," Cita shot back. "For someone so in control of himself, I doubt that is the case." Now Cita stood and walked away from the fire leaving Trevon looking after her.

****

After a sleepless night for Trevon, the party rode north again at daybreak. Trevon slumped in his saddle, the night spent deep in thought weighing heavily on his shoulders this morning.

No one approached him that morning, each taking to gathering their supplies, packing their horses, and setting out. Even Bristol gave him space as she seemed to sense his turmoil. They rode along in silence until evening when they intersected a well-worn path where Stern suggested they make camp.

Trevon glanced behind at the weary travelers and nodded his agreement. They set up camp and many of the party ate and took to their bedrolls, Trevon being one. He tossed and turned in the shadows just outside of the campfire where the others sat quietly watching the flames and contemplating their future.

The next morning Stern led them west without hesitation and they rode on the rest of the morning, the scrape of their horses' hooves behind them the only sound. They rounded a sharp turn in the road and the forest gave way to a settlement of wooden structures both single and two stories in size. After seeing that the main group made camp just outside and out of view of the settlement with Bristol and Clastis to see to their needs, Trevon, Linell, and Fedlen trotted into the middle of the town with Cita and Stern. They came to a stop before the largest building in sight.

The wooden two-story structure stretched out more than any two or three buildings in the town combined. A large group of men milled around the square in different stages of readying their mounts for departure. When they saw Stern and his party approaching, they stopped and stared. A large man with long gray hair pulled back and tied into a tail that draped down the back of his green cloak matching Stern's and Cita's, save for much more silver embroidery, approached Stern and took hold of his mount.

"I wondered if you were planning on bringing him back," Commander Wilkin said patting his horse on the nose. "We were just headed out to look for you. Rumor has it something has happened to the weave."

"No rumor," Stern said flatly.

Wilkin's eyes grew wide and he leaned around Stern to stare at Cita and then take in the new riders with them.

"That might explain your companions," the commander said.

"Yes, it does, sir," Stern said, sliding from his saddle. He let a boy take his horse away and strode up to stop before Trevon and his friends who dismounted.

"Commander Wilkin, may I introduce Trevon, Linell, and Fedlen. They agreed to return here with us and explain the nature of Caltoria and the danger it may be to Stellaran."

The commander nodded to each as Stern made introductions. "Welcome to the Weave Patrol, which by the sounds of it, needs a new name. Please accept our meager hospitality and make yourselves at home." He motioned to a boy who ran over. "Show them to the empty troop quarters on the backside of the grounds. Make sure they have everything they need."

The boy nodded and looked to Trevon.

"Thank you commander, we look forward to sharing our thoughts on Caltoria with you," he said with a nod and then gestured for the boy to lead on.

The commander smiled and returned Trevon's nod, watching them until they disappeared around the corner. His smile vanished as he spun on Stern.

"What in the spirits were you thinking?" he shouted, drawing the attention of everyone around him. "Bringing Caltorians here?" He flailed his arms wildly.

"When the weave went down…" Stern began.

"You should have come straight back without delay," the commander hollered, his face turning red. "Not go out and find yourselves some Caltorians."

"But we were so close to Caltoria, we thought if we could discover the state of the country, it might aid our efforts," Cita spoke up and instantly wished she hadn't as Wilkin spun on her, making her shrink from his glare.

"I made the decision. We have only been gone a day longer than if we traveled straight back and we have those who know first-hand what the state of Caltoria is," Stern told his commander sharply.

Commander Wilkin's eyes narrowed at Stern's insubordination, but the seasoned veteran didn't back down, glaring back.

"Okay, what's done is done, but if the council doesn't like it, it's on your head."

Stern nodded his understanding.

"Givan," Wilkin shouted.

"Sir," a thin man with stringy black hair and tiny black beady eyes stepped up next to him, his green cloak twisted awkwardly on his gangly body as he snapped to attention.

"Ride to Lonnex and tell the council what has happened. Tell them we have some Caltorians here who they might be interested in speaking with," Wilkin ordered.

"There is one more thing," Stern interrupted.

"And what is that?" Wilkin said spinning on him.

"There is a larger party of Caltorians camped outside the settlement," Stern said, flinching at the expected response.

"What? An invading force?"

"No, just descendants of the people who were mistakenly caught on the wrong side of the weave and wish to come home," Stern explained.

Wilkin held Stern's gaze for a moment and then turned back to Givan. "Share this extra information with the council as well."

"Yes, sir," the man ran to his horse, jumped into the saddle, and raced off leaving a dusty plume behind him.

"Are you sure that was wise?" Stern asked, bringing Wilkin's eyes back to him.

"No," the commander's face went slack. "But it is procedure and we still have some time to visit with Trevon and his friends to get a clear perspective."

"Funny how what the council sees and what we see are rarely alike," Stern said with a sigh.

"Sad, actually. Not like it used to be when those with the gift ran the council," he said and walked away not looking back.

"What did he mean by that?" Cita stepped up next to Stern as they watched the commander enter the headquarters.

"With the council void of those with magical ability, it seems what we encounter is often interpreted differently than the way we see it. Kind of like the way you were trained by someone who has never patrolled the weave before. It makes no sense. It is only one way; their way."

Stern looked at his newest and youngest partner and gave a shrug before walking off.

Cita felt a strange surge of guilt inside her as she thought of Trevon and his friends who came here in good faith to help them. She hoped there wouldn't come a time where they regretted trusting her and Stern.

Chapter 11

Teah stood at the bow of the Morning Breeze as it entered between the high fog banks on either side of the port city of Stalwart. The protectors spent most of that morning arguing about the possible reasons the protection fog spell now hanging over them when the true heir still hadn't claimed the throne.

Teah pushed their incessant squabbling back in her mind and concentrated on what lay before her. In the distance, she made out the row of warships set as a barricade to all who entered. The ships towered over the diminutive Morning Breeze with long spikes jutting out from their steel bows. These ships had one purpose and one purpose alone...to destroy other ships.

Each ship sat with its broad side facing the entrance the Morning Breeze now entered with rows and rows of archers lining the decks and any portal open to them. Flying high above them at the peak of each mainmast flapped a red flag with a silver tree embossed on it.

Teah frowned at the familiarity of that symbol and her memory flashed back to that small farmstead and the men holding her sister between them as Caldora slapped her sister across her face. The men's red uniforms and silver breastplate focused in her mind and the image of a tree jumped out at her. She snapped back to the here and now and turned to Caslor standing beside her.

Rachel, Raven, and Grinwald walked up behind them and Teah gave them only a passing glance, leaning closer to Caslor.

"That is King Englewood's banner," she said.

Caslor didn't understand the significance of that statement, looking blankly back at her.

Teah turned to the others as they stopped behind them, knowing they heard her statement to Caslor.

"Well?" she said to Grinwald.

"Yes, I believe that is Englewood's banner," the man said with a nod, unable to hide the concern from his face.

"But I thought Logan killed Englewood?" Rachel said as she stared out at the barricade.

"I thought so too," Grinwald agreed, not looking away from the warships. "But I wasn't there to witness it."

They turned to the Viri Magus with questions swirling in their minds and confusion showing in their eyes.

"He did," a voice said from along the rail.

They turned to see Saliday, sitting casually on the rail picking her teeth with a piece of wood. She pulled the wood from her mouth, examining something unseen on the point and then looked up at them. "I saw it with my own eyes. The protector's swords driven through his body and the man shuddering his last breath. I stood beside Logan as each and every man, woman, and child who desired, came and swore fealty to him."

"But those banners are saying that Englewood is still alive," Raven pointed out.

The others turned from Raven and back to Saliday expectantly.

"Not necessarily," Saliday said, flicking her toothpick into the sea before hopping down to walk slowly closer to them. "It means that an heir to the throne, other than Teah, has taken up the crown in the name of the Englewood family."

"Who would do that?" Teah asked and glanced up at the banners high above them again.

"I'm guessing that Englewood's son, Aston, and widow are at the root of this," Saliday said.

This drew gasps from the others and Caslor leaned forward urgently. "You're saying that Logan let the queen and prince survive?" his voice quivered with disbelief.

"Sasha and I tried convincing him to kill them, but he refused," Saliday said.

"Then what did he do with them?" Grinwald asked.

"He exiled them to Sacrifice," Saliday replied.

"Sacrifice?" Teah questioned.

"It is the furthest settlement in the Forbidden. Logan had the queen and prince taken to Sacrifice to live out their years with the Betra who wanted no part of the return of the protector."

Galiven gasped inside Teah's mind.

What is it? Teah asked.

Nothing, Galiven said.

But the instant Galiven's thought touched her mind she knew what he didn't want to say. She understood the possibility he comprehended before any of the other protectors occupying her mind with him. Galiven understood that with the protective spell of the Lassains now circling Ter Chadain, there could only be one explanation.

She looked to the others as they considered her face deep in thought and furrowed with concern.

"What is it?" Caslor asked.

"I think the Englewoods found one of Galiven's descendants in Sacrifice," she said with a nod.

"Do you really believe that a queen with Lassain blood sits on the throne?" Grinwald gasped.

"What other explanation is there?" Teah countered.

Was your wife with child when the Betra killed you? Teah asked Galiven.

A sorrowful silence filled her thoughts and finally Galiven answered. *Yes.*

Teah didn't respond as the others bombarded her with questions or voiced their concerns amongst themselves and the protectors erupted inside her head. She stood, staring out at the daunting sight of the warships of her country, barring her from entering now that Prince Englewood had placed a Lassain queen on the throne. The quest she spent nearly two years of her life trying to accomplish, now seemed moot. The goal to protect the country from Caltorian invasion no longer mattered. That protection hovered around her in every direction.

Teah turned and walked in a daze from the bow, the comments of the others bouncing off her as she went down to her quarters. She shut the door behind her and eased herself onto her cot, staring at the plank wood walls.

It is done, she thought.

But what about Aston Englewood being in control of Ter Chadain? Bastion asked.

I don't know. Wasn't the activation of the security spell around Ter Chadain the reason I needed to be queen?

Yes, Stalwart said. *But, the others can correct me if I'm wrong, it was Englewood who entered into treaty with the Empress of Caltoria and his heir may do the same even with the spell in force.*

He is right, Falcone agreed. *The spell is an important facet to this, but we were with Logan when he removed Englewood from the throne and exiled his queen and son. They held as much hate for magic and what it represented as did King Englewood.*

Maybe more, Galiven pointed out. The others agreed with their silence.

Teah stared off at nothing. She struggled to wrap her thoughts around the fact that a Lassain queen sat upon the throne of Ter Chadain and that queen wasn't her.

The faces of all those lost on the quest to place her upon the throne swam through her mind, threatening to sweep her away. Logan, Sasha, Galena, Caldora, Talesaur, Lizzy, and all the rest who gave their lives to see this mission accomplished. Everything she fought for after the death of her parents, *adopted parents*, she amended, came down to this point. A new Lassain queen sat upon the throne.

"My journey is done," she said, and the protectors in her mind exploded with protests, but were quickly swept behind the barrier she raised in her mind. "I am done."

****

"What does it all mean?" Caslor asked, watching Teah disappear below deck.

"It means that a tyrant's son is now controlling Ter Chadain," Saliday spat.

"You don't know that," Grinwald argued.

"Really? Then how do you explain that?" Saliday said pointing up to the banners flapping high above them on the ships barring their entrance into the harbor.

"Alright," Grinwald conceded, raising his hands to calm her. "Somehow, Prince Aston and his mother have found an heir to the Lassain throne, but we don't know what he is planning to do now that he has taken the throne again."

"I can tell you right now, that it was Englewood who sent the Senji after Logan and I'm sure Prince Aston has by now extended that to include Teah and possibly a few of us as well. This is not going to turn out well until Teah sits upon the throne. She is the most direct descendent and thus possesses the most legitimate claim to the crown." Saliday flailed her hands as she spoke, a rare show of emotion from the typically calm Tarken.

"Well, you better decide what you want to do," Morgan said striding over to them. "They are sending emissaries over to question our entry." He pointed across the water where a dingy rowed away from the barricade and made its way toward them.

"What are we going to tell them?" Caslor asked.

"What I *wouldn't* tell them is that our passengers include a girl with claims to the throne and the son of the empress of Caltoria, but that's just my thought on it," Morgan said with a wave of his hand as he turned back toward the deck to ready for the Ter Chadain boarding party. "But it's your call, Viri Magus."

Everyone turned to Grinwald as he frowned, deep in thought. He looked up and jumped at the sight of everyone studying him for the answer.

"Below deck, everyone gather in Teah's quarters, we need to get our stories straight," he said and ushered them toward the cabin entrances. He reached out and took a hold of Raven by the collar of her shirt bringing the girl up short.

She turned to him, surprised.

"Stay here and see if there are any sniffers or the like with them. You are an escaped slave from Caltoria seeking refuge. There isn't much to hide there. Let me know as soon as you get a read on the boarding party."

Raven nodded and headed off to the rail while Grinwald hurried below to figure out how he was going to hide two royals that posed a threat to the current ruling party.

****

Raven stood at the rail as the dingy moved closer, studying the three individuals inside the small craft.

A young woman stood at the bow of the dingy with her eyes closed and her hands stretched out before her. Her long brown hair swirled around her face in the light sea breeze and the mist of the waves breaking on the dingy's bow wet the woman's silky green shirt tucked into black trousers.

The person rowing strained heavily muscled shoulders, sending the craft cutting through the choppy waves. His red uniform and silver cloth cap appeared too small for his exceptional bulk. He bent his head and his back to his task without looking up, somehow knowing where he headed without seeing it.

The man standing at the back of the dingy held an air of authority, his bright red uniform with silver embroidery enhancing his jacket and glistening medals adorned his chest. His black hat with silver edging tilted back on his head allowed him clear vision to the deck above where Raven observed him. Upon seeing Raven assessing them, he tilted his head curiously and gave a nod and a smile. His white teeth shone across the distance and Raven stepped back out of sight.

She kept her distance from the rail as the crew lowered a rope ladder and helped the man with the black hat and the woman on board, the oarsman staying below with the dingy.

The man stepped lightly onto the deck and then turned to survey the Morning Breeze with wide eyes and a bright smile. He caught Raven's eyes again and gave a slight bow of his head to her.

Raven returned the gesture in kind and hurried to go below, only to be met by Grinwald coming on deck at the doorway. They paused awkwardly for a moment until Grinwald raised an eyebrow in question.

"The man is not magical, but the woman definitely has magic about her. I doubt you will be able to conceal anyone's ability from her," Raven said and stepped back to allow Grinwald to come on deck.

Grinwald walked past her and moved across the deck toward the new arrivals. Teah, Rachel, Caslor, and Saliday followed after Grinwald. Upon reaching the man and woman now talking with Morgan, the group stopped. Raven slipped in behind Saliday.

"…and we only need to assess any concerns with anyone aboard your ship to determine if access to Ter Chadain will be granted," the man concluded as Grinwald and the others stopped next to them.

"I understand," Morgan was nodding. "Other than my crew, here are my passengers." He gestured to Teah, Grinwald, Caslor, Saliday, Rachel, and Raven.

"Excellent," the man said, excited. "My name is Captain Courtney. I am responsible for the armada you see before you." He swung his arm toward the ships looming over them in the harbor entrance. "My duty is to assure that any who enter Stalwart do not have ill intentions toward Ter Chadain or King Englewood and Queen Lassain."

Teah noticeably tensed at the mention of her last name, but fought to relax again as the captain continued to explain his duty.

"With me is Dezare Banderkin. She will assess any magical abilities you may have and give me her opinion on the risk you will pose Ter Chadain if allowed entry." He motioned to the woman in green standing behind him and she stepped forward.

Dezare's deep emerald eyes stared at each of them for a moment, noticeably stopping on Saliday for a longer period of time than the others, then continued on to Raven. She turned to the captain and he gave her a nod to continue.

The woman took a step away from the rest and motioned Raven over to her first.

Raven hesitated a moment, but after a reassuring nod from Grinwald, she stepped in front of Dezare and the woman gently placed her hands on her head.

Raven jumped at the contact, but closed her eyes and bowed her head. Calm crept over Raven's features as Dezare closed her eyes and concentrated.

A short time later, Dezare lifted her head and put her hand under Raven's chin to raise her face until their eyes met.

"You have been through much in your short life. I feel that you will do nothing but better things in Ter Chadain," Dezare said in a soft voice and then looked over to the captain. "She poses no threat," she raised her voice so the others could hear.

The captain nodded his approval and motioned for Saliday to go next.

Saliday moved over closer, visibly tense. She hesitated just out of Dezare's reach before stepping up close. Saliday's nervous hand slipped into her cloak and rested on the handle of one of her daggers as she looked Dezare in the eye.

The eye contact made it clear, Dezare remembered her from their meeting in her father's hall with Logan and Sasha. Dezare's knowledge of that connection could spell disaster for them.

The woman placed hands on Saliday and leaned closer.

"Where is Logan?" Dezare whispered.

"Dead," Saliday answered, trying not to move her lips.

"Our hope is gone," Dezare said as she lifted her head and looked to the captain.

Saliday's grip tightened on the dagger.

"She is of no danger to Ter Chadain," Dezare said to the captain.

He nodded and motioned for Rachel to step over.

Dezare laid hands on Rachel.

"Welcome home," Dezare whispered and then turned to the captain. "No threat."

Next, Caslor stepped forward and bowed his head.

Dezare's eyebrow lifted as she laid hands on him, and then she leaned in closer. "May coming to Ter Chadain bring your heart peace, Prince Caslor," she said softly. "No threat," Dezare reported to the captain.

Teah took a step as Caslor moved back in line, but Grinwald hurried past her, delaying the moment they dreaded.

Grinwald stepped closer and Dezare held up a hand, stopping him. "I know who you are Grinwald, please step back in line. We all know that Viri Magus do not pose a threat to Ter Chadain."

Captain Courtney's eyes grew wide at the mention of the Viri Magus and nodded at the questioning stare from Dezare and Grinwald. He motioned with his head to get back in line.

Teah moved over to Dezare and bowed her head. The moment Dezare made contact with her head, the protectors started to all talk at once.

Dezare recoiled and fell back onto the deck, a stunned look on her face.

Captain Courtney raced over to her and helped her to her feet, a concerned look on his face. "Are you alright?" he asked, concern thick in his voice.

"Yes, fine," Dezare said looking past him to Teah. "I just lost my balance. Did the ship get hit by a wave?"

Captain Courtney looked to Captain Morgan and shrugged. He watched Dezare step away from him and place her hands on Teah again.

This time Dezare flinched, but Teah held the barrier tightly against the protectors so their thoughts stayed shielded from the woman.

Dezare gasped and lifted her eyes to meet Teah's.

"I am so sorry for your loss," she whispered.

Teah nodded slightly as to not let on to the captain.

"We are ordered to stop you," Dezare said.

Teah only stared back into the woman's eyes.

Dezare lifted her head and stepped back.

"I sense no danger," Dezare addressed the captain.

"Strange, since I feel she might be who we are looking for. Her and her brother were known to be traveling with Grinwald at one time," the captain said, his hand dropping dangerously to his sword handle.

"True," Grinwald spoke up. "But I was taken to Caltoria after Caldora captured me. I have not seen the Lassain siblings since."

"Fine, line up here again," he motioned to the others who already began to creep around and encircle the captain.

They fell in line as instructed and waited.

The captain stepped in front of Grinwald.

"I know you are Grinwald, now who are you?" he turned to Teah.

"Lizzy Bridon," Teah said, using the name of her dead friend and fellow Zele student.

He stared at her for a moment and then moved down the line to Caslor.

"And you sir?" the captain questioned.

"Caslor Anthony, once magical slave," Caslor said using his dead father's surname.

The captain moved on and went down the line finishing with Saliday and a slight nod. "Very well, they seem to all be cleared for entrance. Once we clear the rest of your crew, you will be free to enter Stalwart and Ter Chadain," he addressed Captain Morgan.

Captain Courtney strode away to where the crew gathered for inspection with Morgan by his side. Dezare hesitated a moment taking in the disapproving stares of the magicals before her.

"They have my father Duke Banderkin in prison and will execute him as a traitor if I fail to help them," Dezare said and then scurried off after Captain Courtney.

Teah and the others breathed a sigh of relief and watched wordlessly while Dezare touched the crew members and gave her approval for them to enter Ter Chadain.

Captain Courtney and Dezare returned to their ship and soon the warships parted allowing the Morning Breeze entrance to Stalwart's harbor.

Teah stared out at Stalwart from the rail. She wondered if Ter Chadain knew that the rightful queen was home…or if it cared.

Chapter 12

Logan scraped his wooden bowl with his wooden spoon for the last drop of gravy from the lamb stew and then plunged it into his mouth. He closed his eyes as the savory sauce slid across his tongue and down his throat. The stew brought back memories of days gone by when what happened off their homestead meant little to them.

He opened his eyes and realized all the children stared at him. He flushed as he turned to Zeva who smiled softly and chuckled to herself, completely understanding the wonderful change to their recent diet of nothing but fish.

Any residual distrust from their entrance was minor, but a new tension after the meal began forming as Logan and Zeva tried to figure out how to break the news to these children that they just lost their home.

Logan cleared his throat as he looked from one curly, blonde head to the next. All four sets of blue eyes stared at him with wariness as he stretched his arms above his head and yawned.

"Thank you so much for the food. It's been a long time since I've tasted anything so wonderful," he said with a grin.

"You're welcome," the oldest girl said, her eyes betraying her concern.

"I'm Logan and this is Zeva." Even as the words left his mouth, the children tensed at the names and they all huddled around the oldest girl's chair.

"We are so sorry, we didn't know you were coming back from Stone Town," the girl said staring at Zeva. "We'll leave right away." She motioned to the others and they hurried off and began gathering possessions.

"No, wait." Zeva reached out to take hold of the girl's hand as she stood.

"But this is your home," the girl said.

"True, but you have taken such good care of it in my absence. It would be unfair for you to have to leave it."

Logan joined the children in staring at Zeva in disbelief.

"You mean we can stay?" the girl asked in a whisper, afraid if she said it louder it would be false.

"There are four rooms here and plenty of space," Zeva said looking around, considering as she spoke. "We should all stay and see if we can make it work before we start kicking people out."

The girl stood next to the table and stared at Zeva, considering it for a moment and then looked to her brother and sisters. Each sibling smiled and nodded that they liked the idea.

"Very well, my brother and sisters and I would be honored to share your home with you, Zeva." The girl nodded.

"Wonderful." Zeva smiled and only let that smile waver slightly as she looked at Logan's unhappy stare. "You know my name, share with me yours."

"I am Bethany," said the oldest.

"This is Sara," she introduced the next oldest whose blonde hair was tied back with red ribbon. "That is Zack," she said motioning to her brother as he put the things he'd begun to pack back in their places. "And she is Violet." Bethany gestured to the little girl with blue ribbon tying her two pig tails that twisted and bobbed on the sides of her head. She smiled and giggled shyly as everyone looked at her.

Logan forced a smile and then stood abruptly. "Thank you for supper. I'll be in the tool shed for the night," he said and strode out the door.

He just cleared the bushes by the walk when the door slammed behind him and he turned to see Zeva storming his way. He stopped to watch her stomp up to him. Her face turned up to his and shone red in the moonlight just before she unleashed on him.

"What is the matter with you now?" she shouted.

"I did not come here to be responsible for children," he

107

shouted back.

"No, you came here to avoid any responsibility at all."

"That's not fair."

"Fair? Fair? I'll tell you what's not fair; those children without any parents to take care of them. Those children having to fend for themselves in order to survive in this world is not fair. Losing my entire family because they followed me and supported me even though my life was given into someone else's control is not fair. And yes, Logan, you losing loved one after loved one because you have a certain destiny. That too is not fair. But do you see anyone else around here whining and complaining about the fate they've been given? No. They suck it up and do the best that they can."

Logan stared down at the fiery woman. "I'm sorry…"

"You're darn right you're sorry. You have been the sorriest travel companion that I've ever had to deal with. But maybe you have a right to be that way. Maybe you are right that you've done so much and lost so much already that it is time to step back and let someone else sacrifice everything important to them. I'm not saying you don't have that right, but what I am saying is don't forget that you are a person and as a person, you should always understand that others have burdens to endure as well. I'm not minimizing your sacrifices, just don't minimize mine or those children's sacrifices either."

He stared dumbfounded at her.

"You decide if you want to stay or go, but I have decided the children will stay here as long as they wish. You can choose what you want to do." She spun and stormed back into the house, slamming the door after her.

Logan stood staring at the door for a long while after Zeva disappeared through it. He stood wondering how his world came to be in such a place as this. So close to where he started. Now he had the opportunity to live the way he dreamt he could live his life, without the death and destruction of these past two years.

He wanted to be removed from the violence and struggle that consumed him. Even though he missed the voices of the protectors that once roamed inside his mind he now felt grateful that they traveled with Teah instead. She had more use for them. She needed their guidance more than he did.

He turned and walked toward the tool shed with a smile of contentment on his lips. He actually did what he needed to do in order to aid Teah's claim the throne of Ter Chadain. He freed her from the empress, helped assure her safe passage back to Ter Chadain, and even though he had no actual power to do so, transferred the protector's spirits into her mind to help provide her guidance and knowledge in order to finish her quest.

Pulling a blanket from a shelf, he curled up next to the tack box that hid his swords and closed his eyes on dry land for the first time in weeks. Peace crept over him and he drifted off to sleep once more Logan Saolto, not Logan Lassain, Protector of Ter Chadain.

****

The shining sun and singing birds greeted Logan's morning. His spirit felt light and refreshed, the stain and taint of killing far removed from him in that moment. He stepped out into the sunlight and took in his new home. The buildings shone even more than in the moonlight of the night before. The whitewash stood out crisp and clean on the exterior walls of the farmstead's structures. The roofs and eaves looked a bit worn and tattered compared to the rest of the buildings, but Logan felt confident he could remedy that situation. He pushed the thought aside as Zack came outside of the main house and headed for the tool shed.

The boy slowed his walk as he saw Logan and hesitated for a moment in front of him.

"Morning Zack," Logan greeted.

"Good morning, Logan," Zack replied. "Zeva told me to fetch you for breakfast."

"Sounds good, you eat already?"

"Yes sir, headed to get the cows in for some milking," the boy said with a smile on his lips, but doubt hung in his eyes.

"You go get them and I will help you milk after I finish eating," Logan said as he turned and headed for the house.

"Alright," the boy shouted as he took off at a run toward the pasture with a smile on his face.

Logan stopped and watched Zack run, remembering when he was a boy and his father shared in his chores. His best memories were from those moments when he worked side-by-side with his father. He felt the memory of his father's death threaten to creep up and he forced it down, focusing only on the happy days of working on the farm. He whistled and continued to the house.

Entering the house still whistling, he garnered surprised looks from Zeva and the girls. They smiled back, greeting him with "good morning", and went on with their chores.

Violet dusted the shelves she could reach while Sara swept the floor. Bethany helped Zeva in the kitchen, washing the dishes in a basin and then taking time to stir a pot over the hearth.

Zeva smiled sheepishly at Logan and set a plate of eggs and venison in front of him as he sat down at the table. He smiled back and accepted a mug of water she handed to him.

He took a long drink and a deep inhale of the steaming food in front of him. Just as he was about to dig into his food, a smell reached his nose. He turned to Zeva where she stood next to the hearth and then he saw it, a small pot hanging on a hook suspending it over the fire with steam coming out of a narrow spout.

"Is that brewed brown beans?" he asked his excitement almost giddy.

"It sure is. Want some?" she smiled at his recognition of the

110

traditional hot beverage.

"I haven't had that since I left..." he paused as the memories he fought off all morning built up once more.

Zeva hurried over with a tin cup and the pot and poured him a serving.

He lifted it in his hands, bringing it close to his nose and inhaling deeply with his eyes closed. He took a sip, not bothering to open his eyes, and gave a deep guttural moan of pleasure. "Ooh, that is incredible. Better than I remembered."

"That's because this bean is a special bean developed and cultivated over the centuries by my family. We used to sell this specific bean all over Caltoria."

Logan saw the pride in Zeva, a pride she and her family deserved. Building a wonderful homestead and life is a hard thing, but then leaving it in order to keep the family together after Zeva was taken by the empress impressed Logan even more.

"I'm sorry," Logan said.

"About what?" Zeva frowned.

"Last night, the time in the dingy, everything."

"You have a right."

"But I need to move on and live. You don't deserve to hear it."

"I'm a friend, always will be, but friends kick each other in the back side if we need to. It is our duty as a friend."

Logan stared at Zeva for a moment and then began to nod as a smile curled his lips. "I agree," he said with a laugh. "Kick me anytime you feel I need it."

"Don't worry, I will," Zeva laughed with him.

She sat across from him as he ate, pleased to see his appetite. She sipped her hot beverage and felt comfort for the first time in a long while. As she looked to Logan again, she let her magic wander and touch the red weave surrounding him. She eased her magic against the barrier, recoiling as the deadliness of the weave radiated back through her magic. She flinched, nearly spilling her

111

cup of steaming liquid.

"What's wrong?" Logan asked, surprised by her gasp.

"Nothing, it's just the binding weave…" she said and then trailed off as his face turned stormy.

"The weave is what?" Logan stared at her, his reality staring back at him.

"If anyone tries to untie it, it will kill you," she said, holding his gaze.

"Then don't try to untie it," he said flatly and went back to eating.

"Don't you want to have your magic back?"

"Apparently Grinwald thinks I'm too dangerous with it, so maybe I should defer to his wisdom and let it be." He gave her a nod and took a long drink from his mug.

Zeva stared, horrified at his reaction.

"What?" Logan asked upon seeing her stunned expression.

"Even when the empress controlled my magic, I still felt it as I would an arm or a leg. I can only imagine not being able to touch it at all."

Logan thought for a moment, reaching for the magic he once felt flow throughout his body. It still remained within him, but locked tightly beyond his grasp. He looked back to Zeva with a shrug.

"I need to learn to deal with it or let it drive me crazy. What would you have me do?"

"Deal with it, I guess," Zeva said, her eyes filled with sympathy for him.

"Don't."

"Don't what?"

"Don't waste your sympathy on me. Feel sorry for Sasha, Galena, and all those who sacrificed their lives to protect me and Teah. I still live. I have a chance to put that killing behind me and live a life."

Zeva looked incredulously at Logan.

"What?" Logan sighed as he sat back.

"You really think that the battle is over?"

"My part is."

"As long as the empress is in power, she will do everything possible to keep those with magical abilities down. This fight is far from over."

"It is not my battle. I came to free Teah. Obviously, there are those who feel that my part is done and so do I."

"You are a fool," Zeva stood knocking over her chair, sending it banging to the floor.

The girls cleaning stopped, startled by the loud noise.

"You need to stop feeling sorry for yourself and realize that the battle for the greater good rages around you no matter if you acknowledge it or not." She stormed from the house, slamming the door behind her, leaving Logan staring in shock after her.

"You really make her mad," Bethany said as she took Logan's bowl and spoon from in front of him.

"Yeah, I guess that is something I'm pretty good at," Logan agreed glancing up at her.

"How long have you two been together?"

"Together?" Logan asked, confused.

"You two are together, together, right?"

"No, not really, we were kind of thrown together." Logan considered the possibility and then shook his head. "No, not together. Just friends."

"Oh, sorry, just seemed obvious that you have a connection," she said and then hurried back to the sink.

Logan looked around as Sara and Violet quickly turned their attention back to their chores. He thought about Zeva for a moment, really taking time to think about what she meant to him. She had beauty, that he couldn't deny, but her stubborn attitude meant years of conflict. He chuckled and shook his head before looking up and seeing the girls staring at him nervously. He stood and hurried out the door to find Zeva, needing to make sure her view of their partnership matched his.

Memories of Saliday came to him as he exited the door and stood looking out at the surrounding out buildings. The red-headed Tarken still held a special place in his heart that he refused to allow anyone into again.

He strode away from the door and headed to the barn in search of Zeva, pushing the painful memory of his first love out of his mind. That was a part of his past. His future held a different path. One he planned to assure didn't include death and destruction to everyone close to him.

He stepped in front of the barn looking into the darkened shadows of the large structure just as a horse burst through the opening, sending him sprawling.

A wagon pulled up next to him as he lay coughing in the dust. Zeva sat in the seat with the reins held deftly in her hands and staring down at him curiously.

"You need to be more alert living on a farm."

"I grew up on a farm, just been away for too long." He got to his feet and brushed his clothes off.

"I'm headed to town to pick up some supplies. I managed to take some gold from the empress before leaving. It's obvious we need some things around here."

"I'll come with you," Logan said pulling himself up to sit beside her.

Zeva frowned as he settled in next to her. "Aren't you bringing your weapons?"

"I don't plan on doing any fighting."

"Port Shoal is not a very pleasant place. A lot of sailors port there and they can be a seedy lot."

"The last thing I want is to announce my arrival or cause trouble. Those blades are nothing but trouble, trust me."

Zeva held his stare flatly for a moment and then nodded, giving the reins a quick snap and sending the horse forward.

They rode along a winding road through the rolling hills of green pastures and sparse trees before pulling up along the cliffs overlooking Port Shoal. The coastal town spread out along the shoreline to the north and south, disappearing around a bend in the land in either direction.

"Welcome to my home town," Zeva said without emotion. "Be warned that they might remember me and know that I am a magical. It may be unnerving for some of them that I have returned."

Logan nodded. It made perfect sense. A person who the empress took away as a slave returning might make them uneasy.

"What if they ask how we're connected?" Logan asked, still surveying the town below.

"They know my family...knew my family, so telling them you're a relative won't work."

"Distant cousin?" Logan added trying to be helpful. Zeva's look showed he wasn't.

"My betrothed," she said causing Logan to nearly fall from his seat.

He stared at her in disbelief.

"What?"

"You think that will be believable?"

"You're right, you really aren't my type."

"Not your ty ..." Logan sputtered.

"But we will have to convince them we are truly in love if you don't want them questioning your presence here."

Logan held her stare for a moment and then nodded.

"Good. Now come, *my love*, and make yourself known to the townspeople who you will need to deal with to survive in Port Shoal." She snapped the reins and followed the weaving road along the cliff side toward the town below.

Logan watched her carefully, trying to discern the presence of feelings in Zeva he missed or if she just relished in tormenting him. He finally turned away, aware that he could determine neither.

They pulled down the well-worn road into town and stopped in front of the central store. Hopping out, the newcomers tried to ignore the stares from the townspeople as they passed. They entered the store and a bell hanging over the door rang announcing their arrival.

Logan stared at row upon row of shelves lining the walls and spaced evenly throughout the store, packed full of items to be sold. Zeva didn't hesitate, but hurried to the shelves containing fabric and thread. She pulled bolts of fabric out, looked at them, and then slid them back in place, searching for the pattern she desired.

Watching Zeva's antics, considering the twists and turns his life had taken, a grin spread across his face and he started to laugh. He made eye contact with the man behind the counter, his opulent torso edging out from beneath his blue shirt and above his large silver belt buckle, straining the hole of the tightly cinched piece of leather holding up dark trousers that threatened to fall down at any moment. His slicked-back black hair reminded Logan of a hawk, his tiny eyes and pointed nose accentuated the disapproving stare. His rounded cheeks and extra chins added to his comical appearance.

Logan looked around hoping someone else elicited the man's scorn, but he discovered that he and Zeva were the only ones in the establishment. Logan turned back to the man to see his face pinch down even more.

"Get what you need and be on your way," the man said as he turned his critical stare from Logan to Zeva, tilting his head to see her down the aisle.

"I will in good time," Zeva said not looking up or hesitating in her search.

"We don't like your kind much in this town."

Logan spun to stare at Zeva, waiting for her to lash out, but she ignored his comments and continued in her quest unhindered. He turned back to the man behind the counter who now focused his distaste on Logan since Zeva would give him none of her time.

"You must be one of them too if you're with her," he said with a nod toward Zeva.

"It makes no difference if I am or if I am not," Logan said, stretching his full height. He walked over to the counter the man stood behind and towered over him, looking down flatly at him.

The man didn't flinch but pulled a club from under the counter and slapped it into his empty hand with a smack.

Logan's eyes narrowed as he analyzed the threat. The man's arms were far too short to reach him from where he stood and Logan ascertained that his muscle mass would fail to propel him quickly enough to even remotely touch Logan with a blow of the short club.

He relaxed as the bell rang announcing another shopper's entrance.

Logan glanced over at three men entering the establishment and turned back to the man behind the counter just as he lunged, swinging the club for Logan's head. Logan stepped to one side, allowing the momentum of the swing to propel the large man onto the counter and then took hold of his wrist to pull him across the flat surface and send him careening into a stack of produce piled neatly on a nearby stand.

The man crushed most of the merchandise he landed on and slid over the stand landing at the feet of the three men who just entered.

The newcomers stared in shock at the man covered in the juices of smashed fruits and vegetables lying at their feet. They turned as one to Logan who stood ready for their advance.

"Shit, Emmett," one of the men shouted.

"You pissing off the customers again?" another laughed.

They looked over at Logan and nodded their amusement, obviously not surprised by the shopkeeper's situation. Movement down the aisle caught their attention and they turned to see Zeva standing between the rows, a bolt of fabric cradled in her arms.

Instantly the men's demeanor turned sour and they scowled at her.

Zeva strode to the counter, ignoring the glares, and set the fabric down before turning to Emmett now on the floor. Crossing her arms, she waited impatiently to pay for her merchandise.

Logan eased over next to Zeva and the men's angry stares now fell on him as well.

One of the men helped Emmett to his feet and then joined the other three with his arms crossed, considering the couple. "Oh, now I see what the trouble is."

Emmett scurried around the counter still dripping with juices and looked past Logan and Zeva to the men.

Logan never took his eyes from the trio and caught the slight nod from the tallest of his counterparts, wearing a neatly tailored dark green coat and matching trousers. His short hair looked newly trimmed and his skin shone smooth and soft, almost polished.

"That will be ten pence," Emmett told Zeva who pulled a coin from her pocket and dropped it on the counter.

Logan stepped beside Zeva, taking the fabric in his hand and guiding her around the stand of damaged produce, away from the four men who followed their movement with narrowed eyes. The bell rang as Logan opened the door and ushered Zeva out.

The exited the store and took two steps toward the wagon when the bell rang behind them. Logan tensed, knowing where this was headed and having no way of deterring it.

"Hold up," the voice of the tallest man rang out, the activity and the sounds of the street stopping dead.

Logan and Zeva turned to see the four, all holding clubs and lined up along the walk in front of the store.

"We don't want any trouble." Logan raised his hands in front of him.

"We might have believed you at first, but we've seen you in the company of an escaped magical; we know that to be false." He let his club smack his bare hand.

The hair on the back of Logan's neck tingled and he knew Zeva held her magic at the ready. He reached over and took her hand in his, making eye contact to give her a cautioning look.

"Why would you think she is an escaped magical?" Logan asked as Zeva gave his hand a warning squeeze.

"Really?" the man laughed. "We know Zeva, or did she forget to tell you that she grew up here and was one of us until she turned into a magical."

Realization seeped into Logan. How could he be so stupid?

"The stones are gone and the magicals are free," Logan said.

This only seemed to stir the men further and they began to smack their clubs into their hands in unison.

"The empress did not release them, they escaped from her control. They are no more free than before, just more dangerous," the man sneered.

"We mean you no harm," Logan insisted, tossing the fabric into the wagon behind them without looking back.

"But we mean to harm you. There is a price on every magical's head, especially hers." He pointed with his club at Zeva. "A personal magical of Empress Shakata is very valuable and a sniffer patrol has just arrived in town. This will be easy money."

With that, the men launched themselves at Logan and Zeva.

Logan met them head on, leaping in front of Zeva before she could release her magic. He lifted an arm, catching the first two clubs across his forearm and swiping his other across the men's midsections. The two men doubled over, gasping for air.

Logan spun, intercepting the other two advancing on Zeva. Not expecting the move, they collided with his back. Logan leapt up, flipping backwards and over the two men's heads and neatly grasped each head in a hand to smack them together. A sickening thud preceded the unconscious men slumping to the ground.

Zeva stared in surprise as Logan took her by the hand and pulled her to the wagon where he unceremoniously threw her in and leapt to the seat. He grasped the reins and snapped the horse into motion, sending the wagon speeding out of town with Zeva scrambling to right herself in the bouncing wagon.

She looked back as the men slowly regained their feet in front of the general store, then back up at him, sadness filling her eyes.

"Welcome home," he said, giving her a sideways glance.

She turned back around, staring longingly at the town where she could never return.

Chapter 13

Rudnick Curn strode into Commander Wilkins's office and slammed his fist on the man's desk, the commander jumped in surprise.

"Councilor Curn." The commander came to his feet, bowing at the waist. "I only just dispatched the messenger yesterday. I didn't expect you so soon."

"If we needed to wait for messengers we wouldn't get anything done," the man said holding out a device that resembled a simple compass. On closer inspection, it revealed not letters but crystals that shone a dull green in color. Where a needle normally would point in a direction, a small sword teetered toward the illuminated gem.

"What is that?" the commander questioned.

"Let's just say this little artifact has the ability to find what the council requires." Rudnick tucked the device into a pocket of his large flowing black overcoat.

"And what are you looking for?" the commander frowned.

"We were alerted that the weave is down and then the artifact pointed us to this very building indicating there are exiles here."

Wilkins stiffened and took a step back.

"Not to worry I will take full responsibility of any exiles I find on the premises, but I need your full cooperation," Rudnick said unconvincingly.

"We have four from Caltoria who came willingly in order to give us information on the potential threat from their empress," Wilkins explained leaving off the part about the camp just outside of town.

"Where are you detaining them?" Rudnick questioned.

"They are not detained, but resting in the barracks," the commander said and then braced himself as Rudnick's body tensed.

"Gather some men and take me to them at once," Rudnick shouted, slamming a fist upon the table again.

Wilkins rushed to the door of his office. "Get me a security detail and meet us at the rear barracks," he ordered the nearest man walking across the courtyard.

The man jerked to attention and then ran to gather some others.

Rudnick pushed past Wilkins in the doorway as he pulled the small box from his pocket and strode toward the other side of the grounds. Wilkins hurried after, motioning for all who came into view to follow.

Soon a large contingent of men followed behind Rudnick, his black overcoat flowing behind him. Wilkins jogged along in his green patrol attire. Rudnick marched around the barracks to the rear and entered the smaller troop quarters without slowing.

****

Trevon, Linell, and Fedlen lounged on cots discussing what their next move should be.

Linell wanted to get out of Stellaran as soon as possible, calling this move the biggest mistake of Trevon's life. His own sentiments pointed more toward his betrothal to Linell and was about to share this when the door to the quarters burst open and the room filled with men.

A tall, thin man with a dark pock-marked complexion and long black hair wearing a black traveling cloak stood in front of them, a hand on his hip and his other holding a small square box that shone a soft green.

The man nodded and pointed at Trevon. "This one." He smugly tucked the box back into a pocket.

Two men stepped forward, each grabbing an arm to restrain Trevon while the rest of the weave patrol drew steel, pointing it at Linell and Fedlen before they could draw their weapons. Once the members of their party stood disarmed, they watched helplessly as the patrol took Trevon.

The click of a lock confirmed that they now were prisoners instead of guests and proof that this may very well be the worst decision that Trevon had made in his young life.

Linell pounded on the locked door, her anger mixing with tears of fear for Trevon.

"Stern, Cita," she shouted, "you promised. You promised."

****

The alarm rose throughout the compound, causing Stern to step out of his quarters the same time Cita stepped out of her barracks and stared at each other with concern. They raced toward the rear barracks only to find Trevon being hauled off under guard with Rudnick Curn a step behind.

They watched the group pass before spotting Commander Wilkins and rushing to him.

"What in the name of the gods are you doing?" Stern stepped in front of the commander, stopping him.

"It is not my choice." Wilkins raised a calming hand to Stern just as Cita reached them.

"They came freely to help us," Cita shouted, flailing her hands in exacerbation.

The commander's calming hand turned into a pointed finger that tapped heavily on Cita's chest. "Watch it, mind your place," he warned.

Stern pushed between the two. He stared hard at the man, not backing down.

"Now Stern, you know when Rudnick decides something that's it," Wilkins said trying to calm him.

"No, Commander, you need to listen," Stern said putting his finger against Wilkin's chest causing the commander's eyes to widen in surprise. "I promised them safe passage and my word is my bond."

"Then maybe you shouldn't give your word where you have no authority to do so." The commander brushed Stern's hand aside and walked away.

Stern and Cita stared after the commander, their faces a mixture of anger and frustration. In the barracks behind them they could hear Linell calling out to them, cursing their betrayal.

Realization crossed their faces as they turned to each other.

"The others," they said in unison.

"Go," Stern told Cita and she rushed off toward the encampment of the travelers of Caltoria on the outskirts of town.

****

His captors slammed Trevon into a chair after entering the commander's office, nearly sending the chair toppling over backwards. By the time Trevon righted himself, Rudnick stood towering over him, his finger pointed between Trevon's eyes.

"Why have you come here?" Rudnick shouted.

"To explain the dangers of the empress," Trevon said as fear crept up the back of his throat.

"Really?" Rudnick stepped back, pulling the artifact glowing bright green from his pocket. "It says here that you have ties to the original council members of Stellaran."

Trevon stared at the artifact and then back at Rudnick. How could this object know such things?

"At a loss for words, spy?" Rudnick spat. He raised his hand and backhanded Trevon across his face with a loud crack, sending Trevon tumbling to the floor.

The men gathered Trevon from the floor and the puddle of blood beneath his broken nose and righted him in the chair again. Trevon reached for his magic, finding nothing but emptiness. He looked up at Rudnick in shocked surprise.

"You think I'm foolish enough not to bind your powers before questioning you?" he laughed and backhanded Trevon again.

Trevon's vision erupted into bursts of light as he tumbled to the floor and was unceremoniously planted once again into his chair. His head hung forward, blood ran in a steady stream into his lap, soaking his dark pants.

"Now we will try this again." Rudnick turned away as he spoke, beginning to pace around the room. "Is there one in Caltoria who has rightful heritage to the last Chairman of the Council of Stellaran?"

Trevon looked back at Rudnick with ever-narrowing slits as his eyes swelled shut. He was thankful Rudnick couldn't read the expression on his deformed and beaten face, because he knew he had no chance at keeping the shock and surprise from his face. Instead, his features contorted into a grotesque smile that only enraged Rudnick even more.

He pulled back and struck Trevon with his fist full in the face, sending the chair and Trevon toppling backwards onto the floor with a bounce. Trevon lay motionless on the floor, unconscious.

The men went to right the prisoner, but Rudnick raised a hand to stay them. He stared down at Trevon, disgust twisting his lips as he considered the first Caltorian he'd ever met. Satisfied, he nodded and then motioned for the men to right Trevon again.

"Wouldn't want him choking to death on his own blood," Rudnick said, coldly turning away to stare out the window at the setting sun.

When Trevon began to slide from the chair, one of the men stepped forward to steady him.

"How many do we have to question?" Rudnick asked.

"Three, Master Curn."

"Was I mistaken, or was there a woman?" Rudnick said still staring at Trevon.

"There is one woman," the man agreed.

"Good. Bring her in and we will let her sit here until morning. That will soften her up. I find women much more entertaining to

125

interrogate than men." Rudnick waved a dismissive hand for the men to take Trevon out.

****

Commander Wilkins and Stern sat outside the commander's office, not looking at each other but trying to come to some sort of acceptance over what happened on the other side of the door and the part each played in the betrayal of the travelers from Caltoria. They jumped to their feet as the door to the office opened and the two men drug the unconscious and bleeding Trevon out and across the grounds back to the barracks. The two waiting men exchanged incredulous looks and Stern followed Commander Wilkins into his office.

Rudnick stood looking out a window on the opposite side of the office picking his teeth with a small piece of wood.

"What is the meaning of this? That man is under my protection," Wilkins ranted.

Rudnick didn't look back, but Wilkins dropped to a knee holding a hand to his throat, his mouth open and no sound coming out.

"Mind your tongue, Commander," Rudnick growled. "I act with full authority of the Council."

Wilkins struggled to breathe a moment longer and then dropped onto his hands and knees, gasping as he could breathe once more.

"We didn't bring them back to be tortured. They would answer any question you ask of them freely," Stern argued.

"Really?" Rudnick flicked the wood into a corner on the floor and spun on his heels to advance on Stern who back-pedaled away from the man until his back hit the wall next to the door. Rudnick moved close and held his accusing finger a fraction from Stern's nose. "Even if they are hiding an heir to the seat of Chairman of the Council of Stellaran?"

Stern's eyes shot wide in shock. Rudnick spun on him, his eyes narrowing warily.

"Where is the woman who was with you? She possesses more magic than any I've met."

"Cita…" Stern began but stopped as he realized he said too much.

"Ah yes, Cita. I've heard of her."

Stern didn't respond, but did anything he could to hold this man's stare.

"We believe this to be their plan if the weave ever failed," Rudnick said turning away from a much-relieved Stern. "They will never give up that information freely. I needed to set an example of what I am capable of and willing to do to get the answers I seek."

"You nearly killed him," Stern protested.

"That wasn't intentional. I got a little carried away and when I got to my main question, his face was far too damaged to see any signs of knowledge on it. But with the next I will be more patient and coax the needed information out."

As if on cue, the men appeared in the doorway with Linell restrained between them. She looked at Wilkins on the floor and then made eye contact with Stern. She burst free of the men holding her and launched herself upon Stern, sending them tumbling to the floor as she struck him again and again on the way down.

The men pulled her off a bloodied-faced Stern and forced her into the chair. They tied her hands behind her and her feet to the legs of the chair.

Linell reached for her magic, but the aura around her snuffed out as if by a great blanket and Linell's features turned from determined to terrified. Linell looked at Stern, fear gripping her. She begged for help but the men pushed Stern and Commander Wilkins out of the room, slamming the door behind them.

A faint whimper from Linell reached their ears and the cruel laugh of Rudnick Curn that followed.

Stern dabbed the blood from his face with the end of his shirt. "What have we done?" he whispered in horror.

Chapter 14

Teah and her party knew they couldn't just waltz into Stalwart even if Dezare claimed they posed no threat to Ter Chadain. The captain questioned their story and that made Teah feel uneasy about sailing into the port.

Instead of riding the Morning Breeze through the blockade of the armada, Teah, Caslor, Saliday, Raven, Morgan, Grinwald, and Rachel rowed the remaining dingy alongside the ship in the cover of darkness with the hopes of avoiding any unwanted scrutiny from those in charge.

As the ship reached the entrance to the harbor just past the armada blockade, the dingy eased away from her and angled to the far side of the harbor. Everyone in the dingy lay flat against the bottom as Caslor crouched and rowed silently, each stroke lifting out of the water and easing back in soundlessly.

They reached neglected stone steps leading from the water to the wharf and slipped out of the boat, creeping up the crumbling pads. They scurried across the open space between the dock and the buildings hugging the shadows of the structures to avoid detection.

After a long wait to assure their concealment, Saliday took the lead and motioned them to follow as she crept along the cobblestone, staying within the shadows whenever possible. She paused at the edge of any open expanse, studying their path to detect any possible observers before hurrying across the lighted space and disappearing again into shadow.

They made for the edge of town and finally saw their goal ahead when Teah felt a strange tingle around her head. She glanced back at Grinwald who scanned the surroundings, but he never made eye contact.

Saliday moved closer to Teah without warning, leaning in and whispering in her ear, "something's wrong."

As the words left the Tarken's mouth, troops descended and overwhelmed them. Teah, Zeva, Rachel, and Grinwald called upon their magic only to meet a wall of magic blocking them from its reach.

A trap! The protectors cried out as one then went silent.

A large door eased open exposing rows of people with their hands extended before them, concentrating on the magic they held woven around Teah and the others. She saw the red layers of the weave encircling the entire party from the ship, their captors not willing to chance missing a magical in their midst.

Teah scanned the troops, deciding quickly that even with her protector abilities she couldn't overpower them all without endangering her friends. She looked on helplessly as Dezare stepped forward and mouthed the words, "I'm sorry."

A large woman strode up next to the troops dressed in a black flowery embroidered dress that seemed to squeeze her bosom out the low neckline. Duchess Heniton stared at the travelers and smiled.

"Disarm them and lock them in the dungeon. Be sure to tie the weaves binding their magic. Welcome, Teah Lassain, to the new Ter Chadain. One that doesn't need you any longer." She clapped her hands and the troops moved in to disarm them and escort them to prison.

Teah looked over her shoulder at the duchess as they led her away. Their eyes met and Teah relayed her message loud and clear without a word. The duchess would die for this. Not a threat, but a promise, from one of noble blood to another, without uttering a word.

The smile on the duchess's face went slack and a nervous hand went to her throat.

Teah's satisfied smile spread across her face. Her message was received. Teah held no place for traitors and would show no mercy.

The landing party from the Morning Breeze filed into the dungeons beneath the fortifications protecting Stalwart's harbor. The guards placed the men in one cell and the women in another. Teah caught Caslor's eye as they separated, heading toward each cell's opening.

Caslor gave a slight nod before he vanished into the dark cell.

Teah stepped up behind Rachel to enter the cell but a hand on her shoulder stopped her. She turned to see Dezare, her eyes filled with sorrow staring at her.

"You need to come with me," she said softly.

"We don't have those orders," a guard interrupted stepping beside her.

"I was given the order by the duchess herself," Dezare said, her voice filled with authority.

The guard snapped to attention and pounded a fist to his chest in salute. "As you wish, but first we must restrain her." The guard lifted steel shackles from a hook protruding from the stone block wall and fastened them on Teah's wrists. He gave them a final tug to assure they held and then nodded.

Dezare took hold of the short length of chain between the shackles and led Teah away. They wound up the hard stone stairs following the curve of the walls, the sounds of their footfalls mixed with the light ring of the chains attached to Teah's wrists tapping together.

Teah crinkled her nose at the musty smell as the passage gave her a strange feeling of heaviness as the castle loomed many stories above them. She spent so much time at sea this past year that her enclosed surroundings only amplified her feeling of entrapment. The last time she felt like this she sat in the hold of the slave ship that took her to Caltoria.

The image of Lizzy eased into her thoughts and she blocked the memory of her beheading too late. The image seared into her memory bloomed in vivid, gruesome blood red color. She gasped at the strength of the memory and staggered along the steps.

Dezare paused as Teah wavered, steadying her with a firm grip on the chains.

The women's eyes met and they seemed to mirror the other's sadness.

"Are you alright?" Dezare whispered.

Teah nodded, not sure if the sympathy in the woman's voice should be believed.

"I need you to speak with someone before I take you to the duchess, but we must be quick before we are missed," she said and hurried forward, pulling Teah with her.

They came to a landing that expanded out in every direction to introduce rows of doors. Dezare moved to one of the age darkened wooden doors and tapped on it lightly. The door opened inward before her third tap and, with a quick glance around, Dezare hurried inside with Teah in tow.

A man ushered them in and closed the door behind them. Teah looked at the man nearly twice her age, ruggedly handsome, a silken green shirt stretched across his muscular build. His silver-tipped temples wrinkled as his strangely familiar eyes searched her own. She glanced to Dezare and it struck her as she turned back to the man with a nod of awareness.

"Your father?" Teah asked, already knowing the answer without looking at Dezare, but still studying this man before her.

"May I present Duke Banderkin," Dezare said. "Father, this is Teah Lassain."

The duke raised an eyebrow curiously and then bowed deeply at the waist to Teah. "My Queen."

"That is yet to be seen," Teah said, motioning with her shackled hands for him to rise.

"I have no doubt," the duke said.

"Then what is going on here?"

"Logan left me here to await his return but while he was off rescuing you, Prince Aston attacked Cordlain and declared another as queen with Lassain lineage."

"How can that be?" Teah argued.

"It is said this new queen is Betra. A descendent of Galiven Lassain," Banderkin explained.

I suspected she was with child, but I never knew, Galiven said breaking the silence of the protectors for the first time since her capture.

"So this queen is a true Lassain descendent?" Teah asked.

"So it seems. I've been told by the Viri Magus that the spell would never activate if that were not the case."

"So my quest here is done," Teah said, staring blankly past Banderkin.

"But we have the Englewood regime once more and that was vile the first time. I can only imagine what Aston will be like." The duke turned and strode to the window trying to contain his frustration and rage. "It can't be done," he said staring out the window. "I need to speak with Logan."

Teah inhaled sharply, causing Banderkin to turn around. He frowned at her reaction and raised a curious eyebrow.

"Logan is here, right?"

Dezare followed her father's gaze to Teah.

Teah's eyes watered and she struggled to maintain control.

"Logan is with you, isn't he?"

The duke looked from Teah to Dezare for an answer.

"Logan is not with them," Dezare said, hesitating as she looked to Teah unwilling to break the news of Logan's fate.

"Logan is dead," Teah said the words flat without emotion. "And this quest is over."

Banderkin stared at Teah and then slumped heavily into the chair next to the window. "Then Ter Chadain is no more," he said, the wisp of nostalgia for days gone by buoying each word laced with disbelief.

"What are you two talking about?" Dezare shouted flailing her hands above her head. "This entire quest was meant to put Teah, the rightful heir, upon the throne of Ter Chadain."

Teah and the duke looked at Dezare, resignation in his eyes.

"We needed to remove Englewood from the throne and put the protective barrier up around Ter Chadain by having a queen with the Lassain blood line on the throne."

"But the barrier is up and King Englewood is dead and no longer on the throne," Teah said with a shrug.

"Is he now?" Dezare said taking a step toward Teah. "Is he really?"

Teah looked to the duke who raised an eyebrow in consideration of his daughter's reasoning. She turned back to Dezare.

"What are you trying to say?" Teah asked.

"This new queen may be of your bloodline, but only barely. She may be queen, but only as a puppet to the new King Englewood. She is no more the Queen of Ter Chadain than I am." Dezare crossed her arms over her chest and gave a nod.

"She's right," Duke Banderkin agreed. "This is only slightly better than when the first King Englewood ruled Ter Chadain. He has actually taken steps to disband the two houses of magic."

Teah spun on the duke. Now he held her attention. "What?"

"He has ordered the Viri Magus and Zele Magus to disband," Dezare said.

"And are they disbanding?" Teah asked.

"They are defying that order, as you might expect," Duke Banderkin explained.

"No. What gives me more rightful claim than this new queen? If she is of Lassain blood, the throne is her birthright as well."

Dezare opened her mouth to argue, but Teah caught her eye and she snapped her mouth shut, giving a resigned nod.

"So you are to just let the duchess do with you as you wish?"

Duke Banderkin asked.

"You might not know me," Teah said with a chuckle. "But you knew Logan. Do you think it runs in our blood to stay anyone's prisoner?"

Both the duke and Dezare shook their heads.

"There is still the matter that the king and his new queen are trying to oppress those with magical abilities. If there is one thing I discovered in Caltoria, it is that I will not allow the enslavement and mistreatment of magicals as long as I have breath in my body."

"What are you intending to do?" Duke Banderkin asked.

"Go to the aid of the houses of magic," Teah said, holding his gaze with steeled determination.

"I don't want to point out the obvious, but I think you've forgotten that all of us are the prisoners Duchess Heniton," Dezare said.

"Oh, I plan on changing that once I've spoken to her. Which reminds me, shouldn't we be off? We don't want them to get worked up if we're late."

Dezare's eyes shot wide at the mention of their tight timeline and nodded. She strode over and kissed her father on the cheek, then hurried for the door.

"Good-bye Duke," Teah said as she turned to follow. "Please be ready to leave on a moment's notice."

"I was wondering if your plan to escape included me." He forced a grin.

"Why of course, I will need your guidance and relationship with my brother's army of Betra to reach our new objectives." Teah stopped when she saw Duke Banderkin's expression. "What is it?"

"When the queen took the throne, many of the Betra abandoned Logan's quest and either went home or joined Englewood." He held her angered gaze for a moment and then dropped his gaze to the floor.

"No matter," Teah said turning and following Dezare again. "They will soon realize that betraying a Lassain carries a much higher price the second time."

Teah followed Dezare out of the room, the heavy wooden door closing with a solid thud behind her.

Duke Banderkin gave an involuntary shiver at the implications of Teah's words and the fate that now lay ahead for the Betra.

****

Saliday watched through the barred opening in the wooden cell door as Dezare led Teah away in shackles. Her blood boiled at the thought of Dezare's betrayal to Logan and their cause. She felt certain if Dezare helped the duchess that Duke Banderkin must somehow be involved as well. She reflexively reached for a knife in her cloak but felt only empty fabric after being disarmed by the duchess's guards.

Turning to her new accommodations, she nodded with the knowledge that this cell wasn't her first and hopefully wouldn't be her last quarters forced upon her.

Rachel and Raven sat on one of the several wooden cots in the cramped space. The stone walls glistened with dampness and the moldy, musty smell of rotting matter reached her nose. She moved closer to the cot holding Raven and Rachel before noticing a body occupying one of the other cots.

The person in the cot lay covered with a filthy blanket from head to toe, only allowing the dark eyes access to the outside world of the cell.

Saliday sat down across from the person and leaned down to look directly into the scanning eyes.

Without warning, the person bolted upright and stood towering over Saliday who jerked back from the sudden movement. Her eyes ran up the legs, torso, chest, and neck before coming to rest on the smooth dark skin and beautiful features surrounding the black eyes. The posture screamed confidence and deadliness. She wore a black cloak pulled back to expose tight-fitted undergarments and rippling muscles. The Betra before her held her gaze and then a smile broadened her lips as recognition filled the woman's eyes.

"Tarken," she grinned, her white teeth glistening even in the dark cell. "I know now that my quest is near completion."

Saliday frowned in confusion but this only lessened the Betra's smile slightly.

"What are you talking about?"

"I am the Seeker of the Protector and you are his woman. He must be nearby," the woman said with confidence.

Saliday's eyes dropped from the woman's and she hung her head. "You are wrong, my friend. Your quest has been over for a long time now."

"No, it is you who must be mistaken," the Betra corrected. "When our sister, Sasha perished, her essence came to us in Sacrifice and I was then transformed into the next Seeker. I have followed the calling to find the protector and it has led me here."

Saliday then realized what the woman meant. She nodded. "You are feeling the pull of the protector, but that is not Logan, it is his sister Teah for she too is a protector."

"That cannot be, Tarken," the Betra argued.

"I wish it wasn't, but Logan is dead."

The Betra stared at Saliday in disbelief, still not willing to accept that her quest to find and protect Logan could not be accomplished.

"Then the spirits of our ancestors have mercy on us, because without Logan, the prophecy will not come to be." She stared at Saliday and then Rachel and Raven before lowering her head as the confidence drained from her body, her hope taken from her like the air from her lungs.

Chapter 15

Zeva and Logan raced back to the farmstead, Zeva now at the reins and Logan watching for pursuit over his shoulder.

"No one yet," he shouted over the rumble of hoofs and the wheels of the wagon.

"They know who I am and where I lived when I was taken," she cried. "They will come."

Logan stared at her with frustration.

"I know," she said glancing over at his disapproving look.

"We have put them in danger."

"I know," she repeated.

"They were fine until we decided to come here and ruin their lives."

"We can leave," Zeva said, but the words came out hollow and unconvincing.

Logan looked at her, his doubt evident.

"I know, I know, it won't matter now. They will never leave them be."

"How long do we have?" he asked.

"I doubt they will come themselves, they are cowards. They fear my magic and now they will fear your abilities as well. They will go to the patrol and send them here."

They rumbled into the farmyard jumping from the wagon before it stopped moving and raced into the house.

The four children sat around the table talking and stood as Zeva and Logan burst into the room.

"You need to pack up everything you can carry and put it in the wagon," Zeva said to the startled children.

They stood motionless, confused by the order.

"I have done something very stupid and gone to town," Zeva explained. "Now they know I am back and they will come for me."

"Then you must leave," Bethany told her.

"You need to come with us," Logan said.

"We were fine here before you came, we'll be fine when you leave," Bethany insisted.

"You don't understand," Zeva said crouching down to look Bethany in the eyes. "They will come here looking for me. You all are in danger."

"We are not magical so they will have no need for any of us," Sara, the second oldest chimed in.

"But I doubt they will let you be since they know we were here," Zeva explained.

"Don't tell us where you are going and we cannot betray you," Bethany said crossing her arms.

"That isn't what we are concerned about," Logan said taking Bethany by her arm and turning her to face him. "They will not leave you alone now that they know you are here."

"We will take our chances," Bethany declared.

Logan looked helplessly to Zeva who shrugged.

"All right, we will leave you as we found you," Logan said. "Zack, go put the wagon away and the horse to pasture. We will leave at once."

Zack jumped to his feet and hurried out the door.

"I wish you safety," Logan said turning back to Bethany. "All of you."

"You as well," Bethany said as Sara and Violet nodded their agreement.

"Good-bye," Zeva said her guilt heavy in her word.

Logan and Zeva walked out of the building closing the door behind them as the horse and wagon rumbled to the barn with Zack at the reins. They headed out of the farm stopping by the tool shed for Logan to gather his swords and bow. He didn't bother strapping them on but fastened the bundle to his back ignoring Zeva's questioning stare.

They hurried out of the small valley, turning to look back at the white-washed buildings shining brightly in the setting sun.

Zeva looked longingly at her home she abandoned once more while Logan flashed back to his home in Ter Chadain where his life changed forever.

They turned and walked inland away from the coast, avoiding the main road for as long as they could before the heavy forest forced them to the well-traveled route. Once on the hard-packed road they picked up their pace to distance themselves from Port Shoal. The moon rose high in the sky when they finally stopped at a small clearing at the side of the road.

The night held a chill, but they decided to forego a fire with the hopes of remaining undetected.

When they lay their weary heads down Logan fell to sleep in an instant. As the sun shone in Logan's eyes the next morning, he sat up with a sudden sense of something being wrong. A quick scan found Zeva nowhere in sight. He scrambled to his feet looking around for signs of her departure and a sick feeling crept over him as her tracks led back toward Port Shoal. He hesitated for a moment before hefting his pack over his shoulder and running after her.

****

Zeva waited until she heard Logan's steady breathing as he slept before getting up and heading back to Port Shoal. She understood more than Logan and the children that the empress's patrol wouldn't be satisfied that she and Logan were gone. No, she knew that if the men at the general store spoke the truth, the patrol had a sniffer with them and that sniffer would be too determined to let it go. He would take the children from their home to punish them for harboring a magical, especially a magical the property of Empress Shakata herself. She couldn't let that happen. Now that she knew Logan to be out of imminent

140

danger, she needed to be sure the children were also.

She crept to the tree line along the ridge overlooking the homestead taking concealment in the low foliage and waited. As the sun rose along the far hill across the small valley, a group of riders came into sight. She knew instantly that the sniffer, impatient to have her in captivity again, pressed his patrol into this early morning ride to retrieve her.

Fighting her first instinct to rush forward and engage them before they reached the children, she held out hope that this sniffer possessed some compassion for others. She doubted it to be the case, but she needed to be sure her intervention proved a requirement for the children's safety.

The men on horseback rode into the farmyard and stopped at the front walk to the main house trampling the flowers that neatly lined the walk without noticing. The sniffer stayed mounted as half a dozen men dismounted and entered the house. They emerged with the four children in tow, still in their night clothes.

Zeva heard Bethany's protests as she stood restrained by a guard in front of the sniffer. The sniffer gestured and the men not restraining a child spread out to search the rest of the farmstead. After a long wait the men returned with news of their fruitless search. The sniffer motioned dramatically with flailing arms and the guards hefted the children onto horses and climbed on behind them.

The entire company, now including the children, rode off toward Port Shoal disappearing over the far ridge of the valley.

Zeva sat frozen in place unable to believe she watched them take the children and did nothing. Was she afraid her intervention might harm the children? Maybe the idea of being a slave again held too much fear for her to take that obvious step into servitude again? She wiped a line of sweat from her upper lip and stared at the empty farmstead.

She couldn't be sure how long she sat staring at her home

wondering what to do next. Footsteps behind her drew her out of her stupor with a flurry of magic as she quickly wove an air wall and sent it crashing into the creator of those footsteps.

A loud exhale of air came from the person behind her as her wall of air struck them and sent them flying into the forest, breaking branches and small trees as they tumbled.

Zeva jumped to her feet and stormed after her attacker as her anger and fury reached a fevered pitch. She held her hands above her head to deal another blow when she recognized Logan in a tangle of sticks and leaves lying stunned amongst the foliage.

"What are you doing here?" she asked, her voice quivering with her anger.

"Making sure you didn't do something stupid," he said pulling twigs and leaves from his hair.

"I didn't, but now I wish I did," she spat.

"Took them, huh?"

"Like we suspected, they couldn't leave them be." Her tone seethed with hatred.

"Now what?"

"I have to save them," Zeva said turning away from Logan to look back at the farm.

"You'll never get them out."

"I will if you help me."

"I can't," Logan said getting to his feet.

"You mean you won't."

"I gave that part of my life up. It only hurts people."

"They're innocent children. We need to help them."

Logan stared past Zeva to the farmstead. Not too long ago he lived on a farm and his life changed in an instant. His life still tumbled out of control most of the time since he left his home. How would it all have turned out if someone looked out for him?

"Okay, I'll help, but not as the protector, as Logan."

Zeva stared at him not understanding what he meant.

When Logan saw her confusion he nodded. "I will not use the protector's weapons to kill people. I will help you free the children, but I will avoid any killing. Agreed?"

Zeva hesitated for a moment, uncertain that just Logan would be enough, but she slowly nodded, realizing that it would have to be enough.

"We wait until dark and then go in," Logan said. "Now get some rest, it's going to be a busy night."

Chapter 16

"That is crazy talk," Commander Wilkins said as he took one last look into the hallway outside his chambers and closed the door. He turned to Cita and Stern who both stared with burning determination in their eyes.

"What other choice do we have?" Stern said taking a step closer to Wilkins.

"The others are already heading back to Caltoria as we speak," Cita said divulging her mission of the night before.

"They'll have your head for trying and even if you do manage to get away, and that is a big if, you will be wanted for treason the rest of your days." The man strode past Cita and Stern to a small table as they spun to keep their eyes on him. He lifted a bottle from the table and pulled the cork with a pop pouring himself a drink of spirits in a short ceramic glass. He lifted the cup to his mouth, hesitating to look at first Stern, and then Cita, before downing the liquid in one gulp. He promptly poured himself another and looked back to the two members of his patrol.

"They saved our lives and trusted us with their own," Cita railed. "We need to do something to help them."

"But Rudnick has had Linell in there all day, what do you think is left to save?" Wilkins pointed out.

"It is better than leaving her to him for another night," Stern countered.

"So you choose the life of exiles and outlaws?" Wilkins took in their unison nod. He shook his head and then slammed back his drink and set the glass down on the table. He lifted the bottle and extended it neck first to Stern.

Stern looked at him confused.

"I am warning you against these actions," he said holding the bottle until Stern took it from his hand, still not understanding. "But if I am incapacitated I will not be able to warn of the imminent threat of your actions."

Stern still stared at Wilkins with no understanding.

"Thank you Commander," Cita said as she took the bottle from Stern and struck the commander over the head with the bottle, shattering the glass and sending the man to the floor as dead weight.

"Oh," Stern said nodding as he finally comprehended.

"If we fail at subduing Rudnick it will be the shortest rescue ever."

****

The courtyard lay dark and deserted between the commander's office where they interrogated Linell and the empty barracks where Trevon and Fedlen were being held. No guards stood at any posts, Rudnick feeling confident the patrol headquarters remained loyal to him.

Stern and Cita stood in the shadows of the roof overhang along the exterior wall of the commander's office pausing to be sure the courtyard remained empty. The horses they gathered for their escape stood on the far wall of the barracks and the wind blew a whiny and a huff from the mounts across the empty grounds causing Cita to flinch.

Cita looked to Stern, but his features remained lost in the shadows. A slight nod and she turned bursting into motion. They argued while gathering the horses on who should enter the room first. Stern felt he held the best chance at overpowering the two men with Rudnick, but Cita pointed out that Rudnick held magic and she needed to throw a weave around him the instant the door flew open if their plan held a chance at success.

He finally conceded and she now stood in front of the office door. Stern slipped up alongside, his bow in his hands, an arrow nocked and another waiting at the ready over his shoulder. The creak of the bow and the string reached Cita's ears as she turned away and then kicked the door in holding her magic in her hands.

The door burst open and the occupants spun in surprise.

Cita released her weave sending it like a blanket over Rudnick as his sneer vanished from his lips and he fell rigid to the ground with a thud.

Stern's first arrow hit its mark as the door swung inward and his second sprung from the thrumming string an instant later before the first arrow's victim reached the floor.

Cita ran to Linell, her right cheek swollen nearly closing off her eye, untied her and hurried back toward the door.

Linell paused to pick up a dark object from the floor and hurried after Cita with Stern close behind.

Cita hesitated to scan the grounds for only an instant and then sprinted across the open yard lit by the moonlight to the cover of shadows in front of the barracks holding the others.

Linell slipped in behind Cita as Stern kicked in the door without hesitating. Fedlen jumped to his feet and Trevon lifted his head where he lay on the bed, his face badly beaten.

"Grab him and follow us," Stern said.

Fedlen lifted Trevon on his shoulder and hurried out the door where Cita and Linell joined them.

They raced around the corner and lifted Trevon onto a mount, his body slumping forward, unable to hold his own weight.

"What about the others?" Fedlen asked hesitating at the saddle.

"They left the same day Rudnick took Trevon. They are well ahead of us heading toward Port Shoal," Cita whispered. "Now hurry."

Cita slid up behind Trevon and straightened him against her body with her arms as she took hold of the reins. "Bring the other horse along," she instructed Stern.

The others mounted kicking their mounts into motion disappearing into the darkness and the cover of the trees surrounding the patrol compound.

They rode hard all night, Cita holding the semi-conscious Trevon with his head against her shoulder as it jostled around.

The Caltorians noticed the path different from the one that brought them here earlier that week. They headed west, but also angled south as well taking them a good distance from the patrol base.

As the sun greeted them, the horses steamed with sweat and puffed with exhaustion, the vapored breath of the beasts spewing out of their mouths and noses only emphasizing their condition to the riders.

Stern held up his hand at the front of the party to bring them to a halt.

Everyone eased the mounts to a stop and slipped from their saddles.

Fedlen stood at the ready as Cita eased Trevon down into his waiting arms. He gently took his friend over to a blanket that Linell spread out onto the ground under a large tree and gingerly laid him down.

Cita slid from her saddle, stretching her back and looking to Stern.

The seasoned member of the patrol made eye contact with her giving her a weary smile and a nod before turning to unsaddle the horses allowing them to cool down and rest.

Cita did the same and joined Stern as he walked over to the Caltorians to check on Trevon.

Fedlen stood defensively as they approached, but Linell stood and placed a calming hand upon his arm. He spun on her, but softened upon seeing her expression. He gave a nod to Cita and Stern and then sat back down to keep watch over Trevon.

"Thank you," Linell said, the weariness heavy in her voice.

"We are very sorry," Cita said, but Linell raised a hand to stay her apology.

"We understand you and Stern had nothing to do with this,"

she motioned to her injured cheek and then to Trevon. "We owe you our lives. Where are the others?"

"We sent them on ahead of us with Clastis," Cita explained.

"We put your lives in danger," Stern rationalized.

"Understood, but now your lives are as much in peril as our own. I hope you understand the sacrifices you have made to save us?"

"We do, but now we must ask that you divulge your true reason for setting out from the Sacred City and what you seek," Stern said causing Linell's good eye to open wider and Cita to turn to him with a raised eyebrow.

Fedlen stood and walked up to stand beside Linell with his arms crossed over his chest.

"Well, well, Stern Barsten is more than he seems," Linell said with a forced chuckle.

"It would seem that I am not the only one," he said with a wink.

Cita stared at Stern and then at Linell. She missed the implications of their exchange, but understood that her life just became more complicated.

"We need rest and then to be on our way," Fedlen interjected.

"They will be tracking us," Stern warned.

"Trevon needs time to heal," Linell added.

"Can you heal him?" Cita asked Linell.

"I think so, I don't know, I can't believe how bad he is," Linell said shaken by Trevon's condition.

"Can I take a look at him?" Cita asked.

Linell paused a moment studying the girl and then gave a nod. She led Cita over to Trevon kneeling down on one side of the unconscious man while Cita knelt on his other side.

The men watched them for a moment and then Fedlen turned to Stern. "What is your plan?"

"Head west to the coast angling south until we come to your

closest port city," Stern answered.

"That would be Port Shoal," Fedlen said with a nod.

"Good. Now what are you doing venturing out from the Sacred City and what is your mission?" Stern pressed causing Fedlen to stiffen.

"I'm not sure I should…" Fedlen began. "Trevon is our leader, he should be the one to share that information if he sees fit."

"We are in this together," Stern insisted.

"Agreed," Fedlen said. "But Trevon is still our leader and…"

"And he will share with them everything, in the morning," Trevon's weary voice said from behind them.

The two men spun to see Trevon sitting up, his injuries visible as bruises, but healed up neatly by Cita's magic.

"That is amazing," Fedlen said.

"She is quite gifted with her healing weaves," Linell said running a hand across her now healed cheek where only moments ago it swelled to diminish her vision in her right eye.

"So you are willing to explain your mission now that we are in the thick of it with you?" Stern asked again.

"Yes," Trevon said. "But I need rest." He curled up pulling the blanket from his waist to his shoulder and fell into a deep sleep.

They stared at him in disbelief.

"Healing takes a lot out of the injured as well as the one doing the healing," Cita pointed out. "He should be strong enough by morning to leave."

"I'll take first watch," Fedlen offered and strode off to find a good vantage point to keep an eye out for any pursuers.

The others nodded and joined Trevon in some much needed rest.

The next morning they gathered. Sitting cross-legged on the hard ground, they turned their attention to Trevon.

"Since your lives are now tied to ours, I will share our primary goal," Trevon began. "But first I need to know something." He looked to Cita and Stern as he held their undivided attention. "Are you happy with the Council of Stellaran?"

Cita's and Stern's eyes widened, but they held Trevon's gaze without flinching.

"Why do you ask that?" Stern questioned.

"I noticed that people with magical ability have been relegated to patrolling the line between Caltoria and Stellaran, but it appears they hold no place in the council as in the old days."

Stern cleared his throat and nodded. "We have seen less and less value for our kind through the generations. A far cry from the position those possessing magical abilities once held."

"You haven't answered my question," Trevon pressed.

"No," Cita blurted out drawing everyone's attention to her. She blushed as their eyes fell upon her. "I have seen first-hand during my training for patrol that they do not value our kind, but almost fear us."

"It is true," Stern added.

"I am going to share with you the reason for our mission and you must decide if you are to join us," Trevon said bowing his head and taking a deep breath. Without looking up he continued. "We have been chosen by our people, descendants of the magicals trapped on the wrong side of the wall with the Chairman of the Council of Stellaran all those years ago to seek out one who holds claim to that position." He looked up as the shock crossed Cita's and Stern's faces.

"It is like you search for a single flea on a horse," Stern said in shock.

"I never said it will be easy," Trevon agreed.

"But near impossible," Cita added.

"True, but we were headed to Port Shoal and planned to start our search there," Trevon said.

"Didn't any remain in the Sacred City?" Stern asked.

"The chairman left after setting the barrier around the Sacred

City in search of others scattered by the sudden raising of the barrier. He never returned," Linell said.

"So you don't even know if he has any descendants?" Cita said with shock.

"We heard stories of his struggles, but none can say for sure if he survived long enough to have heirs," Trevon explained.

"So how can you be sure there may be one in Port Shoal," Stern argued.

"We can't, but we needed to start somewhere," Fedlen interjected.

"Maybe we can be sure," Linell said bringing their attention to her as she pulled the square compass-like article from her clothing. Trevon and Linell knew this artifact belonged to Rudnick and held magical abilities, but the others looked at it curiously.

"Rudnick used this to track our presence at patrol headquarters. We can use it to track an heir to the chairman," Trevon explained.

"How does it work?" Fedlen asked.

"I'm not sure, but it sure zeroed in on me and Linell," Trevon said.

"Rudnick told me that it tracks anyone who is a descendent of council members trapped on the Caltorian side of the barrier. Since Trevon and I both have ancestors who were council members, it honed in on us," Linell explained.

She lifted the cover and a soft green glow lit up her features as she peered down at it. She gasped.

"What is it?" Trevon said leaning close and gazing at the device.

"All the councilmember's names are engraved upon the face of the dial. A green gemstone is beside each name," Linell said.

"And Linell's and my ancestor's gemstones are lit up," Trevon said not taking his eyes from the dial of the device.

"So, if this thing works," Linell said pointing to the one red stone on the dial glowing faintly, "a descendent of the chairman is in that direction." She pointed southwest in the direction the needle on the dial indicated.

The party sat and thought in silence, the immense implications sinking in. An heir to the Chairman's seat on the Council of Stellaran lay ahead of them, if the device indicated the truth. The flea on the horse now became a reality.

"The question still stands before you," Trevon said looking at Cita and Stern. "Are you joining us?"

"You know what this will mean?" Stern asked Trevon and then turned to Cita.

"A revolution to put magicals back onto the council where they belong," Cita said with a firm nod.

"War that will cost many lives," Stern agreed.

"Peace is overrated," Linell said standing. She lifted a saddle and walked over to a horse and hefted it into place. She turned back to them as she strapped the saddle and cinched it tight. "I choose justice."

The others stood and hurried to saddle and mount their horses. Destiny awaited.

Chapter 17

Teah stood before Duchess Heniton with her head held high as she stared right into the traitorous woman's eyes.

The Duchess of Los Clostern, her large body squeezed into a chair resembling a throne, tried to hold Teah's gaze for a moment and then dropped her eyes uncomfortably, turning to her general to take the lead.

Clearing his throat, he glanced at Dezare standing motionless in the corner and strode up next to his duchess. A reflexive hand came to his throat tracing a thin scar as he met Teah's eyes, eyes that held the same intensity of Teah's sibling when the general met him months ago. That meeting didn't go very well as the general nearly lost his life to the young protector. He planned for this meeting to be more to his liking as he drew comfort in the shackles on Teah's hands.

He bowed at the waist, his bald head leaning to Teah so she could see the scars of battle running across his white skin in dark purple lines, and then rose again tugging on his neatly braided beard with one hand while fiddling with the rings with his other hand as each finger possessed an adornment.

"We welcome you to Los Clostern," the general said drawing a scowl from the duchess and a huff of air from her lungs. The general turned his head slightly but didn't make eye contact with his duchess. He held Teah's gaze steady and confidently, being sure he held her attention. "We have been given direct orders from King Aston and his queen to take you into our custody and send word when you arrived…if you arrived."

Teah noted the general's deliberate choice of words as he spoke. He wanted her to know that he wasn't calling the shots…but why?

"You are to be our guest until an envoy from the king arrives to escort you to Cordlain."

"How long will that be?" Teah asked.

"Around two weeks, your highness," the general said bringing a scoff of disapproval from the duchess. "We sent our messenger out this morning. It will take nearly a week for him to reach Cordlain." The general answered without acknowledging the duchess.

"I thank you for your honesty," Teah said holding the general's gaze to drive home the point. "I take it you have a memento to remember your meeting with my brother?" Teah said motioning to her neck.

The general pursed his lips and nodded. "Yes, he made an impression on me I will never forget. He holds a very rigid ideal on loyalty."

"As do I," Teah replied.

"I do not doubt. May your stay here, no matter how short, be one you feel has shown you where true loyalty lies."

"I believe it already has," Teah said with a knowing nod.

"Enough chit chat, I can hardly hear a word you are saying," the duchess interrupted. "Dezare, return her to her cell with the others."

"Yes, Duchess," Dezare said with a bow as she walked up and took Teah by the arm leading her for the door.

"Thank you for your hospitality, General," Teah turned back and made eye contact with the man and then turned her stare to the duchess. "It will not be forgotten."

"Is that a threat?" the duchess cried out.

Dezare didn't wait, but lead Teah out of the room. The door closed behind them cutting off the hysterical ranting of the duchess.

When they reached the far end of the hallway at the landing of the stairs, Dezare turned to Teah. "Did the general do what I think he did?" she asked.

"He promised to help me escape before the envoy from the

king arrives," Teah said with a smile and a nod.

"Seems Logan scared the loyalty right into him," Dezare said grinning.

"He could do that to people," Teah said with a smile that melted away as she remembered she spoke of him in past tense. "He made people do amazing things even they never thought they could." She dropped her eyes to the floor and allowed Dezare to lead her on in silence.

They marched into the dungeons past the guards and then waited as the guard unlocked the cell, ushered Teah inside, closed the door behind her, and locked it once more.

Teah turned and looked out the small barred window at Dezare as she waited for the guard to wander off. Once he stepped out of earshot Teah gave a jerk of her head for Dezare to come closer.

"Tonight we leave. We will need horses and any supplies you can gather," Teah instructed.

"It is such short notice," Dezare said in a panic. "If I had another day I could be sure to get what we need."

"We don't have time. Just do the best you can. The horses are the most important. We can gather them at the stables but be sure there are enough for everyone." Teah turned and counted the members in the cell, noting an extra. "Five in here and three next door. We will have an extra if Morgan chooses to return to his ship."

"Do you want me to get word to his ship?" Dezare asked.

"No, they'll be watching," Teah assured her. "Include your father and yourself as well."

Dezare nodded and hurried off to ready for their escape.

Teah watched as she disappeared up the stairwell and then turned to the women in the cell behind her.

The new face didn't shock Teah, just saddened her as the Betra bowed low.

"Long may you fight," the Betra greeted her in the old Betra

155

custom.

"How did you come to be a prisoner of the duchess?" Teah asked.

"She came searching for Logan," Saliday interrupted. "She is Sasha's replacement as Seeker."

Teah's face went blank and tears welled in her eyes. "I'm sorry but he is gone," Teah whispered.

"But you are mistaken," the woman said. "I am Machala and Sasha was my 'Sister of the Path', but the calling which leads a seeker to the protector is still leading me on. He still lives."

"You must mean me," Teah said. "I'm a protector as well."

"I tried to explain that to her too," Saliday interjected.

"But it is not you who I feel. With you standing right in front of me, I would know it. The pull I feel is far away in that direction," Machala said pointing to the stone wall of the cell.

Teah's eyes grew wide and a tear ran down her cheek. "Towards Caltoria?" she whispered.

"He's still alive?" Saliday gasped.

"Oh praise the spirits, let it be true," Teah cried.

"I assure you it is," Machala said. "This magic is very old and strong. I feel him and he is out there somewhere." She pointed again toward the sea.

"When we escape tonight, you must go to him," Teah urged Machala who nodded her intent to do so. "Good, good, with you going to him he stands a chance."

"I wish to go with her," Saliday said timidly.

Teah turned to the Tarken and looked at the woman standing before her more humble than she ever witnessed before. "I thought you two no longer…" the thought trailed off as Saliday's pain-filled eyes rose to Teah's.

"I will always love him," Saliday whispered.

"Then go and find him. Take care of him and bring him back to me," Teah ordered.

The two women nodded and hope seeped into their faces.

Saliday then frowned as Teah seemed to be overlooking a very large part of her plan. "How are we supposed to escape without the use of your magic?"

"Oh, that? I found the tie to my weave hours ago," she said with a smile as the shackles unlatched and dropped to her feet. "I just needed to get the lay of the land and how better to do that when they think you are helpless."

Rachel and Raven crowded closer with excitement and Teah turned to them and in short order untied their imprisoning weaves as well.

"Thank Galena for making me untie her weaves around you and Lizzy," Teah said and then wished she hadn't. The smile vanished from Rachel's face at the mention of Lizzy. That was one death Teah caused that Rachel would never forgive her for. Lizzy, the innocent believer who lost her life trying to protect Teah.

Rachel slunk back to the cot and turned her back to Teah and the others as a cloud of pain seemed to hover over her.

"I thank you. I never want to experience being cut off from my magic again," Raven said lightly.

"Then you better practice blocking those weaves, because I can assure you it will not be the last time someone will try to block your magic," Teah pointed out.

The merry look on Raven's face vanished and she went to the other bunk deep in thought.

"You sure have a way of ruining a mood," Saliday said with a forced chuckle trying to cut the tension in the cell.

"Reality often does that," Teah said and walked to the window in the cell and looked out at the gray sky above which seemed to match her mood. She looked back over her shoulder. "We leave tonight so get ready." She pivoted to contemplate the sky and her thoughts of those who lost their lives because of her quest. A

157

quest that seemed to not matter anymore with a new queen in place activating the spell to protect Ter Chadain from Caltoria. The question now remained, who would protect Ter Chadain from King Englewood and his new queen?

Chapter 18

The moonless night fell heavy over Port Shoal and rain began to fall followed by flashes of lightning in the distant sky as a guard strode beside the tall cloaked figure toward the holding cells. Keeping its head low to ward off the rain, the cloaked figure gave a slight nod to the guards on duty. They received one in return and the two went inside without a word or slowing their pace. Once inside, the two surveyed their surroundings, the guard scanning with searching eyes and the cloaked figure turning from side to side, his face hidden within the shadows of the hood.

The cell's occupants turned and stared at the new arrivals and waited.

The guard turned questioningly to the hooded figure and gave a nod as he reached up and pulled back his hood. The guard's body began to shimmer and shift, and where once stood a man now stood a woman.

"Zeva?" Bethany whispered in surprise coming to her feet.

"Logan." Zack said to the now hoodless figure standing beside the transformed guard.

"Shush," Zeva cautioned. "We need to be quick before the real sniffer comes back." She moved over to the cell and sent a weave into the lock exploding it from the inside out with a crack. She pulled the door open and the children ran to hug her.

Zack hugged Zeva for a moment and then went over to Logan who pulled him under his arm in a masculine clasp.

"Getting in was the easy part," Logan said pulling his hood back up and slipping his hands inside his sleeves.

"Let's go," Logan said taking a step toward the door.

Zack's hand on his arm pulled him up short and he turned questioningly.

"Don't you have a sword?" Zack asked.

"He does," Zeva said. "Two of them in fact, but he is too stubborn to use them."

Logan gave her a warning stare and looked back to Zack's questioning expression. "A story for another time," he said and walked out the door into a torrential downpour.

After a slight hesitation, the others followed, Zeva ushering the children before her.

****

The sniffer waited for them as they exited the building unleashing a burst of magic that should have sent them all flying, but his attack struck Logan in the chest and the weave rebounded above Boskin's head stunning everyone for a moment.

Logan took the moment to pounce into the stunned soldiers and Zeva peppered the dazed sniffer with weave after weave not allowing him to concentrate enough to form another weave in defense. She pushed him down before sending a fist of air to his head and toppling him backward unconscious.

The soldiers weren't fairing too well against Logan, but some maneuvered behind him and crept in. Logan moved like the wind, here one moment and there the next taking down the soldiers behind him with swift kicks and punches.

Once the sniffer lay unconscious, Zeva leveled her magic on the others and quickly dispatched those around Logan, freeing him to run off and quickly return with the farm's wagon and horse along with two mounts.

The children jumped onto the wagon, Bethany taking the reins while Logan and Zeva climbed up in the saddles.

Zeva turned without a word kicking her horse into a run and raced off with the wagon and children right behind her. Logan didn't wait and hurried after.

Logan's horse took two strides to follow when he spun violently in the saddle and toppled to the ground. He sat up and lifted his left arm where a crossbow bolt protruded through his forearm. He snapped the barbed side off and slid the bolt free as he scrambled to his feet and gathered his horse's reins. Another bolt struck him between his shoulder blades sending him stumbling into his horse. The bolt fell at his feet in pieces.

Another bolt struck him in the chest sending him staggering backwards as the bolt dropped to the ground.

This is it. He thought as he fought the urge to pull his swords. He leapt to his saddle as another bolt struck his leg embedding deep into his thigh.

"Aw!" he cried out in pain as he leaned to the side. He kicked his horse with his good leg and the mount lurched and then toppled over on top of him. Logan stared at his horse in horror as a bolt protruded from the beast's head. The weight of the horse pinned his injured leg under its body and gouged the bolt crossways into his thigh. He groaned in pain and struggled to pull his leg free.

The activity around him remained calm as the soldiers, who fled moments earlier crept closer, cautiously tightening around their prey.

Logan pulled his leg free and got to his knees as he pulled his dark cloak back to expose the handles of his swords.

The men skittered back at the sight of the swords and began to circle Logan as a unit.

Logan reached for his swords cringing at the pain radiating from the injury to his left forearm. Fighting through the pain he forced his hands to the sword handles. He cried out in pain and cradled his arm against his body while turning in the middle of the circle of guards, his fiery, threatening eyes and his handling of the other guards enough to keep his attackers at bay until he figured out how to escape.

Sniffer Boskin held a hand to his pounding head, a smile curling the edge of his lips as he approached Logan struggling to keep the soldiers at bay from his knees with only the sword in his right hand.

Logan grit his teeth against pain throbbing through his arm as blood pulsed from the wounds with each beat of his heart. A guard too an errant step too close to Logan and he struck out with his good arm, dropping the man unconscious in a heap.

The circle widened only slightly, closing the gap created by the incapacitated man.

"At last. The one responsible for bringing the weave down," Boskin sneered. "The Protector of Ter Chadain is mine."

Logan looked up at the man with narrowed eyes of defiance straightening to his full height and pulling the rod from its leather holder strapped to his leg.

Boskin scoffed at the harmless piece of metal just before it extended into the silver bow causing the sniffer to recoil in fear.

Fighting the pain raging in his injured arm Logan drew back the string as the silver arrow appeared and loosed it. The arrow struck the Sniffer directly in the chest propelling him across the street.

Logan didn't hesitate but used the opportunity to take down the two crossbowmen on the rooftops hitting the first in the throat and the second in the left eye. He then sent the closest soldier hurtling backward into his comrades with a silver arrow in his chest. The other soldiers scattered like roaches in the light.

Logan stood and limped over to a horse tethered to a post in front of the jail, retracted the bow, sheathed it, and gingerly lifted himself to the saddle. He kicked the horse into motion, leaning over the mount's neck struggling to stay conscious.

Zeva raced ahead with the wagon right behind her lighting the way with a ball of glowing energy hovering above her hand. She held her head at an angle so her hood blocked most of the rain from pouring down her cloak, but the rain soaked her from head to toe.

She needn't look back to see how closely the wagon followed as the rumbling of the wooden wheels told her it nipped at the heels of her horse. A thought came to her to turn and see if Logan followed after the wagon, but she knew Logan wouldn't let them get too far ahead.

After racing away from Port Shoal in the storm, the weather let up and Zeva slowed them to a stop and then rode back to check on the children.

Four sets of anxious eyes reflected back the glowing orb at her. She nodded and smiled her encouragement to them and then turned her attention to the road behind waiting for the hoof beats of Logan's horse, but none came. Zeva's confident look soon wavered.

Sounds of a rider approaching reached her ears and she smiled as a horse came into view in the darkness illuminated by the glowing ball floating above her hand. Her smile faded as she saw Logan hunched over his mount, his head lolling back and forth with every step the horse took.

As the horse neared Zeva, she reached out and took hold of the reins pulling the animal to a stop.

Logan dropped to the ground in a heap.

Zeva slid from her mount lifting Logan's head and cradling it in her lap. She surveyed his injuries quickly, unsure of a pursuit behind them. Her heart sank as his wounds revealed themselves in the glowing light.

"Bethany, Zack, we need to get Logan into the wagon," Zeva shouted and the children, except for Violet, scurried around Logan and helped Zeva lift him into the wagon.

"Can you heal him?" Bethany asked, fear lacing her voice.

"We need to get him somewhere I can work on him," Zeva said looking into the girl's eyes.

"The old mill is a short distance off the main road, no one goes there anymore," Bethany suggested.

Zeva nodded and hopped from the wagon and climbed into her saddle after grabbing Logan's horse's reins and tying them to the back of the wagon. She then kicked her horse into a run hearing the rumbling of the wagon wheels right behind her as Bethany snapped the reins and sent the horse pulling the wagon into motion.

Zeva knew the way to the old mill. Her father used to work there. She leaned into her horse as the rain continued to pelt her as she rode, her thoughts consumed with the possibility of losing Logan and losing Caltoria's only hope of surviving Empress Shakata bent on enslaving every magical once more. Tears ran from her eyes mingling with the rain soaking her face almost as if to wash away any sorrow or compassion she might hold for anyone in Caltoria if Logan died. Because deep inside, she knew she couldn't bear to live in a Caltoria like it was before the protector.

Zeva raced ahead once the old mill came into sight. She threw open the large doors to the warehouse with a wave of an air weave and rode inside with the wagon close behind. She slid from her saddle and ran to the wagon climbing inside the back and began examining Logan.

The children climbed from the wagon to give her more room and closed the doors. They found some old lanterns and lit them. Holding them high above Zeva on the edges of the wagon, they watched in anxiety as Zeva ran her hands over Logan.

Zeva noted Logan's injuries all made by crossbows. She didn't recall any crossbowmen when they escaped. A hole caused by a bolt gaped in his forearm and one bolt still protruded from his leg. The hole stretched out in every direction imaginable leaving raw meat hanging through his pants. She yanked the bolt out and put her efforts to this wound first.

She closed her eyes and began the arduous task of mending each and every severed fiber in his leg one strand at a time.

After more than an hour of work, she leaned back, exhausted by her exertion.

Bethany slid in and began wrapping strips of cloth torn from the girl's dresses around his leg and then finished it off by tying it tightly.

Zeva wondered over the girl's deftness at the task and smiled with appreciation at her assertiveness.

Zeva looked at Logan's forearm injury void of the bolt.

"Looks different than when it first did," Zack said holding the bolt Zeva extracted from Logan's leg.

Zeva leaned in closer as Zack picked up a lantern from the wagon seat and held it closer to Logan so she could see. Taking her still damp bottom of her dress, she wiped away the blood to find the wound already healed. Only a small scar remained.

"How?" she said as Logan moaned and lifted his head, struggling to open his eyes and sit up.

Zeva put a restraining hand to his chest and eased him back down. "You're safe with us now."

He looked up at her and gave her a nod and a slight curl of his lips. "We need to get moving to stay ahead of them. They wanted me," he said and it suddenly made complete sense to Zeva. She was never the prize. They wanted the protector.

"Get some rest and we'll leave at first light," Zeva said.

"No, we must move now. I'll rest in the wagon."

"Where do we go?"

"The sniffer said something about wanting me because I brought the weave down. What did he mean?"

"If the weave is down, that means Stellaran lies to the north and an escape from the empress and Caltoria," Zeva said in awe.

"Then head north." Logan leaned back and passed out.

Zeva looked to Bethany and then the other children behind her questioningly. They all nodded their assent, north to Stellaran. \

165

Chapter 19

The party moved at a quick pace as Clastis, Bristol, and the three guards of the Sacred City's garrison pushed everyone to their limits, but with many on foot, the women and children slowed them down drastically.

Clastis sensed something and lifted his hand bringing everyone to a stop and turned to voice his concern to Bristol. The words never left his mouth as a horn sounded and a large group of armed troops, wearing dark red breastplates bearing a silver fist with silver chainmail covering the shoulder and arms approached. Each wore a silver helmet with a snow white feather reaching from the top. Each feather's tip appeared to be dipped in dark red paint. They surrounded Clastis's party with spears leveled at the travelers. Clastis noted the rows of archers behind the pike men with arrows nocked and trained on them as well.

They stopped and raised their hands in surrender as a man with gold stripes across his chest plate approached Bristol as she sat in her saddle with her hands raised. A row of troops barred her advancement and several archers trained arrows on her.

"We mean you no harm; we will return to Caltoria," Bristol said.

The man stiffened in his saddle and removed his helmet as he kicked his horse closer. His dark hair fell to his shoulders and his dark eyes held Bristol's.

"I'm sorry, but I have my orders," the man said, his eyes held remorse as he turned and retreated.

Without warning, as soon as the man passed his line of archers, arrows rained down upon the travelers from the Sacred City, dropping them from their horses and off their feet with numerous arrows imbedded into their bodies.

Bristol fell dead to the ground, an arrow jutting from her throat.

Clastis saw Bristol fall as he drew his sword and pain erupted in his back and he too fell to the forest floor, the dead and decaying matter filling his nose with rotten, earth smells. The pain tore at his back and his vision of bodies all around him blurred and went black.

****

Trevon and his party followed the tracks the fleeing Caltorians left behind them. In all honesty, a novice tracker would have no problem following the path they left, but stealth wasn't the main goal of this group but the need for speed. They hoped to reach Caltoria before being overtaken by Stellaran forces.

They came into the clearing as the moon hung high above illuminating the field and horror assaulted their senses with the smell of rotting flesh serenaded by the cries of scavenger birds and the hum of flies. Bodies lay everywhere with arrows rising to the sky like gruesome heralds claiming them for death.

Trevon slid from his horse, falling to his knees as his physical strength abandoned him as well as his mental control. He covered his eyes and wept as his people lay slaughtered before him.

Linell and Fedlen tried to help him to his feet but he pushed their supportive hands away, gasping for air that wouldn't come. When he lifted his eyes to them, he saw the horror on their faces and followed their eyes to see Clastis sitting close by with his dead horse as a back rest keeping him upright. Arrows pinned him to his horse as his eyes stared blankly at the carnage around him. His sword rested across his lap, just clear of his scabbard but the blade shone clean.

Trevon didn't bother to rise but crawled through the blood and staring faces of people he knew his entire life to his dear friend, lifting up as he reached him and hugging him around the arrows protruding from his body. He wept on his shoulder and sobbed uncontrollably.

167

He then lifted himself away and began to crawl among the dead, placing a hand on each and praying for their eternal souls. He crawled through the blood-soaked mud and grass for nearly an hour while his party watched in silent agony and sorrow.

Linell found her parents among the dead holding hands and staring at each other at the end. She fell to her knees tearing the arrows savagely from their flesh and throwing her body across theirs embracing them and weeping uncontrollably. Her sobs and moans of grief filled the field with haunting echoes as she cried to the spirits to wake her up from her nightmare.

Fedlen found his only remaining relative, his aunt who took him in when his parents died at the hands of the empress's troops. When he approached her, looking with grief at every face he came upon as he searched for her holding out hope that he may find her curled up under a fallen horse still alive, he recognized her instantly even though she lay face-down on the ground, her back riddled with arrows. He knelt down lifting her gingerly in his arms as much as the arrows allowed and pulled her to his chest. Swaying back and forth he moaned in agony as tears ran down his face and he looked to the heavens for answers that did not come.

Stern and Cita knelt at the edge of the field in horror and shock as the Caltorian's wandered in a stupor through their dead, Trevon choosing to crawl and place hands on each victim to bless them until he found his mother and lost all control.

The two weave patrol members wept openly at the sight and the pain Trevon, Linell, and Fedlen felt. They cringed as the wails of agony arose from the lone survivors of the Sacred City of Caltoria who chose to return to their homeland of Stellaran only to be massacred on its soil.

With his head down in concentration, the sweat dripped down to the end of his nose and dropping off into the dead leaves lining the forest floor, Trevon didn't realize he reached Bristol until he saw her hand with the ring of the Stellaran Council bearing the silver fist which she wore as leader of their people.

His eyes reluctantly lifted to her face, her eyes open wide in shock staring off at nothing. The arrow jutted from her neck on either side, the pool of blood spread out beneath her head and shoulders darkening the floor in the moonlight. Her mouth gaped open as she had struggled at the end for every breath as the blood filled up her lungs and she drowned on her own blood.

Trevon caressed her cheek with the back of his dirty hand and then laid his head upon her chest and wept, his body shaking with the overwhelming sorrow that threatened to draw him into death with her. He slipped the ring from her stiff fingers, easing the symbol of leadership for his people into his pocket. It felt much heavier than he recalled now that the burden of leadership fell upon him and him alone.

Time passed and the leaves rustled with approaching footsteps caused Trevon to close his eyes in an effort to still his sobs of pain in the hopes of appearing to be in control.

"Trevon," Linell's voice whispered as a gentle hand rested on his shoulder. "Oh, Trevon, I'm so sorry."

Trevon lifted his head and looked through bleary eyes up at his betrothed. Her sorrow-filled reddened eyes met his as he turned and then reached up wrapping his arms around her.

They wept on each other's shoulders shaking uncontrollably.

She kissed his head and held him tight as they cried. Her body shook with grief, but her tears didn't come as her tear ducts held little anymore. She now felt numb to the pain and horror to this hideous homecoming.

Trevon's sobs slowed and he eased back from Linell wiping his eyes. He placed a hand on each side of her face and pulled her to his lips kissing her hard and deep as if her kiss was the only thing that could sustain him, the one thing that would keep him alive in all this madness.

He pulled away and looked at the surprise mixed with pain in her beautiful eyes. "Did you find anyone alive?" he asked.

"No." She shook her head and he pressed his lips tightly together.

"Who...?"

"Stern said a brigade called the Red Tips," she said leaning back holding up a long white feather with a blood red tip. "He said they are the death squad for the Council of Stellaran."

Trevon struggled to get to his feet and felt supporting hands on either arm. Looking to each side, Stern and Fedlen held him upright.

"I'll be fine," he argued but the men still supported him.

"It may take some time to get your strength back and I'm not sure you will ever be without pain," Linell informed him of the injuries he sustained in the questioning, but the pain his heart felt overpowered everything else.

"I'm alive," he replied without emotion. He straightened, allowing Fedlen and Stern to steady him for a minute and then drew in his magic and began moving bodies to one side of the narrow clearing.

Fedlen, Linell, Cita, and Stern looked on in confusion for a moment and then began to help as they realized his intention. They buried the victims of the massacre in a mass grave taking the time to fell an enormous oak and fashion a marker with all their people's names on it. Along with the names, Trevon inscribed these words:

HERE LIE THE GOOD PEOPLE OF THE SACRED CITY OF CALTORIA MURDERED FOR TRYING TO GO HOME. MAY THEY REST IN PEACE IN THEIR HOMELAND.

As they mounted their horses, looking down at the marker one last time, the sound of hoofs and wagon wheels caused them to turn around and watch as a woman rode into the clearing followed by a wagon bearing four children.

****

Logan recovered in the wagon as Zeva lead them north toward Stellaran in their attempt to escape the empress's pursuit of the protector. He lay flat in the wagon as it jostled from side to side on the path they followed when Bethany brought the wagon to an abrupt halt.

Logan sat up and looked past Zeva as she sat staring across a large clearing at five riders stopped before a large wooden object. The riders' attention turned to the new arrivals in the clearing. Logan eased himself to the back of the wagon and slid his feet to the ground, staggering a bit before gaining his balance.

As he looked to his unsteady feet something struck him about the ground around him. Through the rough and patchy growth of grass, the ground appeared dark red, nearly black. He dropped to a knee and touched the dirt with his fingers, lifting some to his nose and smelled.

He knew the coppery sweet smell anywhere and his stomach turned as he looked around to see more dark spots than light natural earth along the ground.

Zeva rode next to him, glancing over her shoulder at the riders watching them.

"What is it?" She asked not looking at him but keeping her eyes on the others across the field.

"This was a killing field," Logan said holding his hand up and waiting for her to look at him.

"A what?" She said as she turned and saw the blood-soaked earth between his fingers.

"A great many lives were lost here."

Zeva looked at the ground where Logan stood and then scanned the surrounding area to witness his discovery. The ground held more dark soil than light in most places.

"Do you think they're responsible?" Zeva asked giving a slight nod to the still motionless riders across the field.

"Not likely. I'm not sure how things are done in Stellaran, but few bury their enemy's dead and fewer still erect a monument to them." Logan looked past Zeva at the riders as he spoke.

"What now?" Zeva asked.

"Bethany," Logan said and the girl turned in her seat on the wagon to look back at him. "Stay here and keep still. If anything happens, get out of here, understand?"

The girl opened her mouth to protest, but then stopped and nodded.

Logan gave her a slight nod of approval.

"Let's go see what they have to say," Logan said to Zeva as he held up his arm and she reached down helping him climb up behind her on the horse.

Zeva and Logan gave one more reassuring look to the children and then turned and trotted over to the other riders.

As they approached, Logan noted the weary look on their faces as well as the sorrow filling their eyes. He leaned in close to Zeva and whispered in her ear. "This is not their doing, but be careful."

Zeva nodded, her ear brushing against his lips.

"Our heart goes out to you in your loss," Zeva said as she stopped the horse a few paces away.

The riders exchanged numb glances and turned back to the newcomers.

"Your sympathy is appreciated," the man who looked the weariest said.

"We are passing through and happened upon this clearing," Logan said. "May we inquire who did this so as to avoid a similar fate?"

"They're known as the Red Tips," a weathered-faced man said and then bowed his head as if shamed.

"We will be sure to give wide birth to any such men," Zeva said.

****

Fedlen sat on his horse watching the man and woman approach leaving the wagon of children a safe distance behind them. He understood their need for caution given the scene his party now occupied.

As the man and woman stopped in front of them and spoke, his attention shifted to a flash of light coming from Trevon's belt. He turned and stared at the box taken from Rudnick and the green light flashed brightly even in the sunlight. He hesitated on the box for only a moment, but he understood that the lights lit only when descendants of the council members were near. He looked to Trevon as he spoke, dazed by what this might indicate. Before them sat at least one direct descendant of the Crystal Council members.

"Trevon," Fedlen interrupted.

Trevon turned to him, irritation for the interruption showing on his weary face.

Fedlen nodded toward Trevon's belt.

Trevon didn't understand and frowned. "What is it?"

Fedlen pointed at the box on Trevon's belt.

Trevon's eyes grew large as he saw the glow emanating from the box and carefully lifted it from his belt. He held it before him looking uncertain about opening it.

All eyes fell on Trevon including the newcomers as he lifted the lid of the box to witness the gemstone now shining a bright green indicating that a direct descendant of another member of the Stellaran Council sat in their presence.

****

As the weary man lifted the strange box with an expression of disbelief, Logan and Zeva slowly backed away, uncertain as to the nature of the obviously magical box.

"Wait," the man said raising a hand to stop them. "We are no danger to you."

Zeva continued to ease back on the reins edging the horse further away from the others.

"No, please," the man said almost frantic. "You are who we are seeking. You are meant to lead Stellaran."

Logan and Zeva looked to each other in shock and then Logan shook his head in disbelief.

"Does this always happen to you?" Zeva asked in amazement.

"Pretty much," Logan said with resignation.

Chapter 20

As night fell on Stalwart, Teah gathered her cellmates together and explained her plan. With the binding weaves gone, they felt they possessed more than enough magic to fight their way out of their imprisonment and reach freedom outside the walls of Stalwart.

"I'll take the lead," she said and the women grumbled around her in disagreement.

"You shouldn't put yourself in danger like that," Saliday spoke up. "We are expendable, each and every one of us, except you."

"Nonsense," Teah argued. "With a new queen on the throne, the spell protecting Ter Chadain from Caltorian invasions is in place. I feel Saliday and Machala and their mission to find Logan may be more vital."

They are right, let one of them take the lead, Bastion agreed.

Teah slammed her mental wall up again, not liking the protector's dissent.

Her words didn't seem to convince the women either, but she pushed on. "I'll take care of the door. Once we are free of the cell, Raven and Rachel will free the men and remove their weaves as we practiced earlier."

The women nodded their understanding.

"What about the guards?" Rachel asked straightening from their huddle to look out the barred window in the door at the two men sitting at a table in the large outer room that connected all the cells.

"I got them," Teah said without skipping a beat.

"But you have the door and…" Saliday started but Teah's harsh look cut her off.

"I've got it," Teah said in a low controlled voice. "Now let's get out of here."

Without another word, Teah straightened and extended her open-palmed hand toward the door and it instantly exploded outward sending splinters and chunks of wood hurtling into the far wall nearly missing one of the men as he sat eating some stew. She stepped out of the cell with her arm still extended and the dagger hanging on each man's hip lifted from their sheath as the men came to their feet, floated before them for a split second, and then plunged into each man's heart. The men fell back onto their stools shattering them into pieces under the men's dead weight.

Rachel raced out of the cell and released the weave she held between her hands as she lifted them above her head. The door to the cell blew inward with a crash as the men inside scattered to avoid the careening barrier. Once the door skittered to a halt, Raven hurried in and used the specially crafted weave as Teah instructed and freed first Grinwald and then Caslor of their confining weave.

Morgan hurried out of the cell past Raven to a large cabinet with an oversized lock on it.

Saliday raced to his side and hesitated to ponder the lock.

"Teah," Saliday shouted.

Teah glanced their way taking her eyes from the stairwell and any sign of more guards for a second to flick her wrist and explode the lock from the latch before turning back.

Morgan pulled his cutlass from the cabinet and strapped it on. He then handed Saliday her short sword and her vest of throwing knifes which she quickly put on and fastened snuggly before reaching for her cloak hanging with the rest of the prisoner's outer garments beside the cabinet.

"Teah," Morgan shouted and tossed the protector swords toward her.

Teah snatched them from the air and fluidly swung the scabbards upon her back and fastened the straps across her chest.

As she clipped the straps tight, the thunder of footsteps filled the stairwell. Teah extended her hand toward the cabinet, releasing the metal rod from the sheath as it hung on a hook in the cabinet. It shot past Morgan in a flash and instantly extended into a bow as it nestled in Teah's palm.

Her hand pulled the silver string to her cheek as she rotated on her heels, the silver arrow magically appearing only to be released in a flash of silver and replaced by another and then another and then another.

The magical string thrummed time and time again and with each vibration, dropped another guard attempting to enter the dungeons.

When the last man tumbled over the rest to roll to a stop at her feet, she relaxed and allowed the bow to compress to the metal rod once more.

Caslor stepped forward holding the rod's sheath handing it to Teah as she smiled sheepishly and took it from him.

A crossbow string thrummed followed by a bolt's hum through the air.

Teah lifted an open palm and the bolt turned to dust an inch from Caslor's heart.

Saliday was by Teah's side, pushing the stunned Caslor aside and sending a throwing knife into the chest of the crossbowman who tumbled lifeless down the stairs to their feet.

Teah turned to help Caslor to his feet, but stumbled and fell into his arms as he stood.

"Are you alright?" he asked, his voice laced with concern.

"Fine, just a little light headed," Teah said placing a hand to her forehead.

"You can't expect to use such large amounts of magic without feeling the effects," Grinwald said walking forward. "Magic comes from our inner strength and if you pull too much, it will take its toll."

"I felt it, that's why I used my bow," Teah explained. "I didn't expect another attack so soon."

"At least you're okay," Caslor said with a warm smile.

"You too," Teah grinned.

"Thanks for that," Caslor said making Teah blush.

"If you two are through," Morgan asked, "can we get out of here?"

"We need to get to Cordlain as soon as possible to help Teah take the throne from the imposter," Grinwald said in agreement.

"I don't think that is my mission any longer," Teah informed him.

"What?" Grinwald said in shock.

"There is a queen on the throne who apparently has Lassain blood in her so we are all safe from Caltorian invasion. We need to head to Ceait and the houses of magic."

"What are you talking about?" Grinwald said.

"I spoke with Duke Banderkin before being taken to the duchess and he said that the Betra army has fractured into two. Half is still loyal to our cause and the other has decided to follow the new queen who is also Betra."

Morgan and Caslor joined in Grinwald's incredulous stare.

"I plan to gather what remaining army Banderkin and the Betra can form and take them to Ceait. I will not let Englewood destroy the houses of magic in Ter Chadain. It would be no better than Caltoria if he did," Teah explained.

"When do we head out," Morgan asked as he curiously watched Machala stride up to him and retrieve her sword, resembling Teah's protector swords, from the cabinet and strapping it on. She then pulled the loose-fitting, flowing robe and fastened it behind her, exposing the fitted undergarments with a bare midriff and low neck-line along with shorts cut high up her thigh. The men gawked at Machala who didn't seem to notice their shock at the female Betra battle attire.

"You won't be joining us," Teah informed Morgan who still

stared in shock at the muscular, yet feminine shape of Machala. "You will be sailing Saliday and Machala, the new Seeker of the Protector, back to Caltoria."

"You must be joking," Morgan said with a laugh. "I have no intention of sailing back to Caltoria anytime soon. I'm sure there is a price on my head along with a bounty for my ship."

"Either you sail us there, or I take the Morning Breeze and sail Machala there myself," Saliday stated.

Morgan looked to Grinwald and Raven, not liking the turn this journey now took. Neither of his partners showed any signs of speaking up.

"You always have a choice, Morgan," Teah said. "You can be a part of a vital mission to see if my brother still lives, one that I will always be indebted to you for taking part in, or you can join us on our quest to defend the houses of magic."

"There is a third option," Morgan said under his breath.

"And what is that?" Saliday asked.

"Never mind," Morgan grumbled. "But you are a Tarken," Morgan said turning to her. "If Logan lived, your abilities would lead you to him."

"I thought so too," Saliday agreed. "But Machala has magic almost as old as ours saying that the protector still lives."

"How can that be?" Rachel asked.

"Maybe Logan is being shielded from my magic by a spell, but apparently the protector in him is still sending his message to Machala loud and clear," Saliday said. She turned to Machala who nodded her agreement.

"We need get out of here before they send more men down to get us," Caslor cautioned.

"Are you coming or not?" Saliday said turning to Morgan.

"Only I sail the Morning Breeze into peril," Morgan said puffing up with misguided pride.

"Very well," Teah said. "After we reach the courtyard, you,

179

Machala and Saliday head back to the docks and the rest of you head inland."

"The rest of us?" Caslor questioned. "Where are you going?"

"I made a promise to free Duke Banderkin and his daughter when we left," Teah said.

"I'll come with you," Caslor volunteered just before Grinwald stepped forward to do the same.

"No, I will move quicker alone," Teah stopped their objections before they started. "End of discussion. Now let's go."

She reached over to grasp Saliday's shoulder and make eye contact with the Tarken. "You find Logan and bring him back to us." The intensity of Teah's gaze seared into Saliday as the woman gave a curt nod.

Teah spun and raced up the stairs, the sound of battle erupting above them as she engaged the duchess's troops.

Those remaining in the dungeons exchanged shocked glances and then hurried after their queen, protector, and friend.

By the time the others reached the courtyard, the duchess's troops scrambled to stay alive. As the protector, Teah alternated between sending a shower of arrows into the ramparts of the keep, taking out every man who lifted a bow or crossbow, and drawing her two protector swords and ravaging the men who assaulted her with swords and spears. She spun gracefully among her attackers, slashing and slicing through them, deflecting their assaults, ducking beneath their attempts to stop her. She glided across the courtyard as the dirt turned to bloodied mud beneath her boots.

Grinwald leapt in, using blasts of magic to send the soldiers flying.

Rachel, Caslor, and Raven followed suit as Saliday, Morgan, and Machala pushed the enemy back with an assault of steel from their swords.

Soon the soldiers ran for their lives and Teah raced into the palace without a look back at her companions.

Morgan followed Saliday and Machala as they hurried to the stables, mounted the saddled horses waiting there and raced out of the palace back toward the docks and the Morning Breeze.

Raven caught his embroidered coat by the edge, pulling his horse to a stop. Their eyes met, her intensity blazing from them frightened him. Grinwald hurried over to them.

"You cannot let Logan return to Ter Chadain," Grinwald insisted. "The prophecy says he will be our destruction."

Morgan nodded and pulled free of Raven's grip on his coat and kicked his mount to hurry after Saliday and Machala.

"We need to find the Betra and Ter Chadain troops still loyal to Teah's cause and prepare them for departure," Grinwald said.

"Then let's go," Raven said as they retrieved some horses and sprinted out the deserted gate toward the south.

****

Teah raced up the flights of stairs nearly running into the general as he burst from the duchess's chambers that were along the way to Duke Banderkin's quarters.

The general staggered at the sight of her, dropping the bloodied dagger he held in his hand. Their eyes followed the rattling path of the dagger across the stone floor where it came to rest against the base of a wall.

Teah looked to the man whose features now distorted with fear.

"I take it that a traitor duchess is no longer an issue, General?" she asked.

"No, My Queen," he said dropping to a knee and bowing his head.

"Then leadership in Stalwart is now loyal to our cause?"

"Yes, My Queen," the general said and then stood and raced off.

Teah sprinted down the hallway and tapped once on the door

before barging into the duke's chambers. What she found stopped her in her tracks, dropping her to her knees and emptying her stomach onto the elaborate rugs that adorned the apartment.

Dezare hung from the bed posts, her arms and legs bound to opposite posts. Her stomach laid splayed open with her entrails dangling outside her body. The grotesqueness dripped from her bowels onto the floor and puddled in a deep red stain.

The duke sat in a chair, his hands tied to each arm of the chair, except where he appeared to have chewed through the rope which held him. Blood covered the chewed rope and his right hand that he freed by his chewing. His hand now lay limp in his lap on top of a long dagger covered in blood.

Teah stepped over to the duke and eased his head back to reveal a deep slit in his throat and his mouth covered in blood from his efforts to free himself.

She could only imagine the horrible scene that played out in this room only a moment before her arrival.

They made him watch as they tortured and left her in front of him, Bastion said.

Teah realized her mental shield no longer held the thoughts of the protectors back, but they chose to remain quiet until that horrid moment.

She probably was alive for a while, bleeding out painfully slow, Stalwart added.

And by the time he freed himself, she was already gone, Teah surmised.

So he took his life because living without her was not an option, Falcone commiserated.

Teah dropped to a knee again; the thought of the pain and suffering this father and daughter must have endured in their last moments in this world. She recalled the massacre of her own family under the orders of King Aston's father and her sorrow for the Banderkin family soon gave way to her rage and anger toward the Englewood bloodline. She never had the chance to get revenge of her own on the king even though it was by his deeds that she became the Empress of Caltoria's slave. Logan held that pleasure, but now her path that seemed so disjointed and uncertain snapped into vivid clearness in her mind. She needed to rid Ter Chadain of people like the Englewoods and their followers like the duchess. Those who would do such horrible things to others needed to be stopped. And she wanted, no needed, to be the one to stop them. She needed to be sure that the empress never held any sway over a leader of Ter Chadain again. And the only way to be sure of that, was to claim the throne herself.

Finally thinking like the true queen, my dear, Bastion cheered.

Teah gave a nod. ***True queen indeed,*** she agreed and strode from the room.

Chapter 21

It took a lot of talking, coaxing, and convincing by Trevon to get Zeva and Logan to believe that they meant no harm. After Trevon showed Logan the box that lit green gemstones of three members of the Stellaran board from years ago which represented Linell's and Trevon's bloodline and a third bloodline as well, they finally sat down by a fire outside the clearing in a small camp with some fresh rabbit which Fedlen managed to kill.

The children now slept with their bellies full of rabbit stew in the back of the wagon while Logan, Zeva, and the others sat around the fire.

"So you think I'm a direct descendant of one of the original council members trapped in Caltoria?" Logan asked finding it hard to believe.

"It is true," Trevon insisted. "The box is saying it is true."

"But how well do we know the accuracy of the box?" Stern added, bringing everyone's attention to him as he met their stares flatly.

"Why would Rudnick be using it if it wasn't effective?" Linell argued.

"I'm with Stern on this one," Cita said. "Nothing against you, Logan, but it is hard to believe you are a descendant and you just happen to walk into this clearing."

"I agree," Logan said, not wanting any part of this. His complicated life didn't need any more destinies besides the one being the protector forced upon him.

"But you need to help us take back the council for the sake of our people," Trevon continued.

"I'm not one of you," Logan argued. "I'm from Ter Chadain and I have no desire to fight a battle to claim a right I feel I have no business claiming." In fact, he didn't want to claim anything anymore. His days of fighting battles for others were behind him.

"I think right now we need to concentrate on what to do next," Stern changed the subject.

"I didn't want to bring this up in front of the children, but what happened here?" Zeva asked.

The air seemed to suck out of the area surrounding the campfire as Logan and Zeva witnessed their new acquaintances stiffen, their faces turning white as the blood drained from them.

"I'll tell them," Linell spoke up after a prolonged silence.

"No," Trevon stopped her. "I'm the one who should tell them."

The campsite went quiet again and lasted uncomfortably long as the smoke wafted into the air from the crackling campfire.

"Our people, the people from Stellaran who remained isolated from Caltoria for our own safety and denied access to our own country knew we could not stay in Caltoria once the weave had fallen," Trevon explained. "We met Stern and Cita on our way as we returned to Stellaran. Unfortunately, not all in Stellaran welcomed our return like these two members of the weave patrol."

Logan looked to Stern and Cita as their expressions appeared as if they would be sick.

"When we reached the weave patrol headquarters, a man named Rudnick Curn was waiting for us. He questioned us on the whereabouts of any descendants of the chairmen."

"But you didn't know where any descendants were?" Zeva asked.

"No," Linell answered. "We were planning on searching for them after we escorted our people safely into Stellaran."

"But after Rudnick made it apparent that we were not welcome in Stellaran, Cita and Stern sent our friend Clastis and our people ahead toward Caltoria while they freed us," Trevon went on.

Logan felt something deep inside him stir as Trevon told his story. He felt his anger rise as the plight of a people only wishing to go home after so long grew apparent as the story continued.

"We reached them too late," Trevon said and went silent, his head dropping and the words escaping him to continue.

"It wouldn't have mattered," Stern said but his consoling did nothing but release Trevon's anger.

"Damn the spirits, I don't care if it wouldn't have mattered," Trevon shouted. "I would have been here to help my people, to protect my mother, to…

"To die alongside them," Cita added, her eyes filled with tears and wet paths running down her face.

"At least I would have died doing something," Trevon retorted.

"Sharing their fate serves no purpose," Stern insisted.

"You cannot begin to understand," Linell argued.

"Some people must live and carry on when their loved ones die senselessly, otherwise their sacrifice will mean nothing," Logan said in a soft, controlled voice that quaked as he spoke, his anger threatening to erupt at any moment.

They turned to him as he sat with his head down, staring at the dirt.

"Only Clastis and three others were armed. The rest were peasants, women and children, nearly fifty in all," Fedlen said.

"Who did this?" Logan asked in a hoarse whisper.

"They are the Crystal Council's Red Battalion," Stern answered.

"Did you see any of them when you arrived?" Zeva asked.

"No," Cita said when she understood none of those from the Sacred City could answer at the moment. "But we found this." She held up the white feather with the red tip. "The battalion is also known as "Red Tips" by the tip of blood on the end of the feathers in their helmets. It is the custom to dip them into the blood of their victims to keep the red bright." This particular feather's tip was the deep red of fresh blood.

Logan could hardly contain his anger. The thought of trained military massacring unarmed civilians who merely searched for a place in their homeland sent him into a rage. He seethed with the revenge that sent him after King Englewood for murdering his family. Hatred racked his mind with the thought of the Empress Shakata holding his sister as a slave and losing Sasha in his attempt to free the slaves of Caltoria.

"We need to make the council and the Red Tips pay for this," Logan said over the heads of the Caltorians.

"How do you propose we do that?" Stern asked.

"I will do as Trevon has asked and join you in unseating the Chairman of the Council," Logan answered.

"That is an impossible task," Cita pointed out.

"You don't know Logan yet," Zeva said turning to her. "You will soon find that Logan can accomplish anything he puts his mind to."

"I sure hope you're right," Cita said, staring at Logan as if she searched for an answer in his eyes as they met hers.

"I need some rest," Logan stood turning as Trevon and Zeva rose next to him. "I give you my deepest condolences for your loss." He walked off toward their wagon where the children slept.

Zeva hesitated for a moment, watching Logan walk into the darkness realizing her hope for the return of the protector may be at hand.

"He acts as if hearing Trevon's story pained him," Cita said to Zeva as she stood by her. The weave patroller stared up at the woman, perplexed.

"Logan has suffered much loss himself in the last two years. He will not fail you," Zeva said and followed Logan into the darkness.

****

"I have one condition," Logan stated as he rode up with Zeva and the wagon of children right behind him the next morning.

"And what is that?" Trevon asked.

187

"The children can't go back to Caltoria and I won't have them riding into battle with us with the Red Tips. We need to take them somewhere they will be safe." Logan waited as they glanced from one to the other without an answer.

"I know of a place," Cita spoke up. All eyes turned to her. "Shotwarg Cliffs."

"No, absolutely not," Stern objected.

"What is Shotwarg Cliffs?" Logan asked.

"A secret school in Stellaran for the magically gifted," Cita explained.

"The word 'secret' should explain that it is not an option," Stern argued.

"But they will be safe there," Cita insisted.

"And you think that Rudnick Curn won't be tracking us, isn't tracking us at this very instant? We can't lead him to Shotwarg Cliffs." Stern countered.

"I can cover our tracks. Even this Rudnick won't be able to follow us," Zeva offered.

They turned to Zeva for a moment and back to Stern and Cita. Stern looked at each member of the newly formed party and then past Zeva and Logan at the wagon with the children. He gave a resigned nod.

"Very well," he said. "Cita, carry on."

"I'll start covering our tracks from here. Rudnick will never know what direction we went. As far as he can tell, we all perished here," Zeva said and dropped back behind the wagon.

They all fell in behind Cita as she led them off in a northeastern direction. Logan let the Caltorians ride behind her and then fell in behind them. Stern waited until the wagon passed and then slid beside Zeva.

Zeva glanced at him curiously.

"I'm fascinated to see how you do this," Stern admitted.

She smirked and gave him a nod as they started moving. Her

lips moved but no words came out and she closed her eyes for a moment as her horse followed slowly after the others unguided. She tied the weave in place and then focused on the trail ahead glancing back to see that her weave did as she intended.

Stern's mouth dropped open in shock as he witnessed all the tracks the horses and wagon wheels made vanish as Zeva rode over them. He looked to her in admiration.

"How did you do that?" Stern asked.

"A weave of air and water makes the ground fluid and it fills in like a mud slide on the side of a hill," she explained proudly.

"Incredible," Stern whispered. "You must show me how to do that."

"I will need to reform the weave after a few hours, I will take you through the steps when I do," Zeva said with a smile.

Stern grinned with excitement and turned back to witness the smoothing of their tracks behind them.

****

Logan rode with his head down through the lightly forested terrain, his mind racing with thoughts of struggle between helping these people with their quest and the desire to put aside his past two years of death and destruction as the protector. Did destiny steer him so rigidly that his life as a protector would overshadow everything else that could be? He hoped not, but Port Shoal did prove something that he couldn't deny. If his life or the lives of those he cared about were in peril, he couldn't allow failure by ignoring the powers he possessed. He needed to use those powers and realize that in doing so, he would kill people opposing his goals and his quest. He didn't like the feeling, but he knew that for him to succeed on his mission and protect those around him, killing needed to be a part of it, no matter how much he despised it.

He looked around at the party he now rode in the middle of

and realized that these people all deserved his help. They seemed like good people and worthy people, but most of all, the people they opposed definitely showed that they valued life very little. And that underlying current of hatred and fear for anyone with magical abilities seemed to rear its ugly head again. Where could they find a balance between those with magical powers and those without?

He smiled at Bethany as she steered the horses behind him. Such a brave girl, he thought. She deserved a chance to live in happiness with her sisters and brother.

He turned back to the front as a movement off to his right side caught his attention. He kicked his horse into a run as he flipped his cloak away and drew a sword from his back. He sped past the stunned Caltorians just as the thrum of a bowstring sounded from a rise in the woods to his right. He swept his sword in front of him shattering the arrow as it flew toward Cita.

"Take cover," Logan shouted as the others scrambled from their horses. Logan kicked his horse up the rise toward the attackers, not waiting for the next arrow but closing the distance between him and their attackers.

He reached the top of the rise and found the archer, fumbling to notch another arrow. He swept down across the man's face as he rode by, removing the top half of his head and spraying blood across his legs and his horse.

Another thrum came from his left and he swept his sword in front of him deflecting the arrow targeting his heart. He smoothly sheathed his sword and drew the metal rod as his eyes scanned for the archer. The rod expanded into the bow as he found his target and smoothly let fly a silver arrow, striking the archer in the chest, sending him toppling backwards.

An arrow struck Logan's chest, shattering on impact with the magical chain mail, but driving the wind from his lungs. He held his breath, scanning the trees in the direction the arrow came from. He spotted the man in the trees and sent an arrow through his neck, bringing the man down bouncing off the branches as he descended from his hiding spot to land dead on the forest floor.

A horse huffed in the distance to his right and Logan spun in his saddle, his bow string drawn back and the arrow flying as the target fell into his sights.

The horse only strode two strides before its rider toppled from the saddle with a silver arrow imbedded between his shoulder blades.

Logan scanned the hillside and trees as he listened for any more signs of assailants. He twisted in his saddle as leaves rustled on the forest floor behind him to find Cita in his sites.

She gasped as he twitched to one side and sent a silver arrow into the ground beside her.

"What in the spirits of our ancestors are you doing?" Cita cried out, a hand to her chest.

"Saving your life," Logan said and let the bow retract to a rod once more and slid it back into its sheath.

"But you could have gotten yourself killed racing up here like that," Cita scolded.

"This is what I do," Logan pointed out.

"Who is so reckless as to charge into an enemy like that?" Cita continued.

"He is the Protector of Ter Chadain," Trevon said walking up the hill and staring at Logan, the pommels of the swords of the protectors jutting out from over his shoulder.

Logan glanced over a shoulder at the tell-tale handles which couldn't be mistaken for anything but what they were. The Swords of Salvation, the weapons of the protector, and covered them up again with his cloak.

Fedlen and Linell walked up beside Trevon, staring at Logan as if seeing him for the first time. They obviously knew of the tale of the protector being in Caltoria.

Stern and Zeva hurried up the hill to join the others as they stared at Logan.

"So your secret is out already then?" Zeva said to Logan, her voice woven with amusement.

"What secret?" Stern asked. "Who is the Protector of Ter Chadain?"

"You're looking at him," Zeva said with a nod to Logan. "A legendary warrior who rises to help put a Lassain Queen on the throne of Ter Chadain in times of strife in Ter Chadain."

Stern and Cita stared at them at a loss.

"Many magicals from Caltoria fled across the sea to Ter Chadain to escape the tyranny of the Emperor of Caltoria. Ter Chadain has been a land of magical freedom ever since, ruled by one with Lassain lineage. It is with that magic that Ter Chadain has remained safe from Caltoria all these years."

Stern shook his head as if to shake cobwebs from it. "So there is another country at war with Caltoria which lies across the sea?"

"Enough of the history lesson," Logan interrupted. "We need to keep moving. I don't want to keep the children in danger any longer than needed."

Cita moved over to the first archer Logan partially decapitated and bent down to retrieve a blood-tipped white feather. She held it in front of her for all to see as she strode back to them.

"Red Tips were expecting us," she said.

"I'm guessing they left archers behind in every direction to catch whoever came upon their battle site," Logan pointed out. "I doubt they knew which direction we would take."

"True, but they will discover our direction when these men fail to report back to the main company," Stern said.

"Then we must find the rest and eliminate them as well," Logan replied, bringing incredulous stares from the others. "What? Do you have any better ideas to hide our retreat?"

They looked to one another but said nothing.

Logan gave a nod and spun his horse back down the hill.

Cita grasped his horse's reins and stopped him. "You can't go by yourself."

"I'm faster alone," he argued.

"I'll come with," Cita insisted.

"No, you're the only one who knows where Shotwarg Cliffs is," Logan pointed out.

"I'll go," Stern volunteered stepping up. "I'm the only other one who knows the area."

Logan nodded his acceptance to Stern's accompanying him.

"I will be heading northeast for twenty miles and then due east for a long time," Cita told him.

"I know where you head, but will need help finding the entrance. It has been too long," Stern said bringing a surprised stare from Cita. "You're not the only one who has been to Shotwarg Cliffs."

Logan looked over to Zeva. "Look over them and I will catch up in a day or two," he said.

She nodded confidently, but her eyes betrayed her concern. "Hurry back."

Logan waited for Cita to release his mount but she hesitated for a moment, staring up at him, her deep blue eyes swirling with emotions and thoughts. "Thank you for saving my life."

Logan nodded and she stepped back letting him ride down the hill and then trot off with Stern by his side to hunt down the other scouts from the Red Tips.

The others stood in shocked silence trying to digest what just happened.

Cita looked at Zeva, her face awash with confusion.

"Told you he would surprise you," Zeva said with a satisfied smile and hurried down the hill to check on the children waiting in the wagon.

Chapter 22

Teah slipped through the remaining defenses of Stalwart and met up with Grinwald, Raven, Rachel, and Caslor as they camped well outside the view of the city. She stood just outside the firelight watching the others for a moment, hoping Saliday, Machala, and Morgan reached the Morning Breeze safely and now sailed back toward Caltoria in the hopes of finding Logan.

She moved to enter camp when something caught her eye and she stopped, studying the moment.

Caslor stood toe-to-toe with Grinwald, the two locked in a heated argument. Rachel and Raven looked on, their eyes wide and nervous at the tension between the Viri Magus and the magical son of an empress.

"She needs to claim the throne as was the plan," Caslor said flailing his arms in frustration.

"You heard her, she feels the best plan of action is to go to the aid of the houses of magic since the shield is around Ter Chadain to protect against any further assaults from your mother's forces is already in place," Grinwald argued.

"But if she took out the king and his new queen, the siege on the houses of magic would be over and you would end both threats," Caslor reasoned.

"But the time it will take us to defeat the king in Cordlain could mean the end of the houses of magic and the deaths of many Viri and Zele Magus. We can't risk decimating the magical power in Ter Chadain like that." Grinwald took a threatening step toward Caslor, but the young man wouldn't back down. He stood, glaring at the wizard.

Teah waited a moment longer and when Grinwald spotted her observing them, he backed off. She strode into the firelight and stopped by the fire, her eyes drawn to the flames, not wanting to let her inner turmoil spill out.

"Teah," Grinwald greeted and walked to her, placing a hand on her shoulder.

"Grinwald," Teah said with a nod.

"We were starting to get worried," the Viri Magus continued. "Where are the duke and his daughter?"

"Dead," Teah said flatly, not looking up from the fire.

"Who?" Caslor asked.

"The duchess had them tortured and killed, for helping me, I believe." Teah's eyes were cold and hard at the memory of that scene in the duke's chambers.

"She is a nasty and vile woman," Grinwald said.

"Was," Teah stated.

Grinwald raised an eyebrow at Teah.

"Not me," Teah said. "Her own general took care of that. I suspect he realized he would be next, so he acted first."

"So the general is in charge of Stalwart?" Grinwald asked his concern evident.

"He will see that the port is held by those loyal to our cause, I have no doubt. Logan seemed to make quite the impression on him," Teah couldn't help but grin at her brother's persuasiveness sometimes.

"Come have something to eat," Caslor said as he squatted beside the fire and pulled some meat from a spit hanging over it, dripping juices into the flames with a hiss. He handed the hot meat to Teah and she sat down on a boulder next to the fire and took a bite, the juice dripping down her chin. She didn't bother to wipe it away but took another big bite.

"Would you mind if I had a word in private with Caslor?" Teah asked not looking up from her meal.

Grinwald, Rachel, and Raven nodded and then moved off to give them space.

Careful, Bastion warned, reading Teah's thoughts.

I need to do this. Can you all please give me my thoughts for a few moments?

The protectors went silent and Teah felt certain they didn't listen in.

She turned to Caslor who stared at her, concern on his face, but with the confidence one would expect from a son of an empress; a son who needed to hide his magical ability from his mother in order to survive.

"I heard you and Grinwald arguing," Teah started.

"I'm sorry you had to hear that," Caslor looked at her, his eyes filled with regret.

"I can handle hearing it, but I can't have people questioning my decisions."

Caslor nodded, looking away at the fire.

"I have my reasons and they are mine. You may choose to agree with my decision or not, but I ask you to please keep any discussions of doubt for conversations with me," Teah spoke softly, but firmly.

"I feel that your choice is shortsighted," Caslor said.

Teah wanted to lash out at him, to ask him what he knew about what she had gone through to allow him to make that statement, but she fought it back, drawing in a deep breath and taking another bite of meat to regain her composure.

"I care for you greatly," Teah said after the pause.

"And I do you, more than anyone in this world," Caslor assured her.

"But my life has never been about being a queen until two years ago. My life was my own until destiny turned to becoming Queen of Ter Chadain." She held his gaze for a moment and then continued. "Now that there is a queen with rights to the throne…"

"Her rights are weak at best. You are the true and rightful queen."

"Be that as it may," Teah agreed nodding, "by the spell being cast around Ter Chadain, she does have a legitimate claim that we can't deny. She is fulfilling a large part of the reason a Lassain queen needs to be on the throne."

Caslor stopped his forming retort, clamping his mouth shut with a snap. Instead, he stared at her until she looked up into his eyes. He moved closer and pulled her into his arms. Teah resisted at first, but then gave in and wrapped her arms around him.

"What happened back there?" he whispered in her ear and her body began to shake.

She cried on his shoulder as he caressed her golden hair. She leaned back, wiping tears from her cheeks and eyes and held his gaze; horror still huddled behind her deep blue eyes.

"They did something to a father that should never be done," she said staring at him, haunted.

"Duke Banderkin and his daughter Dezare?"

Teah nodded. "They disemboweled his daughter in front of him and then left him to watch her die."

Caslor gaped at her in shock.

"I don't know if I can continue fighting these evil, vile people," Teah said turning away from him.

Caslor wrapped his arms around her and she leaned her head back against his chest.

"It may seem unimaginable to do such things, cause you to question if what you do is the right thing or why so many people faithful to your cause must suffer and die for you, but if you don't stop this king, then who will?"

"But so many have died for our cause already," Teah said as a tear ran unhindered down her cheek.

"Yes. Good people. Kind people. Brave people. But they all had one thing in common."

Teah didn't want to hear the next statement. She knew already. "Me."

"Yes, you. From the start, it is a new queen the people have wanted, have needed to believe in to go on."

"They have a new queen," Teah said stepping away and turning on him. "I will do what I feel is right and that is to go to the aid of the houses of magic. We leave at first light." She strode off to find a place to sleep. She needed sleep.

I thought you were going to replace King Aston and his queen? Galiven asked, confused.

I am, but the houses are in grave danger. First things first.

The protectors eased their condemnation of her choice and gave her a sense of approval.

Grinwald, Rachel, and Raven filtered back into the campsite around the fire, watching Teah as she went through the saddlebags hanging on some low-lying branches near the horses.

"So what did she decide?" Grinwald asked Caslor.

"To defend the houses of magic," Caslor said not giving any inkling that he didn't agree. "We leave at first light. I'll take first watch." He strode off to take up a position on a large rock at one end of the site, giving him a good vantage point to see anyone approaching.

"She chooses wisely," Grinwald told Raven and Rachel as they looked to him. "With the houses safe, their aid will ensure a victory over King Englewood and his false queen."

"I wouldn't count on anything," Rachel said. "If I know Teah, she is not certain her destiny still lies with the throne. I think she is choosing the obvious path since the other is clouded in doubt." Rachel turned and joined Teah where she was pulling blankets from the supplies.

"She's right," Raven admitted. "Even the girl knows our goal of putting Teah on the throne is not a certainty now that Englewood has shown his cards."

"True," Grinwald agreed. "But there are many factors yet to come into play that might change all that, like Logan's hate for the Englewoods."

Raven turned to him, her eyes questioning.

"Saliday told me of the day Logan killed King Englewood and exiled his son and wife," Grinwald explained. "I guess Prince Aston ranted about his hate for anything magical after he tried, but failed to kill Logan. I have no doubt that if Logan is still alive as the Betra claims, he will be able to convince Teah the only course of action she should take for the best interest of Ter Chadain, is to claim the throne."

"That might be all well and good, but remember, if Zeva survived as Logan did, she will have told him about our treachery. I hate the idea of facing his wrath."

Grinwald held Raven's gaze and gave a shudder at the thought. Logan's anger coupled with the full use of his magic and protector's abilities could burn him and Raven to a crisp.

"Then let us hope that Zeva didn't survive, or that if she did, Logan does not believe her."

"And why would he doubt her?" Raven asked.

"Because he trusts me," Grinwald said confidently, but his eyes betrayed his fears.

"Let us hope that remains the case," Raven said and turned to bed down for the night.

****

Saliday stood at the rail of the Morning Breeze staring out at the vast expanse of water disappearing in every direction. She never imagined having a desire to return to Caltoria ever, much less this soon after escaping that horrid land and its equally horrid empress, but according to Machala, Logan still lived.

She shook her head as if to clear it, trying to focus on her need to find him, but her Tarken abilities failed her. She only found emptiness and a disturbing lack of direction.

Looking down the rail, Saliday grimaced as the Betra Seeker leaned over the rail and emptied her stomach's contents into the sea. With less than a day behind them, the journey looked as if it would prove to be a painful one for the Betra.

Machala straightened and wiped the back of her hand across her lips. She glanced around, making eye contact with Saliday and then spun away.

Saliday walked over and placed a hand on the woman's shoulders. "It is alright, Machala," Saliday comforted. "Some people never get the feel for the sea under them."

Machala nodded her understanding of that concept and flashed a quick look and a halfhearted smile at the Tarken. "Thank you for your kindness, but my sickness is over now and I will be a much better companion in planning for our search for the protector."

Saliday nodded, believing the strong woman's word, but expecting that word hard kept.

"You seem to be struggling a bit yourself," Machala said.

"Me? No. Tarken are born to the sea as much as we are to the land," Saliday said, confused.

"It is not your control of the sea that I speak of, but the control of your powers," Machala said.

"Ah, yes, I'm having trouble focusing on Logan enough to get a direction on him, yet you know exactly where to go. That is a bit disconcerting," Saliday admitted.

"Your magic is very old and born to you naturally," Machala pointed out. "Our magic is specific to one purpose and one purpose only…find the protector. The spell has no other function."

Saliday's eyebrow furrowed in thought as she concentrated on what that meant. Her eyebrows rose in realization. "I've been trying to fill my need to find Logan, the man I love, when I should have been concentrating on…"

"Finding the protector," Machala said with a nod.

"But why are the two different? Logan is the protector." Saliday shook her head, unable to determine the separation.

"It must be magic," Machala deduced. "If the protector's magic was somehow concealed by magic, then I would not be able to find him."

"But if it wasn't Logan's protector magic, but his magic as a Viri Magus that was being concealed or suppressed…"

"Then you cannot focus on that which is concealed," Machala said proudly.

Saliday nodded at the logic. She closed her eyes and instead of seeing Logan, his soft brown eyes and his gentle smile, she concentrated on the protector, wielding his swords and shooting his magical bow. Instantly, the image of the protector clarified in her mind and she knew where she needed to go to find him.

"So you now feel it?" Machala asked seeing the expression on Saliday's face.

"Yes, yes I do. It's as clear as day. He is far inland in Caltoria, almost as if he is beyond Caltoria altogether. But what is beyond Caltoria?" She smiled blissfully and then frowned in confusion.

"Stellaran," Morgan said from behind them.

Both women spun on him, surprised that he stood so close and listened to their exchange.

"But that has been barred from access for hundreds of years. If he is in Stellaran, then the magical weave dividing the two countries is gone and our problems have only begun."

"Why is that?" Machala asked.

"Because Caltoria was formed when Stellaran exiled dissenting factions from Stellaran and if the weave is down, the empress will surely seek her revenge on Stellaran. War is certain."

"Then we must hurry and find Logan," Saliday said.

"I say we turn around and try to save Ter Chadain and leave Logan where he is, dead and buried," Morgan urged.

"But that is where we have a problem," Saliday said, her anger rising as she took an aggressive step toward the captain. "Logan is not dead. Machala and I both sense him."

Morgan raised his hands defensively before him and his eyes widened. "I was told he was dead."

"Now you're being told he isn't," Saliday said not backing down.

"I'm not going to waltz into Bellatora for the empress to put my head on a spit," Morgan complained.

"Nor would we ask you to," Saliday seethed.

"No, we shall sail to this, what did you call it, Stellaran and find the protector there," Machala stated.

"Only one problem," Morgan complained.

"And what is that?" Saliday pressed.

"We can't tell if Stellaran is a friend or a foe. If we sail in there and they want no part of us, it might be a quick end to finding Logan," Morgan explained.

"Then what do you propose?" Machala asked.

"I say we travel to the closest port in Caltoria to where the weave separated them from Stellaran. You can begin your search there," Morgan proposed.

"That sounds like a reasonable idea," Machala agreed.

"What is the name of this port?" Saliday asked.

"Port Shoal," Morgan answered.

"Then Port Shoal it is," Saliday said with a nod to Machala who returned the gesture.

Chapter 23

Logan and Stern rode back to the memorial site of the massacre where they turned west. Since Logan and Zeva never encountered any troops on their way north, they surmised that the troops were ordered not to let any more Caltorians into Stellaran, not worrying about keeping them from fleeing back into Caltoria.

The two traveled silently, scanning for troops and finding them in their usual groupings of four on several occasions along the way. They came across the next group and Logan unceremoniously dispatched each archer from a distance with a well-placed silver arrow.

They turned north and traveled most of the night until they encountered a camp with more than four men, but no Red Tips in the party. No, no Red Tips, but much worse, Stern informed him.

"Rudnick," he whispered to Logan as they lay on a ridge overlooking the fire.

"The man who tortured Trevon and Linell?" Logan asked.

"The very same," Stern confirmed.

"I can take him out if you'd like," Logan offered.

"No, there are members of the weave patrol down there who are doing nothing but following orders."

Logan stared at Stern in the blackness, barely able to see the whites of the man's eyes as he looked back at him.

"How does that differ from the Red Tips we killed. Aren't they just following orders to kill us on sight?"

"Yes, but…" Stern stammered.

"And how about those that killed those innocent people from Caltoria, weren't they just following orders?" Logan's tone rang sharp as the edge of his swords.

"Well…"

"We choose sides, and sometimes those choosing the wrong side, according to the situation, die for it. It isn't fair, but it is either our side or their side and right now, they are on the wrong side since I'm the one with the bow and they're the ones standing in our way."

"Get up slowly with your hands up," a voice said from behind them as they each felt a sword press the middle of their backs.

Logan did a quick scan from his stomach and spotted two archers standing with arrows drawn back, ready to strike. He might survive the attack, but he held no doubts any struggle would prove fatal for his companion.

Stern looked at Logan with a helpless expression.

"Guess we might be on the wrong side now," Logan said standing as his weapons were pulled from his back by several men. They left the metal rod in its sheath on his leg with a chuckle as to its usefulness and shackled their hands behind their backs. They escorted Stern and Logan to stand before Rudnick by the campfire.

"Well, well, Stern Barsten," Rudnick said rubbing his hands together before the fire on the chilly night. "Seems we will have a little payback tonight."

He glanced at Logan dismissively. "And who is this boy?" Rudnick sneered. "Another weave patrol trainee you're leading down your treasonous path?"

"Nobody," Stern answered just before Rudnick stood and drove a fist into his gut, doubling the weave patrol veteran over.

"By the look of these swords, he isn't a nobody," a man said to Rudnick handing the protector swords to him.

"Why, you know, I think you're right considering they bear the code of arms of the exiled Chairman of Stellaran in their pommels," Rudnick said as he looked closer at the swords.

Stern turned to Logan in surprise and confusion.

"Didn't spot that yourself?" Rudnick asked with a chuckle. "You have been on patrol too long. Basic information given to every student with magical ability."

Rudnick leaned closer to Logan, scanning him up and down, trying to measure him up. "Humph," he grunted with indifference as he straightened. "How did you come by these, boy?"

"Found them," Logan said, not taking his eyes from Rudnick.

"A likely story, but you will come with us until we can be certain you have no connection to the old chairman." Rudnick motioned dismissively with his hand and the prisoners were pulled away from the fire toward the horses. "Oh, and in case you are considering to use magic to free yourself, the stone in those shackles will keep you from using your abilities."

Logan and Stern were forced to the ground and then fastened to a tree to keep them from running off.

Stern stared at Logan through the dim light provided by the distant campfire.

"What?" Logan said annoyed.

"Why didn't you tell me?" Stern answered.

"Tell you what?"

"That you are a descendant of the chairman?"

Logan glared at him and even in the darkness, Stern pulled away.

"I never even knew Caltoria existed a year ago, much less Stellaran, and you want me to know that I am a descendant of the Chairman of Stellaran? Yeah, right, that's logical."

Stern nodded, agreeing that it sounded a little unrealistic. "But the swords bear the code of arms for the chairman who was trapped on the wrong side of the weave when it went up hundreds of years ago."

Logan watched the troops around the fire, studying them. "That may be, but in Ter Chadain, the symbol in the sword's crystal on the pommel is the sign of the protector, a legendary warrior who rises to secure the throne for the true Queen of Ter Chadain." Logan turned back to him.

"That could very well be true," Stern began, but then stopped at the sight of Logan's frustrated expression. "Okay, let's say it is true. But a code of arms is passed down from generation to generation. One does not just choose a code of arms from another family. The one who created the magical spell of your protector must have been a direct descendant of the chairman."

"That sounds a bit farfetched," Logan argued.

"Answer me this," Stern said waiting for Logan to give him his attention. "Can anyone be the protector, or must they be of a certain lineage?"

Logan paused at the question, not liking the way this conversation was headed. If what Stern said was true, he not only was the Protector of Ter Chadain, but also tied to this Chairman of Stellaran. He didn't like the sound of that. His destiny filled him with turmoil in the best of times, now Stern wanted to add another layer to it.

"How can we be sure that I am this descendant of the chairman?" Logan asked.

"Only the eldest teachers of Shotwarg Cliffs have access to the prophecy that tells of this."

"Didn't Rudnick say that you and he were magical students?" Logan asked.

"Every person with magical ability attends Shotwarg Cliffs for schooling at some point in their lives," Stern confessed.

"Then how can it be secret since a person loyal to the council like Rudnick attended?"

"Upon departure from the school a spell is used to erase the location of the school from the student's memories."

"Then why does Cita know where it is?" Logan pressed.

"If the elders of the school feel a person will need to return to the school, they will leave their memory intact. This is normal for those seeking a position outside the school for the first time. Cita stayed at the school for a long time after her basic education was complete. For what reason, I do not know, but most students do not remain as long as she did."

Logan turned back to watch the men around the fire as he contemplated Cita. Something about her made him feel uncomfortable. He couldn't put his finger on it, but she wasn't like anyone he ever met before.

Logan woke the next morning as a soldier yanked him to his feet, still shackled and now sporting a rope around his waist leading to a rider on a horse. He looked over and saw Stern fastened the same way.

"We have determined that Cita and the rest of the prisoners are headed toward Shotwarg Cliffs," Rudnick said as he rode up behind them as they stood waiting to move out. The protector's swords sat fastened to the back of his saddle.

Logan and Stern exchanged concerned looks.

"Even though I would never be able to find the school itself, we can find the general location and catch up to them before they reach their destination." Rudnick observed their reactions and laughed. "I see I am right. Head out." He kicked his horse into a trot and took the lead at the head of the party.

Logan and Stern yanked into motion as the horses tightened up the slack with a snap. They walked at a quick pace heading straight for their companions. Logan and Stern could only hope that the others did as they were told and didn't wait for their return, but kept moving. If they kept a steady pace, they would reach Shotwarg Cliffs before Rudnick and his party could catch up.

Those hopes fell to the wayside about midday when a soldier rushed up to Rudnick from up ahead. He pulled his running horse up abruptly and it skittered and pranced with adrenaline.

"Spotted them," the man reported, out of breath.

"How far?" Rudnick asked.

"They have a camp a few hours ahead," the man answered. "Seem to have a broken wagon wheel they're mending."

"Perfect," Rudnick said with a grin. He spun in his saddle and smiled at Logan and Stern. "You see, it will be a quick chase after all." He turned to the men holding Logan's and Stern's ropes. "Follow at a normal pace. By the time you catch up we will have the others either captive or killed."

"What about their magic?" one of the men spoke up, obviously nervous.

"The stone in their shackles prevents them from using it. Keep them moving and you should be fine." Rudnick gave them a stern nod and kicked his horse into motion as the rest of the party followed after, racing out of sight.

The two men nudged their horses into an easy walk, slower than the pace before which kept the ropes between the prisoners and the horses leading them less taut.

Looking at the slack rope in front of him, an idea came to Logan. He stared at Stern until the man looked over. With an expression and a nod, he assured that Stern knew to pay attention.

Logan watched the rise and fall of the road as well as the land adjacent to it. When he found the suitable rise in the side of the road with a dip in the trail, he burst into action. Logan sprang into a dead run, racing up the hill on the side of the road and past the horse leading him. Once ahead of the rider, he jumped, throwing the rope high and dove across both horses as they marched side-by-side and rolled on the far side of the trail. Coming to his feet, he slipped behind a stout tree and braced his legs against the trunk.

The rope, high enough to clear the heads of their mounts, tightened in front of the riders, knocking them from their saddles where Stern stood ready. He kicked the first rider in the head, spinning him to land dizzy in the dirt. The second rider hurried to his feet causing Stern's kick in his direction to miss the mark. The soldier drew his sword and struck at him, but Logan dove between them, sending the soldier plunging over backwards, the blade striking flat across Logan's back.

Logan tried to advance on the soldier as he struggled to right himself only to find the rope connecting him to the horse tightened around the tree, stopping him dead.

Stern raced to the soldier, kicking him in the ribs and then the head, but the man managed to regain his feet and advance on Stern as the weave patrolman backed away.

Stern backed toward Logan allowing him to rejoin the fight. Logan dove for the soldier's feet and sent him toppling over him which allowed Stern one last strike with a boot at his head, sending a sickening crack echoing through the forest.

Stern dropped to the ground next to Logan as the two lay gasping for air.

After catching their breath, they found the keys in the soldier's pockets, unlocked each other's shackles, and raced after Rudnick and the others.

They crested a ridge when they spotted the wagon, quilled with arrows and the entire party hunkered down behind it.

Rudnick's patrol sat on the ridge below where Logan and Stern observed them, sending arrows toward the wagon sporadically.

"Save them until we can get closer," Rudnick ordered.

Logan watched, confused as to why the men didn't just charge the bowless defenders when Linell stepped from behind the wagon and released a ball of fire hurtling toward the men on the ridge, sending them scurrying for cover.

Logan smiled at the much smaller party's standoff with the patrol. Even better armed, the patrol still couldn't match the magic wielded by the Caltorians.

"What now?" Stern asked, staring at the standoff below them.

"We give our friends the edge," Logan grinned and pulled the metal rod from the sheath on his leg. The rod extended to a bow with a snap and he pulled back the string as a silver arrow magically appeared. He let the first arrow fly, striking the man next to Rudnick in the back as he crouched next to his leader.

Rudnick spun in shock to see a barrage of arrows hitting his troops, one after another, with the precision of a surgeon removing a tumor. He spotted Logan on the ridge with Stern next to him and ran for his horse, but Logan sent a volley of arrows that kept him from his mount.

In a panic, Rudnick ran to his closest man as he attempted to climb into his saddle. Rudnick pulled the man backward just as an arrow meant for him struck the man in the chest. He leapt into the saddle and raced off with the few remaining survivors following after. Most of those men didn't last long enough to get out of range of Logan's bow and fell to the canyon floor leaving Rudnick and a mere handful of his patrol fleeing back toward the weave patrol headquarters, away from Shotwarg Cliffs.

Logan rode down to the dead troops and retrieved his swords still fastened behind the saddle of Rudnick's mount. After slipping them on, he glanced to Stern who stared at the weapons curiously, and decided not to bother covering them with a cloak anymore. It seemed that keeping his secret and the importance of the crest in the pommels was no longer an option for him. He feared that tonight around the fire his identity and anything tying him to his destiny in Stellaran would soon be shared with all.

As they rode to the wagon, the children ran over to greet him, but the others huddled around someone on the ground. To his dismay, Zeva lay on the ground, an arrow jutting from her side. Beside her, Cita sat with an arrow in her leg. Both women, though in pain, seemed more irritated than anything else.

"I told her to stay back," Cita said as Logan and Stern dismounted and came over.

"They had already shot you and you couldn't concentrate long enough to weave any protection," Zeva said and then sucked air between her teeth as Fedlen pulled the arrow from her stomach.

Linell knelt beside her and Logan watched as magic hovered

over her and then eased into the open wound.

Zeva sighed as the magic worked and she laid her head back, closing her eyes as the magic took hold.

"She should sleep for a few hours to make sure the healing is complete," Linell said.

"We'll put her in the wagon," Bethany said from behind them and stepped through with the other children behind her. They carefully cradled Zeva in their arms and stepped around to set her gently in the back of the wagon.

"Now you," Linell said moving closer to Cita.

"Oh, no, I can't afford to be asleep for a few hours," Cita protested.

"I will just close the wound and make sure there is no infection," Linell promised.

Cita nodded and let her proceed. Fedlen stepped close to pull the arrow free and then moved aside for Linell to do her work.

Cita looked up at Stern and then to Logan. "Where have you been? You both look terrible."

"Nice to see you too," Stern said with a grin.

"What made Rudnick take off so fast?" Cita's eyes caught the swords jutting over Logan's back, the first time she had a chance to see them this closely and uncovered. Her eyes opened wide and her mouth gaped.

"What are those?" She asked, gasping when Linell's magic entered her wound.

"Something we need to discuss," Stern said.

"But if he is the heir to the chairman, then he brought down the weave?" Cita tried to wrap her head around the idea.

"How would you know that?" Logan asked, instantly regretting it.

"It is prophecy," Cita said. "A prophecy that only a few in Stellaran know and definitely no one from Caltoria would know."

"You are the only one who could bring the weave down and

now you are the only one who can fulfill the prophecy to save us all," Cita said, her words coming out airy as if saying it louder might make it not true.

"Great," Logan moaned. "Another prophecy I need to deal with. Don't I have enough already?"

"I guess not," Stern said with a shrug.

Chapter 24

Teah rode down the winding path with dense forest bordering either side. Her mind wandered as she bounced up and down in the saddle letting the horse pick a path through the rutted trail. She missed Logan. Thought she lost him for the longest time, but now held out hope that Saliday and Machala might find him alive and well. She nodded curtly to herself. Alive would do. Well, she could take it or leave it as long as he still lived.

The path proved too narrow for more than one horse at a time and she led the others, to their dismay and emphatic protest that her leading put her in too much danger. But queen apparent or not, she possessed the best abilities for leading them and they could not articulate to the contrary, so she now rode at point and scanned the surroundings.

The tunnel-like path flanked by towering trees seemed to stretch on forever before her. She lifted in her saddle and peered back from where they rode from and then turned back to the front, frowning at the reality that this path seemed to bear no beginning or ending. She lifted her hand and the company pulled their mounts to a stop. She dismounted and strode back to the others as they pulled their horses up tightly to each other so all could hear.

"How long do these woods go on for?"

"This is almost as densely forested at Treebridge," Grinwald answered her.

Teah looked at him, unimpressed. "I grew up next to Treebridge," she said crossing her arms over her chest. "I want to be rid of this path as soon as possible. It feels as though we're being watched." She scanned the trees as if expecting to find someone lurking there, but found no obvious signs of anyone or anything.

The others also looked around at her comments, but then turned back to her having seen no evidence of followers either.

"These woods are said to have eyes," Rachel said drawing their attention. She sat in her saddle with her arms wrapped around her as if trying to calm her nerves. Her eyes stared wide at them and back at the imposing forest.

"Rubbish," Raven said. "Do you wish me to take point for a while?"

"You have even less experience on horseback than I do," Teah pointed out.

"True, but…" Raven began to protest.

"I'll do it," Caslor said.

"You?" Raven guffawed.

"I am trained to ride as well as fight from the saddle," Caslor defended, patting his small sword on his hip.

"That will do you little good against an archer," Raven argued.

"None of us are protected from the archer's arrow in this shooting gallery," Teah said.

"We can do something about that if we feel it is warranted," Grinwald offered.

"What do you mean?" Teah asked.

"We can combine our magic and put a barrier against the arrow, if they come, but there is a danger to doing this," Grinwald explained.

Teah nodded her understanding even before Grinwald finished. "There are those that can detect our magic weaves if we were to put them around us."

"Exactly," the Viri Magus agreed.

"I feel stealth is our best weapon right now," Teah said. "If they detect us, they will send vast numbers after us. We are safer to avoid detection at all cost than to defend ourselves against a potential discovery."

They fell silent, digesting the decision, and nodding one by one as they realized her way was best.

"I'll take point," Caslor said and rode past Teah to stop ahead

214

of her waiting mount.

"I will cover him," Teah said taking the rod from its sheath and letting it expand to a bow. She strode to her horse and leapt into the saddle. With a nod to Caslor, the company started off again.

They rode a short distance down the trail and an arrow hit Caslor in the chest, sending him toppling from his horse.

Teah found the archer in a tree and sent a silver arrow through his chest propelling him backwards out of the tree and crashing to the forest floor. She leapt from her horse still scanning the surroundings with the bow, string held firmly against her cheek and an arrow notched in the silver strand.

She crept up on Caslor, loosing an arrow into the trees with a thrum of her string and sending another assailant tumbling to the ground. The bow shrunk into the rod of steel and she deftly slipped it into the sheath as she crouched to tend to Caslor as the others hurriedly gathered around.

The arrow protruded out of his right chest, just missing his heart as he lay gasping for air, blood coming out in vaporized droplets with each exhale.

"It hit his lung," Teah said as the others huddled closer, Raven looked up, scanning for threats every so often.

Teah glanced to Grinwald as he released a green weave that floated over Caslor and then narrowed to slip along the shaft into his chest.

Caslor arched his back in pain as he gasped one last time and then passed out. His head slumped to the ground and his face went slack.

Teah reached her power into him, searching for injuries as Grinwald pulled the arrow free and sent another weave into the wound to mend the torn flesh.

Teah ignored Grinwald's efforts and searched deeper, following the slicing path of the broad head as it drove deeper into pink tissue. She paused as an artery pumped blood into the lung with every beat of Caslor's heart. The nick tiny in comparison to the initial wound, but large enough to cause the boy to bleed out in a matter of days if unattended to. She sent a weave of magic into the breach and wove the tissue together. She leaned back from her hovering as Raven cried out.

They spun to see a large party bearing down on them from the rear, scarlet uniforms ruffling and Englewood's banner flying over them as they rode.

Teah and Grinwald lifted the unconscious Caslor across his saddle and raced for their mounts as Raven unleashed a weave of air that rolled down the trail and struck the advancing troops. Men and horses flew into the forest as the weave bowled them over.

Teah kicked her horse into motion, holding tight to the reins of Caslor's and raced down the trail. She crouched against the neck of her mount as arrows flew overhead. She lifted her eyes to see a clearing ahead and urged her horse faster looking to get clear of the confined trail that hindered their maneuvering and left them exposed.

As they broke into the clearing, she knew instantly that her hopes of breaking free were dashed as the twang of a chorus of bowstrings greeted them and a shower of arrows rose into the sky arching above and then turning and plummeting down upon them.

Teah reacted reflexively as she threw up her hands over her head pausing only to glance behind her in assurance that the others remained close. Her mind registered their tight formation and she released the magic through her hands into the sky above. A weave of air and fire rose from her hands as heat rising from hot cobblestone. When the arrows and the magical weave met, the weave continued burning upward through the barrage of arrows, leaving only ash and broad heads behind to drop to the ground around Teah and her party.

Teah pushed her horse forward even as she extended her arms and sent another weave from her hands in the vicinity of the archers on the hillsides.

Cries of agony rose from the archers as Teah's magic hit them, burning and scorching them and the surrounding hillside as it rolled over them.

Grinwald, Rachel, and Raven turned their magic on the horsemen to their rear, sending them scattering and then diving from their mounts, seeking cover.

The narrow valley clearing raced past them as they pushed their horses to keep up with Teah and Caslor.

As they reached the far end of the valley which broke between two large hills, Teah slowed to let the others pass and take a hard turn in the trail that led them away from the troops. The others raced past and Teah kicked her horse as her ears picked up the faintest sound of a bowstring thrum. Her body lurched to one side as the arrow struck and pain erupted in her hip.

She held on with all her strength to the reins and grasped at the saddle for support as she looked down to see an arrow protruding from her hip, only a broad head width below her invisible chain mail. Gritting her teeth against the pain, she kicked her horse again and raced after the others with Caslor in tow.

Teah followed the others until dark when they pulled up and felt certain that the troops now lay far behind them. As she rode up to the others, she slumped across the neck of her horse and gasped for air trying to keep the pain from causing her to black out as it nearly did several times along the ride.

Grinwald and Raven took an unconscious Caslor from his saddle and laid him gently on the grass growing alongside the trail.

Rachel came up to Teah in the dimming light and stopped in shock, a hand to her mouth as she stared wide-eyed at the arrow protruding from Teah's side.

"Grinwald," she shouted as Teah slipped from her saddle into Rachel's arms. Rachel lowered her to the ground, cradling Teah in her arms.

Grinwald hurried to them and crouched next to Teah.

"Why didn't you stop us?" Grinwald scolded.

"We needed to get clear," Teah said drawing a hissing breath through her teeth as the Viri Magus touched the arrow to see the damage.

"It may be stuck in your hip socket," Grinwald informed her.

"I can't move my leg." Teah fought to speak through the pain.

"I need you to rest," Grinwald said.

Teah stared back at the Viri Magus hard, knowing what he meant. "I can't rest now; it will put everyone in jeopardy."

"It is the only way I can be sure I heal everything. I will need Raven and Rachel to help me as well."

"No, I will stay awake," Teah insisted.

"I don't doubt your resolve," Grinwald said. "But I guarantee if you don't let me put you to sleep, you will pass out from the pain anyway."

Teah held the man's gaze for a moment and conceded with a nod.

Grinwald passed his hands over Teah's face sending a calming weave into her as she closed her eyes and slept.

****

When Teah eased her eyes open, her side noticeably ached, but she felt rested and alert. But as she sat up, it became far too clear that something was off. She moved her leg and sighed in relief as it moved under her command, but then she reached down and touched her leg below her injury and panic filled her. Her hand felt her leg under her hand, but she felt nothing in her leg. She struck her leg in the thigh, her calf, and finally her foot. Tears welled up in her eyes. Not because her blows, which increased in intensity with each strike hurt her, but because they didn't. She felt nothing.

218

Caslor sat a short distance away, his eyes watching her as her gaze lifted to him. The sorrow in his eyes said it all. He knew what she lamented over and he couldn't do anything to fix it.

"What?" Teah said in a hush.

"Grinwald said the arrow struck the nerve in your hip along with chipping bone. The combination made it difficult to save your entire leg and impossible to save the nerve after it was shredded." Caslor spoke softly, but firmly, trying to assure Teah that all would be well.

Teah stared down at her leg as if it was some sort of foreign growth she couldn't be rid of. She stood and staggered a bit, trying to balance on one good leg and an unfeeling appendage lacking any sort of feedback. She fell to the ground and didn't move.

Caslor hurried to her and touched her quaking shoulders to gently roll her into his arms.

"It will be alright," he said as he pressed his lips to her forehead.

Teah didn't respond, but continued to cry silently into his chest as he held her.

Chapter 25

Logan and his party sat around their fire as darkness thickened around them. They looked up expectantly as Linell stepped into the firelight.

"The children are asleep in the wagon," she said taking a seat.

"It was an intense day," Zeva said. The color slowly returning to her features as Linell's healing continued to work.

"Tell me about it," Logan said with a moan.

No one yet spoke of the revelation as to Logan's identity and the new insights into his destiny in Stellaran, but Cita sat straighter as she came out of her thoughts when Logan spoke and regarded him.

"We now have some insight into the council's plans though," Cita said.

"And what would that be?" Trevon asked.

"There is a prophecy pertaining to the return of the Chairman to Stellaran. That is why Rudnick and the council are looking for him so fervently."

Logan moaned and Zeva stifled a laugh.

"What's so funny?" Stern said, obviously insulted by their doubt of the prophecy.

"Logan has a prophecy that seems to follow him everywhere," Zeva said and then went silent as her eyes met Logan's warning stare.

"What kind of prophecy?" Trevon asked.

"It's nothing," Logan said trying to pass it off.

"Listen, if we're going to figure this out, you need to tell us of other prophecies that pertain to you," Trevon pressed.

"It isn't as ominous as it sounds," Logan said with a shrug.

"Please," Cita said.

Logan met the weave patroller's gaze and stared into her eyes. He nodded slowly in thought as he tried to break eye contact, but instead of pulling away, he found himself slipping deeper and started to speak.

"Just before my sixteenth birthday I was informed of my destiny to kill the King of Ter Chadain and place my sister upon the throne as queen," he said still holding Cita's gaze. Her eyes widened slightly, but she didn't look away.

"Then he came to Caltoria and fulfilled the prophecy that stated a brother and sister from a distant land would free the slaves of Caltoria," Zeva said, repeating an old ancient prophecy known by the slaves of Caltoria and ignored by all others.

Cita still stared into Logan's eyes, even as the others turned and shared amazed looks.

"And did he?" Trevon asked. "Did he free the slaves?"

"Yes," Zeva said raising gasps from those around the fire except for Logan and Cita locked in their stare.

"If Logan is truly the heir of the chairman," Stern explained, "he would have needed to do something nearly impossible."

"And what is that?" Trevon asked.

"The heir to the chairman will destroy the weave of protection," Cita said still in a trance-like state with Logan. "And return to Stellaran to take his rightful place as king of all he sees."

"King?" Trevon cried out in shock. "No one said anything about a king."

"That is what our prophecy says," Stern reiterated. "But surely this man, this very young man at that, could never have destroyed the weave of protection."

"And why is that?" Zeva asked.

"Because in order to destroy the weave, he would need to destroy a source stone and that is impossible," Stern said confidently.

"But that is exactly what he did," Zeva insisted.

"Impossible," Stern said unconvinced.

Logan still stared at Cita and her at him.

"It is true," Cita said. "Logan is the first King of Stellaran in over a thousand years."

"No, this can't be happening," Trevon groaned as his plans took a bad turn. "I needed a chairman to reinstate the bloodlines lost on the wrong side of the weave to the council. Not a king to rule over us as the empress has."

Logan backhanded Trevon so hard it sent him tumbling. Though he looked away from Cita, he felt her eyes on him still.

"I will never be compared to that vile empress again," Logan said as Fedlen began to draw his blade.

Linell reached over and pushed her hand down upon Fedlen's hand, staying his movement.

"There is only one way to be certain he is who he claims," Stern pointed out.

"I claim nothing," Logan said, feeling his life spinning out of his control again and not liking it one bit.

"The new king is said to be marked with the Lassain crest," Stern continued.

"And what would that be?" Zeva asked.

Logan cringed even before Stern spoke, afraid he already knew what he would say.

"A silver crown over crossed silver swords," Stern said.

"And where is this marking to be?" Zeva asked, feeling her emotions race as she already knew Logan bore the mark on his left breast.

"Over his left breast," Stern finished.

"This is absurd," Logan said standing and backing away from the fire as Trevon stepped back into the firelight rubbing his sore chin.

"It is him," Cita said confidently.

Logan spun to see her still looking at him, sure that she never turned away from him this entire time. She stood and walked over to stand before him, looking him in the eye, nearly his same height.

"Please," she whispered. "Let me see it."

Logan stared at her, his promise to himself to no longer be the protector and kill others lost in his need to escape Port Shoal, but if he divulged his identity to these people, he would certainly never be able to lay down the gauntlet of the protector now that he knew it melded seamlessly with his new destiny to be King of Stellaran.

Cita gently unbuttoned his shirt and slipped it open exposing his left breast. The symbol of the protector shimmered magically in the firelight as the others, including Zeva who already knew it to be there, gasped.

Cita touched the tattoo, sliding her finger across the smooth metallic surface. She looked into his eyes and something surged in him, something he hadn't felt in nearly two years when he dressed in the same room as Saliday in preparation to meet the Betra Council in Courage. That day seemed so far away and long ago.

****

Cita felt it too. She eased in closer to him as she examined the tattoo. She lifted her eyes to his and their lips brushed. In that instant, no one else mattered but Logan as she lost herself in him, her lips reaching for his, finding them as hungry for hers as hers were for his. She didn't know how long they kissed, but it felt to go on forever and that was what she wanted, what she needed. His lips were all that sustained her, kept her breathing, and kept her alive.

When they finally eased apart, the campsite echoed an awkward silence. She looked up at Logan, his eyes still closed as she knew hers were only a moment before, overwhelmed by passion and ecstasy.

She felt her face flush as she turned and raced into the darkness.

****

When Cita's lips touched his, Logan felt himself swept away to a place he may have dreamt of, but never dared hope for. His feelings clouded his mind like a river sweeping away a village in a flash flood. He felt as though he might drown with the pure pleasure of it, but wanted, no needed more, more, more. He knew he would never get enough to satisfy his need, but he pressed on, filling that empty space one very special woman had held control over and torn out to let wither and die.

Then it was over. As quickly as it began, it was over nearly as soon. He stood with his eyes closed, almost afraid to open them to see Saliday in front of him, knowing she belonged to another, but instead, he saw Cita race off into the darkness beyond the firelight, leaving him behind to bear the embarrassment alone in front of Zeva and his new companions.

He managed a weak smile, a nod, and a grunt before hurrying off toward their wagon and the relative safety of the innocent children sleeping inside.

He sat leaning against the wagon wheel when Zeva walked up in the darkness, the glow of the campfire backlighting her approach. He felt relieved she couldn't see his face as the heat from embarrassment told him his cheeks flushed.

Zeva sat down next to him, not turning her head but looking back at the glow from the fire.

"You deserve happiness," she told him.

He didn't turn to her but stared ahead.

"Even a hero needs someone to love and who loves him back," she continued.

"I don't want to hurt her," Logan said.

"From what Teah told me, you might have fears of being hurt yourself."

"That was a long time ago."

"Those kinds of scars don't heal so quickly, but you need to allow yourself to feel."

"But I cause so much death and suffering," Logan turned to Zeva and found her looking at him. Even though the darkness hid her eyes, he felt them upon him.

"But you also have done many good things. Don't diminish that."

"Why does it have to be like this?"

"Prophecy and heroes don't happen without a reason. You need to realize that what you do is for the greater good."

"Damn prophecy. Who is to say that one ruler is better than another?"

"You are doing what needs to be done."

"Tell that to the soldier who is doing his duty to protect his country and king, as he lay dying by my sword or with my arrow in him. Tell his widow and orphaned children that he died because he was on the wrong side of the battle between right and wrong. What gives us the right to declare our side the right side?"

Zeva sat in the silent darkness not turning her head but staring at him.

"What brought you back to being the protector in Port Shoal should resound inside of you and keep you going."

"And what is that?"

"That you choose to survive and will kill in order to ensure that survival," Zeva said.

"That is self-preservation..." Logan started but she cut him off.

"But you choose to kill those who would harm those you care about, or harm innocent people. I don't see the empress's troops leaving innocent people alone, do you?"

Logan shook his head.

"And this council, they sent that nasty little man, Rudnick, to extract information from Caltorians who just wished to return to their homeland."

Logan turned to stare at the fire again.

"Let us not forget the Red Tips and their massacre of those unarmed people from the Sacred City; Trevon's, Linell's, and Fedlen's family and friends. Would you do anything like that?" She stared at him hard in the darkness and he turned to her again.

"No, no I would not."

"Then stop whining about being the protector and do what needs to be done. Keep lamenting over the lives you need to end, that is honorable, but you need to realize that their deaths are the high cost paid for freedom." She stood and stepped around the back of the wagon to climb in and lay down to sleep.

Logan looked deeply into the fire as the faces of his lost loved ones appeared before his eyes. His parents and sister, everyone who raised a sword to defend him, the people who aided him in Stone Town and died at Empress Shakata's command, and...his thoughts caught as a lump formed in his throat, the image of Sasha, her rare but endearing smile tugging a smile from his lips, tears forming in his eyes. She sacrificed her life for his. She sacrificed to ensure he continued on his path to fulfill his destiny. Who was he to ignore that destiny and lessen her sacrifice for him?

He wiped a tear from his cheek and gave a nod. He couldn't question his duty as protector again. He owed that to Sasha and he could never dishonor her memory like that. He pulled his cloak around him and curled up by the wheel, the bulge of his swords digging into his back strangely gave him comfort as he drifted to sleep.

They rose early the next morning, eager to be on the trail to Shotwarg Cliffs. Logan felt a growing sense of urgency to get the children to the safety of the school and out of harm's way.

An awkward silence fell over the group as Cita led the way and Logan chose to ride in the back behind the wagon. Even the children sensed the change in the mood of their group, looking to each other in confusion.

As they crested a rise the forest gave way to open prairie and in the distance a large butte rose above the flat surrounding landscape.

Cita stopped as the others rode up to her and spread out along the rise to stare out at the wide expanse.

"Shotwarg Cliffs," Cita said.

"This was so mysterious to find?" Linell asked. "It is sticking out like a beacon."

"It is not the butte that is hard to find, but the school it conceals," Stern said.

"Only a few know the way in," Cita explained.

"But if all magicals go to the school for training, how is it such a secret?" Trevon asked.

"Didn't Stern go to the school as well?" Fedlen added.

"I did, but once you leave the school behind, its location is wiped clean from your memory," Stern said.

"Then how is it that Cita still remembers?" Zeva asked the obvious question.

"I am one of a few who still retain the memory of Shotwarg Cliffs's entrance since they expected me to return," Cita said looking at Logan for the first time that morning.

"You mean to deliver me to them as written in some sort of prophecy?" Logan concluded.

"Yes," Cita said with a nod and lowered her eyes as if ashamed to admit it. "I hold a place in the rebellion that charged me with finding you and bringing you here."

Everyone joined Stern in staring at Cita in shock, everyone except for Logan. He smiled warmly, happy to know that Cita didn't choose to lie to him about her mission.

"Then we should get me and the children there so the next step can be taken," Logan said and kicked his horse into motion down

227

the rise.

Cita and the others followed after as the sun loomed high in the deep blue cloudless sky above them.

Cita let her horse catch up with Logan and rode at his side for a moment without looking at him. He glanced her way and a smile curled the edges of his lips at the memory of their passionate kiss.

She looked up at him, their eyes locked, and he knew she held the same thoughts in her mind as well. They both bowed their heads turning away as heat rushed to their faces.

"About last night," Logan started as her eyes lifted to his once more.

"Yeah, stupid," Cita blurted out.

"Totally," Logan eagerly agreed.

"Impulsive," Cita added.

"Completely," Logan concurred.

"So we agree we shouldn't let it get in the way of our mission," Cita said flatly.

"I agree," Logan said holding her gaze. He saw the light behind her eyes dim. "But I'm glad we kissed."

Cita's face lit up as she lifted her chin to stare over at him. "You are?"

"You have made me feel something I thought I would never feel again."

"I did?"

"We shouldn't let it interfere with our goals, but I ignored my feelings for someone very special because of what I believed to be my destiny, and I won't do it again."

Cita stared at him with her mouth gaping.

"Unless you didn't feel what I felt?" Logan asked, his eyes begging her to not break his heart.

"No," she said letting herself get lost in those eyes as they turned sad and she realized he didn't understand. "I mean, no, I felt it...did I ever," she added and then blushed at having said too much.

"So we keep it under control until we finish our mission," Logan stated.

"Agreed," Cita said with a nod, and then turned back to him with a curious look on her face. "What is under control?"

"I guess we'll need to play that by ear," Logan said and then glanced back to acknowledge Zeva riding up, still obviously tender from her injury.

"If you two don't stop your flirting up here you're going to make us all sick," Zeva said, amused by the embarrassed reactions from Cita and Logan. "Plus the children are asking questions none of us are willing to answer right now.

Logan looked over his shoulder at the wagon as the children watched him intently. He turned away with a nod. "Got it."

Zeva let her horse drop back into the group leaving Logan and Cita at the front by themselves again. They rode on in silence as the day went on, until in the distance hanging over the butte, a large thunderhead, black and ominous rolled toward them. The deep thrumming of thunder came to their ears as the ground shook beneath them.

Cita frowned as she surveyed the sky and then scanned the barren scruff surrounding them on the open prairie and shook her head.

Stern rode up next to her and gave a nod at the storm ahead. "We have to find some cover," his face showed his obvious duress over the approaching storm.

"Any suggestions?" Cita asked gesturing with her hand at the vast emptiness around them.

He stared ahead again at the black cloud, as expansive as the butte, rolled their way spewing lightning strikes that erupted into the prairie ahead and a black wall of rain stretching to the earth. "This is not good," Stern moaned.

"It's only a storm," Logan said, not looking forward to getting soaked, but not as upset as his companions.

"You must not get these storms in Ter Chadain," Stern said.

"Sure we do. Thunderstorms are very common," Logan replied.

"These are magical thunderstorms," Cita pointed out.

Logan turned and motioned Zeva to come closer. She kicked her horse and it trotted up to where they walked their horses ahead.

"Have you seen magical thunderstorms before?" Logan asked her as she pulled alongside of him.

"Not magical thunderstorms," Zeva answered. "What makes them magical?"

"These storms are a release of magic that has built up in the atmosphere," Cita explained. "Kind of like a discharge of pent of energy."

"So we just let it pass?" Logan asked.

"If we didn't possess magic, that would be the case, but since we do, we are in grave danger," Stern said.

"How do you mean?" Zeva asked.

"The lightning strikes randomly as it crosses the prairie ahead of us, but if there is someone with magic caught in the storm, the lightning will strike the greatest source of magic in the area," Cita explained.

"That could be any one of us," Zeva pointed out.

"Or all of us if we are standing too close together," Stern said.

"There is a rise up ahead, maybe we can seek shelter on the side away from the storm," Logan suggested.

Cita and Stern shared concerned stares for a moment and then nodded.

"Tell the others about the storm and keep the children close," Logan told Zeva.

"No," Cita said stopping Zeva and turning her in her saddle. "Tell the children to wait under the wagon here until the storm passes."

Logan looked questioningly at Cita.

"They have little or no magic, they are safer away from us," Cita said.

"Then we are safer to split up," Logan suggested.

"No, that will only give more targets to strike," Stern disagreed. "If we are closer to each other, it might hit one of us out of the group, but if we split up, it will strike each of us since we are the most magical thing in the surrounding area."

Zeva held Logan's gaze for a moment until he gave her a nod and she rode off to tell the others.

The storm advanced on them quickly and they reached the ridge as light rain began to fall. Logan leapt from his horse and started digging into the side of the ridge, the soft prairie dirt flying out behind him as he dug. He soon opened a large enough hole for him to crouch down in. He took his belongings and tucked them under him and swatted his horse on the rump, sending it racing away from the approaching storm.

The others did likewise a short distance from one another.

Logan glanced back toward the children to see Fedlen with them sitting nervously under the wagon.

They all hunkered down in the holes and waited as the thunder boomed deafening overhead. The rain pelted them in walls and lightning struck the ground around them.

Logan lifted his head trying to see if any strikes hit his counterparts and that was when his head erupted in pain and his eyes saw nothing but white. He shook his head to clear his sight as it came back in a blurry swirl showing him that he lay nearly twenty paces from his makeshift shelter.

The others lifted their heads out of their holes as an image of the prairie rodents from Tumbleweed Plain ran through his mind from when he was a child. He thought to laugh, but the looks on their faces proved too much to keep his amusing thought clear in his mind. Terror etched each of their faces as Logan realized his body smoked from the lightning strike.

He rolled from his back to his hands and knees when the next lightning struck sending him careening across the ground, bouncing and tumbling as pain erupted through his body, reaching into every limb and appendage. He slid to a stop halfway between the ridge and the wagon. Smoke rose from his body as he coughed in an attempt to rid his lungs of the dust and dirt he inhaled as he struck the ground. Another strike sent him rolling closer to the wagon and the terrified children screaming at the sight of him being tossed around by the lightning made him realize that if he allowed himself to continue on this course, he would put the children in danger.

He struggled to his feet, his swords feeling like lead weights upon his back. He reached back clasping each handle and did the only thing he could think of and drew his swords. Holding them out before him, he crossed the blades and lifted them to the sky as the next strike burst from the clouds.

The electricity hit the metal blades, ran down their length and entered the handles. The crystal balls with the protector's symbols in them shone white as the energy grew inside of them. But that was where the lightning ended. The force of the blast slid Logan along the prairie floor as his feet dug in to keep his balance, but he still stood as the strike ended.

Logan's arms ached and his head pounded, but he stood tall as he met the next strike and then the next and the next as the storm threw its fury at him. A deafening boom of thunder followed each strike, one after the other and Logan stood with his swords crossed before him taking the force but holding his ground.

Its wrath finally spent, the storm began breaking up, dissipating as quickly as it had formed, giving way to blue skies once more.

Logan stood for a moment longer as the sky opened above him

and then fell face-first to the ground, his arms dropping lifeless to his sides just as he hit the ground sending the energy dried dirt billowing around him. Blackness greeted him before the ground did as his eyes rolled back into his head and he lost consciousness.

Chapter 26

Teah tried pushing Caslor away as he tried helping her into the saddle only after a long argument over if they should rest longer or move out.

She understood Caslor's thinking, but their destination still laid a far ways off and the king's troops still pursued them. After staring him down she hobbled to her horse and pulled herself up into the saddle, grimacing in pain as her hip refused to cooperate. She wondered at the pain radiating through her limb when all other sensations in her leg remained absent. Waiting a moment for the others to mount up, she kicked her mount with her good leg sending it trotting off.

Her party exchanged worried looks and then hurried after her in silence, unsure how to proceed with her in her current condition.

Everyone rode in silence, deep in their own thoughts, but Grinwald seemed to be taking it the hardest, disappointed in his healing of her. He rode in sullen silence with his head down and shoulders hunched.

After riding hard and steady all morning, Teah pulled up at a small stream to let her horse drink. She slid from the mount and dropped to a knee when her damaged leg didn't support her.

Caslor hurried to her side, but she lifted herself up against her horse and extended a hand to stop him before he reached her.

"I've got it," she said, fighting back the pain with effort.

"Why do you have to be so stubborn?" he mumbled.

"Because it's the only thing keeping me going," Teah said and hobbled to the stream. She dropped down to her knees and cupped water in her hands, raising them to her mouth and drank.

Caslor stood and watched as the others led their horses to the stream and let the animals drink.

Teah stiffly rose to her feet and stumbled as she took a step falling into Caslor's arms. She leaned back glaring at him, the determination simmering behind the deep blue orbs filled with pain.

"I told you I've…" she protested but Caslor cut her off with a fiery kiss. She fought it at first then gave in as he pressed further. She soon became a willing participant and met his passion with her own. When they pulled apart, she stared at him with a wanting that made him shiver.

"You need to let me help until you get your strength back," Caslor said.

"Why do you fight me so much," she said her tone sensual voice sounded hoarse.

"Because only a son of an empress can match the thick headedness of a queen."

"I think you may be pressing your luck." She raised an eyebrow teasingly.

"If I get kisses like that when I do, I will continue to press my luck," Caslor said with a grin.

She laughed, surprising herself, and then wrapped her arms around his neck again and kissed him deeply, but this time she didn't let her passion take control. She pulled away and turned to see the others milling uncomfortably nearby.

"What do we do now?" Rachel asked after they drew apart.

"We continue to Ceait," Teah answered.

"But now that your leg…" Raven began but couldn't finish.

"My leg is just an inconvenience, nothing more. Our mission is the same," Teah said, studying each of them. When she reached Grinwald, she exploded. "Get that look off your face," she shouted.

"But I couldn't heal it completely," Grinwald said, his normally sure demeanor wavering uncharacteristically.

"You saved my life and didn't have to cut off my leg," Teah said. "I'd say you did wonderfully."

"The bone chips injured so much that when I tried to heal the nerves, there was nothing to repair," Grinwald explained.

"I don't want to hear any more of it. You saved me and I can walk. In time, I hope to walk better."

They stood looking at her, uncertain if they should believe her or not.

"Can you do something for the pain?" she asked.

Grinwald's eyes shot wide at her request and he grinned with delight. "You have pain?"

"Don't be so happy about it," Teah grumbled.

"I'm ecstatic about it," Grinwald beamed. "It means that your nerves aren't completely destroyed."

"So you're happy you saved the painful ones?" Teah growled.

"This is a good sign, Teah. It means you may be able to recover from this," Grinwald said, his spirits buoyed.

Teah held Grinwald's optimistic stare and smiled at the possibility. Her smile turned to a grimace as she pulled the weight she let down on her injured back to her good leg.

"It will take time," Caslor assured her.

"We don't have much time," Teah pointed out and hoisted herself up into her saddle again. She tugged on the reins turning her mount's head around and nudged the horse's side with her good leg, sending it into a trot once more.

The others scurried to their horses and joined her as she headed for Ceait again.

A thought crossed her mind as she rode, one that sent a chill down her back. What if they arrived too late and the houses of magic had already succumbed to the king's forces? The thought of Ter Chadain becoming like Caltoria where those with magic were persecuted or enslaved terrified her. As it should worry every person with an ounce of magic in them.

Teah stopped on the ridge and stared down at the town below as the others rode up next to her.

"Troinka." Grinwald identified the town for her.

The sun crept below the horizon behind them and the valley below began to flicker with twinkling lights as the townspeople lit candles in their homes and streetlights lining the thoroughfares.

"It sure will feel good to sleep in a bed," Rachel said longingly.

"It will, but not tonight," Teah said bringing a moan from Rachel and the incredulous stares from the others.

"But we haven't seen anyone all day and a warm meal will go a long way in energizing us for the arduous road ahead," Grinwald protested.

"But if King Aston has men looking for us, there are sure to be others who seek us as well," Teah pointed out.

"Bounty hunters," Raven groaned.

"And most of them will be looking to kill us without question," Grinwald agreed.

"So?" Teah asked waiting for them to agree with her decision.

"We bypass Troinka and continue on," Caslor replied.

"Dead Lake is on the other side of Troinka, we can make camp there tonight," Grinwald said.

"Dead Lake? I don't like the sound of that," Rachel complained.

"It is the site of one of the greatest battles between Ter Chadain and Caltorian forces early in the history of Ter Chadain, shortly after Queen Tera arrived in Ter Chadain," Grinwald said.

"It is said that nearly ten thousand men lost their lives at Dead Lake," Caslor said causing everyone to turn to him in surprise. "What, you don't think we have studied great battles of our country?"

"I guess," Teah agreed.

"The lake actually was no more than a large, deep valley where the battle raged for days," Grinwald explained. "Until Tera unleashed a spell rerouting a river to the valley, flooding it and destroying the invading Caltorian army."

"It is said that she also killed more than a thousand of her own men," Caslor added in disgust.

"Sometimes leading means you have to make hard decisions," Teah said coldly thinking of all those people already lost in this battle for Ter Chadain. She nudged her horse into motion, taking a path skirting Troinka.

The others sat silently in thought for a moment and then, one by one, followed after her. Their heads seemed to hang a little lower and their shoulders slouched a bit more as the heavy words and the ominous destination for this night's camp weighed them down.

They rounded the southern side of Troinka in the dark cover of night and neared the lake when a bright flash of light blinded them and a concussion of air knocked them from their horses. By the time they got to their feet, a large group surrounded them.

Teah reached for her magic and found it beyond her grasp. She looked at the shadowy figures surrounding her, able to pick out her companions. The figure she reasoned to be Caslor drew a sword, but the others stood in apparent shock at the loss of their magic.

Teah drew her blades; the grind of steel against their scabbards caused those surrounding them to back away with caution.

"Hold," a voice came from behind the enemy and a light rose illuminating those figures nearest to Teah.

The group parted as an old woman walked into the circle, a glowing ball of light floating above her outstretched palm. She walked hunched over, but with purpose, toward Teah coming to stop in front of the protector with her swords crossed before her.

"Magus Matris?" Teah said in surprised recognition dropping to a knee in a bow.

The others followed suit except for Raven who stood glaring at the old woman with distrust until Grinwald grabbed her arm and yanked her down.

"Rise," the old woman said, her voice young and vibrant, betraying the withered exterior.

They stood and Teah gaped at her in shock at the degradation of her body over the years since they last saw each other.

The woman stared back at Teah with milky white pupils, but smiled broadly as she spread her arms wide inviting Teah's embrace. The glowing ball floated above them as Teah sheathed her swords and stepped into the woman's arms to hold her tightly.

Teah held the woman for a moment and then stepped away as she noticed those surrounding her were a mixture of Betra and Magus, men and women alike. The Betra women who stood with their black robes pulled back to expose their bare midriffs and muscular legs now let the robes fall back to conceal their sinewy bodies.

"I thought King Englewood was laying siege to the Citadel?" Teah asked.

"That is true, but we needed to find allies to aid us in the defense," the Magus Matris explained.

"Surely you possess enough magic within the Citadel that Englewood's forces hold little chance at breaching its walls," Grinwald said stepping into the light.

"Viri Grinwald, it is wonderful to see that you have returned from the dead," Magus Matris said with a bow that Grinwald returned.

"Back from the dead and back from Caltoria," Grinwald added.

"Normally you would be correct, but it seems that factions of every sort have taken up sides in these dark times," she said.

"How do you mean?" Teah asked.

"Zele Magus and Viri Magus alike have sided with Englewood, sensing that his side is the one to be on," Magus Matris informed them bringing a groan from Rachel and

Grinwald.

"There were many on the last King Englewood's side too," Grinwald pointed out. "I suspect the majority of those have chosen to align with King Aston as well."

"Indeed," Magus Matris agreed.

"At least the Betra have remained loyal to our cause," Teah said looking around at the dark robed figures.

"Not as many as you would imagine," Magus Matris said with a sigh.

"What aren't you telling us," Teah asked picking up on the woman's hesitation, very uncommon for the Matris.

"Many of the Betra have sided with the new Queen of Ter Chadain," Matris said.

"What kind of betrayal is this?" Teah shouted. "After everything my brother has done for them they choose to repay him by betrayal?"

"It is to be expected under the circumstances," the Matris said calmly.

"No," Teah shouted. "There is no excuse."

"My dear," the Magus Matris said taking a step closer to Teah. "You must know that the new queen is a Betra."

Teah, Rachel, and Grinwald gasped as did the protectors inside Teah's head. Their suspicion, now fully exposed as truth, held no less shock for them. An heir of Galiven's survived and continued the Lassain line through the Betra all these years. One of those descendants now sat upon the throne.

"Instead of uniting Ter Chadain, all Logan and I have done is divide it even further," Teah groaned. "What are we to do now?"

"You are to lead us to overthrowing Englewood and his false queen and bring the duchies of Ter Chadain under one banner again," a tall, majestic man dressed in long, flowing brown robes said as he stepped through the crowd.

"Magus Patris," Grinwald said greeting the leader of the Viri

240

Magus.

Teah stared at the leader of the Viri Magus, his tall muscular frame still distinguishable under his robes and his long brown hair flowing across his shoulders. His face showed years of hardship and accumulated wisdom, but his handsome features caught her off guard.

The Magus Patris strode up stopping before Teah and dropped to a knee. He reached up taking her hand and kissed the back of it gently.

"I, Magus Patris, leader of the Viri Magus, swear my loyalty to you in your quest for the throne of Ter Chadain," he said and then stood. "Get them food and drink and see to their horses."

The Betra and Viri Magus around them jumped into motion ushering them toward the lake where the glow of campfires now shone brightly around them.

"Does he do that often?" Teah asked Grinwald as he walked next to her.

"Never in the history of our order has a Patris sworn loyalty to anyone," Grinwald said, his eyes wide in his amazement.

They stopped around a large fire near the lake where enormous white tents were erected to house the Matris and Patris.

"For the Matris and Patris to be traveling together and working this closely together, you know these are dire times," Grinwald added as the others from their company crowded closer.

"So what does this mean for our mission?" Caslor asked.

"If the leaders of the houses of magic feel we need to overthrow Englewood and his new queen, then I think our mission has changed from that of defending the houses of magic, to joining them in their attempt to reclaim the throne of Ter Chadain," Teah said looking to her party.

They all nodded their agreement as the protectors chimed in. All the protectors except Galiven.

Galiven, what are you thinking?

Nothing.

That is not true, Galiven, please tell me your thoughts of going to unseat your descendant from the throne.

I must admit I am torn, Teah.

And I don't blame you for being torn Galiven. I am torn also. This woman is my blood as well.

You can't be considering leaving her on the throne, Bastion protested, *not with Aston controlling her.*

That is the sticking point in all of this. He is controlling her. What would you do about that if you were me, Galiven?

A long pause filled Teah's mind as she sat on a log by the fire and ate the roasted meat handed to her. She purposefully ate in silence, keeping her mouth full so as to not to have to engage in conversation with those around her. Not that it seemed necessary; they devoured their meals in silence as well.

I feel we should remove Aston without judging the woman's part in it until we can discern that level of participation for ourselves, Galiven finally responded.

A smile curled Teah's lips as she felt the other protectors' consensus.

That is what you felt as well? Falcone asked.

You know she did, else she would never have raised the question to Galiven, Stalwart said.

A true leader lets her people make their own decisions as long as they can be nudged to the decision she wants, Bastion said with admiration.

Oh, but it was I who hoped that Galiven would feel as I did. I find that often those closest to the players in the game can be harder on the participants.

Thank you, Galiven said.

Teah looked up from her food with a new sense of peace to find the Magus Matris and the Magus Patris standing next to the same fire, watching them. She motioned them over and they came to stop before her.

"I must ask one thing of you and this cannot be up for debate," Teah started.

The two leaders of the magical houses looked curiously to each other and then back to Teah. Each gave a nod in understanding.

"The new queen must not be harmed in our assault on the palace," Teah stated bringing a burst of outrage from everyone around her, including the two Matris. She raised her hand to silence their outbursts. "If I am correct, this woman is a pawn that Aston has taken from her home in Sacrifice and put upon the throne for the sole reason of activating the magical spell. If that is the case, she may be a hostage and a victim here."

The others remained silent as the possibility of this sank in. Slowly they voiced their agreement and looked approvingly back at her.

"Only after we assess her part in this can we lay blame, understood?" Teah finished.

Each gave a curt nod.

"We march for Cordlain in the morning," Teah said. She took her bedroll that a Betra must have dropped next to her without her knowing and slipped from the log to cover up in front of the fire. She looked up at everyone as they still stared at her.

"I suggest you all get some rest."

This sent the Matris and Patris striding for their tents and her party scurrying to bed down for the night.

That is a true queen and leader right there, Bastion said proudly.

Goodnight, Teah replied with a satisfied grin. She didn't want to admit it to the protectors, but she liked it when they were proud of her.

Her thoughts of approval drifted to Logan, hoping he still lived as Machala believed and that he too would be proud of her.

Chapter 27

Morgan rowed the new dingy, the one that replaced the one that vanished along with Logan and Zeva, away from the Morning Breeze as Machala and Saliday watched the coastline for any indication they'd been spotted.

The Morning Breeze dropped them off around the point not far from Port Shoal to avoid detection and would wait two weeks at Scalded Island before returning to Port Shoal and pick them up, hopefully with Logan.

They made it to shore without detection and pulled the dingy up into some trees and covered it with branches for their return.

Once they secured all their supplies and hid their weapons under long brown cloaks, they headed to town in the effort to discover what news they could about Logan or Zeva. They understood their actions might be a long shot at finding Logan's trail, but using Machala's Betra sense to find the protector and Saliday's Tarken abilities now that she zeroed in on Logan as the protector and not Logan himself, they felt confident their path held true.

They entered town from the east along the high walls of the coastline and walked into the town square. Everything seemed relatively normal until Saliday noticed blood stains in the hardened dirt road when they approached what appeared to be the town jail.

People milled around and a large number of troops occupied most of the village square.

Morgan tapped Saliday's shoulder to get her attention and then motioned with a jerk of his head toward a tavern off to one side.

She nodded and gestured to Machala who followed after her and Morgan into the drinking establishment. Saliday placed a hand on the daggers inside her cloak, gaining comfort from their touch against her fingers. She understood that anything might happen in a place like this, especially if there had been some sort of event that necessitated bringing in troops. No one liked troops.

Morgan took the lead, motioning the women to a small vacant table and then stepping up to the bar to place his order.

Saliday and Machala sat down, watching their surroundings in the habit of someone trained to always be on guard. They waited as Morgan visited jovially with the bartender and then walked back to the table carrying three steins of ale and sat down with them.

Machala sniffed the contents of the stein and crinkled her nose in distaste.

"I know you don't drink ale, but pretend for appearances," Saliday whispered, remembering how Sasha told her Betra never partook in spirits. A pang of remorse filled her as she remembered the Betra Seeker who named her sister.

"I guess there was a jail break about a week or so ago where two people broke out some children being held. They took out an entire garrison, sniffer included," Morgan said, respect evident in his voice.

"It sounds like something Logan would do," Saliday agreed, "always standing up for those who can't stand up for themselves."

"They said it was a man and a woman. The man was injured before he escaped, how badly no one knows," Morgan added.

"He still lives," Machala said holding the stein up to her mouth but keeping the liquid from touching her lips.

"I feel it too," Saliday agreed.

"Which way now?" Morgan asked.

"Inland," Saliday and Machala said in unison.

"Alright, let's head out before we draw any unwanted attention," Morgan said getting to his feet.

"Too late for that," a man said standing behind Morgan between them and the door.

Morgan turned to the man who measured them up and down

with his hands on the hips of his golden uniform. Half dozen men in golden uniforms and gold breastplates embossed with a golden eye stood behind him tensed and at the ready.

"Greetings," Morgan said with a warm smile.

"My sniffer here says you three have some magic about you," the man said gesturing to the small woman standing off to one side away from the others.

"I think that maybe her nose is out of whack," Morgan declared mildly.

"Ha, you may be right. She has had issues lately, but I'd rather check you out first and make sure," the man informed him.

"Normally I would be open for that, but we are in a bit of a hurry, so we're going to have to decline," Morgan said, his tone staying calm and steady.

"Good, so if you would follow us…" the man started before he realized that Morgan refused his order. His eyes snapped from his men back to Morgan filled with surprise just before Morgan drew his blade and impaled him.

Machala drew her sword and advanced on the stunned men behind their leader and Saliday released her daggers, one after the other, sending them to the floor.

Machala reached and dispatched the last standing man as Morgan drew his blade from their leader. They turned to the sniffer, a girl of no more than sixteen with long, blonde hair hanging dirty and uncombed down her back. Her filthy grey dress held patches of different fabric to cover vital spots that were torn away. She stared at them, shaking with fear as her cold blue eyes peered up at them.

"What do we do with her?" Morgan asked.

"Take me with you," the girl begged dropping to her knees and taking a hold of Morgan's cloak.

"She'll only slow us down," Machala stated and turned to the door searching for anyone entering.

"I won't, I promise," the girl pleaded.

"What's your name," Saliday asked.

"No, we can't, this is difficult enough already without bringing a girl along to slow us down," Morgan protested.

"Abria," the girl blurted out. "My name is Abria."

"Why are you helping these men?" Saliday asked.

"Saliday, no," Morgan growled.

Saliday cut him short with a sharp look and quickly turned back to the girl who burst into explanation as soon as she had Saliday's attention again.

"I'm their slave. They hold me against my will and force me to find those who are magical. When I don't, they beat me. If I am wrong, they beat me. And when I try to escape, they beat me and do other things to me."

"What kind of other things?" Morgan asked and received a sharp blow to his midsection from Saliday and a slap across the back of his head from Machala for his insensitive question.

"Things that violate me, take away my respect," the girl said, choking on her answer as she held back tears.

"Come with us," Saliday said turning to retrieve her daggers from the men's chests. She cleaned a dagger and handed it to Abria. "Use this to defend yourself."

The girl took the dagger and tucked it in the rope belt cinching her oversized dress at the waist and nodded.

"Why do I know this is going to come back to bite us?" Morgan asked as they hurried for the door.

Machala peered outside and then stepped into the street motioning them to follow. They eased along the building and then down an alley between two of the structures. They stopped, pressed against one of the buildings looking both ways trying to decide which way to go next.

"You always see the worst in people," Saliday told Morgan, glancing at Abria huddled next to her on the other side.

"I can get us out of Port Shoal without being seen," Abria spoke up suddenly, causing the others to jump.

Morgan, Saliday, and Machala exchanged curious looks and then nodded.

"Okay," Saliday told Abria, "lead on."

The girl slipped ahead of Machala and continued on without hesitation. She led them to the back of the alley where they scurried across a narrow back road and into an opening in the cliffs surrounding Port Shoal. They followed the girl as she went deeper and deeper into the cave until the light from the opening faded from usefulness.

"I can't see a thing," Morgan complained. "How am I supposed to escape when I can't see?"

A light glowed in front of them as the girl lit a torch on the wall, took it from the metal holder, and continued on.

"This is an old smuggler's route into Port Shoal. It was used when the emperor outlawed ale and it had to be brought into town in secret," Abria said and continued on.

They felt the ground beneath them begin to rise and walked for a long while uphill until Abria snuffed out the torch in the dirt floor and stepped into the daylight.

The others stepped out facing a thick wooded area. Moving around the raised earth that accommodated the cave entrance, they stared out at the ocean from the top of the cliffs that lined Port Shoal.

"Where now?" Abria asked.

"Nowhere for you," Morgan said. "We can take it from here."

"I can tell you aren't from Caltoria. I know this area, I can help," Abria pointed out.

"That is true, a guide would make our journey easier and quicker," Machala agreed.

Saliday held Morgan's disapproving stare for a moment until he let it go, resigned to his lack of input on this decision.

"I think they are northeast of here," Saliday said and Machala nodded her agreement.

"Then northeast it is," Abria said and turned to head out but then paused. "How far northeast?"

"We are a fair distance off," Machala said.

"Why, is that a problem?" Saliday asked seeing Abria's concerned face.

"No, no problem if you don't mind entering Stellaran," Abria said.

"Stellaran?" Morgan interjected.

"Haven't you heard, the weave is down?" Abria asked.

"This changes everything if Logan is in Stellaran," Morgan groaned sliding a hand through his hair in frustration.

"Is Stellaran bad?" Saliday asked.

"Only the dreaded enemy of Caltoria who exiled everyone's ancestors here. This is bad. Very bad. We are putting ourselves right in the middle of a war between Caltoria and Stellaran," Morgan said as he began to pace.

"No one said this was going to be easy," Saliday pointed out.

"No one said this was going to be suicide either," Morgan argued.

"It is what it is," Machala stated. "I'm going to find the protector no matter where he is or what war is raging around me."

"Protector?" Abria said in surprise. "You are looking for the protector?"

The three from Ter Chadain turned to Abria, shocked she knew the name.

"He set all the magical slaves free, dropped the weave, and then helped free four children from the troops and a sniffer in Port Shoal. It will be an honor to help you find him," Abria said beaming with pride.

"See, even a girl isn't afraid of a little war," Saliday said elbowing Morgan in the ribs.

"Ya, but she hasn't had to live through one yet," Morgan moaned.

****

After days on the trail, Saliday, Morgan, Machala, and Abria stopped for a much needed rest well inside Stellaran's borders. Machala and Saliday agreed that they remained on the right path to reach Logan; they felt that he kept moving further away from them.

"Did you two ever think that he is riding while we are walking?" Morgan pointed out, sitting around their small fire as the sun set and rubbing his tired feet after removing his boots.

"That's it!" Saliday exclaimed, shoving Morgan so he toppled from his perch on a downed log.

They all laughed as Morgan righted himself and then Machala and Saliday fell silent, horror across their faces.

"What is it?" Morgan asked as he stared at their expressions.

Saliday and Machala looked to each other as the air rushed from their lungs and appeared to not want to return.

"He's gone," Saliday said even as the sky darkened to the north.

"How can that be?" Morgan asked, and then realized what it could be. Logan was dead.

"I can't feel him anymore," Machala lamented.

They sat in silence as Abria turned to the north and watched the sky light up with an awesome display of lightning in the distance.

****

"Logan, Logan?" Cita's voice echoed in Logan's head. He strained to open his eyes only to find the images of blurred figures without defining lines to separate them from each other.

"He's coming round," Zeva whispered as the mass of colors

250

crowded in around him.

"Logan, are you alright?" Cita pressed.

"I, I, can't see straight," he croaked, his voice raw and painful to the vibrations required to create sound. He swallowed with effort and then blinked slowly, deliberately, trying to clear the blurriness before him.

"Take your time, the storm has passed," Stern said. "We'll make camp a short distance from here. Bring the wagon around so we can get Logan up off the ground."

Some of the images shrunk to nothingness in his vision and he struggled to sit up, but a hand pressed firmly against his chest, forcing him to lie back again.

"Oh, no you don't. Lie back and let us take care of you for a bit until you get your bearings," Cita insisted.

"Let me have a look at him," Linell said as her dark image hovered over him, the whites of her eyes standing out against her dark skin. She turned to one side, whispered something he couldn't make out and then leaned in closer to him again. "I don't know how you survived that, but you did. Now we need to see if we can correct the damage that has been done."

"Such as?" Logan rasped.

"Well..." Linell hesitated until Logan grasped her arm and looked at what he thought to be her eyes.

"Tell me." He said and then coughed from the dryness in his throat. "Water."

Linell turned away again, and Logan soon felt the soft cool water-skin against his lips and drank deeply, ignoring the pain when the water hit his scorched throat until it receded with each gulp. As he coughed again from the water going down the wrong path, he felt a pulsing in his side with each cough and felt his side warm with something fluid that spread out along his side and then pooled beneath him.

Hands clasped against his side, putting painful pressure against him and slowing the flow of blood coming out of his wound.

"What are my injuries?" he asked again, this time without coughing and with less pain in his throat.

"The lightning appears to have entered you and blown a hole in your side that we are now trying to mend, but your coughing just tore open the mending we already did, so hold still," Linell ordered him.

He relaxed, waiting in silence as he felt the magic enter him and mend his broken body causing him to clench his teeth against the pain. She took a long time sending her weave through him and he felt her mend other injuries she encountered in her examination. Just when he thought he couldn't stand anymore, Linell gasped and leaned away from him.

"What is it? Trevon asked, kneeling next to Linell as she sat beside Logan.

"His…" she began and then hesitated, looking down at him.

Logan saw her fuzzy face move from Trevon back to him as she hesitated. "Tell us what you sensed."

"Your entire insides seem to have been shredded from the inside out. I have done what I can, but only time will tell if I have found all the holes," Linell said, her voice lacking any confidence.

Logan nodded, not letting the possibility of his life coming to an end overwhelm him. He always knew that his days were numbered. He actually felt lucky to have survived this long. He also understood that being a protector held some benefits that included rapid healing and recovering from injuries that would prove deadly to anyone else.

Cita and Stern returned with Zeva accompanied by the rumbling of the wagon wheels.

He sat up not wanting the children to see him like this and resisted as Cita leaned down to press him back down. He took a hold of her hand and looked into her eyes as they focused a little better in his sight.

"I need you to help me up and get me to the wagon. Do not carry me, assist me," Logan told her.

"But you're too weak," Cita argued.

"I need them to see that I'm going to be alright," Logan whispered.

"But you might not be," Cita said, her voice wavering with a multitude of emotions.

Logan squeezed her hand, not looking away from her worried face. "I'm going to be alright. I just need time to heal." He said it with such conviction that she nodded and helped him to his feet without another word.

He leaned on her shoulder with his severely injured side away from her and his arm around her shoulder. They made their way to the wagon where she helped him sit and then slide back into the wagon.

He felt everyone's eyes upon him and he turned to the blurred shapes of the children and forced a smile upon his lips. "Did you enjoy the fireworks?" he asked.

The children looked at the others in confusion and then turned back to Logan, nodding.

"I overdid it a bit and need to ride with you a while if that's okay?" Logan explained.

"Of course," Bethany spoke for them. "Are you going to be okay?"

"I'll be fine. Thank you for your concern. I should be riding again by tomorrow."

This brought an exchange of stares from the others around him as they saw what Logan didn't. Even with the healing Linell managed to do, blood still oozed out of his side and coated his face, hair, and any skin visible from under his clothing. It seemed as though his body seeped blood from every pore. If this continued, he would soon bleed to death with nothing anyone could do to save him. His bloodied body looked even more

253

horrifying when he smiled in an attempt to comfort them.

"I will ride with him and see what else I can do," Linell said, being the most adept at healing out of their party. She climbed up next to Logan and eased him to lie back and began sending weave after weave into him without hesitation.

"We can camp not far from here. There is a small river that runs across a shallow valley," Cita said and then strode to her horse and mounted to lead the way.

The others mounted their recovered horses and followed after, Trevon riding behind the wagon to be close if Linell needed anything from him.

By the time they reached Cita's campsite, Linell leaned back with exhaustion and discouragement, shaking her head when Trevon looked at her with a questioning stare. He hung his head at her uncertainty as to Logan's chances and kicked his mount to gather with the others as they made camp.

The wagon rolled into a spot next to the river and the children climbed down as Zeva beckoned them to come and get water and something to eat.

Linell left Logan laying semi-conscious in the wagon and spoke a moment to Cita. Cita then came over and climbed up next to Logan, lifting his head to rest in her lap.

He looked up at her as her image floated on the edge of his blurry vision. She hung her head over his.

"I will get through this," Logan told her.

"I know you will," Cita said unconvincingly.

"I've come back from nearer death experiences."

"Oh, so you've been closer to death than being hit by lightning over and over again until it burst from your body in all direction leaving your insides shredded? You have been closer to death than that?"

"I am the Protector of Ter Chadain. You don't know what that means. By the spirits, sometimes I don't know what that means, but I'm pretty darn near indestructible. My vision is already getting better and I feel myself gaining strength."

"But Linell said," Cita began before Logan cut her off with a raised hand that he extended to her lips placing a bloody finger against them.

"Tell Linell I appreciate what she has done to save me and she has indeed helped, but now I need to let the protector spell do its work. Keep everyone away from me for a while and stop trying to heal me. Let me be." His words held no anger, but came out flat and direct leaving Cita no room for discussion.

She nodded, leaned down and kissed him on his bloodied lips, holding him close. "I don't want to lose you," she whispered in his ear.

"You aren't going to. Not today at least," Logan assured her. He lifted his head and kissed her cheek lightly. "You can't get rid of me that easily."

"Being electrocuted by a lightning storm is easy? I'd hate to see hard," Cita said as she gave a miserable laugh.

Logan smiled and grasped Cita's hand giving it a squeeze. "I need to rest."

Cita nodded and slid out of the wagon, pausing a moment, still holding Logan's hand and then reluctantly let go to walk toward the fire where the others sat.

Logan eased his head back and closed his eyes, feeling the pain engulfing every inch of his body. He exhaled slowly and deeply, letting the fatigue win and pull him into a heavy sleep.

As he slept, he dreamt of times with Teah and the days of happiness back at the farm. He missed her so much, his heart hurt at the thought of not being with her. He needed her more than ever and even in this dream, he felt a bit happier just holding her in his thoughts.

I miss you so much sister, his thoughts reached out to her. But somewhere deep inside of him, he knew she remained beyond his reach.

Chapter 28

Teah sat up in her bedroll with a start, the words of her brother still echoing in her mind. Did she imagine them, or did Logan actually speak to her?

She looked around at everyone still sleeping, the sky showing sunrise still hours off. She turned her thoughts inward and the protectors snapped to attention with her thought.

Did you hear Logan? She asked them.

I thought I did, Galiven spoke up.

Something entered your mind, but it is hard to tell where it came from and who it was, Bastion said.

Stalwart and Falcone didn't add their thoughts, but their silence confirmed their agreement that someone spoke to Teah in her thoughts.

Logan? Is that you? Teah tentatively reached out, fighting to keep her hope in check.

Teah? A voice replied.

Teah's heart leapt as she recognized Logan's thoughts in her mind instantly. *Oh brother, I have missed you. We feared you dead.*

No, not yet, but it took a near death experience to allow me to reach out to you again.

Where are you?

I am in Stellaran, Logan replied raising gasps of disbelief from the protectors.

Where is Stellaran? Teah asked, confused at the reaction from the protectors at its mention.

Stellaran lies north of Caltoria, Logan told her.

It has been separated from Caltoria by a magical weave for many years, Bastion explained to her. *He could not possibly be in Stellaran unless...*

Unless what?

Ask Logan if the weave is down, Bastion told her.

Is the weave down between Stellaran and Caltoria? Teah reached out to Logan.

Yes, how did you know? Logan replied after a long pause. *Bastion.*

Oh, right, he lived in Caltoria before escaping to Ter Chadain. He would remember the weave, Logan realized.

The destruction of the source stone and the spire stone must have triggered a reaction with the two stones on the Stellaran side, Bastion explained. *Ask him if the empress has attacked Stellaran yet?*

Has the Shakata attacked Stellaran yet?

Not that we know of, but there is something you should know..., Logan hesitated.

What's that?

They say I'm the heir to the throne of Stellaran, Logan's thought carried his concern.

There has long been rumor that we were direct descendants to the Chairman of the Crystal Council of Stellaran, Bastion said.

Oh Logan, isn't being a protector enough for you? Teah groaned.

It is for me, but I guess this tattoo is actually the code of arms for the Stellaran Chairman and prophecy says that upon my return I will take control of Stellaran as king.

Ask what happened to him on the ship? Stalwart changed the subject, unnerved by king talk.

What happened on the Morning Breeze? Where did you go?

I woke up in the dingy with Zeva, Logan told her.

So she was a Senji?

Senji? The spirits, no! She saved me and has been by my side helping me ever since. She said Grinwald, Morgan, and Raven were behind it.

Everything went silent inside Teah's mind at the thought of

such a betrayal.

Why?

They didn't need me anymore now that they discovered you were also a protector, Logan shared.

It is very possible Grinwald felt two protectors with your powers were too much for Ter Chadain to handle, Falcone reasoned.

But you're okay? You have people around you to help you? You're safe? Teah pelted Logan with questions. She waited for a response but none came and fear gripped her. *Logan?*

I'm here. I kind of had a run-in with a thunderstorm.

How do you have a run-in with a thunderstorm?

It was a magical thunderstorm. I got hit by lightning...a lot.

Now Teah sat in silence, trying to picture her brother battling a thunderstorm, being struck by lightning over and over again.

I will be okay, just trying to heal. How are you?

A bit banged up, but nothing to worry about, Teah told him simply, deciding not to go into detail since she didn't have anything to compare to battling a thunderstorm.

Are Grinwald, Raven, and Morgan still with you? Logan asked.

Grinwald and Raven are, Morgan has returned to Caltoria with Saliday and Machala, the new Seeker of the Protector, to find you. Teah felt the pain at the mention of Saliday and then even greater pain vibrated across their connection when she mentioned Sasha's replacement.

I should rest now, Logan told her. *Work out the best course of action to deal with Grinwald and Raven with the protectors. They should offer some sound counsel on the matter.*

I will. Be safe my brother. I love you.

Love you too.

And as quickly as he popped into her mind, Logan's presence vanished from her thoughts. Teah looked around at her surroundings with new insight and hope for the future. Her brother lived, but in the same thought she now needed to deal with the traitorous actions of Grinwald and Raven. The only problem she saw at confronting the two magicals lay with exposing her connection to Logan. The secret connection they held put them in a great position to keep in check those who may wish to play the siblings against each other. She wasn't certain she wanted to give up that secret just yet.

So we wait to confront Raven and Grinwald until the time is right, Galiven stated.

Teah nodded and sensed the other protectors' agreement.

She stretched out on the bedroll again as a smile crept across her lips. She felt whole again. Knowing that Logan lived and once more was connected to her gave her a renewed confidence to push forward. She then realized she didn't share with Logan that another queen now sat on the throne with a new King Englewood. She felt he needed to rest and not worry about that right now. He couldn't do anything about it while he strove to take the throne of Stellaran. She would share that information with him later.

Closing her eyes, Teah exhaled as all the weight of Ter Chadain lifted a bit as if her brother now helped her carry her burden. In reality, he always carried more than his share and his sister respected him for it. She tried to relax her smile as her cheeks began to hurt, but try as she may, she couldn't remove it from her lips and fell asleep with that silly smile still on her face.

Chapter 29

Logan slept deep feeling a sense of completeness that eluded him since being abandoned in the dingy with Zeva. Now that Teah and he shared a connection once more, he possessed a spark deep within him that started a chain reaction rushing over him from head to toe, healing and repairing everything in its path. He opened his eyes as darkness still hung over the camp.

Cita leaned closer as his eyes flitted open and smiled down at him. He saw the worry on her face and only then realized that his vision was whole once more. She bent down and kissed him gently and he pulled her closer, kissing her back with passion. When he released her, she sat back with a look of pleased shock, panting for air.

"Wow, I wasn't expecting that," Cita said as red flushed her cheeks.

Logan smiled proudly as he sat up realizing he wore no clothing under the blanket draped over him and noticed the absence of blood which caked his body before. His clothing sat folded neatly next to Cita and a blood soaked cloth draped over the edge of the wagon.

"Thank you for caring for me," he said.

"You saved us all that night," Cita told him. "If you hadn't run from us to draw the lightning to yourself, we may all have been killed."

"Don't let it go to his head," Zeva said walking up to the wagon with the fire backlighting her approach. She smiled and then stared at him curiously.

"What?" Logan asked.

"The weave around you is weaker, not gone, but weaker," Zeva told him.

Logan looked at her and then wondered about his dreams while he slept.

Teah? He reached out.

I am here, Teah replied.

Just wanted to be sure I wasn't dreaming.

No, I'm with you.

"I still can't touch my magic?" Logan told her.

"I think the weave goes deeper. There are patches here and there, but I will have to remove it completely for you to have access to your magic again," Zeva explained.

He looked back to Zeva. "Can you remove the rest?"

"I will try, but I think it still poses too much danger. I will study it further while we ride on tomorrow."

"Tomorrow? Shouldn't you all get some rest too?" Logan argued.

"We've been here for two days," Cita said.

"I've been out for two days?"

"We thought we lost you," Cita replied. "It took all my convincing to keep Linell from trying to heal you with her magic again. I explained you insisted to be left to the protector's magic."

"Was she angry," Zeva said with a chuckle. "I think if you didn't heal yourself, she would have killed you after you were dead."

"Yes, I would have," Linell said standing behind Zeva who jumped with a start.

"We're all glad to you see you well," Stern said as he walked up with Trevon, Fedlen, and the children.

Logan looked to every member of his party and smiled with the knowledge that each was true to their cause. He slid to the edge of the wagon and hopped off holding his blanket across his waist.

"I'm starving. How about I get some food and we can discuss our next move," Logan said, not waiting for an answer but striding toward the fire with his blanket dragging behind him, giving them a glance of his naked back side.

Cita groaned and hurried after him with his folded clothes in her arms. "Shouldn't you get dressed first?"

"Nope, that rabbit over the fire smells too good," Logan said as he walked to the fire and tore off a piece of the meat on the spit over the fire shoving it into his mouth, the juice running down his arms and dripping from his elbow onto the ground.

The others watched the antics from the wagon and then looked awkwardly at each other.

"Good to have him back," Trevon said with a smile.

"Sure is," Stern agreed.

"He seems a bit happier," Fedlen said drawing everyone's attention.

They looked at him and then to each other when they realized Fedlen spoke the truth. Logan seemed more jovial, as if a weight was lifted from his shoulders. They nodded and joined Cita and Logan at the fire where Cita still hadn't convinced Logan to dress before stuffing more rabbit into his mouth.

They sat around the fire as the children shared their perspective of watching Logan getting hit over and over again with lightning. Everyone, including Logan, enjoyed the children's vantage point now that they knew Logan to be recovered from those strikes. They stayed up later than they should, laughing and joking, Logan sharing stories of his life as a farm boy and his sister Teah, the Queen of Ter Chadain.

They finally climbed into their bedding and were fast asleep when Cita, lying on the ground next to Logan after insisting on giving the wagon back to the children, stared into this strange man's eyes and searching for the reason he held her affection so deeply.

"You can't choose who you love," Logan said with a smirk.

"How did you?" Cita asked, unnerved that he knew her thoughts.

"Because I feel the same as you do. But don't fight it. We love who our hearts choose to love at that moment and there is nothing we can do to change that. We can deny it and refuse to act on it," he said recalling Saliday, "but it will always be there if our heart chooses it to be there."

Cita stared at him, seeing a depth in his character never divulged to her before. She slid closer, turning her back to him and pressing against his chest. She took his top arm and pulled it over her, holding his hand in hers.

"I know I have prepared many years to have you in my life, but never like this," Cita said raising his hand to her lips and kissing it.

"If not like this, then how?"

"To be by your side and help you take control of Stellaran."

"Great, another woman who wants to protect me," he said pulling his hand away.

Cita pulled his hand back in front of her and held it firmly as she turned her head to look up at his face. "I'm here to do as you say. If that entails protecting you, so be it, but my heart, as you say, has chosen you and that complicates things."

"In what way?"

"Now that I have feelings for you, I must learn to keep sight of what is best for Stellaran and not let those feelings get in the way."

"It always seems to be the case," Logan groaned.

"And what is that?"

"My heart chooses those who feel that the greater good should come before our happiness."

"Isn't that what heroes are required to do? To put the needs of others ahead of their own?"

"I'm really getting tired of being the hero." Logan leaned his head against Cita's shoulder and went silent.

Cita remained quiet as well, taking in the moment of his warmth and the stillness of the world around them. Her eyes opened wide at that realization. The world around them was too quiet.

She sat up with a jolt. "We're under attack!" she shouted as the first Red Tips entered the firelight.

****

Teah woke the next morning refreshed and ready to take the next step toward her destiny. She held no reservations at removing the puppet queen who sat upon her throne. Speaking with Logan gave her a renewed confidence in her goal. She needed to claim the throne and rid Ter Chadain of the Englewoods once and for all. She felt the protectors' emotions rise at the thought of the king and she knew that Logan's mercy would never be repeated by her. Not if she wanted Ter Chadain to be at peace with itself. The hatred Englewood held for anyone with magical abilities kept the family's rule out of the question.

When are we to confront Grinwald and Raven about their treachery? Bastion said what all the protectors felt.

I can't understand why Grinwald would betray Logan like that.

One thing I learned while dealing with lying Viri Magus, is that they always have a reason for their treason. Though it is twisted with their own sense of what is best for Ter Chadain, Stalwart offered.

But to betray the protector who he helped make sure would come into being doesn't make any sense.

We can't count on sense, Bastion reminded her.

Teah's blood went cold as a memory came to her. When she was at Grinwald's home in Tumbleweed and glanced into the book of the Protector's Prophecy.

I caught a glimpse of a warning in the book of the Protector's Prophecy. I didn't get a chance to read it before Grinwald slammed it shut, but he didn't want me to see it, that's for sure.

265

Magicals have long followed prophecy to guide their actions, right or wrong, Falcone weighed in.

You think that prophecy told Grinwald to get rid of Logan? Teah couldn't wrap her head around such a thought.

The Magus have often feared the power of the protector and now that there are two of you, it may have driven Grinwald into eliminating Logan since he still needs you to sit upon the throne, Bastion reasoned.

And he still has a protector in Ter Chadain as well, Galiven added.

Teah's breath left her as she sat staring at the smoldering fire. For Grinwald to be so heartless as to cast Logan overboard at sea stirred a fire deep inside of her as her anger imitated the fire before her.

Grinwald will pay for his treachery, Teah reached out to Logan.

Don't make it too easy, Logan replied.

No, brother, he will suffer as we did.

Good. Logan said.

"What are you thinking about?" Caslor asked making Teah jump with a start.

"Oh, nothing, just getting my thoughts in order," Teah said smiling up at him.

She slapped her palm into his extended hand and pulled herself to her feet, looking around the campsite.

"Where are Grinwald and Raven?" She asked.

"I believe they are meeting with the Matris and Patris," Caslor said pointing to the large tent nearest them which housed the Patris.

266

Chapter 30

"I had no other choice," Grinwald said, his arms flailing in despair as he told his story. "It was either him or the girl and we all know this quest cannot continue without the girl in Ter Chadain."

Raven stood a few paces back in silence watching with concern etched across her face. She took in the reactions of the two leaders of the houses of magic, or the lack of reaction. They sat emotionless as Grinwald recounted casting Logan off the Morning Breeze in the dingy.

The milky blue eyes of the Matris stared straight ahead while the deep brown eyes of the Patris took in Grinwald flatly.

"But both would have assured our success," the Patris said.

"But the prophecy states that a protector with additional magus powers would spell our doom," Grinwald ranted. "What would *two* such protectors do to Ter Chadain?"

"Tear it apart," the Magus said softly.

"Exactly!" Grinwald agreed, extending both arms to the Matris as she condoned his actions.

Raven fidgeted as her involvement in that betrayal filled her mind and she felt a slight tingle of guilt over hurting Logan. She quickly swept the thoughts away and concentrated on the conversation before her.

"What's done is done," the Patris said without emotion. "Now how do we get the girl on the throne where she belongs?"

"I suggest the first thing is not have meetings without her present," Teah said, hands planted on her hips in the doorway with Caslor by her side.

"Come in my dear," Magus Matris said motioning Teah into the tent. "We felt you needed the rest and didn't want to disturb you."

"That will not happen again, understood?" Teah stated and the

267

two leaders bristled at her tone.

"Now listen here…" the Patris began, but Teah cut him off with a raised hand.

"No, I don't think you understand," she said looking him in the eyes. "It is you who will do the listening."

"Teah," Grinwald scolded, appalled.

"You," Teah spun on Grinwald with a threatening finger pointing at him, "Need to keep quiet."

Grinwald's mouth gaped but he remained silent as Teah turned back to Matris and Patris.

"One thing you need to realize is that I have gone through much these past few years and I am no longer the farm girl you first encountered," Teah said.

"Apparently not," Magus Matris said with amusement in her voice.

"I will now be taking control of my own destiny and anyone who wishes to influence that destiny needs to come and speak with me. Any other actions concerning me and my destiny taken behind my back without my knowledge will be considered an act of treason."

The shock on everyone's face in the tent told her that her message got through to them. The protectors in her head pulsed with a sense of approval and respect as she set the new ground rules for their quest to take the throne.

"Teah, you need to understand." Grinwald approached to calm her down.

She lifted a hand and he flew across the room, careening off the furniture set up in the tent, tumbling to the dirt floor.

She spun on the two leaders and held their eyes in a threatening stare. Her words came in a hissing whisper as she seethed with anger, the source she kept secret. "I will not tolerate any more insubordination when it comes to me, my brother, or Caslor as he is my equal in this. Do you understand?"

268

"You can't believe that we will sit idly by and let a girl order us around like lap dogs?" the Patris said, his anger rising.

"Not lap dogs, my dear Patris. I see you as advisors, so advise me. But I warn you, if you have any plans to take actions behind my back without my knowledge, I will destroy you," Teah held his gaze and saw his eyes widen with shock as she spoke. She held that gaze until she felt certain he did not mistake her resolve.

She lifted her eyes to take in the tent again, noting Grinwald brushing himself off and straightening his hair and glasses. She fought back the urge to smile as he kept his distance watching with a worried expression.

"We need to speak to the Betra who are still with us and see if we can sway the other Betra who are currently supporting King Aston to come back to our side," Teah told them.

"What will entice them to come back after they feel Logan abandoned them?" Magus Matris asked.

"Perhaps understanding that only a Lassain with my powers can remove the curse from them and that the Protector of Ter Chadain has returned and requires their allegiance." She emphasized her statement by opening her cloak and tearing her undershirt to reveal the protector's tattoo on her chest. "They shall return to the protector or be cursed forever."

Even Caslor joined in the shocked expressions as Teah Lassain, Queen of Ter Chadain and Protector of Ter Chadain flexed her powers. He shuddered as her power eclipsed even his mother's and he feared for anyone foolish enough to cross her.

****

After making it perfectly clear to the leadership of the Betra accompanying them that those Betra supporting Englewood must return, messengers left the camp to spread the word of the Queen Protector of Ter Chadain as they now dubbed her.

They soon packed up camp and headed out toward Cordlain at

the snail's pace of a large army. Teah rode at the head of the group with a contingent of Betra charged with her protection. Caslor rode beside her. Grinwald, Raven, and the two magical leaders rode behind them, still unable to articulate or digest what transpired in the tent. A shift of power never felt so draining as when Teah took control of her own destiny and offered to take them along only if they promised to behave.

Grinwald remained timid, still in shock over Teah's reaction to him while Raven's suspicion grew over Teah's sudden change in attitude. Something changed overnight and Teah somehow possessed much more confidence and strength like in Caltoria. Like when she and her brother were together. Raven paused in her thoughts, the plausibility hanging over her like a cloud. Could that be it? Could she have some sort of connection to Logan across the sea? She shook her head, dismissing the idea as ridiculous and turned her thoughts to the task at hand; staying on Teah's good side and putting her on the throne.

****

"That was some show," Caslor said, glancing back at the others over his shoulder.

"It's needed to be done for a long time," Teah said, her voice soft but firm.

"You have what it takes to be a great leader," Caslor said respect heavy in his voice.

Teah looked at him with a raised eyebrow.

"My mother may have some messed up views, but she wields her power skillfully," Caslor explained.

"I guess I will concede that, but please don't compare us beyond that," Teah said, her voice light for the first time since the tent.

"I won't, but you drew your line in the sand and then backed it up with authority, very impressive."

"I hope I didn't scare you?" Teah said half teasing.

"Ha, no, I've seen a lot worse, but it was out of character. What changed overnight?"

"There are things about protectors, and Logan and me specifically that you don't know," Teah began.

Careful, Stalwart warned.

"Like what?" Caslor asked his curiosity tweaked.

Teah, don't, Bastion cautioned.

"There are special connections between protectors present and past," Teah said and felt the panic in her head from the protectors.

"What kind of connections?" Caslor prodded.

Teah, no, Falcone shouted. *You must not share this. Not even with him.*

Please, Galiven pleaded. *I, more than the rest understand your desire to trust the one you love, but as a protector, you can't afford that luxury. It cost me my life and cursed an entire people. Don't do this!*

Teah hesitated for a moment and let the words of caution from the protectors sink in. She nodded at their argument and glanced at Caslor waiting for an explanation.

"As a protector, you just feel a deep connection to all the protectors that have come before you. Since Logan is also a protector, I have a deeper connection to him than I ever did before."

Caslor nodded. "It is a 'brotherhood' so to speak and an exclusive one at that."

"Especially for me since I am the first woman protector in history."

The protectors gave a collective sigh of relief.

I will wait to tell him, but he will be told.

This stirred feelings of apprehension in her head from the protectors, but she slid up her wall and the feelings vanished behind it.

They rode in silence for the remainder of the day and marched through the night, keeping a steady pace. The next day the march continued into the evening where they made camp and let the troops rest as they set up camp between the towns of Bridgerton and Octava on the border between the Cranberg and Ter Chadain duchies.

Teah found that even though most of the troops were Betra, a large contingent of Ter Chadain troops from the southern duchies also marched with them, the general of each southern duchy leading their division. She remembered Duke Banderkin and Dezare with remorse and shame over being unable to save them, but his general marched with her and that gave her hope for their duchy.

As they made camp the Magus Patris approached her and offered her his tent. She began to decline, but a look from Caslor told her that a leader needed to be a leader and look the part. She thanked him and immediately called for a meeting with all the duchy generals.

After changing into fresh clothes provided by the Magus Matris and the other Zele Magus with her, she sat down on the large high-backed chair adorned with gold gilding along the arms and legs which the Patris traveled with. The lush red velvet cushioned seat made her sigh with pleasure as she eased into it, a far cry from the stiff leather saddle she resided in the past two days.

Caslor stuck his head in the tent and tentatively looked for her signal. After getting a nod from Teah, he lifted the tent flap to allow the generals of the southern duchies entrance and take audience with the Queen Protector of Ter Chadain.

Four generals, three men and a woman, marched in and stood at attention before her, seeing her up close for the first time. They stared at her impressive image with admiration. Her long blue gown contrasted the riding pants, high boots, and split cloak she normally wore. The neckline cut low to show the hint of her breasts which gave a glimpse of the top of her protector tattoo. Silver embroidery with lace edged the hem, neckline, and cuffs as well as adorned the dress with intricate swirls of silver along the body. Around her neck a golden chain held a gold locket given to her by her mother, Gianna, the last Lassain Queen of Ter Chadain.

The swords of the protector leaned against the side of the chair within easy reach, but with the Betra surrounding her tent and the generals being disarmed before entry, there was little chance of her being in danger. The close proximity of her weapons gave her a calming sense of security as well.

Caslor stepped forward becoming the impromptu herald for the generals. "Generals, may I introduce Teah Lassain, heir apparent to the throne of Ter Chadain and Protector of Ter Chadain."

The generals all bowed in respect to Teah who nodded her head in return.

"Thank you Caslor," Teah said motioning for Caslor to take a small chair next to her. She waited for him to be seated and then turned back to the generals. "Would you do me the honor of introducing yourselves and then we can get down to the business at hand."

A tall, lean man dressed in pale red from the beret on top of his head to the red riding boots all trimmed with golden embroidery and lace stepped forward, bowing deeply with a flourish. His brown hair tipped by grey showed a bald spot as he bowed. He looked up at her with intense hazel eyes as he straightened.

"General Cyrus Bree, Stalosten Duchy, Your Grace. At your service," he said and then stepped back into line.

Teah nodded as he spoke and then bowed slightly at the waist as he finished.

The next general, a much broader and muscled man than General Bree, but standing a good hand shorter stepped forward and bowed. His bow was less dramatic and he stood quickly to study her with his deep brown eyes. His clean-shaven face and head held several scars that curiously added to his handsomeness. His muscled neck looked like a block of stone attaching his head to his solid shoulders. His black riding cloak over an unadorned black shirt and tight fitted riding pants tucked into black calf-high riding boots bulged in attempt to keep his muscles at bay.

"General Darius Covrent of Mellastock Duchy, in your service," he said with all formality and then stepped back into line with a click of his heels.

Teah bowed her head the same degree he bowed to her and looked to the two remaining generals.

"General Griffin Orr from Granstel, My Lady. Honored to be at your service," the man said with a slight bow and stepped back into line.

He looked at Teah as she studied him, the least impressive figure in the line. His wiry grey hair pulled back in a tail showed the white scalp underneath and his pock-marked face held divots and trenches running through his skin making him look aged and feeble. His build fell between the tall and sinewy of General Bree and the muscled General Covrent, but something beneath that exterior cried dangerous to Teah. His body appeared as a notched arrow ready to strike at a moment's notice. His dark grey riding cloak hid most of his grizzled arms and taut muscles with a white shirt possessing light grey embroidery along the fabric edges. His dark grey trousers hung baggy on his frame much like the black garb of the Betra which Teah knew hid a deadly adversary.

Teah gave the man a nod and turned to the remaining general for her introduction.

The woman nodded and stepped forward to bow deeper than the others and held that position as she spoke, face to the floor. "Cecily Haveben, General of Fareband Duchy," she said and remained in her bow.

Teah tensed as she named the duchy of Duke Banderkin.

"Please rise," she whispered.

The woman straightened, her long blond hair tied in a tail lifting from hanging in front of her while she bowed to resting over her right shoulder and running down the right side of her chest. Her dark green cloak, shirt, and riding pants reminded Teah of a dress Dezare wore while aiding her in Stalwart. The black riding boots reached above the woman's knees, a slight heel elevated her above the other generals. Her blue eyes stared at Teah as the heir to the throne searched for words amongst her memories of the horrific end to Duke Banderkin and Dezare. The pain behind those blue eyes swirled as the two shared a silent look.

"My condolences to you and Fareband Duchy," Teah said.

General Haveben stared at Teah in confusion. "Of what do you speak, my lady?"

Teah then realized the fate of Dezare and the duke had not reached the general. She swallowed hard, turning to Caslor who gave her a commiserating look in return.

"While in Stalwart I had the honor of meeting Duke Banderkin and Dezare," Teah began, hesitating as hope surged on the general's face. "It is also in Stalwart that I witnessed their deaths at the hand of Duchess Heniton."

The general's expression went from hope to horror at the news of her duke's demise. She fought back her emotions and her face turned to stone.

"I want you to know, they died fighting for the goal that I intend to see accomplished…with all of your help," Teah said turning her eyes to the rest of the generals.

"I would have expected nothing less," General Haveben said stoically. "What do you wish of us?"

The other generals nodded their agreement, each of them fighting back the emotions they felt hearing the loss of Duke Banderkin and his daughter. They glanced at General Haveben uncomfortably out of the corner of their eyes.

"I wanted to assure you that your interests as well as those of your individual duchies will be held in the highest regard as we move forward. You will all be rewarded for your loyalty to our cause."

Teah hesitated for a moment and then continued with a curious expression. "Weren't there five duchies supporting our cause?"

"That is true," General Cyrus spoke up. "But General Clive of Ackerton Duchy is currently defending the houses of magic in Ceait from Englewood's forces."

"Very well," Teah acknowledged. "We need to move forward with our plans to siege the palace at Cordlain as quickly as possible to bring an end to the assault at Ceait. How many troops are in Cordlain?"

"According to our sources," General Covrent said, "fifty thousand duchy forces and seventy-five thousand Betra forces are camped just outside of Cordlain."

"And where do we place our numbers?" Teah asked.

"Thirty thousand duchy troops and around fifty thousand Betra troops," General Bree said.

"A third greater force than us," Caslor said with dismay.

"True, but we have many more Magus and the protector with us," General Haveben added.

"But they have a palace we need to breech and that may take months," Caslor countered.

There may be a faster way, Bastion spoke up.

What's that?

The Protector's Doorway, Bastion said.

What?

Logan used it to get inside and kill Englewood without laying siege to the palace. It is linked to a matching magical doorway that a protector can travel through, Bastion explained.

Where do I find this doorway?

You need to speak to the Betra. It was in Courage when Logan used it, but it can be brought here, Galiven said.

"Get me the head of the Betra at once," Teah said to Caslor.

He leapt to his feet and raced from the tent.

"What is it?" General Bree asked.

"A way to shorten this war, if it works," Teah said as the generals exchanged confused looks with each other.

Chapter 31

Saliday and Machala sat up with a start at the same moment as their eyes snapped open with realization. Morgan and Abria still slept next to the fire, but the two women exchanged looks that only validated their feelings.

"He is alive," they said in unison.

"He's alive?" Morgan said sitting up and rubbing his eyes.

"Yes," the women said at once.

"Will you stop that," Morgan said. "It creeps me out."

"Sorry," they both said and began to laugh. Their laughter came as a result of relief that Logan still lived and that he lay ahead of them only about a day or so.

"So we continue into Stellaran?" Abria asked cheerfully.

"We do indeed," Saliday said.

"That is wonderful news," Abria said getting to her feet and straightening her clothing.

"Yeah, wonderful," Morgan mumbled.

"What was that?" Saliday asked.

"Wonderful," Morgan said forcing a smile across his lips.

"That's what I thought you said," Saliday chirped and rolled up her bedding.

"Why do you think we lost contact with him?" Machala asked Saliday as they packed up.

"I've learned never to ask too many questions about how magic works," Saliday said. "It is just easier that way."

Machala nodded her comprehension of the sentiment and swung her bedroll across her back. Her black robe hung loose around her solid frame and she pulled the hood up over her head as she strode out of the camp.

"Good thing we kept on going after you lost contact with him," Abria said. "Are we headed in the right direction?" She eyed Morgan who tried to convince them to give up their quest once contact with Logan became severed.

Saliday and the others followed close behind. She felt anxious to reach Logan before he vanished from her senses again. Her desire to find him and make him understand that she needed him, wanted him, consumed her thoughts. The last time she spoke to him on the Morning Breeze, she felt his walls were finally coming down. She couldn't afford to miss what might be her last chance to make him understand how she felt about him.

They walked all day and into the night, pushing on as Machala and Saliday felt Logan close up ahead.

On a slight rise they spotted a campsite's fire with a wagon sitting off to one side. They counted four in the wagon, smaller, possibly children. Seven others lay around the fire as it burned steadily. A small river ran next to the site and the travelers licked their lips at the thought of fresh water instead of the water from the plants they harvested along the way, something Machala proved proficient at.

Movement beyond the camp on the other side of the river caught Saliday's attention as Machala leaned in to the Tarken.

"Someone is infiltrating the camp," Machala whispered.

Saliday watched as a group of two dozen or more crept into the camp, obviously with dangerous intentions. She looked to the camp, hoping to discern Logan from the others. A figure sat up in surprise as the aggressors entered the camp. The figure next to the first burst into action with such fury, Saliday knew it be Logan instantly.

Saliday stood from her crouched position drawing her throwing knives and raced toward the camp. She glanced to her right as Machala matched her stride for stride, her sword drawn and her black cloak fastened behind her back in the fighting position.

How did she have time to do that? Saliday wondered, but then the thought vanished and she entered the place of muscle memory, where she went from tracker, to killer, to survivor.

Machala and Saliday out-distanced Morgan and Abria as they raced ahead, the sounds of battle coming to them as they ran up a small rise just before the river and collided head on with the rear guard of the troops attacking Logan's camp.

The men spun in surprise as the two women bore down on them. Saliday's first throw took a man in the throat and the second another man in the chest. By that time Machala reached the men and slashed into them with powerful strokes of her curved sword, a replica of the protector's swords. The Betra adeptly dispatched the first three men she encountered and engaged the fourth before the rear guard of about ten men reacted.

Saliday hit one more with a dagger and then drew her short sword, hacking at the man rushing her. She deflected his assault and then slid back as he lost his balance due to her sudden retreat. She swept in and drove her sword through his chest.

A blade swung down on her as she pulled her sword free, but the blade met Morgan's sword and the Tarken Captain leapt over Saliday to drive back the attacker.

They fought the superior numbers now without the element of surprise and with some of the men returning to the rear defense when hearing the battle behind them, their odds shrank drastically.

Morgan, Machala, and Saliday stood their ground as the men regrouped and advanced fifteen strong on the three foreigners. The three braced for their charge when a bright light flashed overhead and the men cried out in pain, clawing at their eyes. They fell to the ground writhing in agony as Abria strode past Saliday and the others into the camp.

Morgan, Machala, and Saliday exchanged surprised, but relieved looks, and followed after the freed sniffer.

****

The campsite exploded with the sounds of battle as Cita cried out her warning.

Logan raced past her and she leapt to her feet with her sword drawn, but he already engaged the leaders in the assault, his swords striking out and deflecting blows so quickly that he scored hits after each deflection, sending man after man to the ground dead or dying.

The sight of the red-tipped feathers only fueled his aggression with anger making the protector even more deadly. His fury surged through him and his rage took over, sending him into the midst of the Red Tips hacking and slashing as he went, dropping limbs and heads as he drove through their ranks.

The Red Tips began to retreat, but only after discovering their greater numbers were no match for this foe. When the others from the camp joined in the fight, adding their swords and their magic to the battle, the Red Tips found their fate already sealed.

They turned to retreat as a bright light scorched the sky behind them and screams of agony filled the air. The Red Tips hesitated, looking back to Logan and his companions, and then toward the mysterious light and cries of their comrades. They darted to the sides, running for their lives. Logan reached for his bow before realizing it still lay in its sheath next to his bedroll.

"Logan," Zeva shouted as she tossed the solid metal rod to him.

Logan caught the rod and it instantly expanded to a bow as it touched his hand. He drew back the string and struck Red Tip after Red Tip in the back, dropping them one after another.

As a straggler veered into the clear of Logan's hail of arrows, Zeva, Linell, Stern, or Trevon would hit them with a blast of air or a well-placed burst of fire.

When the last Red Tip lay dead around their campsite, Logan shrunk his bow back to its original size and turned to the others as they stared at him in awe.

A sound of someone approaching brought the extended bow up

again, a notched arrow in the string held to Logan's cheek as four figures came into the firelight. Logan relaxed, instantly disqualifying the figures as Red Tips. He lowered the bow removing the tension on the string as the silver arrow magically vanished and then the bow retracted once more. He stood with his mouth open as the figures were illuminated by the firelight.

"Saliday Talis," Zeva shouted and hurried to greet the Tarken with a hug. "And Morgan," she hissed, drawing back and wrapping a weave of air around the captain, securing him.

"Zeva, what are you doing?" Saliday cried out in shock.

"Protecting Logan from a traitor," Zeva said, not taking her eyes or weave off Morgan.

Saliday began to argue, but Logan raised his hand to silence her. "We will sort this out, but first we need to be sure there are no more Red Tips about. I'm sure this was only a small regiment from their larger force."

"You can count on it," Stern said. "We'll go check it out." Stern motioned for Trevon and Fedlen to follow him and the three rushed to the horses and rode out of camp.

Linell and Cita joined Zeva in a defensive stance between Logan and the newcomers. They remained within an arm's reach of Saliday, Morgan, and the other two women standing before them.

"I'm fine," he said looking to the protective females. When they didn't move or soften their stance, he slipped between Cita's and Zeva's shoulder glancing at them as he passed. "I said I'm fine." Logan stood before Saliday looking down at her green eyes shining up at him.

"I found you," she said softly.

"You did," he answered with a nod. He glanced past her to Machala who now let her black robes drape down over her body. "Welcome Betra," he addressed her.

She took two strides toward him, bringing the women up to his side in defense, but he extended his arms out from his sides stopping them as the Betra knelt down in front of him.

She bowed her head to him. "I, Machala, Seeker of the Protector, lay my life at your feet and in your hands."

"Rise Machala, Seeker of the Protector," Logan said reaching down to help her to her feet. "I acknowledge you as the new seeker in keeping with your sister Sasha's mission."

Machala bowed her head to him in respect at the mention of Sasha. "You have honored Sasha and all of the seekers who shall follow by your treatment of the seekers."

"And Sasha honored me as a seeker and my friend in giving her life to save mine," Logan said, the words choking off at the end.

"My body and soul are yours to command," Machala said drawing raised eyebrows from Linell, Cita, and Zeva. Only Saliday didn't flinch at the implications of Machala's statement.

"What does she mean by that?" Cita asked.

"Sounds like she just became your slave," Linell said.

"No, not slave, betrothed," Machala stated matter-of-factly.

Saliday saw it coming and watched for it as the faces of the three women contorted with shock at the statement, but Cita's reaction told Saliday everything she needed to know about her feelings for Logan. Cita's eyes watered and she fought to control her emotions, but her reaction mirrored Saliday's own reactions nearly two years ago.

"It is their tradition," Logan tried explaining, but none of the women, especially Cita, would hear any of it.

They abandoned their protective positions around Logan and stormed from the campfire.

Logan watched them go, refraining from hurrying after them to explain. He shrugged. "I guess I need to give them time to calm down." He looked resigned to Machala. "Could that have waited for a better time? Did you need to just announce it?"

Now Machala did the shrugging.

Logan shook his head and lifted his chin to look over Saliday's shoulder at Abria standing alone in the dark. He extended his hand to her. "Come here, little one."

Saliday opened her mouth to warn him about her not being so helpless, but she snapped it shut.

"And who are you, my reformed sniffer?" Logan asked.

Abria stiffened at the mention of sniffer, but came closer to Logan and stared up at him. "My name is Abria. How did you know?"

Logan grinned as he reached out to clasp her hand in his. "I have seen sniffers before, all types, but you seem haunted by regret."

"I, I, never wanted to help them," she stammered.

Logan pulled her into a hug wrapping his bloodied arms around her, but Abria didn't seem to notice or care about the blood. She closed her eyes as he pulled her tight to his chest, holding her close. She smiled contentedly, wrapped her arms around him, and hugged him in return.

Saliday stared in awe at his transformation from a boy into a compassionate man. *When did that happen?*

"We are headed to a place where you might feel you truly belong. Would you like to come with us?" Logan asked looking down at her as he released her from his embrace and she beamed up at him.

Abria nodded with excitement.

"Very well. I will introduce you to some other children traveling with us and you can ride with them in the wagon," Logan said. He spotted Bethany hovering on the edge of the firelight and motioned her over.

Bethany walked closer and stopped expectantly next to Logan, evaluating Abria.

"Bethany, this is Abria. Will you please introduce your brother and sisters to her and see that she gets anything we have that she needs?"

Bethany smiled at Abria and then nodded as she looked back at Logan.

"Thank you."

Bethany extended her hand to Abria which the girl grasped and they hurried off.

Now Logan stood before Saliday, his first love who scorned him and the man she chose over him. The same man who happened to play a part in Logan finding himself adrift in a dingy according to Zeva. His eyes narrowed and his soft disposition hardened as he took in the two Tarkens.

"What are you doing here?" Logan asked. "And what is he doing here?"

"I don't know what Zeva is talking about," Morgan began, but a sharp look from Logan and Saliday silenced him.

"I lost touch with you once you were set adrift and didn't realize you lived until meeting up with Machala at Stalwart," Saliday explained.

"Why come back?" Logan questioned.

"Machala was coming to look for you..." Saliday started.

"Machala would have found her way to me, that is what a seeker does, but that doesn't explain why you thought you should come looking for me as well."

"I love you," Saliday said and then looked around self-consciously.

"You made your choice, you chose him," Logan said pointing at Morgan.

"I was wrong," Saliday pleaded. "I thought keeping the Tarken bloodline alive was enough, but I was wrong. I love you and always will."

"Oh, great!" Cita said sharply. Everyone turned to her as she stood with her arms crossed over her chest. "Now you have a betrothed *and* a past lover? How does a girl stand a chance?" She spun and stormed off.

"Cita, wait," Logan cried, but Cita didn't stop. He looked back to Saliday, his face twisted with conflicting feelings as he searched for the words. "I will always love you."

Saliday's hopes soared at his words, but then came the statement that changed everything.

"But, you have chosen a different path and I have come to accept that, now you must too," Logan said gently.

"I want us to be together," Saliday pleaded.

"I can't do that, not now, possibly not ever. You broke my heart, Saliday, and I can't trust you won't do it again."

"But I won't. I promise. Give me another chance," Saliday begged. "I love you."

"This isn't you," Logan leaned in and whispered firmly. "You are stronger than this. I can't risk my heart with you again after doing so nearly destroyed me and my quest."

"So you're rejecting me?" Saliday said as the tears began to flow down her cheeks.

"Not rejecting, that would be what you did to me and I could never hurt you like that. I am denying your request to open up my heart to you again. I will not risk it." He leaned down and kissed her on the forehead as her body shook with her sobs.

He turned to leave and caught Machala's eye. "See to her, please. And see to my prisoner until I decide what to do with him."

"Yes, Master Logan," Machala said with a nod.

Logan nodded and took a step before stopping and leaning back to the Betra. "Oh, can you please keep the betrothed thing to yourself until you have a chance to explain it to Cita and she understands that the choice of marriage lies with me?"

Machala smirked. "Yes, Master Logan."

He nodded his approval and walked off, shaking his head at

the turn this night took.

Saliday and Machala have made it here, he reached out to Teah.

Good, how about Morgan? Teah thought back.

Now my prisoner. I will decide his fate soon.

Remember, our side needs ships and captains.

But treacherous ones like Morgan?

Your call. I'm already dealing with Grinwald and Raven.

Your call on them, but remember, Grinwald has been a good ally in the past and Raven has skills our side can use.

Maybe some attitude adjustments might be in order?

Make them realize treason is a path better repented.

Exactly!

Teah's thoughts echoed in his head, although he didn't buy into the forgiveness route for Morgan easily. Grinwald and Raven needed to stand on their own merits and sins, but Morgan had undermined Logan's path since they met. He needed to understand why before he could even consider trusting him again. He paused a moment when he realized he never did trust the Tarken, but was that because he gave Saliday a reason to break his heart?

Chapter 32

Teah's forces marched across the western corner of Ter Chadain halting where the Bastion River empties into Lassain Bay. Reaching that point put them a day's march from Cordlain and also allowed them some protection from assaults using the bay and the river as protection, leaving them with only the west and south to defend. They planned on resting for a day and then heading out on the last leg of their journey.

That evening, as the camp fell silent and the patrols roamed the boundary, Caslor rushed into Teah's tent, surprising her as she sat going over maps on a large table. She looked up with a start as he smiled with excitement.

"It's here," he said beaming.

"Already? The Betra only left a week ago."

"They rode straight to Courage and then turned around and came right back. Needless to say they are worn out, but your Betra are a strong and determined people," Caslor said.

"Yes, yes they are," Teah agreed standing and wrapping a heavy cloak across her shoulders to cover her nightgown and ward off the night's chill. "Let's go have a look, shall we?"

Caslor drew back the tent flap and led Teah and her guard contingent to where the group of weary Betra huddled around a wagon with a large, canvas draped object protruding. They stopped and stared at the covered object.

Magus Matris and Magus Patris strode up, their faces showing the excitement of the moment.

"How did you...?" Teah asked in surprise.

"You can't think to keep something as important as the Protector's Doorway a secret from us," Magus Patris replied.

"I guess not." Teah shrugged. She looked to the waiting Betra and gave a nod.

The tarp pulled back to expose a solid silver doorframe that shimmered in the darkness as the firelight bounced off the highly polished surface.

Everyone went silent, only the sound of breathing and the crackling fires around them imposed on the quiet.

Teah walked up, carefully laying a hand on the shiny surface, flinching a bit at the coldness to her touch, but then running her hand across the smooth frame with respect.

"So this is how Logan got into the palace unseen?" she asked one of the Betra.

"The council confirmed that they witnessed the Protector, a Tarken, and the last Seeker enter the frame and then shortly after that the announcement of King Englewood's death reached them. A day or so later, the Protector appeared through the doorway with the dead king's wife and son and ordered them to be brought to Sacrifice," the Betra replied.

"Very well," Teah smiled at her reflection in the mirrored surface. "I will go through the doorway tomorrow."

"You can't put yourself in harm's way like that," Magus Patris objected.

"But you heard the Betra, only a protector can use the doorway," Caslor defended.

"Then you must take someone with you, like Logan did," Magus Matris said, breaking her silence.

"Take Grinwald and Raven," Magus Patris offered.

"No, I won't put anyone else in danger. I go alone," Teah said. "That is final," she added as Caslor, Magus Matris, and Magus Patris opened their mouths to object. She turned and strode off to her tent leaving them looking after her.

You know we were with Logan on that step through the doorway, Falcone told her.

And he did take Sasha and Saliday with him, Stalwart added.

Take someone with you, please, Galiven pleaded.

Take the two people you trust with your life the most, Bastion said making her stop just inside her tent's doorway.

Caslor and Rachel.

They have never failed you, Bastion agreed. *Even when they didn't agree with your decisions, they never betrayed you.*

Teah didn't know if she agreed with that reasoning, but she needed to sleep on it before she decided. The protectors continued to discuss the options and encourage her to make that choice as she lay in bed in the dark.

I told you all I would think about it, now quiet. I need some sleep.

The voices in her head went silent and she sighed with relief. Closing her eyes, she let her mind lose its thoughts and go blank.

"Teah?" Caslor's voice reached her through the tent fabric.

"Yes?" she answered.

"Can I come in?" he asked.

"I'm in bed, Caslor, what do you want?" she questioned, irritation rising in her voice.

"I want to come in."

"Enter," she said as her eyebrows rose with curiosity.

Caslor slipped in without lighting any candles or torches. She heard him strike a piece of furniture and curse the spirits for his lack of memory, but he finally reached her bedside and hesitated.

"Couldn't it wait until morning? What do you need?" she grumbled.

"You," he whispered as he lifted the covers and slid between the sheets, pressing up next to her.

She stiffened with surprise then relaxed as his gentle arms embraced her and pulled her to his warm, bare chest. She turned her head and searched for his lips. When she found them, she devoured them hungrily. Her feelings for him, which she'd forced down and tried to control since they left the ship, pressed against her control. Those pent up feelings now erupted running freely through her and into him through where their flesh touched, consuming them both. She held him close, needing him more than she needed anything or anyone before.

She felt the protectors stir and she lifted her wall, shutting them out. She purposefully disconnected with Logan, only too aware how he would feel if she let her feelings at that moment transfer. She remembered the unfortunate instance where Logan and Saliday found themselves in these exact same circumstances and just the memory caused her to blush.

With all of her walls up to protect her from projecting her feelings to anyone else, she concentrated on Caslor and allowed herself to fall into his passion. Their feelings mixed together and rose to a new level unlike anything she might have imagined. She let herself go and trusted him like no one before. And it felt right.

****

Sunlight streaming through a slit high in the tent's ceiling shone on Teah's face as she opened her eyes to find herself alone. She sat up and scanned the tent to find no signs of Caslor or any indication what went on the night before. She flopped back down on her bed with her arms spread wide over her head, a satisfied smile on her face.

She felt different somehow. She felt relaxed, at peace, content. She never imagined letting herself love someone so completely would feel this way. Her mind drifted to Talesaur, the first man to ever show any kind of love, but she now found it hard to recall his face. She felt a pang of sorrow for him as she knew he sacrificed so much defending her from Ordestan and then ultimately gave his life to assure that Logan succeed on his quest to reach her.

A tear ran down her cheek and she lifted a hand to wipe it away and with it, her sorrow for Talesaur lifted and she forced her thoughts back to Caslor, making her heart soar.

She got up from her bed with a light heart and dressed for her step through the doorway, confident with her decision on who to take with her.

She stepped into the sunlight from her tent and surveyed the camp as the Betra guarding her tent snapped to attention. She wore a long green riding cloak with the hood pulled up over a deep green shirt and matching pants tucked into her thigh high boots. Her swords jutted over her shoulders and the bow rested in the sheath strapped to her leg. Striding through the camp, she headed for the doorway with one thing on her mind…kill King Aston.

The mass of Betra around her drew the attention of her troops, but she continued on without hesitation as they cheered at her passing. She reached the silver doorway to find a large contingent of Betra surrounding it and Caslor in his traveling garb waiting for her.

He stepped forward to greet her with a knowing smile and a slight bow and she felt the heat of her embarrassment flush her cheeks.

"Good morning," Teah said softly.

"Indeed it is, My Lady," Caslor answered.

His simple words held new meaning for her this morning as she truly felt like his lady. She smiled at the thought and looked at the others gathered.

Rachel, Grinwald, and Raven stood in their accustomed traveling clothing waiting patiently for her arrival. Now that she'd appeared, they looked questioningly to her as her plan to step through the doorway was murmured among their ranks.

Magus Patris and Magus Matris stood beside the others with their long flowing robes, the mother in white and the father in black.

Teah smiled at the sight of the most powerful Magus in Ter Chadain waiting for her decision on who to take into the doorway.

So you have decided that now is the time? Bastion spoke up.

The time of repentance is upon us.

"Grinwald and Raven will accompany me," Teah announced.

Caslor and Rachel burst into protest as the other four smiled in victory.

"You can't leave me out of this," Caslor argued. "I will do anything to protect you."

"That is why I made my decision," Teah said spinning on him. "You are too close to me and it may cloud your choices in crucial moments. I need someone with me who can make the hard decisions even if that means letting me go."

Caslor opened his mouth to continue his objection, but then snapped it shut as he realized she was right.

"But Teah, I will be by your side and defend you to the end," Rachel pleaded.

"As I have no doubt," Teah agreed. "But you were right when you said that it was my bad decisions that get those around me killed, like Lizzy. I will not take that chance with you. You're the only true friend I have left from my childhood. I won't lose you too if I can help it."

Rachel's eyes watered at the mention of Lizzy and she bowed her head in agreement.

"And you two," Teah said turning to a gloating Grinwald and Raven. "I have decided that you will accompany me, not because the Magus Patris and Magus Matris wished it, and not because I trust you, but actually the opposite."

Grinwald's and Raven's confident smirks slipped from their faces.

"I'm taking you with me to allow you to make amends for your treasonous actions on the Morning Breeze against my brother," Teah continued.

Grinwald's and Raven's faces went white as ghosts as Teah announced their secret. They stood stunned, staring at Teah in shock as she accused them.

"So, this mission is a chance for redemption. If you choose to come, then I will consider your honor and your loyalty to me and my cause restored. If you decide to stay, then you will be taken prisoner and wait to stand trial on my return."

"And what if you don't return?" Raven asked.

"Then you will be considered guilty and be put to death," Teah said flatly.

"You must be joking," Magus Patris scoffed.

"Not at all. If they come with me and I don't return, they too will be either dead or prisoners of Englewood's since they cannot return through the doorway without me."

"So we have no choice but to go with you and assure that you survive," Grinwald said coming out of his stupor.

"Now you understand. I only want loyalty from those who follow me. Since you have shown your disloyalty in casting Logan off the Morning Breeze, you need to show me you are truly loyal and that action was one rare lack of judgment."

The gathering went silent as Teah's words sank in.

"Caslor will be in charge of the army with Rachel to help him. The Magus Matris and Magus Patris will also aid in the decisions, but Caslor has final say."

"He is from Caltoria, not Ter Chadain," the Magus Patris objected.

"This is true, but his father was their greatest general and he has as much knowledge of battle as anyone else here," Teah pointed out. "If I do not return by the morning, you are to start your assault on Cordlain Palace."

"Are you sure about this?" Caslor asked stepping in front of her and placing a hand on each of her arms.

"Yes," she answered holding his gaze until he nodded his head in support and stepped back.

"Take the doorway down and place it against that boulder," Caslor ordered the Betra who loosened the ropes and unloaded the doorway from the wagon, setting it against a large boulder that towered over them all.

Teah stepped in front of the frame and paused to look back at Grinwald and Raven. The two chosen companions glanced to the Magus Patris and the Magus Matris and then strode over to flank Teah.

Remember, Logan used this once already to enter the palace, Stalwart reminded her.

So they may have moved it to a cliff, or the moat, or raging fire pit, or any number of unfavorable locations for you to walk into, Bastion shared.

Teah grimaced at the possibilities she hadn't envisioned. *How do I react to that?*

You use your magic to protect yourself in that event, Falcone instructed.

Teah nodded at his advice and turned to Grinwald.

"Weave a protective shell around you," she said and finished her statement as she looked to Raven. "We don't know where the other doorway is and need to be prepared in case we step off a cliff on the other side."

Raven and Grinwald shared apprehensive looks and nodded their understanding.

Teah drew her swords and extended a hand to Grinwald and Raven. Each grabbed hold of her wrist and she saw their weaves go up. Teah thought of a protective weave and her weave rose around her. She gave one last glance over her shoulder at Caslor and Rachel, forcing a smile and then stepped into the doorway.

The sensation hit her like cold river water, taking her breath away and causing her to shiver. Her eyes blurred and hurt with the coldness. She continued walking as the frigid feeling gave way to warmth and her eyesight cleared as stones and metal bars appeared before them.

A sleepy guard sitting on a stool on the other side of the bars tumbled off his seat at the sight of them and quickly pulled a rope strung through several pulleys.

Teah followed the rope and spun around in time to see the doorway slide through the bars, out of the cell and out of their reach, successfully eliminating their escape route.

"We've got them," the guard shouted as he rushed down a long hallway past other cells and out the door. "We've got them," echoed down the corridor as he ran.

Teah looked to Grinwald and Raven as their predicament sunk in. King Aston now held the Queen Protector of Ter Chadain in his dungeon. In one step through a doorway, the revolution crashed to an end.

Logan, I'm sorry I failed you, Teah reached out to her brother as her despair overwhelmed her.

Chapter 33

The party rode in silence as they crossed the last distance to the Shotwarg Cliffs and the school hidden within. Logan stayed next to Cita, even though she chose to ignore him since discovering Machala was betrothed to him and Saliday was his ex-lover. She withdrew into herself, leading them out of necessity and nothing more.

Logan didn't approach her that morning and decided to let her have some space to work her thoughts out. He glanced back at the others as they followed, smiling as he witnessed Bethany and Abria chatting excitedly. He felt good about the sniffer finding someone she could be friends with. He couldn't see Morgan, but he knew the Tarken lay in the back of the wagon still restrained by Zeva's weave. Logan ignored Morgan while trying to work out the best solution for his treasonous prisoner.

Machala and Saliday rode double next to him a few paces behind, close enough to protect him but far enough back they weren't hovering.

The others rode behind the wagon, scanning the surroundings and chatting back and forth, laughing and joking as they kept their heads on a swivel looking for any lurking dangers. Zeva watched Morgan in the back of the wagon, her look one of hatred that melted away as she interacted with Stern, Fedlen, Linell, and Trevon only to return when she considered the captain once more.

The cliffs rose ahead of them and Logan searched the flat walls for any sign of life or openings that might indicate a human presence. He found none.

They continued riding into the cliffs and finally stopped at the face of the slick, grey stone walls. Cita waited, looking at the group until they all gathered around her and then pulled her horse to the back of the wagon.

Logan followed and soon everyone gathered around the

wagon. They stared expectantly at Cita as she hopped from her horse and reached into the wagon bringing out her bed roll. She unrolled her bedding as everyone exchanged confused looks.

Logan was about to comment that the time wasn't right to be taking a rest when Cita began tearing strips of the blanket off. She motioned for Bethany to come to her and the girl jumped from the wagon and walked over. Cita handed the strips of cloth already torn to the girl.

"Distribute these to all but Stern," she instructed. "Tie one over the eyes of the prisoner as well."

Logan nodded his understanding as he hopped down from his mount and pulled a rope from the wagon. He began looping the rope through the bridles of the horses then attached one end to the back of the wagon. Then he cut the rope and looped the rest to his and then up to Cita's horse.

"I can't have anyone see the entrance," she said to them. "Stern and I will lead you in."

She strode to her horse and climbed into the saddle. She turned back as they all tied the strips of fabric over their eyes. Logan glanced at her and then slid the cloth in place, blocking out his surroundings. He felt his horse lurch into motion at the tug of Cita's rope and heard the wagon creak as it moved behind him. He held on tight as they began to climb, the light filtering through the blanket strip went black and the horse's footsteps along with the sound of the wagon's wheels echoed around him.

He spent far too much time underground on Scalded Island to feel comfortable being led blindly in the darkness. The urge to pull off his blindfold rose as anxiety crept up on him and threatened to send him into a panic. Just when he felt his control vanish, sunlight hit his blindfold and the echoes around him dropped away.

They slowed to a stop and he sat waiting.

"You can remove your blindfolds," Cita instructed.

Logan lifted his blindfold and glanced back to witness the others blinking in the bright sunlight as well. He turned to Cita and their surroundings rising above her, dwarfing her as a city carved in the stone walls liberated from the mountain stood inside the vast opening stretching for the open sky above them.

"Welcome to Shotwarg Cliffs," Cita said. She slipped from her mount and strode off without a glance behind at her companions.

Stern took up her guide position as he freed the connecting ropes from each horse and then motioned them to dismount. As they dropped one-by-one to the stone ground, he collected their mounts and motioned for a young boy who ran into view. The boy rushed to them and took the horses, staring at the newcomers with curiosity before leading the horses away.

A girl, slightly older than the boy, hurried over and helped the children out of the wagon, pausing to stare at the strange man struggling to inch his way to the back of the wagon and finally slipping off to stand without movement of his arms or legs.

Morgan glared back at the girl who shrugged before taking hold of the horses and leading the wagon away.

Zeva walked over to Logan as he stood staring in awe at the massive city.

"Glad I put a gag on that man as well as restraints," Zeva chuckled.

Logan nodded and laughed. Morgan could talk his way out of most anything. He thought that might be the Tarken's greatest weapon.

Logan and the others waited a while longer before a large contingent of armed soldiers dressed in grey armor matching the stone walls marched up on them. Their helmeted heads hid everything but their eyes. They clamored to a halt and parted to allow a slender, dark-skinned man with a white beard matching his white hair cut short against his head, walk through accompanied by Cita. Cita now wore a long grey dress, split at the thigh exposing her bare legs visible just above her thigh-high grey boots. Her dark hair pulled back from her face in a thick braid that flowed down her back shown in the sunlight.

The two stopped before him and the man gave a generous bow.

"Welcome to Shotwarg Cliffs, home to magicals who wish peace and learning away from the oppression of the Stellaran Crystal Council. I am Miso Tallar, head master of the school and caretaker of the city."

"I am..." Logan began, but Miso raised a hand to stop the introduction.

"I know who you are, as well as your companions," Miso said. "It is an honor to have you here, Protector Logan."

"Thank you," Logan said with a slight nod of respect.

"Doyen Cita has cleared you all, except the one named Morgan. Where is the prisoner?"

"Doyen?" Logan questioned looking to Cita with surprise.

"Yes, Cita is the leader of our troops trained to aid in the fulfillment of the prophecy," Miso explained.

"This is Morgan," Zeva said taking a step and giving Morgan a shove. The restrained captive hopped for a few feet in an attempt to retain his balance, but then toppled onto his face against the stone with a thud as the air rushed from his lungs.

Two guards shuffled over and lifted the man, his nose bleeding profusely, and dragged him away.

"I will have you shown to your quarters. I hope keeping you all in the same wing is acceptable?" Miso said.

"That will be fine," Logan agreed, staring at Cita as if he was seeing her for the first time.

Miso clapped his hands and several teenage children appeared. They bowed to Logan and the others.

"Please show our guests to their quarters," Miso said.

Logan looked to Cita and she gave a nod.

Logan waited for the others to walk past following the guides and then stepped in behind.

"I will see you shortly," Cita whispered as Logan passed.

He continued after the others as they headed into a large stone building and the great stone entrance. The floors shone a finely polished grey as their footsteps echoed around them. They climbed a wide staircase and proceeded down a long hallway where each member of his party entered their room designated by the guide.

As each stepped into their room the others continued on, Logan hesitated at their doorway telling them he would send for them shortly. They nodded and closed the doors behind them.

When Logan reached Saliday's door, he stopped and searched for the right words. She looked at him without emotion.

"Are you in this with me?" he asked.

"From day one in that tavern in Ceait," she replied proudly.

"I will send for you shortly," he told her and walked on.

Machala paused at her doorway but refused to enter to the consternation of her guide. When Logan walked up, they both turned to him in frustration.

"She won't take her room, she says she wants to be with you," the teenage girl said, her hand running through her long brown hair as she tried to stay composed, but her brown eyes said she neared her breaking point.

"I am here to protect you. How am I to do that if we are not in the same quarters?" Machala stated.

"Do my quarters have enough space to house two of us?" Logan asked the girl.

"Yes, inner and outer quarters, sir," the girl said nervously.

"Then she will remain with me," Logan instructed.

The girl nodded and led them to the last set of doors in the long hallway. She unlatched and swung inward the large double doors into the giant outer room adorned with lush paintings and tapestries. Along the far wall, a fireplace capable of fitting an entire tree butted up against a large bank of glass windows looking out over the courtyard below. A large desk sat on the other wall with ornately carved tables and lushly upholstered chairs and couches set into groupings around the giant space.

"Your bed chambers are through the door to your right," the girl pointed to the large double doors opposite the fireplace tucked in the corner along the wall of windows.

"Thank you," Logan said, overwhelmed by the opulence of the space. Even though he encountered many extravagant places in his travels since leaving his farm, all this wealth never failed to make him feel unworthy.

Logan waited for the girl to leave and turned to Machala.

"Sleep wherever you like, I will be next door." He stepped through the doors into the sleeping quarters and stared at the massive room every bit as graciously adorned as the outer chambers. He stood in front of a large mirror and slipped from his clothes, then took the pitcher of water from the table and carefully poured some over his head, letting it run down his face and chest to drip on the floor. He took the towel neatly folded next to the small basin on the table and dabbed his face and chest before leaning forward and pouring the rest of the pitcher over his head into the basin. After drying his head with the towel, he dropped it to the floor and dabbed up the water he spilt. He stared at himself in the shiny wooden floor for a moment and then back at himself in the mirror as he straightened before it.

When did he become so old, he thought as he ran a finger along the deep creases on his face he never noticed before?

Logan, I'm sorry I've failed you, came to his mind as Teah's thoughts leapt into his head.

What is it?

I used the Protector's Doorway and have stepped right into a trap.

Don't panic, there has to be a way out. Logan's mind raced as he tried to come up with a solution for his sister.

We're in the dungeons in Cordlain.

Who is with you?

Raven and Grinwald.

More than enough magic to get out of there. Get out of the cell and use the doorway to escape.

But we will never be this close to Aston again without laying siege to the palace. That could take months and cost many lives. Not to mention the houses of magic will fall in that amount of time.

Your safety is the most important thing here. A long silence fell and then it came to Logan. *Escape the cell and then have the protectors lead you to the hidden passages. If Aston hasn't discovered them, you can stay in there until you have your chance.*

And if they come back and discover we're gone…

They'll think you retreated through the doorway.

Thank you, brother.

Good luck.

He dropped down onto the large bed, the down mattress nearly swallowing him with softness.

Slipping off his pants he kicked them to the floor, stretched out his arms over his head, and closed his eyes. He drifted toward sleep, hovering somewhere between dream and reality when he felt the bed move and then a warm body press up against him.

Opening his eyes, a soft glow of candlelight filled the room and he stared into the deepest brown eyes. He started to sit up, but a hand gently pushed him back as Cita stared at him with a curious smile. She leaned on her elbow with her hand holding her head inches from his.

"What?" he asked, but his question vanished as her lips touched his and Cita gave a deep sigh. They held the kiss for a long, sweet moment and then she pulled away.

Logan opened his eyes and took in her beauty in the candlelight, smiling back at her contented expression. Her skin shown under the light white fabric of her nightgown and his breath caught in his throat at her beauty.

"I'm sorry," she whispered.

"For what?"

"Doubting you."

"I don't blame you."

"No, I shouldn't have," she said shaking her head.

"Really, first a woman from my past appears and then I have a Betra proclaim I am her betrothed, which is just crazy."

"I guess when you put it that way, I'm not sorry," she said and unsuccessfully tried to wipe her smile from her face. She gave up and leaned in, kissing him again.

As she leaned back, Logan frowned at her.

"What?"

"Doyen?"

"I should have told you, but there was no need. It doesn't change anything."

"Except that you're the leader of some sort of order sworn to aid me in claiming the throne of Stellaran?" Logan didn't sound pleased.

"That is true, but like I said, it doesn't change anything."

"I don't need a faithful order of followers to throw down their lives for me. I won't have that weight on my shoulders."

"I guess that's just one more thing," Cita said matter-of-factly.

"One more thing what?"

"One more thing you don't have any control over. Like me having feelings for you."

"I don't want anyone to die for me," Logan continued to protest.

"You really don't get it, do you?" Cita said, at a loss.

"Get what?"

"No one is dying for you, Logan Lassain, Protector of Ter Chadain," Cita said leaning back on the bed and throwing her hands over her head.

"What are you talking about? Many have died defending me."

Cita looked at him and the amusement faded from her expression as her brown eyes held his, serious.

"People are protecting you and dying for you for only one reason."

"And what is that?"

"You represent a better life for them, their children, and their children's children."

Logan's jaw dropped, gaping as he felt the truth of her words. It all seemed so clear now and he saw his future tied to everyone he ever came in contact with differently.

"Their future hangs on your success. You hold their future in your hands."

Logan rolled back and stared at the red canopy over his bed, the golden silk embroidery lining the edges.

The weight of the world fell upon him as he struggled to catch his breath. In that dingy adrift at sea with Zeva he threw the weight off and felt uplifted for the first time in over a year. Now, that weight came tumbling back tenfold as the future of Stellaran, a country he didn't even know, dropped upon him, threatening to crush him.

Cita rolled on top of him, straddling him as she stared down at him, his eyes wide gazing back at her.

"Don't fear, I will be by your side, guiding you every step of the way," she said and leaned down to kiss him deeply.

He accepted her kiss and added his need for her to it, intensifying it until they gasped for air.

Shield brother, shield, Teah's embarrassed thoughts pinged off his mind.

Sorry, Logan replied, instantly throwing up a shield in his mind and barring her from his thoughts as he reached up and pulled Cita back to his hungry lips. Those lips were the only thing keeping him from exploding with the responsibility threatening to destroy him and he abandoned himself to them…gladly.

Chapter 34

As Teah, Grinwald, and Raven vanished through the doorway, Caslor motioned for the Betra to load the doorway onto the wagon.

"What are you doing?" Rachel asked taking hold of his arm.

"What I was born to do," Caslor said flatly. "Lead."

"But she said we aren't supposed to start the siege on the palace until tomorrow," Rachel protested.

"True, but we are going to prepare and have our troops ready to start that siege if she doesn't show. I want every chance at getting into the palace and saving her if she doesn't make it out on her own." He stared at Rachel who held his gaze for a moment and then gave a curt nod.

"You heard him, let's get everyone packed up and moving toward Cordlain," Rachel shouted causing anyone within earshot to jump into motion.

By midmorning, the entire army marched across the Bastion River heading for Cordlain. They moved steady, but slow and Caslor grew concerned they wouldn't be in place by the next morning.

"Can't they move faster?" he grumbled sitting astride his horse on a rise and watching the massive force lumber along.

"This much might is not swift," Magus Patris said, his tone placid.

Rachel raced up, excitement spread across her face as she pulled her horse up in front of Caslor and the Magus Patris.

"The Betra are coming." Rachel pointed out ahead of their advancing force.

Caslor and Magus Patris lifted their gaze to the east to see an enormous mass of troops bearing down on their army.

"Sound the halt and prepare to defend," Caslor shouted as he straightened in his saddle.

"Wait, you don't understand," Rachel said reaching over to lay a calming hand on Caslor's arm.

Caslor turned to her in confusion and then back to the advancing Betra force. As the first line of Betra reached the front line of their troops, they pulled up and slipped from their horses to greet the Betra in the army with welcoming gestures. Caslor turned back to Rachel.

"It seems that Teah's message resonated with them," Rachel said grinning.

"How many?" Magus Patris asked.

"From what the leaders of the Betra with us say, nearly all of them, except for a few who came from Sacrifice with Aston," Rachel said.

"That should be nearly one hundred thousand troops," Magus Patris said with a sense of wonder.

"More than enough for a successful siege," Caslor sighed.

"But remember, Cordlain has thick walls and a large number of duchy troops within those walls," Magus Matris said riding up behind them. "Not to mention the Viri and Zele Magus who have chosen to side with a King Englewood once more."

"And how many magicals do we need to worry about?" Caslor asked.

"Each and every one," Magus Matris said stoically, not truly understanding the question, but her statement making a valid point.

Caslor turned back to the group of Betra now melding with his troops. He needed to worry about the magicals because every magical could do the damage of hundreds of troops. He needed a way to neutralize them and remove them from the equation else the siege might be prolonged for weeks, maybe months. He couldn't chance being delayed when time might prove crucial to saving Teah if she failed to return through the doorway.

He turned to Rachel, Magus Matris, and Magus Patris. "How

do you control a magical here in Ter Chadain?"

"We weave a shield around them severing their connection to their magic, why?" Magus Patris asked hesitantly, not liking where this was going.

"Can you do it over a distance?" Caslor pressed.

"Yes, but they could do it to us as well, unless we defend it," Magus Matris explained.

"Then we must do it first," Caslor insisted.

"It is something we do not make a practice of," Magus Patris said.

"Many Viri and Zele Magus don't even know how to weave such a spell," Magus Matris added.

"I would start to show every magical we have how to defend against it as well as weave it around our enemies," Caslor said as he turned back to the army finally moving forward once more. He wasn't going to leave anything to chance. The one person he cared about most depended on it.

****

"Hurry, we need to escape back through the doorway," Grinwald said as he stood in front of the smoking bars of the cell that once separated them from the silver frame.

He and Raven hurried to the doorway and then turned, perplexed at Teah's hesitation as she stood staring blankly at them. She shook her head.

"No, what do you mean no?" Raven hissed. "They knew we were coming. We need to get out of here."

"No, we will never have this chance again," Teah said distracted by the thoughts in her head.

"The chance to be King Aston's prisoners?" Grinwald asked.

"A chance to get this close and end it," Teah corrected.

Footsteps sounded on the stairwell outside of the room holding the cells and they turned toward the door in apprehension.

"So we fight through all of Aston's men then?" Raven asked looking at Teah expecting her to take up the protector role and become the legendary warrior.

Teah hurried to the furthest wall from the silver frame and pushed a brick inward then stepped back as the wall opened exposing a passageway.

"Get inside, quickly," Teah ordered.

Raven gave Grinwald a look of misery and stepped past Teah without acknowledging her, disappearing into the darkness beyond.

Grinwald opened his mouth to protest but Teah's look stopped him short. He hung his head and followed after Raven without a word.

Teah went inside and the wall slid closed engulfing them in darkness.

They sat in darkness as they listened to the room they just vacated fill with soldiers. The murmured voices became frantic, building to a muffled crescendo and then the hurried footsteps trampled from the room leaving them in silence.

Grinwald produced a ball of light floating over the palm of his outstretched hand. He looked to Teah and Raven as they surveyed their new surroundings.

The slick stones shone back from the magical light exposing their dampness and Raven crinkled her nose at the musty odor in their hiding place.

"This hasn't been used in many years," Grinwald observed.

"How did you know it was here?" Raven asked causing Teah to hesitate at the unexpected, but logical question.

Teah drew in a deep breath and then regretted it as she coughed the dusty, moldy smelling air in the passage. Once she quieted her cough, she paused for a moment and then looked the rebel fighter from Caltoria in the eye.

"There are things through my travels I have discovered that I prefer not to share," she stated firmly. "This is one of those discoveries. Just be happy I possessed this knowledge."

"No, I can't agree with that one," Raven said with a shake of her head. "I guess going back through the doorway would have been preferable to hiding in an old secret passage and cutting off our only chance of escape."

"Watch your tone," Teah warned her.

"My tone is my own to regulate," Raven shot back edging closer to Teah, the glow of magic filling the passageway as the tension rose.

"Enough," Grinwald said forcing himself between them. "This is a mission to put Teah on the throne. We cannot lose sight of that."

The tension held for a moment longer as the women glared at each other, but then subsided as logic began to permeate the hostility.

"What is our next step?" Raven sighed, resigned.

Teah gave Raven a slight nod at her request and then turned inward to her advisors.

What now?

This passage connects to the main hall upstairs, Bastion informed her.

You should wait until everyone retires and then make a break across the great hall to the passage behind the grand fireplace in the hall, Galiven added.

That will lead you up to the outer rooms of the king's chambers, Falcone said.

And King Aston, Stalwart said, his seething anger evident in his tone.

Then perhaps we can end the Englewood bloodline and threat to the throne once and for all, Bastion finished.

I will not be as merciful as Logan, Teah agreed. *We see where that got him.*

"We follow this passage up to the great hall and wait for tonight when everyone goes to bed," Teah told Grinwald and Raven. "From there we can get into a passage that leads us to the king's chambers."

"And be done with this nonsense for good," Raven growled.

"That's right," Grinwald agreed. "And put the true queen on the throne."

"Indeed," Teah said and slipped past them to lead the way through the narrow winding tunnel that sloped upward to the levels above them.

Raven hesitated a moment beside Grinwald as Teah lit a ball of magic for herself and continued on. "Are you sure she is better than Logan?" Raven asked.

"No, but she was the logical choice," Grinwald pointed out.

"But now that she knows what we did to him, how safe are we?"

"About as safe as we ever were dealing with magic this powerful," he said with a shrug and hurried after Teah.

"Great," Raven groaned and shuffled after them.

Chapter 35

Logan opened his eyes to the darkened room feeling the warmth of Cita next to him. He smiled at her touch, but something gave him pause. He felt uneasy. He scanned the room searching for the source of his discomfort, but nothing revealed itself. He turned to kiss Cita on the forehead and as his eyes fluttered to the shadow of her face close to his, he caught movement out of the corner of his eye.

From his prone position on the bed, he leapt over Cita taking the bed linens with him and barreled into a figure inching closer to Cita's side.

The maneuver left Cita completely exposed on the bed, shocking her awake not only by his sudden movement, but also the chill on her bare skin. She sat up as the bedding undulated on the floor with its occupants.

"Machala," Cita shouted as she scurried to the writhing fabric.

The Betra burst into the room, lending the light from the other room to the bedchamber as a night gowned Cita circled the bedding on the floor and the struggle underneath.

Machala surged forward without hesitation and pulled the fabric away to reveal Abria who slammed a crooked dagger into the Betra's midsection and then spun on Logan as he untangled himself from the bedding.

Abria pulled the blade from Machala who slumped to the floor and lunged at Logan.

Cita hurtled herself into Abria sending the much smaller girl sliding across the polished wooden flooring and crashing into the furniture. Cita scrambled to her feet and sent a weave at Abria who deflected the weave with a raised hand and sent it into a table and chairs, shattering the wood with the impact of the magic.

Abria released a weave of her own at Cita who dove out of the way, but the weave struck her with a glancing blow and sent her spinning across the floor and into a large couch with a loud crunching sound.

By this time, Logan stood with the protector swords crossed in front of him, facing the Senji with her crooked bladed dagger.

Abria smiled her sweetest smile bending down to pull an identical dagger from her boot and spun both skillfully in her hands as she circled Logan looking for an opening.

Logan took a moment to glance at Machala lying still on the floor as he stepped carefully over her and Abria sent a weave into him.

The magic struck the swords, impacting them with force and sending Logan sliding across the floor bracing against them. He held the blades firmly against the magic and concentrated on the Senji as she lightly stepped over Machala's body.

"Why are you doing this, Abria?" Logan asked, glancing quickly over his shoulder at Cita who lay still on the floor.

"Once you have a mark on you, you are marked until the job is done," Abria said, her voice light and musical.

"But the man who hired you is dead," Logan argued.

"The first man who hired us is dead," she agreed. "But not the second or third."

The admission caught Logan off guard at the thought of multiple contracts taken out on his life.

"Fine, Aston has obvious motives to put out a contract on me," Logan said. "But who is the third?"

"Oh, I have told you only the one who is dead, but I cannot reveal those still living. It is against the Senji code," Abria said. Her tone remained conversational as if they spoke over tea instead of stepping over a body and brandishing blades.

"What hopes do you have of killing me now that your element of surprise is gone," Logan pointed out.

"It is what I must do," Abria said raising her hand and sending another weave into the raised swords.

The weave parted harmlessly around Logan's swords and struck furnishing behind him in a jumble of crashes.

"But others have failed before you," Logan said and regretted his comment as Abria's sweet face turned to fury.

"One of those Senji was my brother," Abria screamed. "And the reason I asked for this contract." She hurtled toward Logan, her crooked blades slashing.

Logan backed away, deflecting the slashes of the Senji blades with his own. Sparks flicked from the contact of steel on steel. He knew all too well that the assassin's blades were dipped in poison to increase their lethalness. He arched back as Abria aimed both blades for his chest, bringing a sword up to swipe them away and spin out of her reach. He searched her eyes for any sign of talking her down from her frenzy. Instead, he saw nothing but madness as her mouth foamed at the corners in her rabid attack.

She raised her hand sending a weave of air into him, knocking him backwards into a chair and crushing it beneath him as he crashed to the floor. She dove on top of him, straddling his waist and driving her blades down toward his chest with all her might.

The blades struck Logan in the chest, hit the chain mail, and twisted painfully from Abria's hands. She cried out in frustration and agony as the daggers skittered across the polished floor and out of her reach. She raised her hand as she drew in the magic to weave a deadly blow.

Logan saw the weave building over Abria's hand as it turned blood red. He swung both arms up from the floor at his sides and crossed them as his blades slid into the girl's midsection and continued his arc until they reverberated with a metal ring as they struck the floor on either side of him.

The magic building over Abria's hand vanished and she stared down at him, shock and surprise across her young, seemingly innocent face, as her body from the waist up toppled off him leaving her lower extremities still sitting him. Blood gushed from the severed body covering Logan in the hot, nauseating gore of his own creation.

Logan dropped his swords and rolled to his side, forcing the severed remains from him and vomiting into the blood and guts surrounding him. He struggled to his feet, pausing a moment at the blind staring eyes of Abria, the latest victim of the Protector of Ter Chadain. Picking up the discarded bedding, he wiped as much of the entrails from his face and chest as he could but it dried surprisingly quickly to his skin.

He knelt beside Machala as she lay with her eyes closed on the floor. Touching her chest to check for a heartbeat, he already knew that poison-dipped blade spared few. He reached over and lifted some of the linens to cover her body and bowed his head in respect.

Cita moaned and he scrambled across the floor to her, taking her in his arms to hold her tight. She opened her eyes and screamed at the sight of him.

"Oh, oh dear spirits," Cita cried out in shock.

"I'm fine," Logan said calmly.

"But the blood? Whose?" she hesitated glancing around first to the lump under the bedding and then to the two pieces of Abria. "Logan, what happened?" she gasped.

"A member of a brotherhood of assassins," Logan explained.

"Abria was a Senji?"

"You know about Senji in Stellaran?" Logan said in surprise.

"Where do you think they started? Everyone has roots in Stellaran. Their band is strong here as well."

"Great," Logan said helping Cita sit up and then standing to turn and offer her a hand to help her to her feet.

She gripped his hand and he pulled her up beside him.

"Are you okay?" Logan asked as Cita rubbed the back of her head grimacing.

"Yeah, just a bit rattled. I'll be fine."

"She came closer than the rest have," Logan nodded toward Abria.

"There have been others?"

"She is the third who has tried and failed."

"What happened to the others?" Cita asked trying to wrap her head around it.

"All dead. I killed one in Ter Chadain, one on the ship coming over to Caltoria, and then Abria," Logan said with a shrug.

"Don't you realize that once you kill one of them you are marked for life by all of them?" Cita moaned in disbelief.

"So I've heard."

"And that doesn't bother you?"

"I've been a target for many people and am still here. Does it really matter who is after me? I have to kill them to survive no matter what group they belong to."

"That's true, but the Senji are trained assassins. They are everywhere and obviously, can be anyone," she said motioning to Abria's body but not looking at the gory sight.

"If I'm dead, it really doesn't matter to me who kills me. The result is the same."

Cita stared at him hard, not knowing how to take his candor about his mortality and the likelihood of his lifespan being very short.

"Come on," she said motioning him to follow her as she walked toward the door. "Let's get you cleaned up and have someone come in here and move Machala and clean this room up."

Logan glanced over at the lump under the bedding and nodded sadly before following after Cita.

****

Trevon, Linell, Fedlen, and Stern sat at the long table in the kitchen to the chagrin of the kitchen staff as their urges to sit in the main hall went unheeded by the newcomers.

Stern felt meeting in the kitchen brought less scrutiny, but by the reaction of the cooks and servers scurrying around them, he wasn't so sure now. Still, he needed to speak with the Caltorians and decide if they too sensed something was amiss.

"I can't put my finger on it," Trevon agreed with the patrolman.

"Something is not quite right here," Stern said with a shake of his head.

"We feel setting Logan up to be the King of Stellaran is the biggest thing out of place," Linell added.

"There has been a council in Stellaran as far back as history goes," Fedlen concurred. "Who is to say that Logan should be king and do away with the council?"

"According to the teachings of Shotwarg Cliffs, the prophecy states that Logan needs to destroy everything to save everyone," Stern said.

Linell, Trevon, and Fedlen stared blankly at him, unconvinced.

"Fine, let me show you and you can see for yourselves," Stern said slamming his hands on the table and standing as the kitchen staff stopped and gaped at him. He blushed with embarrassment and stepped away from his seat. "Follow me."

The others followed him out of the kitchen and through the halls containing the classrooms filled with students and then through a long narrow corridor that unexpectedly opened into a room of white marble. Stern strode to the far wall containing gold lettering carved into the pristine white marble.

Trevon, Linell, and Fedlen stopped behind Stern and silently read the passage on the wall.

"It doesn't say Logan needs to be King of Stellaran," Trevon said turning to Stern. "Why do they think he needs to be king?"

"In order to accomplish what the prophecy says, they believe that he needs to be king," Stern argued.

"But nowhere in this does it even mention king," Linell agreed with Trevon.

"But it does say he will do away with what is," Fedlen pointed out.

"Don't tell me you agree with their interpretation?" Trevon said turning on his friend.

"I don't think their interpretation of the prophecy is necessarily wrong," Fedlen defended his point.

"But what would Logan becoming king do to our plans?" Linell asked.

"How do you mean?" Stern interrupted. "What are your plans?"

"We need to remove the pretenders on the council and replace them with actual descendants to the rightful councilmembers," Trevon said standing a bit straighter.

Stern frowned at this comment as he considered the three in a new light. "I am not saying that you do not have legitimate claims here, but in order for Logan to fulfill the prophecy, he will need to remove all members of the council," Stern pointed out.

"And that will allow us to take their places," Linell jumped in.

"Or not, if he decides to take control of Stellaran as king," Fedlen said drawing everyone's attention.

"If you didn't realize it yet," Stern said nodding. "Logan is a force that is hard to direct and control."

"We've noticed," Trevon said.

"So you are with us?" Linell asked seeing a waver in Stern's resolve.

"I feel that a council is better to rule than one person, unless that one person acts for the good of the people. Then he may be the one to protect us against a council corrupted by power," Stern explained.

"I think we need to see this through," Fedlen spoke up. "If Logan becomes king, we need to be in a position to remove him if he becomes a tyrant."

"Tyrant?" Linell questioned. "Logan, really?"

"People change when they have power," Trevon agreed.

"So, we stay close and aid Logan in his overthrow of the council and are prepared to step in and form a new council if the need arises?" Stern questioned.

"Step in, do you mean we would kill Logan?" Linell asked her face awash with conflicting emotions.

"If that is what is needed to keep Stellaran safe from misguided people in power," Trevon said.

"We are in agreement?" Stern asked once more, looking to each Caltorian who held claims to a seat on the Stellaran Council. Each gave their nod of agreement.

"Very well then, let's get ready to depart," Trevon said and they turned and strode from the prophecy room with a new purpose.

Chapter 36

The general in his dress reds knelt before King Aston in the throne room, his bald head beading with sweat and his eyes searching the crowd around him for assistance. None stepped forward as the king addressed him.

The new queen sat on the throne, her eyes swollen with tears as she watched. Her long black hair braided neatly and then curled into a bun on the top of her head becoming the perfect perch for the crown of silver and gold imbedded with rubies, diamonds, and emeralds. She held her lace-gloved hands in the lap of her elaborately embroidered, pearl adorned cream dress. Her eyes dropped uncomfortably to her lap as the king berated the man. She knew where this treatment led and understood the man would likely be headless by morning.

Aston reached over and grasped the queen's chin, forcefully lifting her head to look at the man.

"Oh no, you will watch this. This man's incompetence has allowed the intruders to escape and has put our rule in danger. You will bear witness to his fate or I will send you back to that filth-ridden village for you to starve in your own squalor." His eyes burned with anger as he glared at her.

"Let me go then, I need not sit on a throne that is not mine to occupy," she said and received a slap across the face for her words.

As Aston's handprint reddened on the queen's cheek she raised her chin and defied him, fighting back the tears now threatening to overflow from her eyes. "My people may be outcasts, but we have honor. Something you would know nothing about," she said glaring back at him.

The room stilled as the king admonished the queen. None dared step forward or speak up, fearful that the king would behead them as he had done to any speaking out against him upon his return. If they needed a reminder of their precarious position, the heads of all who opposed Aston were easily seen outside the throne room windows on stakes, staring with eye sockets picked clean by the birds.

This time Aston reared back and struck her with a fist directly in her face sending her sprawling across the dais. She leaned on an elbow and wiped the blood from her nose and lip, pushing herself to her knees before standing to tower over the smaller king.

She knew how he hated when she stood on the same level as him, insecure with his small stature, but she puffed up her chest and fumed down at him, her ire reaching her limit with him more than ever before.

He stepped to strike her again, but she deftly deflected his blow bringing a gasp from the audience forced to gather whenever the king wanted to make an example of someone. She spun him around and slipped the blade from its hiding place in her dress's belt, pressing it against his neck as he struggled, before recognizing his precarious position.

Men around the dais drew swords and surrounded them, but Aston raised a hand to stay them as the queen pressed the blade harder against his throat drawing a line of blood from under the steel.

"Hold," the king said in a raspy, horrified voice. He looked to his side where the old man and woman sat watching the fiasco. He gave a slight nod and the queen lifted from the dais as the blade dropped from her hand in surprise, clanking against the stone flooring as she hung helplessly above.

The queen's eyes darted like a cornered animal as she sought a way out, but the magical weave surrounding her held her tight, cutting off the air needed to cry out.

The king motioned for the magicals to lower the queen and she eased down before him, hanging inches off the floor. He stared at her panicked eyes and smiled as he pulled back and struck her hard in the face. The crunching of bone and cartilage echoed in the chamber followed by many groans from the crowd, but no one spoke out or objected to his treatment of the queen.

She stayed upright, levitating off the floor as her head hung limply at the end of her slender neck.

Aston lifted her bloodied face by the chin and smiled, pleased with himself. He turned to the man still kneeling before them and then to the audience. The throne room remained deathly quiet.

"I will spare your life, this time, since the queen has availed herself to bear the brunt of my anger for you. You may now thank her by being in her guard detail," Aston said boastfully. "Now take her to her chambers and remain there until you are summoned."

The man stood, reaching for the floating queen and she dropped into his arms as the magicals removed their weaves. He lifted her to his chest, cradling her in his arms and walked out of the room leaving the king staring triumphantly after them.

****

Teah sat behind the stone block wall the protectors said led into the grand hall. She trusted them, but felt she needed to know what Aston was plotting before she burst out from their hiding place to confront him. She needed a better understanding of her odds.

"I need to sleep before tonight," she said sitting down on the stone floor. "Can one of you take first watch?"

"I got it," Grinwald offered drawing no argument from Raven who nodded.

"Wake one of us up in a few hours. By my calculation it is only midday."

Grinwald nodded and sat down closest to the wall to take watch.

Raven moved down the passageway the way they came and curled up on the floor without a word.

Teah sat down with her legs crossed and leaned against the wall. She closed her eyes and drew in her magic, lifting her spirit from her body and letting it float above her for a moment. Her mind instantly lost contact with the protectors and she wondered if they knew her consciousness no longer occupied her body. She smiled to herself and slipped through the wall into the grand hall.

Many people filled the hall as they ate their noon meal. She realized she didn't even know what King Aston looked like, but felt confident that she would know him when she saw him.

The people in the room appeared to be a mixture of noble men and women and magicals. Zele Magus's faces drew names of recognition to mind as she stared at them in disgust. Viri Magus also sat eating at the tables. All magicals betraying the leadership of their order and were considered traitors to their cause, but their presence here concerned her more as to how their magic could come into play to stop their attempts to kill the king and queen. These numbers could easily overwhelm her and her two companions and end the rebellion very quickly.

Her thoughts seemed to skip a beat as she peered into the eyes of a young female magical and the bright red stone placed prominently on her forehead. Panic filled her as she turned to see another, and yet another and still more in every direction that she turned. More magicals, male and female alike, stoned and enslaved by King Aston. But she never heard of a source stone being in Ter Chadain. She only encountered them in Caltoria so how did Aston come into the possession of soul stones? She gasped as she realized that the majority of the magicals in the palace in the hall possessed stones. For Aston to possess that many stones he must have gotten them from Caltoria or possibly where Logan was, Stellaran.

Rage overwhelmed her and when it became clear the king was

not in the hall, she let her spirit move up the stairwell to the upper level of the palace. She allowed her intuition to guide her to the most luxurious and elaborate area of the palace where she stopped outside a door guarded by a dozen armed soldiers. She slipped past unseen and slammed into a wall of magic that made her head ring with pain. She waited for the pain to subside and scanned the large outer chambers of the king's quarters.

Viri Magus and Zele Magus filled the room except for a small walkway that lead to the bedchamber doors. Each magical sat either on furniture or on the floor with their eyes closed in concentration, a colored stone set upon their forehead.

Teah studied a Zele Magus close to her, a girl with long blonde hair no older than herself. She looked at the weave rising from the girl as it took form and intermingled with the other weaves coming from all the other magicals. As the weaves melded into one, it took on a red transparent appearance. Teah noted that the weave started a few paces inside the door and extended to every corner of the room except the narrow path leading to the bedchambers.

Teah realized this must be the source of her painful collision just moments before. This barrier kept everyone and everything out. She frowned at the existence of the path. If this was meant to protect the king, the path left him very vulnerable. She then remembered that only magicals could see the weaves and Aston was defending himself against Logan and not against someone thought to possess magical powers.

She stepped to the beginning of the path and let her spirit float along until it reached the door to the inner chambers. She hesitated, wondering at how easy this defense would be for her to defeat, but her rage at seeing all the stoned magicals sent her surging forward with a vengeance.

She burst into the chambers and her spirit screamed out at the sight of the aged man and woman sitting in two high-backed chairs looking directly at her. Her instinct told her to flee, but as her spirit turned to retreat, a wall of magic slammed around her on all sides and pain erupted in her like she never felt before. No pain inflicted by the empress wielding her controlling stone ever came close to that which wracked her spirit as she crumpled to the floor.

"What is going on?" a stern male voice said from the other side of the room.

"Just as you suspected," the male magical said in a ragged old voice. "We have captured a spirit walker."

"Aha, I thought they may try something like that," the man cheered in victory. "And whose spirit do we now hold captive in your invisible cell?"

"Oh, dear spirits," the old woman whispered in fear as Teah forced her head up to look her captors in the eye.

"What, what is it?" the man pressed.

"We have captured the greatest prize," the old man rasped.

"Whose spirit are you holding? Tell me," the man ordered and now Teah understood this man to be King Aston.

"We have trapped the spirit of Teah Lassain," the woman said holding Teah's venomous gaze and shuddering at the sight.

"I know you can see spirits with your magic, but how can you be so sure it is her?" Aston said looking around at the doorway where his mortal eyes saw nothing.

"In this form, no one can hide their identity. It instantly is known to whoever comes in contact with it," the man explained. "This spirit belongs to Teah Lassain, heir to the throne and ..."

"And what?" Aston demanded, irritated by his hesitation.

"She is also the Protector of Ter Chadain," the man finished, his voice filled with fear.

"How can that be?" Aston said spinning from the two magicals who held their magic around Teah's spirit. "I met the Protector of Ter Chadain. I saw him run his blades through my father and mock me and my mother after doing so."

"It appears this woman is also in possession of the protector's powers," the old woman said. "Hold your weave tighter," she scolded her counterpart without looking at him. "If she gets free, we're all dead. Tighten it up."

Teah felt her confinement squeeze against her spirit, restraining her tighter. She wanted to cry out, but only the two holding her prisoner would hear her. She wondered how long it would take for Grinwald and Raven to realize she no longer resided in her body and to come searching for her.

Her hopes sunk at the thought of her two companions coming to her aid. They were severely outnumbered and all the magicals in the outer room were waiting for any magical who came uninvited through those doors.

She let her anger build as she looked at the two magicals with the king pacing excitedly behind them, hoping she might at least make the two magicals uncomfortable looking at her as she seethed with the thoughts of tearing them apart. She refused to let pity or fear enter her consciousness, but only concentrated on getting out of this prison and exacting her fury upon them.

The magicals fidgeted nervously as they averted their eyes and then glanced back only to avert them again. That was when she saw it. A silver circlet sat upon each of their heads. Their circlets shone with alternating dark blue and dark red stones, six in all. She stared hard at the stones wondering if they were soul stones, but something about them gave her the feeling these magicals were different.

She felt confident that her demeanor toward them was starting to wear on their resolve. She could only hope that while they worried about her wrath, they might not notice her carefully studying their weave around her and begin to untie the strands with her mind. One by one.

****

After a couple hours of listening to the monotonous drone of voices from the other side of the wall, Grinwald stood and stepped past a sleeping Teah to shake Raven awake.

Raven stirred at Grinwald's touch and yawned with nod as the Viri Magus slid down the wall to the floor to get some sleep.

Raven eased past Teah but caught her foot under one of Teah's bent knees as she sat cross-legged on the floor with her back resting on the wall. Teah toppled over as Raven stumbled over her, slamming both of them to the ground with a sickening thud.

Raven scrambled to her feet turning to help Teah only to find her unresponsive. "Teah, are you okay?" Raven looked to Grinwald who sat up at the sound of their collision and watched with concern.

He slid closer to Teah and helped Raven set her back up. Her body remained in the same cross-legged position as if frozen in place. He looked to Raven with a frown and then placed a hand upon Teah's forehead.

"She's gone," Grinwald said.

"What do you mean, 'she's gone'?" Raven whispered harshly. "I barely touched her. She has suffered mightier blows many times in battle."

"I mean she has left her body," Grinwald corrected.

"She spirit-walked?" Raven gasped. "I've heard of it, but I thought no one has done it for hundreds, maybe thousands of years."

"I have never known one who could spirit-walk, but I believe that is exactly what she has done."

"So what do we do now?" Raven asked.

"Wait for her return," Grinwald said flatly. "She knew when we needed to go across the great hall to the next passageway. She will return."

Raven looked at him, not too certain with his assessment of the

328

situation.

"What else can we do?" Grinwald said throwing his hands up in frustration. "Can you spirit-walk?"

"No, can you?" Raven replied.

"Then we will have to wait for her return."

Raven nodded and moved next to the wall between the passage and the great hall while Grinwald lay back down and tried to sleep.

Raven looked back to Teah and shook her head, uncertain things were going to work out as smoothly as Grinwald hoped.

****

Caslor surveyed his army spread out in the valley below him as he sat with the two leaders of the houses of magic of Ter Chadain and Rachel on a rise. He looked up at the sun high in the sky, wishing Teah speed in her mission.

He couldn't tell her, but he held out little hope for her success. A more likely scenario would be her return after discovering the king too well-guarded to get to and then the army would take a turn at breaching the city of Cordlain. Once the city fell, the palace would soon follow.

The army lumbered along moving closer to Cordlain, but at a snail's pace giving Caslor angst in his desire to reach the city before nightfall. Even though he felt confident of Teah's return, he needed to be able to launch his siege the instant it became apparent she would not. Time would be of the essence in that situation in order to have any hopes of saving her from a certain death.

A rider raced toward the group and they turned to watch her ride up pulling her horse to a sliding stop at the last second.

"Word from Ceait," the woman said, panting.

"Yes?" Caslor asked.

"The army laying siege to the houses of magic in Ceait have

broken through the defenses," the woman said. "The houses are lost."

Caslor turned to Magus Patris and Magus Matris as they reached out to each other and clasped hands in painful support.

"Go get some rest and something to eat," Caslor told the messenger who nodded and rode off.

"Hundreds of magicals will be either dead or taken prisoner," Magus Matris said to no one in particular.

"Let us hope it is the latter, but with the house of Englewood's history, that is truly doubtful," Magus Patris said sadly.

"This poses a greater problem for us as well," Caslor said bringing their attention to him. "That army will undoubtedly begin marching to Cordlain to aid the city against our siege. It will take some time, but it shortens our window to take the city. If we are in full siege when they arrive, they will be able to flank us and break our siege ending any hopes of reaching Teah."

"Then let us hope she will not require our help," Magus Patris said flatly.

Chapter 37

Logan sat in the outer chambers of his room staring out the large windows overlooking the city. Guards stood at the ready outside his doorway after Abria's attack, anyone entering surrendered their weapons or was turned away. The security didn't bother Logan, but he knew that if Senji wanted to reach him, they eventually would find a way. His best security lay across his lap in the form of the protector's swords. He laid his hands on the handles and drew comfort from their familiar feel in his palms.

The door opened and he turned to see Cita enter in her thigh-high boots and fitted pants, a cloak over the top of the dark shirt.

He stood, swinging the baldrics in place and fastening the swords across his back. He reflexively checked for the sheath holding the bow on his leg.

"Are we ready to leave?" Logan asked as she strode over to him.

"The others are getting our horses, but there is something I need to show you before we leave."

Logan raised an eyebrow in question but nodded and motioned with his arm for her to proceed.

They exited the chambers and walked down to the main entrance. Instead of going out into the common area where they came in, Cita turned and moved deeper into the building.

As they walked, Logan heard voices of children as they passed classrooms of children with an adult in front of the room giving the children instruction. Outside one classroom a guard stood with a group of children who smiled brightly as they strode up.

Bethany, Violet, Sara, and Zack rushed up to embrace him.

"Is it true? Are you leaving us?" Bethany asked her forehead furrowed.

"Yes, it is true, we must continue on," Logan said as the

children gave a collective groan. "But you will be safe here, you have my word." He looked to Cita for reinforcement and she nodded her guarantee.

As Logan looked at them he noted that each wore a slender silver bracelet with a sliver of colored stone in it. His heart sank as he instantly understood the purpose of those stones, identical to those that once imprisoned him and his sister and so many more in Caltoria. His face flushed red and he spun on Cita.

"What is the meaning of controlling them with soul stones?" he asked, taking hold of her arm and pulling her away from the children.

"The bracelets are tools that help the children control their magic until they can do it on their own," Cita explained. "Every student wears one until their last year here."

"I destroyed the source stone in the catacombs of Bellatora," Logan said, confused.

"There is another source stone in use and others possibly still yet to be found in the earth."

"Where is it?"

"In a prison not far from here."

"Who holds the controlling stones of these?" Logan demanded gesturing at the children.

"The children," Cita said. She took him by the hand leading him back to the children where she extended a hand to Bethany. "May we see your bracelet?"

Bethany extended her arm to them as Cita showed Logan the bracelet. "This is the soul stone," Cita said pointing to the light red stone on the back of Bethany's wrist. "And this is the correlating control stone," she finished turning Bethany's wrist over to show an identical stone on her palm side of the bracelet. "Only the children control their stones, no one else."

Logan looked at her, the confusion and anger draining from his face as he drew a deep breath. He looked to the children and dropped to a knee. The younger children stepped into his outstretched arms and hugged him back. He stood, messing Zack's hair with a playful smile and then turned to Bethany who stood patiently waiting.

"You're an incredible woman," Logan said causing her to blush. "Take care of your brother and sisters and they will turn out as strong as you are." He pulled her into his arms and kissed the top of her head.

She stepped back from him and smiled proudly. "I will. Are you coming back?"

The question caught him off guard as he never made it a habit to think returning anywhere since he felt he already well outlived his life expectancy. "I'll try."

She stretched on her tiptoes to kiss him on the cheek and then turned to usher the children away without looking back.

Logan watched them leave, touching his cheek where Bethany kissed him goodbye.

"You always steal the heart of every woman you meet?" Cita asked kiddingly.

"No, she is like a sister to me," he said brushing her comment aside.

"Maybe, but you are more than a big brother to her, at least she wishes you were," Cita insisted.

Logan looked confused at Cita as he considered the statement. "She has a crush on you."

"Well, I might not survive another Senji attack, so we might not have to worry about that now will we?" He turned and started down the hallway before Cita took hold of his hand and stopped him.

"This way, there is one more thing to show you." She led him down the hall and turned down a long narrow corridor that suddenly widened into a large room with white marble from floor to ceiling.

Logan instantly noticed golden words etched into the far wall. He moved closer and his skin began to crawl even as he did. He knew what the words were and he hated everything about them. He stopped short and spun on Cita.

"I don't believe in prophecy," he said leaving no room for doubt.

"I wanted you to see the words that drove our preparation for your arrival," Cita told him.

He looked at her a moment longer and then turned to read the words aloud. "An ancient sign will rise again to conquer and destroy what has become, saving the future for all." At the end of the message was a symbol matching his tattoo. He reflexively touched his chest upon seeing it.

Cita stepped to him and pulled his shirt down to expose his tattoo and then looked up at the prophecy again. "You cannot deny this is your destiny."

"I make my own destiny," he grumbled. "But if you're lucky, I will fulfill the prophecy while I'm doing it." Logan turned and strode purposefully from the room. "Let's get moving," he said over his shoulder as he disappeared down the hallway.

Cita hesitated a second to read the prophecy one last time, still a bit stunned by being an active part in it, and then hurried after him.

Logan exited the building to find the courtyard filled with people mounted and waiting for him. He smiled at his companions, fighting back the anger over being told once more what his destiny would be.

A stable girl led a horse over and he mounted. "Thank you," he said giving the girl a wink.

His face turned hard again as Cita exited and climbed into her saddle. She looked to him, questioning.

"You're the Doyen, where do we need to go to fulfill your precious prophecy," Logan told her.

"We need to get more troops," Cita said.

Logan looked around at the wide range of people in the courtyard. Most were close to his age, but a few were older. They all carried either a sword or a bow on their saddle or strapped across their backs. None wore armor or a uniform of any sort.

"I would say we need to find some seasoned soldiers if we are to defeat a council who has the Red Tips at their command," Logan pointed out.

"There is a place not far from here that has just the type," Cita said.

Logan looked at her, hearing the tone in her voice he knew she kept something from him. He raised an eyebrow.

"It is Scardalon Prison. A place where the council houses those who oppose their views or anyone they deem too dangerous to be free," Cita said.

"You know what they say," Stern said breaking his silence where he sat mounted, next to Logan. "Enemy of my enemy is my ally."

"That may be true, but what happens when that enemy is defeated?" Zeva piped up on the other side of Cita.

"Then we will have to deal with them," Stern replied.

"Let's take it one enemy at a time, if we can," Logan moaned. "Lead on." He gestured to Cita with a sweep of his arm.

Cita nodded and kicked her horse into motion with Logan and the others falling in behind her.

Saliday pushed through the group and pulled up next to Logan. "What about Morgan?"

"What about him?" Logan asked, not looking at her squarely.

"He is sitting in a prison in a foreign land in a hidden location where we cannot find him without a guide."

Logan turned to her, his face devoid of emotion. "And?"

"And it isn't right," Saliday shouted.

Logan pulled up short, creating a chain reaction of riders

335

bumping into each other behind him and crying out in disgust.

Saliday pulled up and turned back to him.

"What isn't right is him joining in a plot to kill me." Logan glanced over at Zeva as she stepped her horse up beside his. "If it wasn't for Zeva, we wouldn't be here right now."

"But he aided us in the past. If it weren't for Morgan, you would have never reached Teah in Caltoria," Saliday argued.

"I would have found another ship," Logan countered.

"But you didn't, and he risked his life to help us," Saliday pressed.

"So what would you have me do with him, let him go?" Logan said, his voice hard.

"You're blaming him for what happened between you and me," Saliday said and her hand went to her mouth, eyes wide in shock.

Logan's face turned dark as he fought to stay in control of his anger. He glared at Saliday, lips thinning as they pressed together. "I release him to you. Go where you wish, but if you choose to come with us then know this …I will not guarantee his safety," his words came out in an intense whisper.

By this time Cita rode back to where Logan stopped and sat listening to the exchange. When Logan turned to her, she nodded. "You there," Cita addressed a man just behind Logan and Saliday. "Ride back with Saliday and have them release the prisoner Morgan to her. Keep him shackled and let her be responsible for freeing him."

The man nodded and kicked his horse into motion as those following parted to allow him passage. They waited as Saliday looked hopelessly to Logan and then raced after the man.

An awkward silence hung over the party as Logan watched Saliday ride for a moment and then turn back to Cita. "Lead on, Doyen, this place is depressing me."

Cita spun her horse around and took up the lead again, the

others falling in behind her. Trevon, Linell, Stern, and Zeva shot quick glances to Logan that he noticed, but didn't acknowledge. Instead he kept his eyes focused on the road ahead, letting what he had with Saliday be left behind as she once again chose Morgan over him.

When they reached the exit to the city Cita handed each of the newcomers a cloth hood and motioned to riders to guide their horses through the tunnels leading out of the secret location.

Logan looked flatly at Cita who didn't waiver, but motioned for him to put on the hood. Logan glanced back at the others who didn't appear any happier than he, but then nodded to them and slipped the hood over his head.

The familiar echoing of the horse's hoofs on the stone path reverberated around them and Logan tried to think of something else. He reached out to Teah, checking in with her for the first time since Cita entered his bed the night before.

His mind touched Teah's, but it seemed hazy, unclear, and distant from what he usually felt.

Are you alright, sister?

I seem to have gotten myself captured.

You're a protector and a Zele Magus, you can get out of it. Fight your way out.

I normally would agree with you, but I kind of...

What?

Got my spirit captured outside of my body, Teah hesitantly shared.

Logan's thoughts skipped a beat and he paused, dumbfounded by this admission. *How?*

I can spirit-walk. I went to locate Aston and they were waiting. They have two very old magicals who trapped my spirit in some kind of woven prison. I can't get back to my body. Her thoughts were panicked.

I don't have any experience with spirit-walking, but you are powerful enough to spirit-walk, you should be powerful enough to undo their weaves. Slow everything down and concentrate on cutting each strand of the weave, one at a time. Trying to escape by bursting through all the weaves at once will only prove futile. Attack a strand at a time.

No thought came back to him from Teah.

Teah?

Got it. Good thinking. I believe that might work.

Logan noticed his horse stopped and the hood lifted from his head leaving him squinting at the sunlight on his face.

Free yourself and be safe. I have to go now.

Be safe brother, Teah replied and then their connection went silent.

Logan looked to Cita who stared at him curiously.

"What is it?" Logan asked.

"You seemed to be somewhere else," Cita said. "Are you ready to go?"

"Lead on," Logan said with a nod.

Cita kicked her horse into motion and Logan followed after, hearing the others do the same behind him.

They rode on for a long time across the flat prairie until the terrain began to change. The prairie shrubs and scruff gave way to small trees and bushes, the vegetation turning greener. Trees dotted the distance and soon became discernable from the horizon. Logan scanned the terrain ahead as a building took shape from the tree line with its dark grey stones dimming the bright green foliage around it.

"Scardalon Prison," Cita called over her shoulder.

As they approached a cloud of dust arose from the distance and a lone rider took shape, racing toward them. He pulled up in front of Cita as she eased her mount to a halt and the others followed suit.

The rider's grey uniform covered a thin body with bony hands

338

and arms protruding from the far too large sleeves of the enormous shirt. A patch over the man's left breast showed golden swords crossed over the golden words, 'Protection of All'.

"You are entering the restricted lands of Scardalon Prison. By order of the Stellaran Crystal Council, you are ordered to vacate this area at once or risk the council's punishment," the man said straightening in the saddle and puffing up his frail chest.

"We wish to speak to the Keeper of the Keys," Cita addressed the man.

"Ha, I doubt that is going to happen. The Keeper of the Keys does not see just anyone who stops by," the man said with amusement.

"As I thought," Cita said and raised her hand above her head and made a circle motion with her index finger.

Two soldiers raced to the man, one with an arrow trained on him and the other pulled the reins from the man's hand.

"What is the meaning of this? You will become a tenant of Scardalon for these actions," the man warned.

"Let's go." Cita ignored the man's outburst, riding her horse past the man, the soldiers falling in behind her with their new prisoner.

Logan watched, leaving this to Cita who seemed to have it all well at hand. He followed after with the rest of the party and soon stood at the gates of the prison.

A man on the wall shouted down to them. "Release our man and go on your way or face the judgment of the council for your actions."

"We wish to speak with the Keeper of the Keys," Cita shouted back.

The man opened his mouth to reply, but then snapped it shut and spun from the wall.

Cita exchanged a look of caution with Logan and then turned her attention back to the wall when a man in a black uniform bearing the same symbol on the chest as their captive stepped up to the grey stone wall.

"I am the Keeper of the Keys, what is it that you want?" the man said his voice revealing his irritation.

"We are asking for admittance and your peaceful surrender," Cita said.

The man laughed as he bent at the waist, unable to contain his amusement. "Oh, this is a new one and very entertaining. You want us to surrender to you, just like that?"

"I do," Cita said without emotion.

"And why should we do that when we are secure behind our gates and walls?"

"Because you have few men inside and only enough provisions to last a few days without sending your men out for their normal supply run," Cita told him.

The man's face turned white as her words hit home.

Logan smiled as he saw the man's confidence drain from him. Cita prepared for this day and knew their routine, giving her the advantage.

"I have plenty of men inside these walls to defend us, or are you forgetting our control of the prisoners inside?" the man showed a small boost of confidence as he spoke.

"Use of your prisoners in that manner is forbidden and you know it," Cita countered.

"Oh, I think the council will forgive me that indiscretion if it is required to hold the prison," the Keeper smiled down at her. He lifted a chain from around his neck and colors glittered in the morning sun.

Logan hadn't noticed the chain until he lifted it and the sun glinted off the colorful stones held at the top of individual keys. His heart stopped as he instantly identified the soul stones in the keys and knew that with each colored stone, a matching stone set in the forehead of a prisoner.

Logan's anger rose to boiling in that instant and he drew the silver rod from its sheath. It extended to a bow and he smoothly pulled back the string to materialize the silver arrow pointed directly at the Keeper's heart.

"Tell him to let us in and release the prisoners or he dies...now," Logan hissed in hatred.

Cita stared over her shoulder at Logan in shock, but then shook off her stupor and turned back to the Keeper on the wall. "I advise you to surrender, now, or you will perish this very instant."

The man flicked his eyes from Cita to Logan and opened his mouth to argue, but the words never left his mouth as a silver shaft vibrated in his chest before he toppled over backwards.

"Get us in there. Now!" Logan shouted.

Zeva unleashed the powerful weave she created while watching all of the events unfold from behind Logan that struck the doors and buckled the steel supports holding the massive oak panels upright.

Linell released her weave that splintered one of the doors sending broken wood flying everywhere and leaving a gaping hole into the prison.

Logan didn't hesitate, but deftly sheathed his bow after it shrank and pulled his swords free. He kicked his horse and raced into the breach, vanishing from view.

Cita and the others stared in stunned silence before racing after him.

Chapter 38

Teah crouched under the oppressive confining weaves of the two magicals as she searched for a tie in their weaves. Alone and without anyone to guide her, she needed to find her own escape. She wondered on where the protector spirits went when she spirit-walked, but then turned her attention back to the weaves. They wound around intricately, overlapping and doubling back without warning. She traced one strand only to discover she mistakenly jumped to another strand as it looped back on itself. She sighed with frustration and worried at the idea of being held until her body failed and withered away. She surmised that her spirit remained eternal, but her body had no such luxury needing sustenance to survive.

As she concentrated on the weaves, she also listened hoping to discover something useful to use against Aston if she escaped. When she escaped, she corrected, trying to stay optimistic.

"So this spirit you say is captive in your invisible weave before me is the sister of the Protector of Ter Chadain and the heir to the throne?" Aston asked.

"That is correct. She also possesses the powers of the protectors as well," the woman replied.

"How is that even possible?" Aston ranted as he paced behind the two chairs the magicals sat in concentrating on holding the weave around Teah.

"We are not certain, but we theorize that due to the Lassains being twins the magical spell of the protectors was compelled to become part of each of them," the man explained.

"And she is a Zele Magus as well?" Aston shouted in dismay, clearly frightened.

"To spirit-walk, she is very powerful," the woman said.

"She cannot escape, you hear me, she cannot be allowed to escape," Englewood cried, on the verge of hysteria.

"We have her spirit, but if we find her body and destroy it, she will be of no threat to you even if she does escape," the man pointed out.

"Guards, guards," Englewood barked.

A group of men burst through the doorway stopping short of Teah's spirit as the male magical raised his hand to stop them.

"Search for the intruders that came through the doorway," Englewood ordered.

"We have been, but there are no signs of them. We believe they returned to where they came through the doorway," the man said.

"No they haven't," Aston shouted. "We have one woman's spirit captured. Her body is still in the palace somewhere. Find them."

"But we have searched everywhere," the man said reluctantly.

"May I suggest taking magicals to search them out?" the female magical suggested. "They can sense those with magic and help if need be."

Teah's heart sank at the thought of magicals finding her body's hiding place and a cold chill ran through her. She wanted to cry out but she had no voice in this state. Terror mixed with fear as her memory of the days she spent in slavery under the empress came flooding back.

She reached out to Logan and felt his fury as the news reached him.

"Make it happen," King Aston ordered and the men scrambled from the room.

Teah's heart sank as she realized that if they killed her body, she would remain a spirit forever. Never to see Logan or Caslor again.

She concentrated on taking her magic and striking at each strand, one at a time. She cut one and waited to see if the magicals holding her noticed. When nothing happened, she cut another with a sharp strike of her magic. She continued, one after another, removing the weaves that imprisoned her. She felt the magic around her weaken and instinctually quickened her pace, knowing that it wouldn't be long and the two magicals would also feel it.

"You fool, tighten your weave, it is weakening," the woman scolded the man.

"Me? You need to tighten your weaves, they are not bonding with mine like they should," the man shot back.

"Oh, dear spirit," the woman gasped.

"What? What is it?" Aston rushed up behind the chairs looking at the magicals with concern.

"She is cutting the weaves from within," the man explained.

"Should she be able to do that?" Englewood said frantically.

Both magicals looked back over their shoulder at the king and shook their heads. "No."

Her escape plan discovered, Teah worked at a fevered pace as new weaves joined old only to be severed by Teah before they could fall into place. She cut the weaves with mere thought faster than the magicals could layer them on her prison. They couldn't keep up and their faces contorted with horror as she gained ground by the second.

"We can't stop her, she is too powerful," the man shouted.

"Guards," Aston shouted and two men appeared looking to their king. "Hurry and find the intruders or we all will die for it."

****

Raven and Grinwald sat watching the motionless body of Teah when the first wave of sound rushed into the tunnel causing them to drop to their knees in pain, covering their ears and fighting to keep conscious. The wave passed and Grinwald looked with concern to Raven wiping tears from her eyes and cheeks.

"What was that?" Grinwald questioned.

"It is a search weave that sends out a sound and then bounces

344

back to the sender telling them what it encountered. They will be upon us quickly once they narrow down our location. A few more of those weaves and we're caught for sure."

"We can still fight," Grinwald pointed out.

"That's true, but we are definitely out-manned."

"You've been out-manned before, we can do this," Grinwald encouraged.

"Just like the caves of Scalded Island," Raven agreed.

"At all cost, we must protect Teah…what's left of her."

"Not much use to us without her spirit," Raven argued.

"But we are defeated if her spirit has no place to return."

"True," Raven said with a nod.

A resounding noise reverberating off the walls of their passage dropped them to the floor again and they staggered to their feet with their hands over their ears.

"Weave a sound barrier around your ears so we can withstand the next pass," Grinwald suggested and turned his thoughts inward as he wove the weaves together to do just that. Once his weave was in place, he nodded and turned his attention to Raven who indicated she too was ready.

The weave came down the passage again. This time they felt the vibration on their skin, but didn't succumb to the overwhelming sound that accompanied it. Another weave followed, then another, and another in quick succession as the searchers zeroed in on their location. Once the weaves came in rapid succession, Grinwald nodded to Raven and they both drew in as much magic as they could hold, waiting to be discovered.

The wall leading to the great hall exploded inward. Grinwald deflected the blast back into the great hall. He waved his hand, removing the sound barrier weave and turned to Raven as she held her hands above her head preparing to repel the assault.

A blast came in and met Grinwald's wall of air again, pounding into the bodies gathered around the opening on the other side. He dropped to a knee and continued to repel each weave sent at them. Raven understood, sending weaves of her own into the great hall, holding them tight until they escaped the passage and entered the larger room beyond before releasing the weaves to expand and level everyone in the hall.

The passage and hall went still. Grinwald caught his breath, giving a smile to Raven, grinning proudly from ear to ear.

They didn't hear the approach of another group of Aston's troops from behind them and Raven propelled forward as a weave struck her from behind. Her eyes went wide and the smile turned from triumph to resolute, knowing her fate as she flew above a ducking Grinwald who tried to catch her with a hasty weave of his own in the narrow space. She struck what was left of the wall separating the passage and great hall with such force the stone blocks crumbled under her impact.

Raven's blood sprayed, covering Grinwald and Teah and she slid down the wall in a wet slick, dropping across the opening to the floor.

Grinwald scurried to her after throwing up a weave barring the advancing troops. He rolled her over on her back and she coughed blood that misted over the front of her and down her already bloodied face.

"Oh Raven, I'm so sorry," he said after sending his magic into her and finding he could do nothing to stop the massive internal bleeding. She only had seconds left.

"Don't be," she said and coughed again. "Tell Teah I'm sorry," she coughed again and pain wracked her expression. "About Logan. And thank her for letting me see what freedom was like…" She grimaced one last time before her eyes stared blankly past Grinwald.

He hung his head as he slid her eyelids closed and then quickly wove another barrier, dropping it over him and Teah's empty body as he crouched close to the Queen Protector and readied himself for the final assault.

****

Teah made headway on severing the weaves one after another and her hope surged.

"We need to weave faster," the man said panting with exertion.

"Guards," Aston shouted.

A man appeared instantly inside the door, waiting for his king's orders.

"Bring in four magicals, two men and two women, at once," Aston ordered and the man disappeared only to return a moment later with two women and two men, each with a darkly colored soul stone on their forehead.

The man forced the four new arrivals to their knees next to the old magicals and stood at attention.

The magicals looked to their elders waiting to be told why they were summoned.

"We need you to wrap weaves around a spirit we have captured. Just form the weaves and we will lay them. Weave as quickly as you can or we are all doomed," the male magical instructed.

The magicals all began to weave frantically as the man and woman holding Teah laid them.

Teah's hope crumbled as the new weaves overpowered her. She lost ground and soon felt the weaves weighing upon her spirit. Her chance to escape evaporating as her strategy no longer proved viable.

Chapter 39

Logan raced through the gaping hole in the prison gates in time to see the guards pulling the lifeless form of the Keeper of the Keys into the main building and slamming the doors behind them. He slowed as he surveyed the grounds and the lack of guards.

Zeva, Cita, Trevon, Linell, Stern, and Fedlen pulled up behind him and sat staring at the empty courtyard.

"Where is everyone?" Fedlen asked glancing back as the remaining troops filtered into the prison.

"I've heard that the prison has very few guards, but nothing like this," Stern said in a stunned voice.

"The Keeper has control over all the magic of the prisoners within these walls, that is all the force they need," Cita said.

"Until Logan put an arrow through the Keeper's heart," Zeva pointed out.

"What will they do next?" Logan turned to Cita.

"There should be another on site to control the soul stones of the prisoners," Cita said thinking out loud. "He should be gathering those keys about now and I would guess counter attack at any time."

As the words left her mouth, Logan saw a wall of weaves appear in the courtyard and then rush toward them.

Zeva and Linell saw it too and threw up a defensive wall in front of them. The courtyard boomed with the collision of the two massive weaves of magic. The impact of the two weaves shook the ground unseating many of the riders and sending them sprawling to the ground. Logan tumbled from his mount with Stern and Cita hanging on to their saddle horns, struggling to stay seated. Trevon, Fedlen, and Linell fell beside Logan as he rolled to his back and caught a falling Zeva in his arms.

She smiled at him as she stood and brushed herself off before extending a hand to clasp his and help him to his feet.

"Right on cue," Logan said looking at Cita and then at the prison wall. "How long can you hold them off?"

"I don't know how many prisoners they have or how strong each is. With the men and women we have here we should be able to hold our own, though I doubt we can make any advancement." Cita and Stern slid from their horses and faced Logan.

Logan looked around at the men and women around him as his mind churned with options. He gave a nod, coming to a conclusion.

"Stern, Fedlen, Trevon, and I will advance on the prison while you keep them occupied," Logan said. Surprise spread across the faces of the men he named and Cita spun on him with concern.

"How do you expect to fight off the entire prison guard with only four of you?" Cita protested.

"I'm the Protector of Ter Chadain. This is what I was created for. We will get to the new Keeper of the Keys and eliminate the magical threat, but you need to keep his mind on you."

Cita nodded and motioned her troops to her as she stood with Zeva and Linell.

"We will attack and repel attacks so I need you to form into three groups lead by myself, Zeva, and Linell. Weave on our cue and direct it where we instruct. We need to do this in succession to conserve strength. The key here is to maintain a consistent barrage to allow Logan and his party to get into the prison and remove the Keeper. Understood?"

The troops nodded and began to divide into the three units as directed.

Cita turned to Logan with a nod.

Logan gave her a wink and looked to his chosen men waiting for his instruction.

"I can deflect any magic coming our way with the swords. I will take anything head-on while Stern and Trevon will protect us from the side." The men nodded their understanding.

"Fedlen," Logan turned to the only non-magical member of his party. "How good are you with a bow?"

"More than adequate," Fedlen answered honestly.

"Get a bow and remove any distant threat you see while staying within our circle of protection."

"Got it," Fedlen said and hurried off to secure a bow from one of the troops.

"Are you sure about this?" Stern asked.

"It will work, but we need to act as a unit and stay focused. The Keeper is who we need here."

Fedlen returned with a longbow and large quiver of arrows slung over his back. He gave Logan a curt nod indicating his readiness.

"Let's go," Logan said and stepped to the front drawing his swords, sending the sound of metal singing throughout the courtyard.

He moved swiftly across the open space to the main doors where the dead Keeper and his men retreated. Without hesitation, a weave raced toward them that he deflected with his swords held crossed in front of him.

Trevon sent a weave of his own into the door and the thick wood barring their entrance splintered inward.

They stepped through the door to find the main entrance empty as the grey stone echoed their footsteps around them. The room arched high above them where archers stood on raised walkways unleashing arrows at them.

Logan deflected those directed at him while Stern and Trevon sent weaves of fire up to meet the arrows in midflight and turn them to ash. Fedlen's string hummed behind them dropping an archer from the walkway to the entry's floor and then strummed again and again, hitting mark after mark.

The men on the walkway turned and retreated.

Logan raced ahead forcing the others to run after him. He

kicked in a door barring their path and continued through a long corridor leading to the back of the prison where Logan thought the new Keeper of the Keys might hide.

Men stepped into the passage to bar their advancement, but Logan cut them down before they could mount any serious threat. They stepped through the doorway, entering a room that loomed massively around them, dwarfing them by the high ceiling and curved walls. In the center sat something Logan never wanted to see again and his skin crawled at the sheer magic emanating from the object.

"A source stone," Stern said in a hushed whisper.

The stone hummed with power as someone drew magic from it and directed it into the soul stones of the prisoners.

Arrows rained down from above, but Trevon and Stern sent out a weave deflecting them harmlessly against the walls.

Logan spotted the Keeper on a balcony high on the wall. He spun to tell Fedlen, but the man already loosed an arrow at the Keeper. The arrow made it to the edge of the balcony and then turned to ash.

The Keeper turned and disappeared from view.

"We need to get him and the controlling stones," Logan shouted and then raced into a passageway across from him leading to a staircase spiraling upward. They hurried up the stairs reaching the level the Keeper stood on only moments before, to find it empty.

They turned to an outside window facing across the plain on the backside of the prison to see two riders, one a prison guard and the other the Keeper of the Keys.

Trevon, Stern, and Fedlen hung their heads in defeat, knowing that without the keys, the Keeper would continue to have control over the prisoners and holding them captive.

"We lost," Trevon said with disgust.

"Not yet," Logan said, striding from the room and rushing

down the stairs to the room containing the source stone. He was considering the powerful stone when Stern, Trevon, and Fedlen came up behind him.

"What are you thinking?" Stern asked him.

"I destroyed a stone like this in Caltoria with my sister," Logan told him.

"That is suicide," Fedlen said.

"I need to free these prisoners," Logan argued.

"From what I've heard, your sister is even more magically powerful than you," Trevon pointed out.

"True, especially since I think there is a binding weave on me, but that is nothing more than a tattered web right now, barely hanging on and keeping me from my true powers." Logan spoke more to himself than anyone else.

"You can't do this alone," Stern insisted.

"I won't have any of you help me, you don't know the kind of power we're dealing with. I do." Without another word, he flipped his swords around in his hands so that the blades pointed to the floor like daggers and he rushed the stone.

"No!" Stern, Fedlen, and Trevon cried out in unison, but he didn't slow.

He leapt as high as he could and came down with all his might, burying his blades hilt deep into the stone. He knew the power of the stone would fight him, but he didn't remember this much pain; the magic ravaged inside his body threatening to blow him apart. He clenched his teeth and dug deep inside, searching for his magic hidden away for so long.

When he thought his head might explode, he felt a surge deep within him building from a spark to a raging inferno. He grasped at the magic, trying to control it or at least direct it, but the magic ignored his bidding and filled every cell of his body to the bursting point. He dug deeper, fighting to stay in control of his magic as it surged again. He focused it on the blades impaled in

352

the stone and sent his magic through the blades like a conduit directing lightning, something he felt he could relate to.

He mind raced as voices came to him. Voices that once gave him comfort and direction as well as irritated him at times. The voices shouted to him, telling him to stop. Begging him to stop. He understood their concern, but he also knew the magicals who depended on him to free them from a slavery he himself had witnessed and never wished on another living being.

You must stop or you will die, one of the voices warned.

He's done it, the stone is failing, another voice said with hope.

Run Logan! You've done it, but now the stone will be destroyed along with you and your friends if you don't flee, the first voice said, panic filtering through the words.

Logan opened his eyes with effort as the stone glowed bright white causing him to squint in pain. He pulled one blade out with considerable effort. Then pushed himself away from the stone with his free hand holding his blade and he slid the second blade free, sending him to the ground.

Numerous hands lifted him and half carried, half dragged him from the room rushing down the long hallway and out into the building's entrance. They didn't hesitate, but raced through the gaping opening blown in the doors and into the courtyard. As they reached the courtyard the ground shook and then suddenly, everything went still.

Logan began to right himself and stand on his own feet when the rumble erupted from inside the prison and debris mixed with magic burst from the doorway and into the courtyard sending everyone tumbling backwards into the outer wall of the prison.

It ended as rapidly as it began and they slowly picked themselves from the mess and started to assess damages.

Logan lay in the rubble, unable and a bit unwilling to move as his strength abandoned him and left him immobile. He tried to move, but every inch of his body screamed out in pain so he lay still, unwilling to tempt that feeling for the moment.

You did it boy, a voice said inside his head.

Bastion?

I am here as well Logan, the second voice he heard while battling the stone said.

Stalwart, he said recognizing the protector instantly. *Falcone and Galiven? Are you back as well?*

A silence hung in his mind at the mention of the other two protectors who inhabited his mind at one time in his life.

I believe they did not make the journey, Bastion explained.

They're still with Teah? Logan asked a bit disappointed at the prospect of not having all of the protectors back in his mind.

It is possible, but the magic of the stones can pull us out of a mind, this we know for sure, but I doubt there is a guarantee that we will be put in another's mind. Stalwart's explanation felt sorrowful.

Let us hope that Galiven, Falcone, and Teah are safe, Bastion agreed.

Teah was in danger?

When we left her she was out of her body somewhere in the palace at Cordlain, Stalwart said.

And?

The silence that filled his mind made his painful skin crawl.

Teah? Teah, are you alright? Logan reached out to his sister.

The protectors in his head went silent as the possibility sank in. How could he gain two of the protectors only to lose Teah? The reality brought tears to his eyes and sorrow threatened to rip what was left of his heart out of his chest.

Chapter 40

Teah cried out in pain as her head exploded with colors and blinding light. She felt as though she was missing something, but she couldn't put her finger on what. In that instant the weaves fell away from her and she stared into the shocked faces of the six magicals who once held her prisoner.

The oily spots on four of their foreheads were the only remnants of the stones that once held them under Aston's control. Their eyes shone brightly with renewed life as they realized their magic once more belonged to them.

Teah looked at the old woman with the circlet as she stared down at her spirit, invisible to all in the room but her and her male counterpart. "Run child, return to your body and we shall hold the king here for you as long as we are able."

She raced through the outer room avoiding the evaporating layers of weaves appearing like different colored snakes all around her, writhing in threatening twists and turns.

She reached the great hall and gasped at the devastation; bodies and body parts lay scattered across the floor amongst the broken furniture. Blood pooled in the low spots of the stone floor reflecting the carnage in red.

She entered the passage to see Raven's broken form lying in a heap by the exposed entry. Grinwald crouched over her body, covering it with his own as several Zele Magus bombarded his weave protecting them over and over again. Teah noted that the weave weakened with each blast and Grinwald reinforced the weave after each blast, but by the sweat beading on the old Viri Magus's face, he couldn't hold out much longer.

Teah slipped into her body with a relieved sigh even with the carnage all around them. She felt in her element once more as the presence of the protectors sprang forth in her mind again, but it did not feel the same. She heard them shouting their concerns at her absence, but she blocked them and turned her attention to Grinwald.

As she stirred beneath his protective arms, Grinwald pulled back with a gasp and then a look of exhausted relief.

"Welcome back," he said out of breath.

"Good to be back," she said getting to her feet. "Raven?"

Grinwald shook his head and she nodded sadly.

Grinwald stepped away and she drew her swords from the scabbards on her back. She looked to two Zele Magus standing side-by-side filling the passage leading to the cells. She instantly noticed the lack of oily dots on their forehead and understood they were willing accomplices to Aston's plans. She flicked her wrist sending a pulse of magic down the length of her sword. She pointed it at the Zele Magus and they burst apart, sending gore everywhere.

Teah staggered a moment, leaning on one of her swords to catch her breath, surprised that the combination of powers would do so much damage but take so much of her strength.

"I can't do that very often," she shouted to Grinwald who watched over her shoulder.

"Then use each separately unless you have no other choice," Grinwald counseled.

Grinwald spun to the opening leading to the great hall and placed a weave over the access to the passage.

"What now?" he asked over his shoulder, keeping an eye on the weave.

"We need to get to Aston's chambers. A group of magicals is holding him there for us to return."

"But there are too many magicals to fight off, not counting the soldiers. We'll never make it," Grinwald argued.

"Somehow Aston enslaved some magicals with soul stones and now they're free," Teah explained.

"Soul stones? Here in Ter Chadain?" Grinwald gasped in

horror.

"They must have been tied to a source stone in Caltoria or Stellaran," Teah replied.

"You speak in the past tense. You don't think they're tied to the stone anymore?"

"The slaves under the stone's spell are now free and some are holding Aston in his chambers."

"But what could break the spell of the stones?" Grinwald asked.

"There is only one force I know that could do that," Teah said with a knowing smile.

Grinwald nodded, catching her meaning.

"Logan," they said in unison.

She turned and raced with blades slicing into the troops blocking her way to the king's chambers. She felt victory within her grasp and she wouldn't let anything or anyone stand in her way. A thought from Logan reached her, but she let it slip past unanswered as her focus remained on reaching Aston and ending this.

****

Caslor waited only until the sun set. He used the opportunity to surround Cordlain and begin the siege. With the sun at his back the city's defenders who saw his massive army's approach didn't realize he now effectively cut them off from any supplies.

As the blinding sun edged below the horizon Caslor gave the order and the Zele Magus and Viri Magus began their magical assault on the city pounding their defenses. The attacks caught the garrison on the walls by surprise sending many of the troops toppling from their positions to their death.

The advantage proved short-lived as magicals appeared on the ramparts and began deflecting the assault, nullifying the results and effectively causing a stalemate.

357

Caslor sent in the battering rams constructed of enormous trees with metal tips to shatter the city's gates. Under the protective weaves of the magicals moving with them the battering rams, held in a large carriage pushed and pulled by his men, lumbered up to the gates as the defenders showered them with arrows and weaves that bounced off their defensive weaves and sent anything unfortunate enough to be in its path flying.

The battering ram started its slow, painful process of destroying the gates with a deep drumming that radiated through the walls of the city and echoed throughout the plains.

Caslor sat on a stand built for the directors of the siege to observe and make adjustments to the attack and orchestrate the massive force now assembled to claim the city.

Rachel stood next to Caslor as she watched silently at the force being brought to bear. Her eyes welled with tears as the knowledge of the innocent people within the city and their plight until the siege came to an end. Those not forced into the defense of the city would eventually starve as the siege drug on.

"Please take the city quickly to shorten the suffering of the innocent people of Cordlain," Rachel asked.

"It will take as long as it will take," Caslor said with a shrug.

The Magus Patris and Magus Matris stood next to Caslor witnessing the largest siege to Cordlain in over five hundred years. Their faces showed no emotion as they watched and listened to the drum, drum, drumming of the rhythmic pounding of the battering ram against the wooden gates.

Several messengers stood at the ready for any orders Caslor needed relayed to the generals who chose to stay on the field with their troops.

Caslor watched as his troops stood at the ready as the gates creaked and buckled under the force of the ram. He glanced back at the stairs leading to the viewing stand hoping news of Teah's return would come. He sighed and turned back to the assault as the gates cracked and then broke from their metal hinges, falling inward. Without hesitation, the troops surged through the opening like a tidal wave breaching a dam.

From his vantage point he witnessed his forces spread out into the streets, dispatching anything that stood in its way. He smiled as he saw his orders not to kill except in self-defense as they swept through the city followed. Troops paused to usher innocent people into their homes and out of harm's way. He ordered them to gather any male of a certain age and hold them until the offensive was done. He needed the people to rally behind his cause, not rebel due to innocent people being murdered.

He argued with his generals over this tactic, his foolishness being pointed out, but he couldn't afford a rebellion fueled by something he might have avoided.

Watching as a camp formed in the central square with some of his troops standing guard as others brought men to the encampment, he nodded and then turned his attention to the rest of his force rolling forward.

Soon the entire city lay under his control, but he didn't find any comfort in that. This happened far too quickly. It should have taken days to move through the city fighting toward the palace.

A messenger rushed up the stairs and those on the platform turned as the man stopped and waited at the top on the edge of the platform.

Caslor motioned him over.

"We have reached the palace," the man said gasping to gain his breath.

"How was the defense?" Caslor asked, already knowing the answer.

"There was no more than an initial hold as we advanced, then they retreated to the palace."

Caslor looked over the city to the massive palace on the hill. Three layers of walls rose out of the hill surrounding it, giving

Aston three layers of defense before reaching the palace itself.

"They surrendered the city, knowing they had no hopes of holding such a large area," Magus Patris spoke up.

"Now they plan to make their stand at the stronger defenses around the palace," Magus Matris agreed.

"Do we stop and regroup?" Magus Patris asked.

Caslor scanned the field surrounding him as more and more troops marched through the open gates to the city proper. He searched for any messenger heading his way from their camp and the doorway he waited for Teah to step through, but he saw nothing. He nodded in thought as he looked back to the palace and the first walls of defense as his troops halted a safe distance in the city to await his next orders.

"Move the battering rams up to the palace and then begin to assault the gates at once," Caslor ordered.

"Yes sir," the messenger snapped to attention and then raced down the stairs, jumped on a horse, and rode off toward the city.

Chapter 41

Logan lay still, waiting for a word from Teah, but none came. His body shook as he felt the emotions in him surge at the thought of losing her. He fought them off, forcing them down. He couldn't afford the luxury of mourning his sister, at least until he knew her fate for certain.

His moment of isolation in the rubble of his destruction of the source stone proved short-lived as Cita raced to him and slid on her knees beside him.

"Logan, are you alright?" she asked, her eyes searching his body for injuries. Her eyes took in his burnt arms and face, seeing they were now blistered.

"Fine," Logan said sitting up with her help.

"What did you do?" she asked searching his eyes for answers.

"Destroyed the stone enslaving these people," Logan said pointing to those wandering by with oily spots on their foreheads and confusion awash in their features.

"You could have been killed, ending our quest before it began," Cita said half scolding, half worried.

"The Keeper of the Keys escaped and it was the only way to free them," Logan pointed out.

"But at what cost?" Cita said looking down at his arms.

Logan followed her gaze to his damaged arms. The skin bubbled with bright red blisters, some already bursting and oozing with clear fluid. He grimaced at the sight and struggled to his feet with Cita's help, his swords still clenched in his burnt hands as he tenderly lifted his arms to put them back in their sheaths. He found his hands and arms wouldn't do his bidding.

"Can you take these for me?" he asked Cita, lifting his arms gingerly toward her.

She took hold of one of the swords, but his fingers remained clenched around them even as he focused on commanding them to relax.

"You need to pry my fingers open," he told her as she looked at him in horror at the suggestion. "Please."

She nodded and reached down to ease one finger at a time from around the handle. She watched his face as she straightened each digit and he grimaced with pain. Her face showed her anguish as she cringed with each movement.

After the painstakingly long process, the swords finally rested in their sheaths and the scabbards lay over the pommel of Logan's saddle on his horse. Logan sat with his back against the outside of the prison wall with his eyes closed and his head tilted back.

Cita stood with Trevon and the others watching as Zeva worked at healing Logan's wounds. She alone understood how to use her magic to aid and not interfere with his protector's magic in healing his injuries. Something they discovered she spent the long hours on their journey studying unbeknownst to Logan.

When Logan opened his eyes he witnessed his now healed arms, minus any hair they might have possessed before his assault on the source stone, but for the most part, completely healed. He got to his feet as Trevon, Fedlen, Stern, Linell, and Cita approached him and Zeva.

"The prisoners are waiting with the rest of the troops," Cita said.

"How many?" Logan asked.

"Enough to take down the council," Cita said with a smile.

"What if we encounter the Red Tips?" Trevon asked.

"Even if they were at full strength, which we know they are not due to the numbers we have encountered and defeated, they would be no match for the power we now possess. The magic of these prisoners coupled with our troops will make us a force to be reckoned with." Cita's confidence encouraged everyone around her.

"Then let's go tell our new recruits what's in store for them,"

Logan said.

Cita nodded and led Logan around the exterior walls of the prison to the opposite side of the gate.

As they stepped into view of the large army gathered before them, the troops all dropped to a knee and bowed their heads.

Logan stopped, overwhelmed by the sight as the two protectors in his mind radiated with approval.

"People of Stellaran," Logan said raising his voice. "I come to you today asking that you aid in ending a rule which has made people like you outlaws and criminals in their own land." His words echoed against the stone walls behind him and over his kneeling force. "I ask you to give me your faith that I will help bring together a better Stellaran. A Stellaran where magical and non-magical alike can live in peace and prosperity. I ask that you have trust in me and know that I seek only to end the slavery of magicals and oppressive rule over all people."

Logan looked out as all the bowed heads remained motionless before him. He glanced back at Cita and his companions to find them also kneeling, their heads bowed.

Turning back to his army, he raised his voice and asked his last question. "Are you with me?"

The army as a whole came to their feet and cheered their response.

"I would take that as a yes," Cita said now standing beside him.

"I guess you're right," Logan chuckled.

Zeva, Trevon, Stern, Linell, and Fedlen walked up behind them.

"Let's go claim Stellaran for its people," Logan said and they all nodded and smiled their agreement.

****

Logan and his army marched toward Lonnex, the capital city

of Stellaran named after the first chairman of the Crystal Council. They avoided any other settlements on the way, hoping to make the journey as quickly as possible and without any unnecessary confrontations. Their fight was with the council, not the individual governing parties in charge of the outlying towns and villages.

Logan knew it to be only a matter of time before the Red Tips made their appearance and they did not disappoint as a large battalion stretched across the prairie half a day's march outside of Lonnex. A lone figure sat on horseback in front of the army waiting for them as they neared and Logan recognized him instantly.

Logan halted the army and continued up to Rudnick as he sat waiting. Cita, Stern, and Trevon rode with him stopping beside him a few feet from the man.

"Still forgetting your place, I see," Rudnick said with obvious hatred.

"I hoped you would have learned your lesson, but you are a slow learner," Logan replied.

"It is you who will learn a lesson this day," Rudnick said. "When this feeble gathering you call an army is decimated by my trained men, you will wish you had just scampered back to Caltoria."

"So the Red Tips are under your command now?" Logan asked.

"Always have been," Rudnick said puffing up proudly.

"So you gave the order to massacre the innocent people from Caltoria?" Logan continued, watching Trevon stiffen in his saddle beside him.

"They were anything but innocent, people exiled and laying claim to something that is not theirs. Very similar to you," Rudnick pointed out.

"We have a born right to a seat on the council," Trevon shouted.

"Foolish boy, you don't understand that the council never will allow you or any like you near Lonnex." Rudnick smiled, pleased at the rage he stirred in Trevon; the young man's face blazed red.

"There is one difference between those Caltorian's you killed and us," Logan said bringing Rudnick's eyes back to his.

"And what's that?"

"They didn't have the Protector of Ter Chadain fighting with them," Logan said.

"Oh, yes, Ter Chadain. I believe we have sent supplies to a King Aston to aid him in his defense against rebels led by your sister," Rudnick said smugly. "I believe soul stones were included in those supplies so your dear sister might be a slave to the king even as we speak."

The mention of Teah being a slave to a soul stone once more sent Logan over the edge. He drew his swords in one smooth motion and kicked his horse lunging forward.

Rudnick turned and ran, kicking his horse over and over, urging it to run faster as Logan surged toward him.

Logan pulled up, watching as Rudnick disappeared behind his men. Logan trotted back to the others.

"We advance at once," he ordered. "Be aware, there is magic on their side other than Rudnick."

"How do you mean?" Cita asked.

"I can sense that every member of the Red Tips is also a magical at some level," Logan said.

The idea of this caught the others totally unaware as they stared blankly back at him.

He turned his mount around and hesitated a moment looking over his shoulder. "Keep the ranks tight and have the strongest members deflect attacks while the others take the offensive."

"What are you going to do?" Stern asked.

"What I do best...kill," Logan said sending visible shudders through everyone within earshot.

Logan's face took on a blank expression as he turned his horse back toward Rudnick and the Red Tips. He let himself be taken to that place where only death waited to walk beside him and claim all who dared confront him or were foolish enough to venture too near him. He would take life this day and not hesitate to consider the action, but take another and another and yet another until none stood between him and his goal.

And today his goal was to claim the country of Stellaran for his name. The name of the Chairman Lassain, the last magical chairman of Stellaran; his rule over this land was unceremoniously taken from him before his time. This country would once more know the rule of a magical whose vision was peace and not war.

Logan heard the bow strings strum and the hiss of the arrows arching toward him. He rode out front of the others who hurried to form ranks and follow. Only Cita rode anywhere near him leading the main force directly behind him, but she was still out of arrow range as the barrage rained down on him.

Stern took the lead of the left flank while Trevon and Linell lead the right flank. Fedlen took up a position in the rear and watched for an assault from the rear.

A thought from Logan turned the arrows hurtling toward him to ash that wafted down over him in a shower of cinders as he rode on. He smiled to himself as his magic flowed freely through him now more than ever after his contact with the source stone. His magic rose up with the mere thought and he relished at the power waiting at his fingertips.

He reached the first line of Red Tips and sent a surge of magic out in every direction, tearing into the soldiers and exploding their bodies apart in a red gory mass. He swept into the next line letting his swords cut the soldiers apart. Limbs and heads fell around him as he slashed smoothly from one side to the other.

Red Tips surged toward him but he extended an arm and sent

them to the ground in unrecognizable bloody lumps.

Cita's forces filled the void Logan's devastation left behind keeping any Red Tips from closing in behind the protector and catching him from the rear.

At this time, Logan's troops now joined the battle with Stern's force pressing from the left and Linell's and Trevon's force pushing in from the right, the Red Tips found themselves surrounded and squeezed tighter and tighter. The carnage erupted in earnest as casualties fell on both sides, but the majority of the dead and injured bore a red tipped feather.

Logan didn't hold back, showing no mercy on any who happened in his path. His goal held one image in his mind and bore one name...Rudnick. He wanted this man dead by his hand and needed to see the life drain from his eyes. He searched as he dispatched Red Tip after Red Tip until only a handful of the enemy still survived.

He held the last Red Tip in his path at the end of his arm as he sat on his horse staring into the man's terrified eyes.

"Where is Rudnick?" Logan asked.

"He retreated to Lonnex," the horrified man screamed.

Logan sent a surge of magic through his hand into the man and the soldier exploded from the inside out, covering Logan in even more blood.

He turned in his saddle as he released the bloody remnants of the soldier's uniform dropping to the ground to see carnage behind him. A few Red Tips battled here and there in pockets surrounded by his troops, but the majority remained on the blood-soaked ground either dead or writhing in the last throes.

Logan watched as Zeva, Cita, Stern, Linell, and Trevon rode to him, the battle behind them wrapping up as the last Red Tips fought to the death, overwhelmed now by the remaining numbers of the makeshift army. He searched for Fedlen, but then turned to see the sorrowful faces of Linell and Trevon stare blankly back at him.

"I'm sorry," Logan said not needing to explain why.

Linell's eyes watered and Trevon fought to stay composed as he nodded and looked away.

Cita, Stern, and Zeva stared at Logan in horror as he sat covered in red gore from head to toe.

"Are you injured?" Cita asked getting a curious stare from Logan.

"You're covered in blood," Zeva pointed out.

Logan glanced down at his person and shook his head. "Not mine."

"Let's get the troops together, tend to our wounded, and head out," Cita said.

"Agreed," Logan said and turned without another word to ride through the battlefield toward the rear of his troops. He dismounted and sat with his swords, still bloody, in his hands resting on his knees. His head hung down and he let the energy and adrenaline from battle drain from his body.

You did well, Stalwart said causing Logan to jump.

I forgot you were there.

It has been a long time, Bastion agreed. *But Stalwart is right. You have come into your own.*

Is that a good thing? When coming into your own means you are a competent killer?

It is what is needed for one of your destiny, Bastion pointed out.

I never thought my destiny would mean being a murderer.

The protectors remained silent, possibly considering their own destinies.

Chapter 42

Teah and Grinwald battled their way toward the king's chambers, joined by freed magicals possessing oily spots on their foreheads. By the time they reached the outer chambers where Teah encountered hundreds of magicals in her spiritual form, the battle raged furiously.

Magicals threw weave after weave at the contingency set up guarding the inner chamber doors. A group of magicals showing no signs of the destroyed soul stones on their foreheads stood side-by-side with palace guards barring entrance to the king's chambers.

Teah and her group came up behind the magicals on the offensive as a group of guards and magicals slipped up behind the assaulting force.

Teah sent a blast of flame into the flanking party scattering them down side hallways for survival.

The magicals attempting to gain access to the king turned at their opportune arrival and nodded their acceptance of her and her party's aid.

"What is the situation? Teah asked the woman who appeared to be in charge, barking out orders and sending strong weaves into the defensive magical barrier keeping them from their prize.

"Queen Protector," the woman said tucking a long strand of black hair behind her ear as she bowed her head in respect.

"How is it that magicals are fighting for a king who would enslave them?" Teah asked, confused by such treacherous loyalty.

"They picked a side to stay free and obviously chose wrong. They are now fighting for their lives for their poor decision." The woman turned and sent another blast of magic into the barrier. It lit up the invisible wall for a moment and then vanished.

"Are the old ones still inside?" Teah asked referring to the two magicals who trapped her spirit while they were stoned.

"I believe so. I think they are holed up with the king, not letting this force in front of us entrance," the woman told her.

"So they are trapped?" Grinwald said as he stood surveying the battle and watching behind them for another rear assault.

"It appears that way," the woman agreed.

A blast of magic sent Teah and the woman hurtling into the hallway chamber wall. Teah's head throbbed as she tried to right herself and blood ran down her face filling her eyes and giving everything a fuzzy red hue. Taking the back of her sleeve, she cleared her eyes of the blood only to have more blood fill them again. She glanced next to her to see the woman's body crumpled against the wall, her neck twisted at an unnatural angle, her eyes staring blankly at the ceiling.

Teah looked around at the carnage that one blast caused as magicals picked themselves up off the floor. Grinwald lay still on the far side of the chamber and she scrambled to his side, giving a sigh of relief as he stirred and opened his eyes.

His face turned, aghast at the sight of her, blood running from a large gash on her forehead down her face. He reached up and touched the wound, weaving it closed and stopping the bleeding.

"Are you okay?" he asked weakly.

"Yes, but we have to get to the king if we have any hopes of surviving," Teah said looking around as the others began to weave protective spells out into the hallway leading to the chambers. She stood and turned to those in her way as the sound of a rear assault on the new magical barriers in place rumbled to her ears.

A burst of fire roared at them and she flung her hand up to deflect it into a lush couch that burst into flames.

"That isn't going to help. We can't stay here if the place is on fire." She raised a hand and sent a weave into the fire encircling the flames and then drawing the air out of the magical containment. The flames flickered and then went out.

Another fire weave hit near her and Grinwald, the impact

sending them sliding along the smooth tile flooring into the outer wall where the woman Teah spoke to moments earlier still lay. Teah's back impacted the wall driving the air from her lungs and causing her to gasp in pain. She struggled to catch her breath and inhaled quickly in a fearful panic.

Deep breaths, take it easy, slow it down, Falcone said calmly.

Something about the protectors wasn't right. The battle kept her from thinking about it until now, but she felt as though something was missing.

Where are Bastion and Stalwart?

We aren't sure, Galiven responded. *One moment they were here with us and the next they weren't.*

How could that be?

The only magic powerful enough are the soul stones... Falcone paused mid-thought not wanting to finish what they all dreaded.

You don't think Logan has been stoned? Do you?

Another blast near her brought her out of her thought and sent her into motion as she realized that King Aston having soul stones and Logan possibly being stoned was too much of a coincidence. A common thread played a part here and she needed to find out what that meant.

Her anger rose at the memory of being stoned and the frustration with losing Logan into slavery again surged inside her. She came to her feet as the magic within her built to a fevered pitch. She drew her swords and strode up to those stopping her from getting to the man who knew the answers she sought.

Reaching the barrier, the magicals behind the wall sent weave after weave from their side through the wall toward her. Teah effortlessly sliced through the weaves with the protector swords sending them spinning apart in harmless wispy shapes.

She sliced the barrier, the blades glowing with enormous amounts of magic pulsing through them. She stepped through the opening she created and expended her arms out to her sides. The

371

swords pulsed with white hot magic, turning magicals and soldiers alike to ash.

She kicked the door in knocking it from its hinges and sending it sliding across the floor of the inner chamber. Striding through the doorway with Grinwald close behind, Teah stopped at the sight before her.

The magicals sat in high-backed chairs with King Aston dangling upside down before them a few feet off the ground. No sound came from his open mouth in his attempt to scream for help which held an effective weave of air cutting off all sound.

The two magicals turned to Teah and gave her a respectful nod, which she didn't return as the fury still swelled in her and all niceties remained far from her mind. She hesitated, feeling that something didn't feel quite right, but not able to put her finger on it. As she turned to see if Grinwald felt it too, the door lifted from the floor and slammed back into the opening.

Grinwald's face contorted with recognition mixed with terror as he stared at the two old magicals. Teah stared at the two circlets filled with glowing stones on their foreheads and terror ripped through her mind.

The Banished Ones, Falcone cried out in warning.

Teah didn't see the weave that hit her before it lifted her from her feet and slammed her against the wall holding her dangling as her swords clattered to the floor below her.

Grinwald threw a weave at the two old magicals but the man easily deflected it and tossed Grinwald across the room slamming him into the mantle over the large fireplace and letting him drop limply to the floor, unconscious.

Teah struggled, but her mind spun in confusion at the change of events.

The king gently rotated and settled on his feet again as the air weave in his mouth vanished and a smile spread across his face.

He strode over to where Teah fought to get free from the

weave holding her against the wall. She stopped thrashing as the king stopped in front of her and looked her up and down triumphantly.

"So I have you now, Queen Protector."

Teah looked past him to the magicals with pleading eyes, but saw no sympathy in their aged features as they stared back at her.

"Oh, those two are on loan to me from some very special friends I've recently made. They have more of them to greet your dear brother when he arrives at Lonnex as well," the king said gloating.

They are two of the ten magicals exiled from Ter Chadain by the Tera Lassain, the first Queen of Ter Chadain, Stalwart explained.

That was before your time, how can you be sure?

Their images were passed on through the protectors from Bastion, to be sure we would always know them, Galiven said.

How can they still be alive?

Their magic was very strong and combining with all those soul stones may have given them immortality, Falcone rationalized.

Teah fought to control her fear, but hearing that there may be eight more of these magicals waiting for Logan, she reached out to him...and failed.

She tried again and her thoughts came echoing back. The panic rose in her as she realized this very well could be the end of her quest. She stared helplessly at her swords lying on the floor where the weave of the old ones took hold of her to trap her against the wall.

She tried moving her arms held tightly against the wall at her sides and slowing eased her right hand toward the sheath on her leg, but the bond held tight just inches from her goal.

She looked back into Aston's victorious stare and felt her hope drain from her. She needed to do something, but no matter how she searched for a way out, and longed for the protectors to give her some insight into her escape, nothing came.

"Guards," Aston shouted and a group of men stepped through another doorway and snapped to attention.

"Summon my queen and all the nobles who are no doubt hiding in their chambers to the throne room once you have dispensed with the rebels still wandering around the palace," he instructed.

Teah held out hope for some of those magicals to come to her aid, but Aston dashed those hopes as he stopped the last man in the unit before he left.

"Kill any magical you find who has a spot where the soul stone once was. They are of no further use to me," the king instructed.

The man nodded, accepting the order and hurrying from the room.

Teah's last hopes of escape seemed to vanish with the man and his orders to kill any of her kind. She stared a bit too long at the circlet on the male magical's head and brought Aston's attention to her.

"Oh, not to worry, the controlling stone for these magicals is far too powerful a magic to be so easily destroyed. These magicals have been enslaved by the soul stone circlets since the time of Tera Lassain. They have come to accept their place as servants to the Council of Stellaran. I may choose to use the old ones to control you and get rid of the difficult Betra Queen of mine…but that may prove problematic. I will need to think on it." His eyes wandered as he fell into his thoughts. They snapped back on Teah with childlike excitement. "Not to worry, I will have decided before we greet our guests in the throne room."

What do I do now?

She asked, but the protectors did not give her any suggestions or any comfort. She understood the direness of her predicament for that to happen.

Chapter 43

Trevon stared at Logan from what was hopefully a safe distance, but he didn't hold any false notions that it couldn't happen at any distance. Logan killed, proficiently and without remorse from what he could tell. He held no doubt that Logan as king was a very poor idea, but how could he tell him that?

"Quit staring," Linell said hitting Trevon in the shoulder as they sat resting with Stern. Her somber tone only hinted at the pain wracking her at the loss of her dear friend Fedlen. He took a sword to the heart and died at the hands of the Red Tips. She didn't even reach him in time to try and help him, or comfort him in his last moments, or say goodbye. Maybe that was why she hurt so badly. This entire journey decimated those in her life leaving only Trevon as the last remnant of her past existence. She hung her head as tears failed to come from her exhausted tear ducts. That seemed to aggravate her sorrow even more.

"But he can't become king. You saw how he lost control and destroyed everything around him," Trevon said motioning in Logan's direction as he spoke. He looked to Linell who stared at her lap and then to Stern, already glancing in Logan's direction then turned to meet his gaze.

"He did most of the dirty work of killing today lessening our losses enormously," Stern pointed out and then wished he could take his words back at the sight of the pain in Trevon's eyes at the mention of the losses suffered this day.

"Granted," Trevon said pushing through his shaking voice. "But can he be a noble leader as well as a deadly warrior?"

"It is impossible to tell, but are you going to tell him your concerns? Are you going to face him and tell him he is not worthy to be king?"

****

Logan leaned against a wagon away from the rest of his party. He'd cleaned himself up as they sat mourning their friend. He knew he lacked the words to ease their pain, so decided no words were better than inadequate ones. He liked Fedlen, but death came hand-in-hand with his way of life since that night in Grinwald's hut. He knew he would never get used to it, but he learned to accept it. Still, he felt sorrow for their loss.

He straightened and walked wearily toward his companions who appeared to be in a heated discussion.

"No, of course not. Telling Logan he isn't fit to be king might prove dangerous," Trevon said and then looked up at Logan from his sitting position, terror in his eyes when he realized who approached.

Logan stopped a few feet away as Trevon went silent, not even taking a breath. Stern gaped at him. Linell didn't move but looked at her bloody hands resting on her lap.

Logan didn't react to Trevon's comment, slipping past the two men and dropping to a knee next to Linell who seemed mesmerized at the sight of blood covering her hands.

Logan wrapped a comforting arm across her shoulders.

Linell looked to him foggily, her eyes widening when she realized who comforted her. When their eyes met, her surprise turned to peace as they held each other's gaze. She draped her arms around his neck and he wrapped his arms around her, hugging her tightly to him.

Trevon and Stern gawked at them, Linell's body shaking as sorrow wracked her body and tears flowed anew down her cheeks.

Logan held her close, not letting up until she finally lifted her head from his newly wet shoulder. He leaned back and looked her in the eyes, she gave a sorrowful grin seeing he shared her pain on her level.

"I'm truly sorry for your loss. Know that he will always be

remembered with honor in the new Stellaran," Logan whispered to her.

She nodded her approval of that thought.

"As far as not being worthy of being king, I couldn't agree more," Logan said to Trevon.

Trevon opened his mouth to explain, but Logan raised a weary hand to stay his comment.

"I have never been interested in power for myself, but to empower people to be able to live a free life the way they want to live it. I'm merely a conduit of a prophecy to make right what has gone so wrong."

He stood and walked away without a look back.

"He is noble," Linell said with reverence. "I think we need to stop worrying about Logan and worry more about how we can help him. If we see that he succeeds, I don't doubt that good will come from it."

Stern and Trevon nodded in agreement and then turned to watch Logan walk through the camp, stopping by each and every small gathering and speaking words of comfort and encouragement.

****

Logan dropped to the ground next to the wagon he leaned against hours before, the sun long since set below the horizon and the moon high in the night's sky. He leaned against the wagon wheel and closed his eyes to the exhaustion begging to take over his body.

You have been honorable to these people, Bastion said with approval.

What did you expect?

Nothing less, Stalwart agreed.

Teah? Are you there? His thought reached out and seemed to echo into the silence. He hung his head at the meaning of her lack of response.

It could mean many things, Stalwart said trying to keep Logan positive.

Like what?

Neither Bastion nor Stalwart offered up an explanation leaving Logan with his worried thoughts. The last communication with Teah found her trapped by two old magicals in her spiritual form. He couldn't imagine magicals as powerful as his sister. He witnessed firsthand her power when they destroyed the source stone in Bellatora. She had more power than many magicals. His thought hung heavy in his mind and apprehension from the protectors trickled to his consciousness.

What is it? What do you fear?

Back in my day, magic was much stronger on average than it is now, Bastion told him. *It is believed that there is a certain group of magicals who were exiled in my time who may have found a way to become immortal.*

From what you say Teah described, these could be some of them, Stalwart said warily.

And...?

If it is true and Aston has some of the exiled magicals aiding him, Teah could be in great peril, Bastion finished.

Logan didn't want to think of the consequences of Teah being captured by the exiled magicals, or worse. He closed his eyes and slid up the barrier between his mind and the protectors' spirits. He forced himself to shut down his thoughts and rest. He drew in a long breath just as a blanket was draped over him.

He opened his weary eyes to Cita as she straightened the blanket and then slid in beside him. She eased a bedroll under his head and laid her head next to his. Her face bore scrapes and scratches from the battle, but she'd escaped any real injuries.

He closed his eyes and let the warmth of her body against his soothe him into relaxing and letting his body and mind recover from the day and prepare for what might very well be his last day alive. He smiled in silence as he thought, that pretty much summed up every day of his life since he stepped outside of Grinwald's home in Tumbleweed all those years ago. He longed for those peaceful times, but let those thoughts drift away as he cleared his mind and allowed sleep to take him.

****

The next morning as the sun came up over Lonnex, Logan sat on his mount beside his friends with an army at his back as soldiers scurried along the ramparts of the walls surrounding the capital city of Stellaran.

Logan gave a chuckle at the inadequate structure meant to protect the city from invasion. *More like a wall to keep the cattle from grazing in the city.* He wasn't impressed.

"There has been no uprising or invasion since the weave went up. The Red Tips are the only army allowed in Stellaran and the council controls them, so there is no need for defenses," Stern explained.

"I don't want innocent people killed...including those in the Red Tips who wish to surrender," Logan said, remorseful of his total annihilation of the last Red Tips battalion.

"We can send a group of magicals in to weave a barrier along our path so we may proceed to the Halls of Council with little interference. Only the Red Tips and those magicals who wish to directly oppose us will be able to confront us," Cita offered.

"Make it so," Logan ordered and watched Cita kick her mount into motion to gather her troops.

****

Logan and his army moved unhindered through the streets of Lonnex as his troops with magical abilities held up a barrier along their path keeping it clear. They pulled to a stop in front of the

379

Halls of Council and Logan saw why they were not confronted in the city. The Halls of Council loomed at the center of the city with high block walls and thousands of Red Tips lining the tops with arrows notched in their bows.

Linell raised a weave of protection as they stopped out of the range of the archers, to be certain.

They gathered around Logan waiting for his orders. He stared at the building and the council's last stand.

We need to lay siege the building if we want to reach the council and remove them, Bastion said.

There is a problem you are not seeing.

And what is that? Stalwart asked.

Look through my eyes at the walls.

The protectors hesitated a moment and then gasped as they surveyed what Logan requested.

I have never seen such a thing, Stalwart said in disbelief.

I have, Bastion said.

Logan looked back at the walls seeing the deep red colors of a deadly weave surrounding the building. If any of them merely touched the weave, Logan held no doubt that death would be the result.

When the Banished attempted to take Tera from the throne they combined their powers, both male and female magicals, and created a deadly weave where a single touch was fatal. This is such a weave.

I thought you said that magicals today don't hold as much power as those from your day?

I did, Bastion agreed.

Then how?

The council has Banished Ones inside, Bastion said in a whisper.

Logan stared at the blood-red weave and his heart sank. If Teah encountered some of these Banished Ones, he held little hope for a positive outcome.

"What now?" Cita said staring at the wall. "Breaking through the weave will be very difficult."

"Keep everyone back," Logan instructed. "The weave is a dark red. It is deadly to the touch."

"You see the weave's colors?" Linell said in awe.

"A skill my sister and I have in common," Logan said with a nod. "Keep them back and let us put our heads together and figure out a way through it."

Good luck lad, Tera couldn't break that weave back then, I doubt you can do it now, Bastion said skeptically.

Maybe I don't need luck. Maybe I have all I need right here, Logan said tapping his chest with his hand.

Bastion's and Stalwart's doubt hung in Logan's mind, but he smiled as he knew they didn't understand what he meant. Yet somehow, he felt confident that he knew what to do.

Chapter 44

Teah felt isolated hanging in a magical cocoon above the shiny stone floor of the throne room awaiting her fate as the nobles filed in staring at her like a traveling carnival act.

Grinwald floated nearby, still unconscious from the beating Aston's men inflicted on the Viri Magus as punishment for his betrayal.

As the room brimmed to capacity, the whispers cut off as Aston strode in with the protector swords slung over his shoulder leading a small woman with long dark hair. Her unflattering grey dress hung like a gunny sack on her frame and her face showed signs of a recent beating. A silver crown rested on her head as if someone just forced it on moments before entering the room.

The woman stared terrified at Teah with one open eye, the other swollen shut. The split in her top lip appeared red and tender as the woman ran a nervous tongue across it grimacing with pain at the forgetful habit.

Teah knew this must be the queen Aston presented to the people of Ter Chadain to reclaim his power. Teah surmised now that Aston had her in his possession, this woman held very little value anymore. She concluded that Englewood decided to control her instead of killing her and potentially making her a martyr in the cause against him.

Teah looked to the woman with sympathy for being used as a pawn by Aston, but her current position remained as dire as the woman's, making her no help.

"I present to you Teah Lassain, heir to the throne and my new queen," Aston boasted lifting the protector's swords over his head in victory.

The room gasped and applause tentatively rose up along with timid cheers from the nobles.

Teah fought against her bonds then stopped and traced the

intricate weaves. They twisted and turned on each other with seemingly no pattern. Her mind soon spun in confusion as the weaves swirled, undulating like a live snake.

You are looking at this all wrong, Falcone said giving her a ray of hope. *Separate the male weave from the female weave.*

Teah looked to the weaves again but could see no difference. She reached inside of herself taking hold of her magic and sent it running along the weaves. As her magic touched the male weave it turned and followed another path leaving her magic's route illuminated. The magic raced ahead and soon came back to the beginning showing clearly the female weave pattern.

She laughed to herself at such an easy weave holding her, but in combination with the male's weave, it became nearly unbreakable. She drew in more magic and turned her attention to King Aston as he continued to bask in his victory, setting the swords against his throne.

"So, as you see, I currently have one too many queens in my kingdom," Aston announced as the applause silenced. "I have come to a decision."

All eyes turned from Teah to the beaten queen standing diminutively next to her guard. She lifted her eyes and waited for her sentence, trembling.

"Since having a queen seems to be a difficult accomplishment, I have decided to keep them both. Each will have their own cell in my dungeon and the Queen Protector will be controlled by the Banished Ones to assure she doesn't get any grand ideas of taking the throne for herself."

Teah's blood turned cold at the idea of being controlled and a slave to Aston for all time. She glanced to Grinwald in his suspended weave as he stirred but didn't open his eyes. She swore he gave her a slight nod, but his eyes remained closed.

The weaves holding Teah lowered her to the floor and then doubled her over to kneel before Englewood. Teah looked at the blank expressions on the faces of the Banished Ones and drew in as much magic as she could hold, feeling it pushing at her boundaries and threatening to explode.

Aston walked up before her holding a circlet containing six clear soul stones in his hand and smiled down triumphantly at her.

"You should have stayed a slave to the empress. She may have been more merciful to you. But since your brother killed my father before my eyes, you will get no such consideration from me." Aston glared down at her. "Now you will join the ten in becoming enslaved to the bloodline of the one who places the circlet upon your head."

He reached to place the circlet and she closed her eyes, waiting for the moment the stones would brush her forehead. She would have mere seconds before it took hold of her. At that moment, she let her magic burst from every pore in her body. The magic came out as a bright flash of light, evaporating the female weave holding her, then incinerating the male weave the next instant.

The force sent Aston flying and Grinwald tumbling from within his imprisoning weave. The circlet on Teah's head melted away and she sent a pulse of magic from her extended arms into the two Banished magicals, sending them careening backwards into the wall.

****

The weaves holding Grinwald vanished and the Viri Magus stood, turning on the guards rushing in. He sent them toppling backwards with a strong weave of air and spun in time to see Teah send the old magicals flying.

Troops mixed with magicals rushed into the room and Grinwald held them back with a woven wall of air. They fought against his defenses, but he held them off. A flash of light drew his attention as Aston picked up the protector's swords and turned on Teah.

Teah sent magic toward Englewood, but the old magicals now on their feet deflected her magical assault causing it to impact the walls behind him sending the Betra Queen and the guards scrambling for cover.

Aston used the advantage and charged Teah. He slashed at her, but she dove away and rolled to her feet. A blast of magic hit her sending her tumbling across the floor to slam into the wall.

Grinwald spun to the source of the magic attacking Teah and sent a male magical slamming against the wall. He turned back to Teah seeing her scrambling along the floor on her back to escape the advancing Aston while trying to pull the bow free from its sheath.

Grinwald sent a weave toward Aston, but the Banished Ones defended him turning it aside at the last moment. Aston towered above Teah raising one sword over his head to strike her down.

****

When Aston picked up the protector's swords, Teah's heart sank. She knew their power, even in his hands. She sent a weave toward him but the Banished Ones deflected it, sending it sailing harmlessly around him.

She avoided his strike and reached for her bow only to be hit with a weave that sent her spinning across the room. She shook her head trying to gain her bearings and scrambled backwards as Aston advanced on her. Her hand reached for her bow, but the king's advance made it impossible to retrieve the bow without allowing him to reach her.

Grinwald came into view just as he crashed into the king, sending them tumbling to the floor. Given the moment of reprieve Teah pulled the rod from the sheath and it expanded to the silver bow. Her hand pulled back on the string as a silver arrow materialized and she loosed it at first one Banished one and then the other, hitting her marks squarely in the chest and sending them tumbling to the floor. As King Aston straightened from the floor leaving a motionless Grinwald behind, Teah sunk a silver arrow into him.

The arrow caught Aston in the chest as he turned toward Teah and a second impacted only a fraction from the first.

Aston's incredulous shock showed in his eyes and he seemed to move in slow motion as his eyes went blank and he fell to the floor. The protector's swords skittered across the polished surface where Teah stopped them with her boot and bent down to retrieve them.

The bow shrank and she tucked it away before grasping the swords and then standing to meet the stares of the guards, nobles, and the Betra Queen.

As one, the entire room went silent and everyone bowed their heads in respect.

Grinwald coughed and stirred next to Aston's body. Teah raced to his side.

Several men and women joined her, all with the remnants of stones on their foreheads as a greasy spot.

Teah knelt beside Grinwald and lifted him to rest his head on her lap. She sent a weave into him and cringed as she knew the wounds caused by the swords would prove fatal before she could heal him.

She looked into his eyes as tears welled up in hers.

"I'm sorry, my child," Grinwald said as he coughed and blood wet his lips.

"It's okay, I forgive you," Teah said honestly.

"I always tried to do what was best for you, Logan, and Ter Chadain," he said and coughed again, sending blood spraying across Teah's face as she leaned close. "Sometimes hard decisions need to be made for the greater good."

"I know and I'm sure Logan does as well," Teah comforted.

"Tell him I'm sorry." He closed his eyes and took a deep

breath. Then he reached up and pulled Teah down close as he gasped for air.

"There are many with agendas yet to be played out," he whispered. "Trust no one." He exhaled one last time and went still in her arms.

Teah leaned down, touching her cheek to his as she sobbed, her sorrow too overwhelming to grasp her victory.

Chapter 45

Logan sat quietly with his back resting against a stone building's wall as he contemplated his next move. Although his external demeanor seemed relaxed, his mind erupted in chaos as the two protectors argued on the best course of action.

Logan listened, not entering the argument but turning the problem over and over again for himself. A deadly weave stood between him and the Crystal Council of Stellaran. But most importantly for him and most of his party, it also stood between them and Rudnick, the man who massacred innocent people trying to return to their homeland. This didn't feel like vengeance, to him it felt more like justice and even in that, Rudnick's death would fall disappointingly short of satisfying.

Cita walked up, hesitating a short distance from him.

He raised his head and motioned her over.

She slid down the wall beside him staring at the deep gray weave before her.

"So you see a deep red color?" she asked.

He nodded looking at the weave and then turning back to her. "A touch would kill any of us, at least most of us."

"I do not like the sound of it. What are you thinking?" Cita placed a hand on his arm and leaned down to make eye contact with his averted eyes.

"I have the magic to get through the weave, but I don't think I have enough magic to take anyone with me," he said flatly.

"No, no way. That is what they want," Cita protested, pulling away.

"It is the only way."

"No it isn't, there are always other ways."

"Not this time. I think I can part the weave with my swords, but I won't be able to hold it open for anyone to come with me."

"And once you're inside, then what? You plan on defeating

whoever put up the weave, Rudnick, the remainder of the Red Tips, *and* the council, all by yourself?"

"Doesn't sound likely, does it?"

"Then you should find a different plan. I doubt that a suicide mission by the one who is to be our king is what we need."

"I'll tell you what, if I can get to the magicals creating the weave and bring the weave down, the rest of you can attack. That way you can take on the Red Tips and whoever else decides to stand beside Rudnick and the council."

That is a foolish plan, Bastion warned.

Do we have any other choices?

He has a point, Stalwart reasoned.

The protectors went quiet giving him their silent, yet begrudging support.

"Gather the others, I want to do this by tonight and we need to have everything in place," he said looking past the council hall at the sun dipping below the horizon.

****

Teah lifted her head from Grinwald as her tears wet her face and noticed the silence around her. Everyone stared, afraid to move and cautious to not upset this deadly woman in her moment of grief.

The Betra Queen stepped over the bodies of the Banished Ones and gingerly approached Teah where she knelt with Grinwald in her arms. She dropped to a knee and bowed her head to Teah as she removed the silver crown and placed it upon Teah's head.

Teah's eyes widened as she realized what was happening.

"As Queen of Ter Chadain I renounce my right to the throne and proclaim you, Teah Lassain, rightful queen," she said softly, but loud enough for everyone present to hear. "My Betra are with you."

"Long live the Queen Protector," a nobleman from the crowd

shouted and was echoed throughout the room as they all dropped to a knee and bowed in allegiance to their new queen.

****

Logan spelled out his plan to his friends, those who had followed him since his going over the side of the Morning Breeze to this moment. Their faces told him their dislike of his plan, but none of them spoke out in opposition, knowing it was their only chance of success.

"So that is it. I'm going to use the swords to get through the weave and then find the magicals controlling it. Once I have the weave down, the rest of you attack and take the council," Logan said to their stoic stares. "Okay, let's get ready." He turned and walked away leaving the others in silence.

"Sounds like a stupid plan if you ask me," a voice said from the darkness as he got further from his gathering.

He knew the voice, never would forget it. He cringed at the timing of her return.

Saliday stepped from the shadows; the outline of Morgan hovered just outside the light.

Logan clenched his teeth at the pirate's presence, but focused on Saliday as she came closer.

"Why would you be so foolish as to risk your life for a people and a country you don't even know?" Saliday asked.

"I know them better than those I've been with much longer," Logan said.

Saliday grimaced at the jab. "I have always been loyal to you."

Logan pressed his lips together, trying to stay composed and concentrate on the task before him. "What do you want, Saliday?"

"I want to stop this, but I know once you've made up your mind, you never turn back, so I want you to know that I love you," she said, her eyes watering in the dim light.

"If you say so," Logan said, unconvinced and then looked past her to the shadow of Morgan.

Saliday took hold of his chin and turned his face down to hers. "I never stopped loving you and I believe you still love me as well."

"I do love you," Logan admitted openly.

Saliday looked up at him in shock at his admittance.

"But I have moved on. I understand we can never be together as long as you have the duty to preserve your race with Morgan."

"But I choose you," she pleaded.

"I don't choose you. I can't be the one who ends the line of Tarkens. I can never live with myself if that happens and I know you can't either."

"I can deal with it, I love you." She started to cry, seeing her pleas going nowhere.

He leaned down and pressed his lips to hers, feeling the passion rising inside of him and pushing it down. He pulled away and stared at her face turned up to him, eyes closed and content.

"This is how I need to remember you," he said and turned away without another word or glance back.

Saliday stared after him, stunned and heartbroken.

Chapter 46

Logan stood before the weave watching the red fluidity of the magic undulating in front of him. His small party of friends stood behind him watching in silence.

Zeva took a few steps to his side and stared at the weave without speaking.

"Thank you…for everything," he said not looking at her.

"I'm honored to be your friend," she said softly.

"See you on the other side," he said in a feeble attempt to sound confident.

She reached over and hugged him tightly, then stretched on her tiptoes to kiss him on the cheek. She turned and walked back to the others.

He heard Cita approaching and his heart sank and soared at the same time. Her effect on him made him wonder how he'd survived so long without that feeling. She wrapped an arm around his waist and he did the same as they observed the weave.

"You know I…" she started and then he spun her into his arms, kissing her deeply.

He pulled away and looked down at her wet eyes as she stared up at him. "I know."

He took a step toward the weave without a second glance to Cita and drew the swords, the ring of their steel echoed in the night.

He wanted to turn back, to take Cita in his arms and feel her passion again, but he lowered his head with determination and strode up to the edge of the weave, pulling in his magic to send it down and into the protector's swords.

The weave hissed and smoked where the blades met it as Logan put the tips of the weapons together and inched forward. The weave held firm at first and then slowly parted, spreading out around him.

Just as he suspected, once he stepped past the edge of the weave it closed behind him leaving him in the midst of the magic trying desperately to reach him, but held at bay by the magic of the swords.

The weave proved to be only a few paces deep and he emerged on the other side and in the midst of Red Tips lounging about, not expecting anyone to breach the weave.

The soldier closest to him opened his mouth to raise an alarm, but Logan cut him down before the man uttered a sound. He used the darkness to find cover behind some wagons as he dragged the dead man out of sight and scanned the walls of the hall to get his bearings. More Red Tips stood at ease around the exterior of the hall and some even sat on the steps leading up to the main entrance.

He undressed the dead man and stripped down to slip inside the Red Tip uniform. It proved a bit snug, but he pulled the red cloak on to complete his disguise and conceal his swords on his back. He felt confident of his masquerade in the dim light, but held little hope that he would pass for a Red Tip once inside the brightly lit hall where the illumination streamed through the windows.

He stood and confidently strode out across the courtyard to the main stairs climbing them one after another, not slowing to observe those around him; acting as though he belonged there. Upon reaching the landing at the top of the stairs with tall pillars holding the entrance's roof high overhead, he met his first test.

Men stood at attention on either side of the doorway and dropped their spears in front of him as he approached, barring his entrance.

A man off to one side stepped into the doorway and put a hand up ordering Logan to stop. "What is your business inside?" the man questioned.

"I was told to report to the magicals holding the weave if I saw anything unusual," Logan said flatly.

"And did you see anything unusual?"

"Yes sir," Logan said snapping to attention.

"And what is that?"

"I was ordered to report only to the magicals," Logan answered.

"By whose orders?" the man asked, incensed by Logan not reporting to him.

"Rudnick, sir." Logan replied.

The man's eyes shot wide with fear. "Let him through, let him through," he ordered the guards who quickly raised their spears to allow Logan entrance.

Logan hesitated for a moment, surprised by the sudden change in their demeanor.

"Go, don't keep Rudnick waiting," the man shouted taking Logan by the arm and pushing him into the corridor.

Logan took a few steps and then hesitated only to bring the anger of the man down on him.

"What are you waiting for, go."

"Where are the magicals?" Logan asked.

"Fool, haven't you been in the hall before? Never mind. Down the hall on the right to the very end in the grand council room." The man pointed, shaking his hand fervently.

Logan turned and hurried down the hall, easing the tension of the man behind him as he watched him go. Logan strode down the marble hallway and paused at the large wooden double doors. He hesitated a moment before opening the door and stepping inside.

He wasn't prepared to see what lay inside as his eyes tried to adjust to the dimmer lighting in the large room. He picked out eight shapes sitting motionless in chairs around the grand table. The candlelight coming from candelabras on the table itself surrounded it, reflecting off the six soul stones in the silver circlet on the foreheads of each of the magicals as they sat with their eyes closed in concentration. Their wrinkled faces showed centuries of life in their deep creases and weariness hung across their features.

The Banished Ones, at least eight of them, Bastion said.

Eight?

There were ten when Tera banished them, Bastion said.

Hurry, kill them before they become aware of you, Stalwart instructed.

They're slaves, I can't just kill them for being slaves of the council.

When magicals are controlled by others for so long they no longer have a mind of their own, only the thoughts and wishes of their masters, Bastion told him. *There is nothing to free inside of them anymore.*

Logan didn't like it, but he drew his blades and stepped up to the nearest chair containing a woman with silver hair staring blankly at nothing.

The door behind him creaked and he spun to stand face-to-face with Rudnick whose eyes shot wide with surprise, and he fumbled for his sword. Logan rushed him as he retreated out the door, screaming for reinforcements.

Logan knew he only had moments before Red Tips descended upon him. He pulled his magic from deep inside and sent it to his swords turning them white with magic. He then climbed on the table with the magicals surrounding him.

He took a deep breath to release his magic and the eight magical's eyes snapped open in unison. His position on the table quickly changed from one of control to one of weakness as the magicals unleashed their powers into him.

Logan lifted from the table and slammed into the ceiling. He hung trapped against the intricate details of the coved roof as the eyes of the eight Banished Ones stared up at him venomously.

He regained his composure and sent his magic back into his

swords turning them white with magic again. He released the magic as a solid white wall down to the table shattering the wood and sending the Banished Ones flying.

The weaves holding him aloft vanished and he crashed onto the remnants of the table, the air rushing from his lungs. As he lay gasping for breath the magicals lifted themselves from the floor scanning the room searching for him.

He raised a sword protectively in front of him as a rush of magic hit the blade and parted around him, striking those behind him, sending them slamming into the far wall.

He jumped to his feet rushing the closest magical, cutting the man in half and sending the woman next to him running for her life only to run into the Red Tips bursting into the room. Logan blocked another barrage of magic and struck down a female Banished with one stroke and a male Banished with another.

That's three, Stalwart told him. *Five left.*

Logan grimaced at the morbid scorekeeping and leapt across the table into the huddled mass of more Banished as they tried to weave protection around them. The protector's swords sliced through the magic and then into three more Banished.

Logan spotted a Banished racing toward the door he entered and another toward the back of the room. He smoothly sheathed his swords, drew the bow lifting it as it expanded, and sent a silver arrow into the man racing toward the back of the room.

The arrow hit the man squarely in the back and burst out of his chest sending him toppling into the furniture surrounding the fireplace.

Logan spun and hit the last Banished One, a female, as she grasped at a Red Tip's uniform begging him for protection. Her eyes went wide and her mouth gaped for air as she slid down the front of the man's uniform leaving a bloody streak.

More merciful than they deserved, Bastion told him.

Still murder, Logan lamented.

An escape from an eternal life of slavery, Stalwart pointed out.

Logan jerked from his internal dialogue with the protectors as more Red Tips rushed in. Logan jumped onto the remnants of the table, raised his bow, and drew back the string letting the silver arrow fly.

He hit Red Tip after Red Tip with deadly accuracy, raining down his deadly barrage into the surging troops. The bowstring thrummed with each loosed arrow as the room soon resounded continuously with the humming of the string keeping the troops at bay and away from him.

He thought of drawing his swords and sending magic through them, but something inside his head warned against it. Almost like a voice of caution not to overuse his magic.

He stayed with the bow and kept dropping Red Tip one after another until their bodies piled up in the doorway so that the soldiers needed to climb over the fallen to get into the room.

The assault halted suddenly and Logan waited for the next push. When none came, he leapt from the table and headed for the door. He paused, wondering how to go about getting past the mound of bodies in front of him when the corpses slid to one side and Zeva walked into the room.

She saw him and rushed to leap into his arms, hugging him tightly. She slid down and looked up at his stunned face with a smile.

"You did it, the weave went down and we attacked. They didn't see it coming. Now the Red Tips are fighting for their lives and we need to find the council before they escape," she told him.

"I saw Rudnick, but he fled before the Red Tips attacked me," Logan said as they hurried from the room and past the main entrance into another wing of the building.

"Trevon, Linell, and Stern are searching for him," she said.

"Cita?"

"Searching for the council with Saliday and Morgan," Zeva

397

said stopping Logan in his tracks. "What?" She turned back to him.

"I don't trust them," Logan said not needing to explain who he didn't trust.

"Then we better get to them before something happens to Cita," Zeva said and ran down the hallway, not waiting for Logan. He caught her after a couple of strides and they raced to the large chambers at the end of the wing.

The doors stood open and the sound of battle echoed down the hallway before they reached the opening. They slowed as Logan drew his bow and pulled back on the string to notch a silver arrow.

Red Tips came into view and Logan cut them down, sending arrows into them.

Zeva sent the Red Tips who rushed them spinning backwards with a wall of air.

They pushed into the room where Cita battled with numerous Red Tips and Saliday and Morgan fought off a group surrounding them.

Logan dispatched the Red Tips around Cita with his arrows as Zeva helped Saliday and Morgan. Saliday's vest of knives appeared depleted.

They came together as they fought off the advancing Red Tips and Logan put his bow away in favor of his swords for close quarters fighting.

Logan made eye contact with Cita who flashed a bright smile and continued to battle the troops pressing in on them.

Logan spun and surged into the oncoming troops, stopping their rush as he slashed his way forward, successfully turning the tide and sending the men into full retreat. No Red Tip survived when they stepped within his swords' radius and many others fled to avoid a battle with the protector.

Logan saw the council for the first time as they sat in their white robes trapped at a large table on a raised dais with their backs to the end wall with no door or windows.

A group of Red Tips stood defensively around them as other Red Tips rushed into the room only to meet Cita, Zeva, Saliday, Morgan, and Logan with devastating consequences.

Even though these men were an elite group of warriors, they could not match the combination of skill and magic the five adversaries possessed. Their numbers dwindled as Cita's army flooded the building cutting off any hopes the council held for an escape.

The Red Tips in front of the council hunkered down for a battle to the death as the council sat terrified behind them. The nine-membered panel remained frozen with fear at the table watching their fate unfold before them.

Logan raised a hand halting his party's advancement on the troops bristling before them. Cita and the others stopped, standing at the ready as Logan sheathed his swords.

"I ask for your surrender," Logan announced.

"And what is our fate if we do?" An opulent grey-haired man sitting in the middle of the table with his head held high asked.

Logan assumed this man to be the chairman.

"Leniency and justice," Logan said.

"By whose standards?" the man questioned.

"By the standard of Logan Lassain, the Protector of Ter Chadain and descendent of Chairman Lassain."

The council members' faces turned pale at the mention of Chairman Lassain.

"So you say we shall live?" A woman with long black hair and dark eyes filled with panic spoke as she sat to one side of the chairman.

"All who surrender will live although they may be imprisoned for a time depending on the crimes they have committed," Logan announced.

"And that pardon of death is extended to all who surrender?" A man questioned from the end of the table as he ran a nervous hand over his bald white head.

"All but one," Logan said bringing a silence to the room. He looked around, but did not see the man he sought. "All but Rudnick Curn will be spared. Rudnick must die for his crimes against the descendants of the council members and their families."

"Done," the chairman said without hesitation. "Put down your weapons," he ordered the Red Tips defending them.

The men obeyed dropping their weapons at Logan's feet and stepping aside.

The chairman then stood and walked to the tapestried wall behind them. He pulled back the cloth to reveal a small golden door built into the wall and then reached beneath his robe lifting a golden key on a golden chain underneath. Taking the chain from his neck he inserted the key into the keyhole. The lock clicked and he opened the door. Reaching in, he lifted something golden from the hiding place and turned back to Logan.

He then stepped around the others at the table and proceeded to where Logan stood. In his hands, Logan now saw the golden crown. The man bowed deeply and then straightened to look Logan in the eyes.

"As prophecy foretold, when the heir returns he shall become King of Stellaran. I now proclaim you our king,"

Logan dropped to a knee so the man could rest the golden crown on his head.

"Long live the king!" the rest of the council shouted and slid out of their chairs to drop to a knee.

A hissing sound reached Logan's ears and he spun just as Morgan tackled him, falling on top of him as they crashed to the floor.

Rudnick dropped the bow and disappeared into the wall behind the dais. Cita, Zeva, and Saliday rushed to Logan. He slid out from under Morgan and saw the arrow protruding from Morgan's back.

Morgan looked up at Logan's confused stare giving a weak smile that showed blood on his teeth and seeping from the corner of his lips. "She loves you, and I couldn't let her feel the pain of losing you. Guess I'm a romantic." He grinned and his eyes closed as his life slipped from his body.

Saliday dropped to her knees lifting Morgan in her arms rocking back and forth as she wept.

Zeva knelt beside Morgan sending her magic into him before turning to Logan and shaking her head.

Logan stood and scanned the room. He took the crown from his head and handed it to Cita. "Stay here, I'll find Rudnick," he ordered.

Cita and Zeva both opened their mouth to object.

"We need to assure the people of Stellaran that their king and their council still rule," Logan said ending their objections.

Logan rushed to the false panel, drew his swords and kicked it into the tunnel behind it. He gave a glance back at his friends and hurried into the passageway.

Darkness engulfed him and he sent magic into his swords like in the tunnels on Scalded Island, racing ahead to their dull white light.

He burst from the passage to find himself in the stables filled with Red Tips. The men turned at his exit from the tunnel and rushed him. He hacked and sliced through them while trying to catch a glimpse of Rudnick.

Hoof beats and a horse racing past showed Logan his prey and he intensified his assault on the unfortunate soldiers to reach Rudnick before he could escape.

Linell, Stern, and Trevon ran into the stable and attacked the Red Tips from behind, successfully ending the assault, sending the men scattering and scrambling from the stables.

"Rudnick is escaping," Logan shouted as he pointed across the courtyard to where the lone rider disappeared through the gate.

Logan and the others jumped onto some mounts and thundered after Rudnick.

They chased him through the city catching glimpses of him every so often as he wove his way through the streets. They followed him out of the city, he stayed just out of reach of Logan's arrows, but the distance continued to close between them.

He appeared on a rise and Logan lifted the rod from its sheath and notched an arrow in the expanding bow letting the silver arrow fly. The arrow flew true and straight, imbedding deeply into Rudnick's back doubling him over against his horse's neck as he disappeared to the other side of the hill.

They hurried after only to pull up sharply at the sight before them. Rudnick's horse continued across an open field carrying an unconscious Rudnick, but what lay before him was what surprised them. A camp containing several tents flying the flag with the symbol of the golden eye along with many troops in golden armor sat on the shallow valley floor.

Logan stared in disbelief as the flag of the Empress of Caltoria flapped high on the breeze over the encampment as the Rudnick's horse trotted into the camp and out of Logan's grasp.

"What do we do now?" Linell shouted.

"Those are Caltorian troops," Trevon pointed out.

"If Rudnick knew they were there, so did the council," Stern surmised.

"Why are they here?" Logan asked.

"Because the council was offering something that the empress wanted," a voice said from behind them and they spun to see Zeva riding up.

"And what is that?" Trevon asked.

"The council said they promised the empress the Banished

Ones in exchange for peace," Zeva said.

"And now that I have eliminated them?" Logan questioned.

"The chairman said the empress promised war if her demands weren't meant," Zeva said.

As if on cue, a group of horses rode out from the encampment below heading right for Logan and his companions.

The golden-armored group pulled up a few feet short of Logan and a man with silver bars on the shoulders of his armor removed his golden helmet to address them.

"I am emissary from Empress Shakata, and who are you?" the man asked with authority.

"I am Logan Lassain, new king of Stellaran," Logan replied.

"Oh, so Rudnick wasn't lying, you have taken control of Stellaran?"

"Yes I have," Logan answered.

"Then the offer given to the council is now extended to you. Give us the Banished Ones and there will be peace between our nations," the man ordered.

"There is a slight problem with that request," Logan said.

"And what is that?"

"The Banished Ones are dead," Logan said.

"That is most unfortunate," the man said with a frown. "I'm sure the empress will not be pleased."

"Tell her that her pleasure is of little concern to me," Logan responded.

The man sat up straighter in his horse and glared at Logan with venom in his eyes.

"Return Rudnick Curn to us," Logan ordered.

"He is a guest of the empress now and will return with us to deliver your message to Empress Shakata," the man said as he spun his horse and kicked it into a run back to his camp followed by the rest of his entourage.

"There is no way I will let her enslave magicals ever again,"

Logan said defiantly watching the riders return to their camp.

"Then as the new King of Stellaran, your first duty will be to win a war against Caltoria," Stern surmised.

"So be it," Logan said pulling back on the reins and spinning his horse around to head back to Lonnex.

Zeva, Stern, Trevon, and Linell exchanged unhappy glances and followed after Logan.

Chapter 47

Teah sat on the throne as she sent word to the city garrison to stand down and allow Caslor admittance to the palace. She reached out to Logan and sighed with relief when he answered.

Yes sister, his thoughts sounded weary.

I have done it. I have claimed the throne of Ter Chadain.

Then our quest for the throne is done, Logan replied with relief.

When will you return to Ter Chadain?

I fear that will not be for some time.

Why is that?

I am now the King of Stellaran and the Empress of Caltoria was trying to secure power by taking control of the Banished Ones.

Teah paused in shock as the new information sank in.

I killed two Banished Ones in Ter Chadain, but she might get one of the other eight, she warned.

No she won't. I killed the rest here in Stellaran.

So Stellaran is now at war with Caltoria? Teah asked.

My forces are no match for hers, Logan admitted.

Then we must join together to defeat her.

And put another in her place.

Exactly, Teah told him as her eyes lifted from staring at nothing to Caslor as he strode into the throne room.

Caslor rushed up to her, took her in his arms, and kissed her. He set her down and she stared up at him seriously.

"What?" he asked.

"It's your mother again."

THE END

This Ends The Return to Ter Chadain, Book 3 in the Protector of Ter Chadain series.

Acknowledgement

I want to thank my wife, Jenny, for her patient support of this passion of mine. Also, to my beta reader, Mike and his wife Kathy for their consistent encouragement "the writing is not the issue." My children for their encouragement and patience as I share rambling plots and storylines with them. And the Roseville Writers Group (Celia, Catherine, Quinette, Michelle, and John) for holding me to a high standard.
To all my readers, without you, there would be no need for this.

Made in the USA
Middletown, DE
23 June 2021